STORIES OF
BOOKS AND
LIBRARIES

EDITED BY JANE HOLLOWAY

T0333087

EVERYMAN'S POCKET CLASSICS
Alfred A. Knopf New York London Toronto

THIS IS A BORZOI BOOK
PUBLISHED BY ALFRED A. KNOPF

This selection by Jane Holloway first published in
Everyman's Library, 2023
Copyright © 2023 by Everyman's Library
Second printing (US)

A list of acknowledgments to copyright owners appears at
the back of this volume.

everymanslibrary.com
www.everymanslibrary.co.uk

ISBN 978-0-593-53627-8 (US)
978-1-84159-634-1 (UK)

A CIP catalogue reference for this book is available from the
British Library

Typography by Peter B. Willberg

Typeset in the UK by Input Data Services Ltd, Isle Abbotts, Somerset

Printed and bound in Germany by GGP Media GmbH, Pössneck

EVERYMAN,

I WILL GO WITH THEE,

AND BE THY GUIDE,

IN THY MOST NEED

TO GO BY THY SIDE

EVERYMAN'S POCKET CLASSICS

Contents

In books I find the dead as if they were alive; in books I foresee things to come; in books warlike affairs are set forth; from books come forth the laws of peace. All things are corrupted and decay in time; Saturn ceases not to devour the children that he generates; all the glory of the world would be buried in oblivion, unless God had provided mortals with the remedy of books.

RICHARD DE BURY, Philobiblon (1345)

Reading is untidy, discursive and perpetually inviting.

ALAN BENNETT, The Uncommon Reader (2007)

RAY BRADBURY

EXCHANGE
(1996)

THERE WERE TOO many cards in the file, too many books on the shelves, too many children laughing in the children's room, too many newspapers to fold and stash on the racks . . .

All in all, too much. Miss Adams pushed her gray hair back over her lined brow, adjusted her gold-rimmed pince-nez, and rang the small silver bell on the library desk, at the same time switching off and on all the lights. The exodus of adults and children was exhausting. Miss Ingraham, the assistant librarian, had gone home early because her father was sick, so it left the burden of stamping, filing, and checking books squarely on Miss Adams' shoulders.

Finally the last book was stamped, the last child fed through the great brass doors, the doors locked, and with immense weariness, Miss Adams moved back up through a silence of forty years of books and being keeper of the books, stood for a long moment by the main desk.

She laid her glasses down on the green blotter, and pressed the bridge of her small-boned nose between thumb and forefinger and held it, eyes shut. What a racket! Children who fingerpainted or cartooned frontispieces or rattled their roller skates. High school students arriving with laughters, departing with mindless songs!

Taking up her rubber stamp, she probed the files, weeding out errors, her fingers whispering between Dante and Darwin.

A moment later she heard the rapping on the front-door glass and saw a man's shadow outside, wanting in. She shook her head. The figure pleaded silently, making gestures.

Sighing, Miss Adams opened the door, saw a young man in uniform, and said, 'It's late. We're closed.' She glanced at his insignia and added, 'Captain.'

'Hold on!' said the captain. 'Remember me?'

And repeated it, as she hesitated.

'*Remember?*'

She studied his face, trying to bring light out of shadow. 'Yes, I think I do,' she said at last. 'You once borrowed books here.'

'Right.'

'Many years ago,' she added. 'Now I almost have you placed.'

As he stood waiting she tried to see him in those other years, but his younger face did not come clear, or a name with it, and his hand reached out now to take hers.

'May I come in?'

'Well.' She hesitated. 'Yes.'

She led the way up the steps into the immense twilight of books. The young officer looked around and let his breath out slowly, then reached to take a book and hold it to his nose, inhaling, then almost laughing.

'Don't mind me, Miss Adams. You ever smell new books? Binding, pages, print. Like fresh bread when you're hungry.' He glanced around. 'I'm hungry now, but don't even know what for.'

There was a moment of silence, so she asked him how long he might stay.

'Just a few hours. I'm on the train from New York to L.A., so I came up from Chicago to see old places, old friends.'

His eyes were troubled and he fretted his cap, turning it in his long, slender fingers.

She said gently, 'Is anything wrong? Anything I can help you with?'

He glanced out the window at the dark town, with just a few lights in the windows of the small houses across the way.

'I was surprised,' he said.

'By what?'

'I don't know what I expected. Pretty damn dumb,' he said, looking from her to the windows, 'to expect that when I went away, everyone froze in place waiting for me to come home. That when I stepped off the train, all my old pals would unfreeze, run down, meet me at the station. Silly.'

'No,' she said, more easily now. 'I think we all imagine that. I visited Paris as a young girl, went back to France when I was forty, and was outraged that no one had waited, buildings had vanished, and all the hotel staff where I had once lived had died, retired, or traveled.'

He nodded at this, but could not seem to go on.

'Did anyone know you were coming?' she asked.

'I wrote a few, but no answers. I figured, hell, they're busy, but they'll be *there*. They weren't.'

She felt the next words come off her lips and was faintly surprised. 'I'm still here,' she said.

'You *are*,' he said with a quick smile. 'And I can't tell you how glad I am.'

He was gazing at her now with such intensity that she had to look away. 'You know,' she said, 'I must confess you look familiar, but I don't quite fit your face with the boy who came here –'

'Twenty years ago! And as for what *he* looked like, that other one, me, well –'

He brought out a smallish wallet which held a dozen

pictures and handed over a photograph of a boy perhaps twelve years old, with an impish smile and wild blond hair, looking as if he might catapult out of the frame.

'Ah, yes.' Miss Adams adjusted her pince-nez and closed her eyes to remember. 'That one, Spaulding. William Henry Spaulding?'

He nodded and peered at the picture in her hands anxiously.

'Was I a lot of trouble?'

'Yes.' She nodded and held the picture closer and glanced up at him. 'A fiend.' She handed the picture back. 'But I loved you.'

'Did you?' he said and smiled more broadly.

'In spite of you, yes.'

He waited a moment and then said, 'Do you *still* love me?'

She looked to left and right as if the dark stacks held the answer.

'It's a little early to know, isn't it?'

'Forgive.'

'No, no, a good question. Time will tell. Let's not stand like your frozen friends who didn't move. Come along. I've just had some late-night coffee. There may be some left. Give me your cap. Take off that coat. The file index is there. Go look up your old library cards for the hell – heck – of it.'

'Are they still *there*?' In amaze.

'Librarians save everything. You never know who's coming in on the next train. Go.'

When she came back with the coffee, he stood staring down into the index file like a bird fixing its gaze on a half-empty nest. He handed her one of the old purple-stamped cards.

'Migawd,' he said, 'I took out a lot of books.'

'Ten at a time. I said no, but you took them. And,' she added, '*read* them! Here.' She put his cup on top of the file and waited while he drew out canceled card after card and laughed quietly.

'I can't believe. I must not have lived anywhere else but here. May I take this with me, to sit?' He showed the cards. She nodded. 'Can you show me around? I mean, maybe I've forgotten something.'

She shook her head and took his elbow. 'I doubt that. Come on. Over here, of course, is the adult section.'

'I begged you to let me cross over when I was thirteen. "You're not ready," you said. But –'

'I let you cross over anyway?'

'You did. And much thanks.'

Another thought came to him as he looked down at her.

'You used to be taller than me,' he said.

She looked up at him, amused.

'I've noticed that happens quite often in my life, but I can still do *this*.'

Before he could move, she grabbed his chin in her thumb and forefinger and held tight. His eyes rolled.

He said:

'I remember. When I was really bad you'd hold on and put your face down close and scowl. The scowl did it. After ten seconds of your holding my chin very tight, I behaved for days.'

She nodded, released his chin. He rubbed it and as they moved on he ducked his head, not looking at her.

'Forgive, I hope you won't be upset, but when I was a boy I used to look up and see you behind your desk, so near but far away, and, how can I say this, I used to think that you were Mrs. God, and that the library was a whole world, and

15

that no matter what part of the world or what people or thing I wanted to see and read, you'd find and give it to me.' He stopped, his face coloring. 'You *did*, too. You had the world ready for me every time I asked. There was always a place I hadn't seen, a country I hadn't visited where you took me. I've never forgotten.'

She looked around, slowly, at the thousands of books. She felt her heart move quietly. 'Did you really call me what you just said?'

'Mrs. God? Oh, yes. Often. Always.'

'Come along,' she said at last.

They walked around the rooms together and then downstairs to the newspaper files, and coming back up, he suddenly leaned against the banister, holding tight.

'Miss Adams,' he said.

'What is it, Captain?'

He exhaled. 'I'm scared. I don't want to leave. I'm afraid.'

Her hand, all by itself, took his arm and she finally said, there in the shadows, 'Sometimes – I'm afraid, too. What frightens *you*?'

'I don't want to go away without saying goodbye. If I never return, I want to see all my friends, shake hands, slap them on the back, I don't know, make jokes.' He stopped and waited, then went on. 'But I walk around town and nobody knows me. Everyone's gone.'

The pendulum on the wall clock slid back and forth, shining, with the merest of sounds.

Hardly knowing where she was going, Miss Adams took his arm and guided him up the last steps, away from the marble vaults below, to a final, brightly decorated room, where he glanced around and shook his head.

'There's no one here, either.'

'Do you believe that?'

16

'Well, where are they? Do any of my old pals ever come visit, borrow books, bring them back late?'

'Not often,' she said. 'But listen. Do you realize Thomas Wolfe was wrong?'

'Wolfe? The great literary beast? Wrong?'

'The *title* of one of his books.'

'*You Can't Go Home Again?*' he guessed.

'That's it. He was wrong. *This* is home. Your friends are still here. This was your summer place.'

'Yes. Myths. Legends. Mummies. Aztec kings. Wicked sisters who spat toads. Where I really lived. But I don't see my people.'

'Well.'

And before he could speak, she switched on a green-shaded lamp that shed a private light on a small table.

'Isn't this nice?' she said. 'Most libraries today, too much light. There should be shadows, don't you think? Some mystery, yes? So that late nights the beasts can prowl out of the stacks and crouch by this jungle light to turn the pages with their breath. Am I crazy?'

'Not that I noticed.'

'Good. Sit. Now that I know who you are, it all comes back.'

'It couldn't possibly.'

'No? You'll see.'

She vanished into the stacks and came out with ten books that she placed upright, their pages a trifle spread so they could stand and he could read the titles.

'The summer of 1930, when you were, what? ten, you read all of these in one week.'

'Oz? Dorothy? The Wizard? Oh, *yes*.'

She placed still others nearby. *Alice in Wonderland. Through the Looking-Glass.* A month later you reborrowed both. "But," I said, "you've already *read* them!" "But," you said, "not enough so I can speak. I want to be able to *tell* them out *loud*."'

'My God,' he said quietly, 'did I say that?'

'You did. Here's more you read a dozen times. Greek myths, Roman, Egyptian. Norse myths, Chinese. You were *ravenous*.'

'King Tut arrived from the tomb when I was three. His picture in the Rotogravure started me. What else have you there?'

'*Tarzan of the Apes*. You borrowed it . . .'

'Three dozen times! *John Carter, Warlord of Mars*, four dozen. My God, dear lady, how come you remember all this?'

'You never left. Summertimes you were here when I unlocked the doors. You went home for lunch but sometimes brought sandwiches and sat out by the stone lion at noon. Your father pulled you home by your ear some nights when you stayed late. How could I forget a boy like that?'

'But still –'

'You never played, never ran out in baseball weather, or football, I imagine. Why?'

He glanced toward the front door. '*They* were waiting for me.'

'They?'

'You know. The ones who never borrowed books, never read. They. Them. *Those*.'

She looked and remembered. 'Ah, yes. The bullies. Why did they chase you?'

'Because they knew I loved books and didn't much care for them.'

'It's a wonder you survived. I used to watch you getting, reading hunchbacked, late afternoons. You looked so lonely.'

'No. I had *these*. Company.'

'Here's more.'

She put down *Ivanhoe*, *Robin Hood*, and *Treasure Island*.

'Oh,' he said, 'and dear and strange Mr. Poe. How I loved his Red Death.'

'You took it so often I told you to keep it on permanent loan unless someone else asked. Someone did, six months later, and when you brought it in I could see it was a terrible blow. A few days later I let you have Poe for another year. I don't recall, did you ever –?'

'It's out in California. Shall I –'

'No, no. Please. Well, here are *your* books. Let me bring others.'

She came out not carrying many books but one at a time, as if each one were, indeed, special.

She began to make a circle inside the other Stonehenge circle and as she placed the books, in lonely splendor, he said their names and then the names of the authors who had written them and then the names of those who had sat across from him so many years ago and read the books quietly or sometimes whispered the finest parts aloud, so beautifully that no one said Quiet or Silence or even *Shh!*

She placed the first book and there was a wild field of broom and a wind blowing a young woman across that field as it began to snow and someone, far away, called 'Kathy' and as the snows fell he saw a girl he had walked to school in the sixth grade seated across the table, her eyes fixed to the windblown field and the snow and the lost woman in another time of winter.

A second book was set in place and a black and beauteous horse raced across a summer field of green and on that horse was another girl, who hid behind the book and dared to pass him notes when he was twelve.

19

And then there was the far ghost with a snow-maiden face whose hair was a long golden harp played by the summer airs; she who was always sailing to Byzantium where Emperors were drowsed by golden birds that sang in clockwork cages at sunset and dawn. She who always skirted the outer rim of school and went to swim in the deep lake ten thousand afternoons ago and never came out, so was never found, but suddenly now she made landfall here in the green-shaded light and opened Yeats to at last sail home from Byzantium.

And on her right: John Huff, whose name came clearer than the rest, who claimed to have climbed every tree in town and fallen from none, who had raced through watermelon patches treading melons, never touching earth, to knock down rainfalls of chestnuts with one blow, who yodeled at your sun-up window and wrote the same Mark Twain book report in four different grades before the teachers caught on, at which he said, vanishing, 'Just call me Huck.'

And to *his* right, the pale son of the town hotel owner who looked as if he had gone sleepless forever, who swore every empty house was haunted and took you there to prove it, with a juicy tongue, compressed nose, and throat garglings that sounded the long October demise, the terrible and unutterable fall of the House of Usher.

And next to him was yet another girl.

And next to her . . .

And just beyond . . .

Miss Adams placed a final book and he recalled the fair creature, long ago, when such things were left unsaid, glancing up at him one day when he was an unknowing twelve and she was a wise thirteen to quietly say: 'I am Beauty. And you, are *you* the Beast?'

Now, late in time, he wanted to answer that small and

wondrous ghost: 'No. He hides in the stacks and when the clock strikes three, will prowl forth to drink.'

And it was finished, all the books were placed, the outer ring of his selves and the inner ring of remembered faces, deathless, with summer and autumn names.

He sat for a long moment and then another long moment and then, one by one, reached for and took all of the books that had been his, and still were, and opened them and read and shut them and took another until he reached the end of the outer circle and then went to touch and turn and find the raft on the river, the field of broom where the storms lived, and the pasture with the black and beauteous horse and its lovely rider. Behind him, he heard the lady librarian quietly back away to leave him with words . . .

A long while later he sat back, rubbed his eyes, and looked around at the fortress, the encirclement, the Roman encampment of books, and nodded, his eyes wet.

'Yes.'

He heard her move behind him.

'Yes, *what?*'

'What you said, Thomas Wolfe, the title of that book of his. Wrong. Everything's *here.* Nothing's changed.'

'Nothing will as long as I can help it,' she said.

'Don't ever go away.'

'I won't if you'll come back more often.'

Just then, from below the town, not so very far off, a train whistle blew. She said:

'Is that *yours?*'

'No, but the one soon after,' he said and got up and moved around the small monuments that stood very tall and, one by one, shut the covers, his lips moving to sound the old titles and the old, dear names.

'Do we *have* to put them back on the shelves?' he said.

She looked at him and at the double circle and after a long moment said, 'Tomorrow will do. Why?'

'Maybe,' he said, 'during the night, because of the color of those lamps, green, the jungle, maybe those creatures you mentioned will come out and turn the pages with their breath. And maybe –'

'What else?'

'Maybe my friends, who've hid in the stacks all these years, will come out, too.'

'They're already here,' she said quietly.

'Yes.' He nodded. 'They are.'

And still he could not move.

She backed off across the room without making any sound, and when she reached her desk she called back, the last call of the night.

'Closing time. Closing time, children.'

And turned the lights quickly off and then on and then halfway between; a library twilight.

He moved from the table with the double circle of books and came to her and said, 'I can go now.'

'Yes,' she said. 'William Henry Spaulding. You *can.*'

They walked together as she turned out the lights, turned out the lights, one by one. She helped him into his coat and then, hardly thinking to do so, he took her hand and kissed her fingers.

It was so abrupt, she almost laughed, but then she said, 'Remember what Edith Wharton said when Henry James did what you just did?'

'What?'

' "The flavor starts at the *elbow*." '

They broke into laughter together and he turned and went down the marble steps toward the stained-glass entry. At the bottom of the stairs he looked up at her and said:

'Tonight, when you're going to sleep, remember what I called you when I was twelve, and say it out loud.'

'I don't remember,' she said.

'Yes, you do.'

Below the town, a train whistle blew again.

He opened the front door, stepped out, and he was gone.

Her hand on the last light switch, looking in at the double circle of books on the far table, she thought: What *was* it he called me?

'Oh, *yes*,' she said a moment later.

And switched off the light.

HELEN OYEYEMI

BOOKS AND ROSES
(2016)

For Jaume Vallcorba

ONCE UPON A time in Catalonia a baby was found in a chapel. This was over at Santa Maria de Montserrat. It was an April morning. And the baby was so wriggly and minuscule that the basket she was found in looked empty at first glance. The child had got lost in a corner of it, but courageously wriggled her way back up to the top fold of the blanket in order to peep out. The monk who found this basket searched desperately for an explanation. His eyes met the wooden eyes of the Virgin of Montserrat, a mother who has held her child on her lap for centuries, a gilded child that doesn't breathe or grow. In looking upon that great lady, the monk received a measure of her unquestioning love and fell to his knees to pray for further guidance, only to find that he'd knelt on a slip of paper that the baby had dislodged with her wriggling. The note read:

1. You have a Black Madonna here, so you will know how to love this child almost as much as I do. Please call her Montserrat.
2. Wait for me.

A golden chain was fastened around her neck, and on that chain was a key. As she grew up, the lock of every door and cupboard in the monastery was tested, to no avail. She had to wait. It was both a comfort and a great frustration to Montse, this . . . what could she call it, a notion, a suggestion, a promise? This promise that somebody was coming back for her. If she'd been a white child the monks of Santa Maria de Montserrat might have given her into the care of a local family, but she was as black as the face and hands of the Virgin they adored. She was given the surname 'Fosc', not just because she was black, but also because her origin was obscure. And the monks set themselves the task of learning all they could about the needs of a child. More often than not they erred on the side of indulgence, and held debates on the matter of whether this extreme degree of fondness was a mortal sin or a venial one. At any rate, it was the Benedictine friars who fed and clothed and carried Montse and went through the horrors of the teething process with her, and rang the chapel bells for hours the day she spoke her first words. Neither as a girl nor as a woman did Montse ever doubt the devotion of her many fathers, and in part it was the certainty of this devotion that saw her through times at school and times down in the city when people looked at her strangely or said insulting things; the words and looks sometimes made her lower her head for a few steps along the street, but never for long. She was a daughter of the Virgin of Montserrat, and she felt instinctively, and of course heretically, that the Virgin herself was only a symbol of a yet greater sister-mother who was carefree and sorrowful all at once, a goddess who didn't guide you or shield you but only went with you from place to place and added her tangible presence to your own when required.

When Montse was old enough she took a job at a haberdashery in Les Corts de Sarria and worked there until Señora Cabella found her relatives unwilling to take over the family business and the shop closed down. 'You're a hardworking girl, Montse,' Señora Cabella told her, 'and I know you'll make something of yourself if given a chance. You've seen that eyesore at the Passeig de Gracia. The Casa Mila. People call it La Pedrera because it looks like a quarry, just a lot of stones all thrown on top of each other. An honest, reliable girl can find work as a laundress there. Is that work you can do? Very well – go to Señora Molina, the *conserje*'s wife. Tell her Emma Cabella sent you. Give her this.' And the woman wrote out a recommendation that made Montse blush to read.

She reported to Señora Molina at La Pedrera the next morning, and the *conserje*'s wife sent her upstairs to Señora Gaeta, who pronounced Montse satisfactory and tied an apron on her. After that it was work, work, work, and weeks turned into months. Montse had to work extra fast to keep Señora Gaeta from noticing that she was washing the Cabella family's clothes along with those of the residents she'd been assigned. The staff turnover at La Pedrera was rapid; every week there were new girls who joined the ranks without warning, and girls who vanished without giving notice. Señora Gaeta knew every name and face, even when the identical uniforms made it difficult for the girls themselves to remember each other. It was Señora Gaeta who employed the girls and also relieved them of their duties if their efforts weren't up to scratch. She darted around the attic, flicking the air with her red lacquered fan as she inspected various activities. The residents of Casa Mila called Señora Gaeta a treasure, and the laundry maids liked her because she sometimes joined in when they sang work songs; it seemed that once she had been just like them, for all the damask and cameo rings she wore now. Señora Gaeta was also well liked because it was exciting to hear her talk: she swore the most powerful and unusual oaths they'd ever heard, really unrepeatable stuff, and all in a sweetly quivering voice, like the song of a harp. Her policy was to employ healthy-looking women who seemed unlikely to develop bad backs too quickly. But you can't guess right all the time. There were girls who aged overnight. Others were unexpectedly lazy. Women who worried about their reputation didn't last long in the attic laundry either – they sought and found work in more ordinary buildings.

It was generally agreed that this mansion the Mila family had had built in their name was a complete failure. This was mostly the fault of the architect. He had the right materials but clearly he hadn't known how to make the best use of them. A house of stone and glass and iron should be stark and sober, a watchtower from which a benevolent guard is kept over society. But the white stone of this particular house rippled as if reacting to a hand that had found its most pleasurable point of contact. A notable newspaper critic had described this effect as being that of 'a pernicious sensuality'. And as if that wasn't enough, the entire construction blushed a truly disgraceful peachy-pink at sunset and dawn. Respectable citizens couldn't help but feel that the house expressed the dispositions of its inhabitants, who must surely be either mad or unceasingly engaged in indecent activities. But Montse thought the house she worked in was beautiful. She stood on a corner of the pavement and looked up, and what she saw clouded her senses. To Montse's mind La Pedrera was a magnificent place. But then her taste lacked refinement. Her greatest material treasure was an egregiously shiny bit of tin she'd won at a fairground coconut shy; this fact can't be overlooked.

There were a few more cultured types who shared Montse's admiration of La Pedrera, though – one of them was Señora Lucy, who lived on the second floor and frequently argued with people about whether or not her home was an aesthetic offence. Journalists came to interview the Señora from time to time, and would make some comment about the house as a parting shot on their way out, but Señora Lucy refused to let them have the last word and stood there arguing at the top of her voice. The question of right angles was always being raised: how could Señora Lucy bear to live in a house without a single right angle . . . not even in the furniture . . .?

'But really, who needs right angles? Who?' Señora Lucy would demand, and she'd slam the courtyard door and run up the stairs laughing.

Señora Lucy was a painter with eyes like daybreak. Like Montse, she wore a key on a chain around her neck, but unlike Montse she told people that she was fifty years old and gave them looks that dared them to say she was in good condition for her age. (Señora Lucy was actually thirty-five, only five years older than Montse. One of the housemaids had overheard a gallery curator begging her to stop telling people she was fifty. The Señora had replied that she'd recently attended the exhibitions of some of her colleagues and now wished to discover whether fifty-year-old men in her field were treated with reverence because they were fifty or for some other reason.) Aside from this, the housemaids were somewhat disappointed with Señora Lucy. They expected their resident artist to lounge about in scarlet pyjamas, drink cocktails for breakfast and entertain dashing rascals and fragrant sirens. But Señora Lucy kept office hours. Merce, her maid of all work, tried to defend her by alleging that the Señora drank her morning coffee out of a vase, but nobody found this credible.

Montse found ways to be the one to return Señora Lucy's laundry to her; this sometimes meant undertaking several other deliveries so that her boss, Señora Gaeta, didn't become suspicious. There was a workroom in Señora Lucy's apartment; she often began work there, and then had the canvases transported to her real studio. Thirty seconds in Señora Lucy's apartment was long enough for Montse to get a good stare at all those beginnings of paintings. The Señora soon saw that Montse was curious about her work, and she took to leaving her studio door open while she etched on canvas. She'd call Montse to come and judge how well the picture was progressing. 'Look here,' she'd say, indicating a faint shape in the corner of the frame. 'Look here . . .' her fingertips glided over a darkening of colour in the distance. She sketched with an effort that strained every limb. Montse saw that the Señora sometimes grew short of breath though she'd hardly stirred. A consequence of snatching images out of the air – the air took something back.

Montse asked Señora about the key around her neck. It wasn't a real question, she was just talking so that she could stay a moment longer. But the Señora said she wore it because she was waiting for someone; at this Montse forgot herself and blurted: 'You too?'

The Señora was amused. 'Yes, me too. I suppose we're all waiting for someone.' And she told Montse all about it as she poured coffee into vases for them both. (It was true! It was true!)

'Two mostly penniless women met at a self-congratulation ritual in Seville.' That was how Señora Lucy began. The event was the five-year reunion of a graduating class of the University of Seville – neither woman had attended this university, but they blended in, and every other person they met claimed to remember them, and there was much exclamation on the theme of it being wonderful to see former classmates looking so well. The imposters had done their research, and knew what to say, and what questions to ask. Their names were Safiye and Lucy, and you wouldn't have guessed that either one was a pauper, since they'd spent most of the preceding afternoon liberating various items of priceless finery from their keepers.

These two penniless girls knew every trick in the book, and their not being able to identify each other was one of the downsides of being an efficient fraud. Both women moved from town to town under an assortment of aliases, and both believed that collaboration was for weaklings. Lucy and Safiye hadn't come to that gathering looking for friendship or love; they were there to make contacts. Back when they had toiled at honest work – Lucy at a bakery and Safiye at an abattoir – they'd wondered if it could be true that there were people who were given money simply because they looked as if they were used to having lots of it. Being blessed with forgettable faces and the gift of brazen fabrication, they'd each gone forth to test this theory and had found it functional. Safiye loved to look at paintings, and needed money to build her collection. Lucy was an artist in constant need of paint, brushes, turpentine, peaceful light and enough canvas to make compelling errors on. For a time Lucy had been married to a rare sort of clown, the sort that children aren't afraid of: *After all, he is one of us, you can see it in his eyes*, they reasoned. *How funny that he's so strangely tall.* Lucy and her husband had not much liked being married to each other, the bond proving much heavier than their light-hearted courtship had led them to expect, but they agreed that it had been worth a try, and while waiting for their divorce to come through, Lucy's husband had taught her the sleight of hand she eventually used to pick her neighbour's pocket down to the very last thread. The night she met Safiye, she stole her earrings right out of her earlobes and, having retired to a quiet corner of the mansion to inspect them, found that the gems were paste. Then she discovered that her base-metal bangle was missing and quickly realized that she could only have lost it to the person she was stealing from; she'd been distracted by the baubles and the appeal of those delicate earlobes. Cornered by a banker whose false memory of having been in love with her since matriculation day might prove profitable, Lucy wavered between a sensible decision and a foolhardy one. Ever did foolhardiness hold the upper hand with Lucy; she found Safiye leaning against an oil lantern out in the garden and saw for herself that she wasn't the only foolish woman in the world, or even at that party, for Safiye had Lucy's highly polished bangle in her hand and was turning it this way and that in order to catch fireflies in the billowing, transparent left sleeve of her gown. All this at the risk of being set alight, but then, from where Lucy stood, Safiye looked as if she was formed of fire herself, particles of flame dancing the flesh of her arm into existence. That or she was returning to fire.

They left the reunion early and in a hurry, along with a small group of attendees who'd found themselves unable to sustain the pretence of total success. Having fallen into Lucy's bed, they didn't get out again for days. How could they, when Lucy held all Safiye's satisfactions in her very fingertips, and each teasing stroke of Safiye's tongue summoned Lucy to the brink of delirium? They fell asleep, each making secret plans to slip away in the middle of the night. After all, their passion placed them entirely at each other's command, and they were bound to find that fearsome. So they planned escape but woke up intertwined. It was at Lucy's bidding that Safiye would stay or go. And who knew what Safiye might suddenly and successfully demand of Lucy? *Stop breathing. Give up tea.* The situation improved

34

once it occurred to them that they should also talk; as they came to understand each other they learned that what they'd been afraid of was running out of self. On the contrary, the more they loved the more there was to love. At times it was necessary to spend months apart, coaxing valuable goods out of people using methods they avoided discussing in detail. Lucy sent Safiye paintings and orange blossoms, and Safiye directed a steady flow of potential portrait subjects Lucy's way. The lovers fought about this; it seemed to Lucy that Safiye was trying to trick her into making a 'respectable' living. Lucy had promised herself that she'd only paint faces she found compelling and it was a bother to have to keep inventing excuses for not taking on portraits.

'It's all right, you're just not good at gifts,' Lucy said, with a smile intended to pacify. Gifts didn't matter when they were together, and gifts didn't have to matter when they were apart, either. But Safiye was outraged.

'What are you talking about? Don't you ever say that I'm bad at gifts!'

If there are any words that Lucy could now unsay, it would be those words about Safiye being bad at gifts; if Lucy hadn't said them, Safiye wouldn't have set out to steal the gift that would prove her wrong, and she wouldn't have got caught.

The lovers spent Christmas together, then parted – Lucy for Grenoble and Safiye for Barcelona. They wrote to each other care of their cities' central post offices, and at the beginning of April, Safiye wrote of the romance of St. Jordi's Day. *Lucy, it is the custom here to exchange books and roses each year on April 23. Shall we?*

Lucy happily settled down to work. First she sent for papyrus and handmade a book, leaf by leaf, binding the leaves together between board covers. Then she filled each page from memory, drew English roses budding and Chinese roses in full bloom, peppercorn-pink Bourbon roses climbing walls and silvery musk roses drowsing in flowerbeds. She took every rose she'd ever seen, made them as lifelike as she could (where she shaded each petal the rough paper turned silken) and in these lasting forms she offered them to Safiye. The making of this rose book coincided with a period in Lucy's life when she was making money without having to lie to anyone. She'd fallen in with an inveterate gambler who'd noticed that she steadied his nerves to a miraculous degree. He always won at blackjack whenever she was sitting beside him, so they agreed he'd give her ten per cent of each evening's winnings. This man only played when the stakes were high, so he won big and they were both happy. Lucy had no idea what was going to happen when their luck ran out; she could only hope her gambler wouldn't try to get violent with her, because then she'd have to get violent herself. That would be a shame because she liked the man. He never pawed at her, he always asked her how Safiye was getting on, and he was very much in love with his wife, who loved him too and thought he was a night watchman. The gambler's wife would've gone mad with terror if she'd known how close she came to losing her life savings each night, but she didn't suspect a thing, so she packed her husband light suppers to eat at work, suppers the man couldn't even bear to look at (his stomach always played up when he was challenging Lady Luck), so Lucy ate the suppers and enjoyed them very much, the flavour of herbed olives lingering in her mouth so that when she drank her wine she tasted all the greenness of the grapes.

From where Lucy sat beside her gambler she had a view through a casement window, a view of a long street that led to the foot of a mountain. And what Lucy liked best about her casement-window view was that as night time turned into dawn, the mountain seemed to travel down the street. It advanced on tiptoe, fully prepared to be shooed away. Insofar as a purely transient construction of flesh and blood can remember (or foretell) what it is to be stone, Lucy understood the mountain's wish to listen at the window of a den of gamblers and be warmed by all that free floating hope and desolation. Her wish for the mountain was that it would one day shrink to a pebble, crash in through the glass and roll into a corner to happily absorb tavern life for as long as the place stayed standing. Lucy tried to write something to Safiye about the view through the casement window, but found that her description of the mountain expressed a degree of pining so extreme that it made for distasteful reading. She didn't post that letter.

Safiye had begun working as a lady's maid – an appropriate post for her, as she had the requisite patience. It can take months before you even learn the location of a household safe, let alone discover the code that makes its contents available to you. But was that really Safiye's plan? Lucy had a feeling she was being tricked into the conventional again. Safiye instigated bothersome conversations about 'the future', the eventual need for security and it being possible to play one trick too many. From time to time Lucy paused her work on the rose book to write and send brief notes: *Safiye – I've been so busy I haven't had time to think; I'm afraid I'll only be able to send you a small token for this St. Jordi's Day you wrote about. I'll beg my forgiveness when I see you.* Safiye replied: *Whatever the size of your token, I'm certain mine is smaller. You'll laugh when you see it, Lucy.* Lucy wrote back: *Competitive as ever! Whatever it is you're doing, don't get caught. I love you, I love you.*

* * *

On April 23, an envelope addressed in Safiye's hand arrived at the post office for Lucy. It contained a key on a necklace chain and a map of Barcelona with a black rose drawn over a small section of it. Lucy turned the envelope inside out but there was no accompanying note. *She couldn't even send a book*, Lucy thought, tutting in spite of herself. She hadn't yet sent the book she'd made, and as she stood in the queue to post it she began to consider keeping it.

The woman in line ahead of her was reading a newspaper and Lucy saw Safiye's face – more an imperfectly sketched reproduction of it – and read the word 'Barcelone' in the headline. Some vital passage narrowed in her heart, or her blood got too thick to flow through it. She read enough to understand that the police were looking for a lady's maid in connection to a murder and a series of other crimes they suspected her of having committed under other names.

Murder? Impossible. Not Safiye. Lucy walked backwards until she found a wall to stand behind her. She rested until she was able to walk to the train station, where she bought tickets and a newspaper of which she read a single page as she waited for the train to come. She would go where the map in her purse told her to go, she would find Safiye, Safiye would explain and they would laugh. They'd have to leave the continent, of course. They might even have to earn their livings honestly like Safiye wanted, but please, please please please. This pleading went on inside her for the entire journey, through three train changes and the better part of a day. A mountain seemed to follow along behind each train she took – whenever she looked over her shoulder there it was, keeping pace. She liked to think it was her mountain she was seeing, the one she'd first seen in Grenoble, now trying its best to keep faith with her until she found Safiye.

Safiye's map led Lucy to a crudely hewn door in a wall. This didn't look like a door that could open, but a covering for a mistake in the brickwork. The key fit the lock and Lucy walked into a walled garden overrun with roses. She waded through waves of scent, lifting rope-like vines of sweetbriar and eglantine out of her path, her steps scattering pale blue butterflies in every direction. Safiye had said that Lucy would laugh at the size of her gift, and perhaps if Lucy had found her there she would have. After all, she'd never been given a secret garden before. But the newspapers were saying that this woman who looked like Safiye had killed her employer, and Lucy was very much afraid that it was true and this gift was the reason. At nightfall she considered sleeping among the roses, all those frilled puffs of air carrying her towards some answer, but it was better to find Safiye than to dream. She spent two weeks flitting around the city listening to talk of the killer lady's maid. She didn't dare return to the rose garden, but she wore the key around her neck in the hope and fear that it would be recognized. It wasn't, and she opted to return to Grenoble before she ran out of money. Her gambler was in hospital. There'd been heavy losses at the blackjack table, his wife had discovered what he'd been up to, developed a wholly unexpected strength ('inhuman strength', he called it), broken both of his arms and then moved in with a carpenter who'd clearly been keeping her company while he'd been out working on their finances. Still, he was happy to see Lucy: 'Fortuna smiles upon me again!' What could Lucy do? She made him soup, and when she wasn't at his bedside she was picking pockets to help cover the hospital bills. They remain friends to this day: he was impressed by her assumption of responsibility for him and she was struck by the novelty of its never occurring to him to blame anybody else for his problems.

*   *   *

A few weeks after her return to Grenoble there was a spring storm that splashed the streets with moss from the mountain-tops. The stormy night turned the window of Lucy's room into a door; through sleep Lucy became aware that it was more than just rain that rattled the glass . . . someone was knocking. Half awake, she staggered across the room to turn the latch. When Safiye finally crawled in, shivering and drenched to the bone, they kissed for a long time, kissed until Lucy was fully woken by the chattering of Safiye's teeth against hers. She fetched a towel, Safiye performed a heart-wrenchingly weak little striptease for her, and Lucy wrapped her love up warm and held her and didn't ask what she needed to ask.

After a little while Safiye spoke, her voice so perfectly unchanged it was closer to memory than it was to real time.

'Today I asked people about you, and I even walked behind you in the street for a little while. You bought some hat ribbon and a sack of onions, and you got a good deal on the hat ribbon. Sometimes I almost thought you'd caught me watching, but now I'm sure you didn't know. You're doing well. I'm proud of you. And all I've managed to do is take a key and make a mess of things. I wanted to give you . . . I wanted to give you . . .'

'Sleep,' Lucy said. 'Just sleep.' Those were the only words she had the breath to say. But Safiye had come to make her understand about the key, the key, the key, it was like a mania, and she wouldn't sleep until Lucy heard her explanations.

From the first Safiye had felt a mild distaste for the way her employer, Señora del Olmo, talked: 'There was such an interesting exchange rate in this woman's mind . . . when-ever she remembered anyone giving her anything, they only

40

gave a very little and kept the lion's share to themselves. But whenever she remembered giving anyone anything, she gave a lot, so much it almost ruined her.' Apart from that, Safiye had neither liked nor disliked Señora del Olmo, preferring to concentrate on building her mental inventory of the household treasures, of which there were many. In addition to these there was a key the woman wore around her neck. She toyed with it as she interviewed gardener after gardener; Safiye sat through the interviews too, taking notes and reading the character references. None of the gardeners seemed able to fulfil Señora del Olmo's requirement of absolute discretion: the garden must be brought to order, but it must also be kept secret. Eventually Safiye had offered the services of her own green thumb. By that time she'd earned enough trust for Señora del Olmo to take her across town to the door of the garden, open it, and allow Safiye to look in. Safiye saw at once that this wasn't a place where any gardener could have influence, and she saw in the roses a perpetual gift, a tangled shock of a studio where Lucy could work and play and study colour. Señora del Olmo instructed Safiye to wait outside, entered the garden and closed the door behind her. After half an hour the Señora emerged, short of breath, with flushed cheeks –

'As if she'd just been kissed?' Lucy asked.

'Not at all like that. It was more as if she'd been seized and shaken like a faulty thermometer. I asked her if there was anybody else in the garden, and she almost screamed at me. *No! No. Why do you ask that?* The Señora had picked a magnificent bunch of yellow roses, with lavender tiger stripes, such vivid flowers that they made her hand look like a wretched cardboard prop for them. Señora del Olmo kept the roses in her lap throughout the carriage ride and by the time we'd reached home she was calm. But I thought there must be someone else in that garden – the question wouldn't have upset her as much otherwise, you know?'

'No one else was there when I was,' Lucy said.

Safiye blinked. 'So you've been there.'

'Yes, and there were only roses.'

'Only roses . . .'

'So how did you get the key?' They were watching each other closely now, Safiye watching for disbelief, Lucy watching for a lie.

'In the evening, I went up to the Señora's sitting room, to see if there was anything she wanted before I went to bed myself. The only other people the Señora employed were a cook and a maid of all work, and they didn't live with us, so they'd gone home for the night. I knocked at the door and the Señora didn't answer, but I heard – a sound.'

'A sound? Like a voice?'

'Yes – no. Creaking. A rusty handle turning, or a wooden door forced open until its hinges buckle, or, to me, to me it was the sound of something growing. I sometimes imagine that if we could hear trees growing we'd hear them . . . creak . . . like that. I knocked again, and the creaking stopped, but a silence began. A silence I didn't feel good about at all. But I felt obliged to do whatever I could do . . . if I left a door closed and it transpired that somebody might have lived if I had only opened it in time . . . I couldn't bear that . . . so I had to try the door no matter what. I prayed that it was locked, but it opened and I saw the Señora standing by the window in the moonlight with her back to me. She was holding a rose cupped in her hands, as if about to drink from it. She was standing very straight, nobody stands as straight as she was standing, not even the dancers at the opera house . . .'

'Dead?'

'No, she was just having a nap. Of course she was fucking dead, Lucy. I lit the lantern on the table and went up close. Her eyes were open and there was some form of *comprehension* in them – I almost thought she was about to hush me; she looked as if she understood what had happened to her, and was about to say: *Shhh, I know. I know. And there's no need for you to know.* It was the most terrible look. The most terrible. I looked at the rest of her to try to forget it, and I saw three things in quick succession: one, that the colour of the rose she was holding was different from the colour of the roses in the vase on the windowsill. The ones in the vase were yellow streaked with lavender, as I told you, and the one in the Señora's hand was orange streaked with brown.'

Lucy mixed paints in the back of her mind. What turned yellow to orange, and blue or purple to brown? Red.

'I also saw that there was a hole in the Señora's chest.'

'A hole?'

'A small precise puncture.' Safiye tapped the centre of Lucy's chest and pushed, gently. 'It went through to the other side. And yet, no blood.'

(It was all in the rose.)

'What else?'

'The stem of the orange rose.' Safiye was shivering again. 'How could I tell these things to a policeman? How could I tell him that this was how I found her? The rose had grown a kind of tail. Long, curved, thorny. I ran away.'

'You took the key first,' Lucy reminded her.

'I took the key and then I ran.'

The lovers closed their eyes on their thoughts and passed from thought into sleep. When Lucy woke, Safiye had gone. She'd left a note – *Wait for me* – and that was the only proof that the night-time visit hadn't been a dream.

* * *

43

A decade later, Lucy was still waiting. The waiting had changed her life. For one thing, she'd left France for Spain. And the only name she now used was her real one, the name that Safiye knew, so that Safiye would be able to find her. And using her real name meant keeping the reputation associated with that name clean. She showed the book of roses she'd made for Safiye to the owner of a gallery; the man asked her to name her price, so she asked for a sum that she herself thought outrageous. He found it reasonable and paid on the spot, then asked her for more. And so Safiye drew Lucy into respectability after all.

Señora Lucy's separation from Safiye meant that she often painted landscapes in which she looked for her. Señora Lucy was rarely visible in these paintings but Safiye always was, and looking at the paintings engaged you in a search for a lost woman, an uneasy search, because somehow in these pictures seeing her never meant the same thing as having found her. Señora Lucy had other subjects; she was working on her own vision of the Judgement of Paris, and Montse had been spending her lunch breaks posing for Señora Lucy's study of Aphrodite. Montse was a fidgeter; again and again she was told, 'No no no no, as you were!' Then Señora Lucy would come and tilt Montse's chin upwards, or trail her fingers through Montse's hair so that it fell over her shoulder just so. And the proximity of that delightful frown clouded Montse's senses to a degree that made her very happy to stay exactly where she was as long as Señora Lucy stayed too.

But these weren't the paintings that sold. It was Señora Lucy's lost-woman paintings that had made her famous. The lost woman was thought to be a representation of the Señora herself, but if anybody had asked Montse about that she would have disagreed. She knew some of these paintings quite well, having found out where a number of them were being exhibited. Sunday morning had become her morning for walking speechlessly among them. Safiye crossed a snowy valley with her back to the onlooker, and she left no footprints. In another painting Safiye climbed down a ladder of clouds; you turned to the next picture frame and she had become a grey-haired woman who closed her eyes and turned to dust at the same time as sweeping herself up with a little brush she held in her left hand.

'And the garden?' Montserrat asked.

Lucy smiled. 'Still mine. I go there once a year. The lock never changes; I think the place has been completely forgotten. Except maybe one day she'll meet me there.'

'I hope she does,' Montse lied. 'But isn't there some danger there?'

'So you believe what she said?'

'Well – yes.'

'Thank you. For saying that. Even if you don't mean it. The papers said that this Señora Fausta del Olmo was stabbed . . . what Safiye described was close enough . . .'

Montse thought that even now it wouldn't be difficult to turn half-fledged doubt into something more substantial. She could say, quite simply, *I'm touched by your constancy, Señora, but I think you're waiting for a murderer.* Running from the strangeness of such a death was understandable; having the presence of mind to take the key was less so. Or, Montse considered, you had to be Safiye to understand it. And, even as herself, Montse couldn't say for sure what she would have done or chosen not to do in such a situation. If that's how you find out who you really are then she didn't want to know. So yes, Montse could help Señora Lucy's doubts along, but there was no honour in pressing such an advantage.

'And what about your own key, Montserrat?'

Lucy's key gleamed and Montse's looked a little sad and dusty; perhaps it was only gold plated. She rubbed at it with her apron.

'Just junk, I think.'

All the shops would be closed by the time Montse finished work, and the next day would be St. Jordi's Day, so Montse ran into the bookshop across the street and chose something with a nice cover to give to Señora Lucy. This errand, combined with the Señora's long story, meant that Montserrat was an hour late returning to the laundry room. She worked long past dinner time, wringing linen under Señora Gaeta's watchful eye, silently cursing the illusions of space that had been created within the attic. All those soaring lines from ceiling to wall disguised the fact that the room was as narrow as a coffin. Finally Señora Gaeta inspected her work and let her go. Only one remark was made about Montse's shamefully late return from lunch: 'You only get to do that once, my dear.'

Montse went home to the room and bed she shared with three other laundry maids more or less the same size as her. She and her bedfellows usually talked until they fell asleep. They were good friends, the four of them; they had to be. That night Montse somehow made it into bed first and the other three climbed in one by one until Montse lay squashed up against the bedroom wall, too tired to add to the conversation.

While Montse had been making up her hours, the other laundry maids had attended a concert and glimpsed a few of La Pedrera's most gossiped-about couples there. For example, there were the Artigas from the third floor and the

Valdeses from the fourth floor, lavishing sepulchral smiles upon each other. Señor Artiga and Señora Valdes were lovers with the tacit consent of his wife and her husband. Señora Valdes' husband was a gentle man many years older than her, a man much saddened by what he saw as a fatal flaw in the building's design. The lift only stopped at every other floor; this forced you to meet your neighbours as you walked the extra flight of stairs up or down. This was how Señora Valdes and Señor Artiga had found themselves alone together in the first place. It was Señor Valdes' hope that his wife's attachment to 'that popinjay' Artiga was a passing fancy. Artiga's wife couldn't wait that long, and had made several not-so-discreet enquiries regarding the engagement of assassins until her husband had stayed her hand by vowing to do away with himself if she harmed so much as a hair on Señora Valdes' head. Why didn't Artiga divorce his wife and ask Señora Valdes to leave her husband and marry him? She'd have done it in a heartbeat, if only he'd asked (so the gossips said). Señor Artiga was unlikely to ask any such thing. His mistress was the most delightful companion he'd ever known, but his wife was an heiress. No man in his right mind leaves an heiress unless he's leaving her for another heiress. 'Maybe in another life, my love,' Artiga told Señora Valdes, causing her to weep in a most gratifying manner. And so, in between their not-so-secret assignations, Artiga and Señora Valdes devoured each other with their eyes, and Señora Artiga raged like one possessed, and Señor Valdes patiently awaited the vindication of an ever-dwindling hope, and their fellow residents got up a petition addressed to the owners of the building, asking that both the Artigas and the Valdeses be evicted. The *conserje* and his wife liked poor old Señor Valdes, but even they'd signed the petition, because La Pedrera's reputation was bad enough, and it was doubtful that this scandalous peace could hold. Laura, Montse's outermost bedmate, was taking bets.

On the morning of St. Jordi's Day, before work began, Montse climbed the staircase to the third floor. *To Lucy from her Aphrodite.* The white walls and window frames wound their patterns around her with the adamant geometry of a seashell. A book and a rose, that was all she was bringing. The Señora wasn't at home. She must be in her garden with all her other roses. Montse set her offering down before Señora Lucy's apartment door, the rose atop the book. And then she went to work.

'Montserrat, have you seen the newspaper?' Assunta called out across the washtubs.

'I never see the newspaper,' Montserrat answered through a mouthful of thread.

'Montserrat, Montserrat of the key,' Marta crooned beside her. The other maids took up the chant until Montse held her needle still and said, 'All right, what's the joke, girls?'

'They're talking about the advertisement that's in *La Vanguardia* this morning,' said Señora Gaeta, placing the newspaper on the lid of Montse's workbasket. Montse laid lengths of thread beneath the lines of newsprint as she read:

ENZO GOMEZ OF GOMEZ, CRUZ AND MOLINA, AWAITS CONTACT WITH A WOMAN WHO BEARS THE NAME MONTSERRAT AND IS IN POSSESSION OF A GOLD KEY ONE AND ONE HALF INCHES IN LENGTH.

Without saying another word, the eagle-eyed Señora Gaeta picked up a scarlet thread an inch and a half long and held it up against Montse's key. The lengths matched. Señora Gaeta rested a hand on Montse's shoulder then walked back up to the front of the room to inspect a heap of newly done laundry before it was returned to its owner. The babble around Montse grew deafening.

'Montse, don't go – it's a trap! This is just like that episode in *Lightning and Undetectable Poisons –*'

'That's our Cecilia, confusing life with one of her beloved radio novellas again . . . so sordid an imagination . . .'

'Let's face it, eh, Montse – you're no good at laundry, you must have been born to be rich!'

'Montserrat, never forget that I, Laura Morales, have always loved you . . . remember I shared my lunch with you on the very first day?'

'. . . When she moves into her new mansion she can have us all to stay for a weekend – come on, Montse! Just one weekend a year.'

'Ladies, ladies,' Señora Gaeta intervened at last. 'I have a headache today. Quiet, or every last one of you will be looking for jobs in hell.'

Montse kept her eyes on her work. It was the only way to keep her mind quiet.

The solicitor, Enzo Gomez, looked at her hands and uniform before he looked into her eyes. Her hands had been roughened by harsh soap and hard water; she fought the impulse to hide them behind her back. Instead she undid the clasp of her necklace and held the key out to him. She told him her name and he jingled a bunch of keys in his own pocket and said: 'The only way we can find out is by trying the lock. So let's go.'

The route they took was familiar. 'Sometimes I go to an art gallery just down that street,' Montse said, pointing. He had already been looking at her but when she said that he began to stare.

'You sometimes go to the Salazar Gallery?'

'Yes . . . they exhibit paintings by –'

'I don't know much about the artists of today; you can only really rely on the old masters . . . but that's where we're going, to the Salazar Gallery.'

Gomez stopped, pulled a folder out of his briefcase and read aloud from a piece of paper in it: 'Against my better judgement but in accordance with the promise I made to my brother Isidoro Salazar, I, Zacarias Salazar, leave the library of my house at seventeen Carrer Alhambra to one Montserrat, who will come with the key to the library as proof of her claim. If the claimant has not come forth within fifty years of my death, let the lock of the library door be changed in order to put an end to this nonsense. For if the mother cannot be found, then how can the daughter?'

Enzo put the folder back. 'I hope you're the one,' he said. 'I've met a lot of Montserrats in this capacity today, most of them chancers. But you – I hope it's you. Are you . . . what do you know of the Salazar family?'

'I know that old Zacarias Salazar was a billionaire, left no biological children but still fathers many artworks through his patronage . . .'

'You read the gallery catalogue thoroughly, I see.'

A gallery attendant opened the main gate for them and showed them around a few gilt-wallpapered passages until they came to the library, which was on its own at the end of a corridor. Montse was dimly aware of Enzo Gomez mopping his forehead with a handkerchief as she placed the key in the lock and turned it. The door opened onto a room with high shelves and higher windows that followed the curve of a cupola ceiling. The laundry maid and the solicitor stood in front of the shelf closest to the door. The sunset lit the chandeliers above them and they found themselves holding hands until Gomez remembered his professionalism and strode over to the nearest desk to remove papers from his briefcase once again.

'I'm glad it's you, Montserrat,' he said, placing the papers on the desk and patting them. 'You must let me know if I can be of service to you in future.' He bowed, shook hands and left her in her library without looking back, the quivering of his trouser cuffs the only visible sign of his emotions.

Montse wandered among the shelves until it was too dark to see. She thought that if the place was really hers she should open it up to the public; there were more books here than could possibly be read in one lifetime. Books on sword-swallowing and life forms found in the ocean, clidomancy and the aurora borealis and other topics that reminded Montse how very much there was to wonder about in this world: there were things she'd seen in dreams that she wanted to see again, and one of these books, any of them, might lead her back to those visions, and then further on, so that she saw marvels while still awake. For now there was the smell of leather-bound books and another faint but definite scent: roses. She cried into her hands because she was lost: she'd carried the key to this place for so long and now that she was here she didn't know where she was. The scent of roses grew stronger and she wiped her hands on her apron, switched on a light and opened the folder Enzo Gomez had handed her.

This is what she read:

Montserrat, I'm very fond of your mother. I was fond of everyone who shared my home. I am a fool, but not the kind who surrounds himself with people he doesn't trust.

I didn't know what was really happening below stairs; we upstairs are always the last to know. Things could have been very different. You would have had a home here, and I would have spoilt you, and doubtless you would have grown up with the most maddening airs and graces. That would have been wonderful.

As I say, I was fond of everyone who lived with me, but I was particularly fond of Aurelie. I am an old man now – an old libertine, even – and my memory commits all manner of betrayals; only a few things stay with me. Some words that made me happy because they were said by exactly the right person at exactly the right time, and some pictures because they formed their own moment. One such picture is your mother's brilliant smile, always slightly anxious, as if even in the moment of delighting you she wonders how she dares to be so very delightful. I hope that smile is before you right now. I hope she came back to you.

Please allow me to say another useless thing: nobody could have made me believe that Aurelie ever stole from me. The only person who could possibly have held your mother in higher esteem than I did was my brother, Isidoro. He told me I should give my library to her. Then he told me she'd be happier if I gave it to her daughter. *Do it or I'll haunt you to death*, he wrote. The rest of this house is dedicated to art now; it's been a long time since I lived here, or visited. But the library is yours. So enjoy it, my dear.

Zacarias Salazar

P.S. I found Aurelie's letter to you enclosed among my brother's papers. I am unsure how it got there.

Aurelie's letter made Montse stand and walk the paths between the shelves as she read, stopping to sit in the cushioned chairs scattered across the library's alcoves. She kept looking up from the page, along the shelves, into the past.

Dear Montserrat,
I should make this quick because I'm coming back for you so really there's no need for it. I suppose really I'm writing this to try to get my brain working properly again. It will be hard to let you go even for a little while, but Isidoro thought that even if worse comes to worst (which it won't) the library key will bring you back here somehow.

I'll tell you about your key: a wish brought it to me. It was my birthday, my thirtieth birthday, and Fausta del Olmo was the only one who knew. There are people who are drawn to secrets as ants are to jam. Fausta's one of them. She searches out all things unspoken and unseen – not to make them known, but to destroy them so that nobody knows they ever existed. That's what makes her heart beat faster, the destruction of invisible foundations. Why? Because she finds it funny. The master once told us about a cousin of his, a lovely, cheerful girl, but touched in the head, he said. This cousin committed suicide one day, quite out of the blue. She did it after talking to her friend on the telephone. That friend now spends her days searching her brain for those disastrous words she must have said, and has become ill herself. As our master was telling us this, I watched Fausta del Olmo out of the corner of my eye. She was laughing ,silently, but the master didn't notice until Fausta's laughter grew so great that she began to choke. She explained that she was overcome by the sadness and the mystery of it all, and she made the sign of the cross. By then I was already so frightened of her that

53

I didn't dare contradict her. There's no stopping Fausta because she believes in hell. The master thinks this belief in hell keeps her on the straight and narrow, but the truth is she's so sure she's going there that she doesn't even care any more. When Fausta brought me a little cake with a candle in it and told me to make a wish, I wanted to say no. It's stupid but I didn't want Fausta to know my birthday, in case she somehow had the power to take it away. If she made it so I was never born, I'd never have had a chance to be me and to hear your father's honey-wine voice and to fall in love with him. He ran off, your father, and if I ever find him I won't be able to stop myself from kicking him in the face for that, the cowardly way he left me here. I didn't yet know I was pregnant, but I bet he knew. He must have developed some sort of instinct for those things. He once said: 'Babies are so . . .' and I thought he was going to say something poetic but he finished: 'expensive.'

I should be making you understand about the key! When I blew out my birthday candle I wished for a million books. I think I wished this because at that time I was having to force my smiles, and I wanted to stop that and to really be happier.

The master has a husband, Pasqual Grec. Not that they were married in church, but that's the way they are with each other. Some of the other servants pretend they've no eyes in their heads and say that Pasqual is just the master's dear friend, but Fausta del Olmo says that they definitely share a bed and that since they are rich they can just do everything they want to do without having to take an interest in anybody's opinion. Your key doesn't seem to want me to talk about it, but I will. I will. The master and Pasqual had fights – maybe three times a week. The master is not an angry man, but he's argumentative in a way that makes other people angry. And Pasqual is an outdoorsman and doesn't like to wait too long between hunts; when he gets restless there are fights – maybe three a week. The master retires to the library for some time and takes his meals in there, and Pasqual goes out with the horses. But when the master comes out of the library he's much more peaceful. I thought it must be all the books that calmed the master down. Millions of books – at least that's how it looks when you just take a quick glance while pretending not to be at all interested. And the day after I made my wish, the key to the library fell into my hands. The master had left it in the pocket of a housecoat he'd sent down to me in the laundry. Of course it could have been any key, but it wasn't. The key and the opportunity to use it came together, for the master and Pasqual had decided to winter in Buenos Aires. I was about four months pregnant by then, and had to bind my stomach to keep you secret and keep my place in the household. I went into the library at night and found peace and fortitude there.

I didn't know where to begin, so I just looked for a name that I knew until I came to a life of Joan of Arc, which I sat down and read really desperately; I read without stopping until the end, as if somebody were chasing me through the pages with a butcher's knife. The next night I read more slowly, a life of Galileo Galilei that took me four nights to finish because his fate was hard to take. I kept saying, 'Those bastards,' and once after saying that I heard a sound in another part of the library. A library at night is full of sounds: the unread books can't stand it any longer and announce their contents, some boasting, some shy, some devious. But the sound I heard wasn't the sound of a book. It was more like a suppressed cough or a sneeze, or a clearing of the throat, or some convulsive, impulsive mix of the three. Everything became very still. Even the books shut up. I looked at the shelf directly in front of me; I read each title on it, spine after spine. There was a gap between the spines, and two eyes looked out of it. Not the master's, or Pasqual's, not the eyes of anybody I could remember having met.

I found the courage to ask: 'What are you doing here?'

'What are YOU doing here?' asked the man. I could hear in his voice that he wasn't well, and then fear left me; I felt we both had our reasons.

'Can't you see I'm reading?' I said. 'Maybe you should read too, instead of SPYING on people.'

'Maybe I should,' he said. 'It's just that I thought you might be like the other one.'

'The other one?'

'Yes. But don't tell her you've seen me.'

'Why not?'

'Because then she'd know that I've seen her . . . and I don't want her to know that until I've spoken to my brother.'

'Your brother?'

'Too much talking, pretty thief. I have to rest now. But promise you won't tell her.'

He didn't need to describe her; it had to be Fausta he was talking about. I didn't even want to know what she'd been up to.

'I'm not a thief,' I said. 'And I won't say anything to her. I haven't seen you, anyway. Only your eyes.'

'Well? What do you think of my eyes, pretty thief?'

'They are an old man's eyes,' I answered, and I held *The Life of Galileo* up in front of my face until I heard him walking away. He walked all the way to the back of the library, and up some stairs – I hadn't known there was a staircase in the library until I heard him going up it – look, Montserrat, and you'll see that there is one, built between two shelves, leading to a door halfway up the wall. Through that door is a wing of the main house that only a few of the servants were familiar with, though we all knew that Isidoro Salazar, the master's younger brother, lived in that part of the house. Lived – well, we knew the man was dying there, and did not wish to be talked to or talked about. A special cook prepared his meals according to certain nutritional principles of immortality that a Swiss doctor had told the master about, and Fausta had told us how she laid the table and served the meals in Isidoro's rooms. He waited in the next room while she did it, and no matter what he ate or didn't eat, he was still dying. When I thought about that I worried that my words might have added to Isidoro's troubles.

The next day, after Fausta had brought him his lunch, I wrote: 'I should not have been like that to you. Rude and thoughtless maid from the library' on a piece of paper, ran up to his rooms and pushed the note under his door. And I stayed away from the library for a while, only returning when the chatter of the books reached me where I slept in the maids' dormitory on the other side of the house. He wasn't there that night, but when I went to my shelf of choice to take down Galileo, I saw a slip of paper sticking out of the neighbouring book. The slip read: *To the pretty thief – read this book, and then look for more.*

I loved some of the books he chose; others sent me to sleep. I turned his slips of paper over and wrote down my thoughts. One of the books he chose was a slim pamphlet of poetry that didn't make much sense to me: I dismissed it with a line borrowed from other poems he'd introduced me to: '*It may wele ryme but it accordith nought.*' He responded with a really long and angry letter – I think he must have been the author of those poems I didn't think were good.

Isidoro wouldn't come near me, even when I began to want him to. We'd spend nights reading together, on separate sides of a shelf, not speaking, listening to the books around us. According to Stendhal it takes about a year and a month to fall in love, all being well. Maybe we fell faster because all was not well with us: every day it got harder for me to keep you to myself, and he could not forget that he was dying; he fought sleep until the nightmares came to take him by force. He fell asleep in the library one night – he had done this twice before, but out of respect for him I had left using a route that meant I could pass him without looking at him. But when I heard him saying: 'No, no . . .' I went to him without thinking and leant over him to try to see whether I should wake him. He was younger than the look in his eyes suggested. I don't know what his sickness was – it had some wasting effect – even as I saw his face I saw that its beauty was diminished. You can read character in a sleeping face, and his was quite a face. The face of a proud man, vengeful and not a little naive, a man with questions he hadn't finished asking and answers to some questions I had myself. He opened his old-man eyes and took a long, deep breath, as if breathing me in. It must have looked as if I was about to kiss him. Our faces were very close and curtains of my hair surrounded us; if we kissed it would be our secret to keep. I kissed him. Then I asked if it had hurt. He said he wasn't sure and that we'd better try it again. And he kissed me back. I didn't want to leave him after that, but I had to be back in bed by the time the other maids began to wake up.

Montserrat, I wrote that being in love with your father was nice, but being in love with Isidoro Salazar was like a dream. Not because of money or anything like that! The man loved foolishly and without regard for the time limit his learned doctors had told him he had; he made me feel that in some way we had always known about each other and that he would be at my side for ever. When Fausta del Olmo took me aside and asked: 'Is there anything you want to tell me?' my blood should have run cold, but it didn't. After all, she could have been asking about the pregnancy.

Beyond Isidoro's staircase is a door that connects to a walled garden. The garden is Isidoro's too: he planted all the roses there himself and took care of them until he got too sick to do anything but just be there with them of an evening. We were often there together. It's a long walk from the top of the garden to the bottom, and I'd carry him some of the way. Yes, on my back, if you can imagine that. He was drowsy because of his medication – he had to take more and more – but even through the haze of his remedies he remembered you: 'The baby!' I told him you didn't mind (you don't, do you?) and that his weight was balancing me out. He grew more lucid when we lay down on the grass. He was so fond of the roses; one night I told him that he wouldn't die, but that he would become roses.

'I wouldn't mind this dying so much if that were true,' he said, slowly. 'But wait a minute . . . roses die too.'

'Well, after that you'd become something else. Maybe a wasp, because then you could go around stinging people who don't like your poems.'

It was around that time that I kept finding gifts on my bed. Little gifts, but they got bigger and bigger. A mother of pearl comb, a calfskin purse, a green cashmere shawl. I told Isidoro to stop giving me gifts. The other servants were asking about them. Isidoro simply smiled at first, but when he asked me to show him the gifts, I saw that he was perplexed and that they hadn't come from him.

'Are you sure there's nothing you want to tell me?' Fausta del Olmo asked, and maybe it was just a beam of sunlight that struck her eye, but I thought she squinted at my stomach. She added that the master would return in two weeks' time. I didn't even answer her. Suddenly she pushed me – if I hadn't clutched the stair-rail I would have fallen – and as she passed me she hissed: 'Why should it be you who sees him?'

That afternoon I found the last gift under my pillow. It was a diamond ring. I put the box in the pocket of my apron and kept it there until night time, when I went to the library. I showed the ring to Isidoro and asked him what I should do. He said I should marry him. He had instructed Fausta del Olmo to put the ring beneath my pillow; he was sure that she had been responsible for the other gifts, even though they were nothing to do with him. She was planning something, but it didn't matter, or wouldn't if I married him.

'Time is of the essence,' Isidoro said. All I could do was look at him with my mouth wide open. And then I said yes. He said I must fetch a priest at once, and I didn't know where to find a priest, so I went and woke Fausta del Olmo up and asked her to help me. She gave me the oddest look and said: 'What do you want a priest for?'

'I'm marrying Isidoro Salazar tonight,' I said.

'Oh, really? And I suppose he's the father of your child, too?' she whispered, her eyes glinting the way they do when she gets hold of a secret at last.

'Please, just hurry.'

Fausta del Olmo put on her coat and slippers and ran

out to fetch a priest, and the man of God arrived quickly; he was calm and had a kind face and took my hand and asked me what the trouble was. 'But didn't you tell him, Fausta, that this is a wedding?'

Fausta shrugged and looked embarrassed and I began to be frightened of her all over again. Something was wrong. I took the priest to the library, and Fausta del Olmo followed us. Isidoro wasn't there, but when I opened the library door, a door at the far, far end of the room slammed shut. Isidoro had seen Fausta and escaped into the rose garden. I went after him, but Fausta and the priest didn't follow me – they were talking, and Fausta was pointing at something . . . I now realize it was the door to Isidoro's rooms that she was pointing at.

Isidoro wasn't in the garden; after searching for him I went back into the library, which was also empty. I could hear a lot of noise and commotion in the rest of the house, footsteps hurrying up and down the wing where Isidoro's rooms were. I saw his rooms, the inside of them, I mean, for the first time that night. The priest Isidoro and I had sent for was praying over a waxen body that lay in the bed. When the priest finished his prayers he said that I must not be afraid to tell him the truth, that no one would punish me, that I'd done well to send for him.

'What do you mean?' I said.

'This man has been dead for at least a day. No, don't shake your head at me, young lady. See how stiff he is. He'd been very ill, poor soul, so this is a release for him. You came here this morning and found him like this, isn't that what happened? And your master is away, so you worried all day about who to tell and what you would say until the worry made you cook up this story in your head about a wedding. Isn't that so?'

61

All the servants were listening, but I still said no, that he was wrong. I put my hand in my pocket to take out my ring and show it to him, but the ring was gone too.

'My ring,' I said, turning to Fausta del Olmo, who replied in the deadliest, most gentle voice: 'What ring, Aurelie? Be careful what you say.'

After that I stopped talking. I looked at the body in the bed and told myself it was Isidoro and no one else. This was a truth that I had to learn – things would go very badly for me if I refused to learn it – but the lesson was very hard indeed.

The priest left, promising to write to the master as soon as he got home, and all we servants went to bed. Fausta was the last to leave Isidoro's room, closing the door behind her as quietly as if he was just sleeping. Then she took my arm and dragged me downstairs to the maids' dormitory, where judge and jury were waiting. Was I mad or was I simply a liar? They'd already taken out the little gifts I'd received and were talking about them: now Fausta told them where the gifts had come from. I'd taken the key to the library from the master's laundry, she announced, and I'd been selling off a number of his valuable books. I inferred that this is what Fausta herself had been doing before I'd interrupted her with my library visits.

'But how stupid, to spend the money on things like this,' the cook said, flapping the green shawl in my face.

'Some people just don't think of the future,' Fausta del Olmo said. A couple of the other maids hadn't joined in and looked as if they didn't entirely believe Fausta del Olmo. Perhaps they'd had their own problems with her. But then Fausta announced that even Isidoro Salazar had known I was a thief. She showed them some of the slips of paper Isidoro had left for me in the library, slips he must

62

have left that time I stayed away. The words 'pretty thief' persuaded them. The master is a generous man and stealing from him causes all sorts of unnecessary difficulties. Now that some of his books are gone he may well become much less generous. The servants drove me out of the dormitory. They went to the kitchen and took pots and pans and banged them together and cried: 'Shame! Shame! Shame!' I stayed in my bed for as long as I could with my covers pulled over my head, but they were so loud. They surrounded my bed, shame, shame, shame, so loud I can still hear it, shame, shame, shame. I fled, and Fausta and the servants chased me through the corridors with their pots and pans and screeching – someone hit me with a spatula and then they all threw spoons, which sounds droll now that it's over, but having silver spoons thrown at you in a dark house is a terrifying thing, you see them flashing against the walls like little swords before they hit you. It would've been worse if those people had actually had knives: they'd completely lost their minds.

I made it into the library by the skin of my teeth and locked the door behind me. I wrote, am writing, this letter to you, my Montserrat. The servants have given up their rough music and have gone to bed. You will be born soon, maybe later today, maybe tomorrow. I feel you close. I know where I will have to leave you. As for this letter, I will give it to the roses, and then I must get out of here for a while. How long? Until I am sure of what happened, or at least the true order of it all. Did I somehow give him more time than he would have had on his own? The entire time I have been writing this letter I have felt Isidoro's eyes on me. He seems to be telling me that we could still have been married, that if I'd only brought the priest and not Fausta we could still have been married. Of course he cannot really be telling me anything: I have seen him as a dead man. Why am I not afraid?

Montse found that she'd walked the length of the library as she read her mother's letter. Now she stood at the door to Isidoro's garden, which opened with the same key. Outside, someone in the shadows took a couple of startled steps backwards. Señora Lucy.

'I saw all this light coming out from under that door,' Lucy said. 'That was new.' She peered over Montse's shoulder. 'Swap you a rose for a book,' she said.

THE TREASURE OF WISDOM

Me, poor man, my library
Was dukedom large enough.

WILLIAM SHAKESPEARE,
The Tempest (1611)

RICHARD DE BURY

From *Philobiblon* (1345)

WHAT WE ARE TO THINK OF THE PRICE IN THE BUYING OF BOOKS

FROM WHAT HAS been said we draw this corollary welcome to us, but (as we believe) acceptable to few: namely,
that no dearness of price ought to hinder a man from the
buying of books, if he has the money that is demanded for
them, unless it be to withstand the malice of the seller or
to await a more favourable opportunity of buying. For if
it is wisdom only that makes the price of books, which is
an infinite treasure to mankind, and if the value of books
is unspeakable, as the premises show, how shall the bargain be shown to be dear where an infinite good is being
bought? Wherefore, that books are to be gladly bought and
unwillingly sold, Solomon, the sun of men, exhorts us in
the Proverbs: Buy the truth, he says, and sell not wisdom.
But what we are trying to show by rhetoric or logic, let us
prove by examples from history. The arch-philosopher Aristotle, whom Averroes regards as the law of Nature, bought
a few books of Speusippus straightway after his death for
72,000 sesterces. Plato, before him in time, but after him
in learning, bought the book of Philolaus the Pythagorean,
from which he is said to have taken the Timaeus, for 10,000
denaries, as Aulus Gellius relates in the Noctes Atticae. Now
Aulus Gellius relates this that the foolish may consider how
wise men despise money in comparison with books. And
on the other hand, that we may know that folly and pride
go together, let us here relate the folly of Tarquin the Proud

in despising books, as also related by Aulus Gellius. An old woman, utterly unknown, is said to have come to Tarquin the Proud, the seventh king of Rome, offering to sell nine books, in which (as she declared) sacred oracles were contained, but she asked an immense sum for them, insomuch that the king said she was mad. In anger she flung three books into the fire, and still asked the same sum for the rest. When the king refused it, again she flung three others into the fire and still asked the same price for the three that were left. At last, astonished beyond measure, Tarquin was glad to pay for three books the same price for which he might have bought nine. The old woman straightway disappeared, and was never seen before or after. These were the Sibylline books, which the Romans consulted as a divine oracle by some one of the Quindecemvirs, and this is believed to have been the origin of the Quindecemvirate. What did this Sibyl teach the proud king by this bold deed, except that the vessels of wisdom, holy books, exceed all human estimation; and, as Gregory says of the kingdom of Heaven: They are worth all that thou hast?

Translated from the Latin by E. C. Thomas

[*Richard de Bury (1281–1345) enjoyed a successful ministerial, diplomatic and ecclesiastical career under Edward III. He became Bishop of Durham in 1333. A great bibliophile, 'he had more books', reported his first biographer William de Chambre, 'than all the other English bishops put together. He had a separate library in each of his residences, and wherever he was residing, so many books lay about his bed-chamber, that it was hardly possible to stand or move without treading upon them . . .' His library was probably sold to pay off debts after his death.*]

UMBERTO ECO

From *The Name of the Rose* (1980)

In which Adso, in the scriptorium, reflects on the history of his order and on the destiny of books. [Nov. 1327]

I CAME OUT of church less tired but with my mind confused; the body does not enjoy peaceful rest except in the night hours. I went up to the scriptorium and, after obtaining Malachi's permission, began to leaf through the catalogue. But as I glanced absently at the pages passing before my eyes, I was really observing the monks.

I was struck by their calm, their serenity. Intent on their work, they seemed to forget that one of their brothers was being anxiously sought throughout the grounds, and that two others had disappeared in frightful circumstances. Here, I said to myself, is the greatness of our order: for centuries and centuries men like these have seen the barbarian hordes burst in, sack their abbeys, plunge kingdoms into chasms of fire, and yet they have gone on cherishing parchments and inks, have continued to read, moving their lips over words that have been handed down through centuries and which they will hand down to the centuries to come. They went on reading and copying as the millennium approached; why should they not continue to do so now?

The day before, Benno had said he would be prepared to sin in order to procure a rare book. He was not lying and not joking. A monk should surely love his books with humility, wishing their good and not the glory of his own curiosity;

but what the temptation of adultery is for laymen and the yearning for riches is for secular ecclesiastics, the seduction of knowledge is for monks.

I leafed through the catalogue, and a feast of mysterious titles danced before my eyes: *Quinti Sereni de medicamentis, Phaenomena, Liber Aesopi de natura animalium, Liber Aethici peronymi de cosmographia, Libri tre quos Arculphus episcopus adamnano escipiente de locis sanctis ultramarinis designavit conscribendos, Libellus Q. Iulii Hilarionis de origine mundi, Solini Polyhistor de situ orbis terrarum et mirabilibus, Almagesthus.* . . . I was not surprised that the mystery of the crimes should involve the library. For these men devoted to writing, the library was at once the celestial Jerusalem and an underground world on the border between terra incognita and Hades. They were dominated by the library, by its promises and by its prohibitions. They lived with it, for it, and perhaps against it, sinfully hoping one day to violate all its secrets. Why should they not have risked death to satisfy a curiosity of their minds, or have killed to prevent someone from appropriating a jealously guarded secret of their own?

Temptations, to be sure; intellectual pride. Quite different was the scribe-monk imagined by our sainted founder, capable of copying without understanding, surrendered to the will of God, writing as if praying, and praying inasmuch as he was writing. Why was it no longer so? Oh, this was surely not the only degeneration of our order! It had become too powerful, its abbots competed with kings: in Abo did I not perhaps have the example of a monarch who, with monarch's demeanor, tried to settle controversies between monarchs? The very knowledge that the abbeys had accumulated was now used as barter goods, cause for pride, motive for boasting and prestige; just as knights displayed armor and

standards, our abbots displayed illuminated manuscripts.
... And all the more so now (what madness!), when our
monasteries had also lost the leadership in learning: cathedral schools, urban corporations, universities were copying
books, perhaps more and better than we, and producing new
ones, and this may have been the cause of many misfortunes.

The abbey where I was staying was probably the last to
boast of excellence in the production and reproduction
of learning. But perhaps for this very reason, the monks
were no longer content with the holy work of copying;
they wanted also to produce new complements of nature,
impelled by the lust for novelty. And they did not realize, as
I sensed vaguely at that moment (and know clearly today,
now aged in years and experience), that in doing so they
sanctioned the destruction of their excellence. Because if
this new learning they wanted to produce were to circulate
fresh outside those walls, then nothing would distinguish
the sacred place any longer from a cathedral school or a
city university. Remaining isolated, on the other hand, it
maintained its prestige and its strength intact, it was not
corrupted by disputation, by the quodlibetical conceit that
would subject every mystery and every greatness to the scrutiny of the sic et non. There, I said to myself, are the reasons
for the silence and the darkness that surround this library:
it is the preserve of learning but can maintain this learning
unsullied only if it prevents its reaching anyone at all, even
the monks themselves. Learning is not like a coin, which
remains physically whole even through the most infamous
transactions; it is, rather, like a very handsome dress, which
is worn out through use and ostentation. Is not a book like
that, in fact? Its pages crumble, its ink and gold turn dull,
if too many hands touch it. I saw Pacificus of Tivoli, leafing
through an ancient volume whose pages had become stuck

together because of the humidity. He moistened his thumb and forefinger with his tongue to leaf through his book, and at every touch of his saliva those pages lost vigor; opening them meant folding them, exposing them to the harsh action of air and dust, which would erode the subtle wrinkles of the parchment, and would produce mildew where the saliva had softened but also weakened the corner of the page. As an excess of sweetness makes the warrior flaccid and inept, this excess of possessive and curious love would make the book vulnerable to the disease destined to kill it.

What should be done? Stop reading, and only preserve? Were my fears correct? What would my master have said?

Nearby I saw a rubricator, Magnus of Iona, who had finished scraping his vellum with pumice stone and was now softening it with chalk, soon to smooth the surface with the ruler. Another, next to him, Rabano of Toledo, had fixed the parchment to the desk, pricking the margins with tiny holes on both sides, between which, with a metal stylus, he was now drawing very fine horizontal lines. Soon the two pages would be filled with colors and shapes, the sheet would become a kind of reliquary, glowing with gems studded in what would then be the devout text of the writing. Those two brothers, I said to myself, are living their hours of paradise on earth. They were producing new books, just like those that time would inexorably destroy. . . . Therefore, the library could not be threatened by any earthly force, it was a living thing. . . . But if it was living, why should it not be opened to the risk of knowledge? Was this what Benno wanted and what Venantius perhaps had wanted?

I felt confused, afraid of my own thoughts. Perhaps they were not fitting for a novice, who should only follow the Rule scrupulously and humbly through all the years to come – which is what I subsequently did, without asking myself further questions, while around me the world was sinking deeper and deeper into a storm of blood and madness.

It was the hour of our morning meal. I went to the kitchen, where by now I had become a friend of the cooks, and they gave me some of the best morsels.

Translated by William Weaver

JOHN BALE

From the preface to *The Laborious Journey and Search of John Leland, for England's Antiquities* (1549)

[The author laments the destruction of monastic libraries during the Reformation – and calls for prompt action.]

... BUT THIS IS highly to be lamented of all them that hath a natural love to their country, either yet to learned antiquity (which is a most singular beauty to the same), that in turning over of the superstitious monasteries so little respect was had to their libraries for the safeguard of those noble and precious monuments. I do not deny it but the monks, canons, and friars were wicked both ways, as the oiled bishops and priests for the more part are yet still: first, for so much as they were the professed soldiers of Antichrist, and next to that, for so much as they were most execrable livers. For these causes I must confess them most justly suppressed, yet this would I have wished (and I scarcely utter it without tears), that the profitable corn had not so unadvisedly and ungodly perished with the unprofitable chaff, nor the wholesome herbs with the unwholesome weeds: I mean the worthy works of men godly-minded and lively memorials of our nation with those lazy lubbers and popish bellygods. . . .

Never had we been offended for the loss of our libraries – being so many in number, and in so desolate places for the most part – if the chief monuments and most notable works of our excellent writers had been reserved. If there had been in every shire of England, but one solemn library, to the preservation of those noble works and preferment of good learnings in our posterity, it had been yet somewhat. But to destroy all without consideration is and will be unto England forever a most horrible infamy among the grave seigniors of other nations. A great number of them which purchased those superstitious mansions reserved of those library books, some to serve their jakes,* some to scour their candlesticks, and some to rub their boots. Some they sold to the grocers and soap sellers, and some they sent over sea to the bookbinders, not in small number, but at times whole ships full, to the wondering of the foreign nations. Yea, the universities of this realm are not all clear in this detestable fact. But cursed is that belly which seeketh to be fed with such ungodly gains, and so deeply shameth his natural country. I know a merchant man, which shall at this time be nameless, that bought the contents of two noble libraries for 40 shillings price – a shame it is to be spoken. This stuff hath he occupied in the stead of gray paper† by the space of more than these ten years, and yet he hath store enough for as many years to come. A prodigious example is this, and to be abhorred of all men which love their nation as they should do. . . .

Yea, what may bring our realm to more shame and rebuke than to have it noised abroad that we are despisers of learning? I judge this to be true, and utter it with heaviness, that neither the Britaines under the Romans and Saxons, nor yet the English people under the Danes and Normans, had ever such damage of their learned monuments as we have seen in our time. Our posterity may well curse this wicked fact of our age, this unreasonable spoil of England's most noble antiquities, unless they be stayed in time, and by the art of printing be brought into a number of copies. The monks kept them under dust, and idle-headed priests regarded

* serve as toilet-paper in their privies or out-houses.
† *gray paper* an unbleached paper used chiefly for wrapping.

them not; their later owners have most shamefully abused them, and the courteous merchants have sold them away into foreign nations for money.

Step you forth now, last of all, ye noble men and women (as there are in these days a great number of you most nobly learned, praise be God for it), and show your natural, noble hearts to your nation. Tread under your feet the unworthy example of these Herostrates or abominable destroyers, and bring you into the light that they kept long in the darkness, or else in these days seeketh utterly to destroy. As ye find a notable antiquity – such as are the histories of Gildas and Nennius among the Britaines, Stephanides and Asserius among the English Saxons – let them anon be imprinted, and so bring them into a number of copies, both to their and your own perpetual fame; for a more notable point of nobility can ye not show than in such sort to beautify your country, and so to restore us to such a truth in histories as we have long wanted.

[*John Bale (1495–1563) was a Carmelite friar who became an enthusiastic Protestant convert. He renounced his vows, married, wrote plays, and preached sermons which sometimes got him into trouble – but he had a powerful protector in Thomas Cromwell. When Henry VIII had Cromwell executed in 1540, Bale prudently departed for Germany. He re-edited John Leland's important work on monastic libraries after his return to England in Edward VI's reign. In 1552 Edward appointed him Bishop of Ossory in Ireland, where his reformist policies proved unsurprisingly controversial. After less than a year, on the accession of a Roman Catholic queen, Mary I, he had to flee for his life, leaving behind the 'two great wain loads' of books he had rescued after the Dissolution. This valuable library, to his chagrin, was in its turn dispersed.*]

ITALO CALVINO

A GENERAL IN
THE LIBRARY
(1953)

Translated by Tim Parks

ONE DAY, IN the illustrious nation of Panduria, a suspicion crept into the minds of top officials: that books contained opinions hostile to military prestige. In fact trials and enquiries had revealed that the tendency, now so widespread, of thinking of generals as people actually capable of making mistakes and causing catastrophes, and of wars as things that did not always amount to splendid cavalry charges towards a glorious destiny, was shared by a large number of books, ancient and modern, foreign and Pandurese.

Panduria's General Staff met together to assess the situation. But they didn't know where to begin, because none of them was particularly well-versed in matters bibliographical. A commission of enquiry was set up under General Fedina, a severe and scrupulous official. The commission was to examine all the books in the biggest library in Panduria.

The library was in an old building full of columns and staircases, the walls peeling and even crumbling here and there. Its cold rooms were crammed to bursting with books, and in parts inaccessible, with some corners only mice could explore. Weighed down by huge military expenditures, Panduria's state budget was unable to offer any assistance.

The military took over the library one rainy morning in November. The general climbed off his horse, squat, stiff, his thick neck shaven, his eyebrows frowning over pince-nez; four lanky lieutenants, chins held high and eyelids lowered, got out of a car, each with a briefcase in his hand. Then came a squadron of soldiers who set up camp in the old courtyard, with mules, bales of hay, tents, cooking equipment, camp radio, and signalling flags.

Sentries were placed at the doors, together with a notice forbidding entry, 'for the duration of large-scale manoeuvres now under way'. This was an expedient which would allow the enquiry to be carried out in great secret. The scholars who used to go to the library every morning wearing heavy coats and scarves and balaclavas so as not to freeze, had to go back home again. Puzzled, they asked each other: 'What's this about large-scale manoeuvres in the library? Won't they make a mess of the place? And the cavalry? And are they going to be shooting too?'

Of the library staff, only one little old man, Signor Crispino, was kept so that he could explain to the officers how the books were arranged. He was a shortish fellow, with a bald, eggish pate and eyes like pinheads behind his spectacles.

First and foremost General Fedina was concerned with the logistics of the operation, since his orders were that the commission was not to leave the library before having completed their enquiry; it was a job that required concentration, and they must not allow themselves to be distracted. Thus a supply of provisions was procured, likewise some barrack stoves and a store of firewood together with some collections of old and it was generally thought uninteresting magazines. Never had the library been so warm in the winter season. Pallet beds for the general and his officers were set up in safe areas surrounded by mousetraps.

Then duties were assigned. Each lieutenant was allotted a particular branch of knowledge, a particular century of history. The general was to oversee the sorting of the volumes and the application of an appropriate rubber stamp depending on whether a book had been judged suitable for officers, NCOs, common soldiers, or should be reported to the Military Court.

And the commission began its appointed task. Every evening the camp radio transmitted General Fedina's report to HQ. 'So many books examined. So many seized as suspect. So many declared suitable for officers and soldiers.' Only rarely were these cold figures accompanied by something out of the ordinary: a request for a pair of glasses to correct short-sightedness for an officer who had broken his, the news that a mule had eaten a rare manuscript edition of Cicero left unattended.

But developments of far greater import were under way, about which the camp radio transmitted no news at all. Rather than thinning out, the forest of books seemed to grow ever more tangled and insidious. The officers would have lost their way had it not been for the help of Signor Crispino. Lieutenant Abrogati, for example, would jump to his feet and throw the book he was reading down on the table: 'But this is outrageous! A book about the Punic Wars that speaks well of the Carthaginians and criticizes the Romans! This must be reported at once!' (It should be said here that, rightly or wrongly, the Pandurians considered themselves descendants of the Romans.) Moving silently in soft slippers, the old librarian came up to him. 'That's nothing,' he would say, 'read what it says here, about the Romans again, you can put this in your report too, and this and this,' and he presented him with a pile of books. The lieutenant leafed nervously through them, then, getting interested, he began to read, to take notes. And he would scratch his head and mutter: 'For heaven's sake! The things you learn! Who would ever have thought!' Signor Crispino went over to Lieutenant Lucchetti who was closing a tome in rage, declaring: 'Nice stuff this is! These people have the audacity to entertain doubts as to the purity of the ideals that inspired the Crusades! Yessir, the Crusades!' And Signor Crispino said with a smile: 'Oh, but look, if you have to make a report on that subject, may I suggest a few other books that will offer more details,' and he pulled down half a shelf-full. Lieutenant Lucchetti leaned forward and got stuck in, and for a week you could hear him flicking through the pages and muttering: 'These Crusades though, very nice I must say!'

In the commission's evening report, the number of books examined got bigger and bigger, but they no longer provided figures relative to positive and negative verdicts. General Fedina's rubber stamps lay idle. If, trying to check up on the work of one of the lieutenants, he asked, 'But why did you pass this novel? The soldiers come off better than the officers! This author has no respect for hierarchy!', the lieutenant would answer by quoting other authors and getting all muddled up in matters historical, philosophical and economic. This led to open discussions that went on for hours and hours. Moving silently in his slippers, almost invisible in his grey shirt, Signor Crispino would always join in at the right moment, offering some book which he felt contained interesting information on the subject under consideration, and which always had the effect of radically undermining General Fedina's convictions.

Meanwhile the soldiers didn't have much to do and were getting bored. One of them, Barabasso, the best educated, asked the officers for a book to read. At first they wanted to give him one of the few that had already been declared fit for the troops; but remembering the thousands of volumes still to be examined, the general was loth to think of Private Barabasso's reading hours being lost to the cause of duty; and he gave him a book yet to be examined, a novel that looked easy enough, suggested by Signor Crispino. Having read the book, Barabasso was to report to the general. Other soldiers likewise requested and were granted the same duty. Private Tommasone read aloud to a fellow soldier who couldn't read, and the man would give him his opinions. During open discussions, the soldiers began to take part along with the officers.

Not much is known about the progress of the commission's work: what happened in the library through the long winter weeks was not reported. All we know is that General Fedina's radio reports to General Staff headquarters became ever more infrequent, until finally they stopped altogether. The Chief of Staff was alarmed; he transmitted the order to wind up the enquiry as quickly as possible and present a full and detailed report.

In the library, the order found the minds of Fedina and his men prey to conflicting sentiments: on the one hand they were constantly discovering new interests to satisfy and were enjoying their reading and studies more than they would ever have imagined; on the other hand they couldn't wait to be back in the world again, to take up life again, a world and a life that seemed so much more complex now, as though renewed before their very eyes; and on yet another hand, the fact that the day was fast approaching when they would have to leave the library filled them with apprehension, for they would have to give an account of their mission, and with all the ideas that were bubbling up in their heads they had no idea how to get out of what had become a very tight corner indeed.

In the evening they would look out of the windows at the first buds on the branches glowing in the sunset, at the lights going on in the town, while one of them read some poetry out loud. Fedina wasn't with them: he had given the order that he was to be left alone at his desk to draft the final report. But every now and then the bell would ring and the others would hear him calling: 'Crispino! Crispino!' He couldn't get anywhere without the help of the old librarian, and they ended up sitting at the same desk writing the report together.

One bright morning the commission finally left the library and went to report to the Chief of Staff; and Fedina illustrated the results of the enquiry before an assembly of the General Staff. His speech was a kind of compendium of human history from its origins down to the present day, a compendium in which all those ideas considered beyond discussion by the right-minded folk of Panduria were attacked, in which the ruling classes were declared responsible for the nation's misfortunes, and the people exalted as the heroic victims of mistaken policies and unnecessary wars. It was a somewhat confused presentation including, as can happen with those who have only recently embraced new ideas, declarations that were often simplistic and contradictory. But as to the overall meaning there could be no doubt. The assembly of generals was stunned, their eyes opened wide, then they found their voices and began to shout. General Fedina was not even allowed to finish. There was talk of a court-martial, of his being reduced to the ranks. Then, afraid there might be a more serious scandal, the general and the four lieutenants were each pensioned off for health reasons, as a result of 'a serious nervous breakdown suffered in the course of duty'. Dressed in civilian clothes, with heavy coats and thick sweaters so as not to freeze, they were often to be seen going into the old library where Signor Crispino would be waiting for them with his books.

LORRIE MOORE

COMMUNITY LIFE
(1991)

WHEN OLENA WAS a little girl, she had called them lie-berries – a fibbing fruit, a story store – and now she had a job in one. She had originally wanted to teach English literature, but when she failed to warm to the graduate study of it, its french-fried theories – a vocabulary of arson! – she'd transferred to library school, where everyone was taught to take care of books, tenderly, as if they were dishes or dolls.

She had learned to read at an early age. Her parents, newly settled in Vermont from Tirgu Mures in Transylvania, were anxious that their daughter learn to speak English, to blend in with the community in a way they felt they probably never would, and so every Saturday they took her to the children's section of the Rutland library and let her spend time with the librarian, who chose books for her and sometimes even read a page or two out loud, though there was a sign that said PLEASE BE QUIET BOYS AND GIRLS. No comma.

Which made it seem to Olena that only the boys had to be quiet. She and the librarian could do whatever they wanted.

She had loved the librarian.

And when Olena's Romanian began to recede altogether, and in its stead bloomed a slow, rich English-speaking voice, not unlike the librarian's, too womanly for a little girl, the other children on her street became even more afraid of her. '*Dracula!*' they shouted. '*Transylvaniess!*' they shrieked, and ran.

'You'll have a new name now,' her father told her the first day of first grade. He had already changed their last name from Todorescu to Resnick. His shop was called 'Resnick's Furs.' 'From here on in, you will no longer be Olena. You will have a nice American name: Nell.'

'You make to say ze name,' her mother said. 'When ze teacher tell you *Olena*, you say, "*No, Nell*." Say *Nell*.'

'Nell,' said Olena. But when she got to school, the teacher, sensing something dreamy and outcast in her, clasped her hand and exclaimed, 'Olena! What a beautiful name!' Olena's heart filled with gratitude and surprise, and she fell in close to the teacher's hip, adoring and mute.

From there on in, only her parents, in their throaty Romanian accents, ever called her Nell, her secret, jaunty American self existing only for them.

'Nell, how are ze ozer children at ze school?'

'Nell, please to tell us what you do.'

Years later, when they were killed in a car crash on the Farm to Market Road, and the Nell-that-never-lived died with them, Olena, numbly rearranging the letters of her own name on the envelopes of the sympathy cards she received, discovered what the letters spelled: *Olena*; *Alone*. It was a body walled in the cellar of her, a whiff and forecast of doom like an early, rotten spring – and she longed for the Nell-that-never-lived's return. She wished to start over again, to be someone living coltishly in the world, not someone hidden away, behind books, with a carefully learned voice and a sad past.

She missed her mother the most.

The library Olena worked in was one of the most prestigious university libraries in the Midwest. It housed a large collection of rare and foreign books, and she had driven across several states to get there, squinting through the splattered tempera of insects on the windshield, watching for the dark tail of a possible tornado, and getting sick, painfully, in Indiana, in the rest rooms of the dead-Hoosier service plazas along I-80. The ladies' rooms there had had electric eyes for the toilets, the sinks, the hand dryers, and she'd set them all off by staggering in and out of the stalls or leaning into the sinks. 'You the only one in here?' asked a cleaning woman. 'You the only one in here making this racket?' Olena had smiled, a dog's smile; in the yellowish light, everything seemed tragic and ridiculous and unable to stop. The flatness of the terrain gave her vertigo, she decided, that was it. The land was windswept; there were no smells. In Vermont, she had felt cradled by mountains. Now, here, she would have to be brave.

But she had no memory of how to be brave. Here, it seemed, she had no memories at all. Nothing triggered them. And once in a while, when she gave voice to the fleeting edge of one, it seemed like something she was making up.

She first met Nick at the library in May. She was temporarily positioned at the reference desk, hauled out from her ordinary task as supervisor of foreign cataloging, to replace someone who was ill. Nick was researching statistics on municipal campaign spending in the state. 'Haven't stepped into a library since I was eighteen,' he said. He looked at least forty.

She showed him where he might look. 'Try looking here,' she said, writing down the names of indexes to state records, but he kept looking at *her*. 'Or here.'

'I'm managing a county board seat campaign,' he said. 'The election's not until the fall, but I'm trying to get a jump on things.' His hair was a coppery brown, threaded through with silver. There was something animated in his eyes, like pond life. 'I just wanted to get some comparison figures. Will you have a cup of coffee with me?'

'I don't think so,' she said.

But he came back the next day and asked her again.

The coffee shop near campus was hot and noisy, crowded with students, and Nick loudly ordered espresso for them both. She usually didn't like espresso, its gritty, cigarish taste. But there was in the air that kind of distortion that bent you a little; it caused your usual self to grow slippery, to wander off and shop, to get blurry, bleed, bevel with possibility. She drank the espresso fast, with determination and a sense of adventure. 'I guess I'll have a second,' she said, and wiped her mouth with a napkin.

'I'll get it,' said Nick, and when he came back, he told her some more about the campaign he was running. 'It's important to get the endorsements of the neighborhood associations,' he said. He ran a bratwurst and frozen yogurt stand called Please Squeeze and Bratwursts. He had gotten to know a lot of people that way. 'I feel alive and relevant, living my life like this,' he said. 'I don't feel like I've sold out.'

'Sold out to what?' she asked.

He smiled. 'I can tell you're not from around here,' he said. He raked his hand through the various metals of his hair. '*Selling out.* Like doing something you really never wanted to do, and getting paid too much for it.'

'Oh,' she said.

'When I was a kid, my father said to me, "Sometimes in life, son, you're going to find you have to do things you don't want to do," and I looked him right in the eye and said, "No fucking way."' Olena laughed. 'I mean, you probably always wanted to be a librarian, right?'

She looked at all the crooked diagonals of his face and couldn't tell whether he was serious. 'Me?' she said. 'I first went to graduate school to be an English professor.' She sighed, switched elbows, sinking her chin into her other hand. 'I did try,' she said. 'I read Derrida. I read Lacan. I read *Reading Lacan*. I read "Reading *Reading Lacan*" – and that's when I applied to library school.'

'I don't know who Lacan is,' he said.

'He's, well – you see? That's why I like libraries: No whos or whys. Just "where is it?"'

'And *where* are you from?' he asked, his face briefly animated by his own clever change of subject. 'Originally.' There was, it seemed, a way of spotting those not native to the town. It was a college town, attractive and dull, and it hurried the transients along – the students, gypsies, visiting scholars and comics – with a motion not unlike peristalsis.

'Vermont,' she said.

'Vermont!' Nick exclaimed, as if this were exotic, which made her glad she hadn't said something like Transylvania. He leaned toward her, confidentially. 'I have to tell you: I own one chair from Ethan Allen Furniture.'

'You do?' She smiled. 'I won't tell anyone.'

'Before that, however, I was in prison, and didn't own a stick.'

'Really?' she asked. She sat back. Was he telling the truth? As a girl, she'd been very gullible, but she had always learned more that way.

'I went to school here,' he said. 'In the sixties. I bombed a warehouse where the military was storing research supplies. I got twelve years.' He paused, searching her eyes to see how she was doing with this, how *he* was doing with it. Then he fetched back his gaze, like a piece of jewelry he'd merely wanted to show her, quick. 'There wasn't supposed to be anyone there; we'd checked it all out in advance. But this poor asshole named Lawrence Sperry – Larry Sperry! Christ, can you imagine having a name like that?'

'Sure,' said Olena.

Nick looked at her suspiciously. 'He was in there, working late. He lost a leg and an eye in the explosion. I got the federal pen in Winford. Attempted murder.'

The thick coffee coated his lips. He had been looking steadily at her, but now he looked away.

'Would you like a bun?' asked Olena. 'I'm going to go get a bun.' She stood, but he turned and gazed up at her with such disbelief that she sat back down again, sloppily, sidesaddle. She twisted forward, leaned into the table. 'I'm sorry. Is that all true, what you just said? Did that really happen to you?'

'*What?*' His mouth fell open. 'You think I'd make that up?'

'It's just that, well, I work around a lot of literature,' she said.

' "Literature," ' he repeated.

She touched his hand. She didn't know what else to do. 'Can I cook dinner for you some night? Tonight?'

There was a blaze in his eye, a concentrated seeing. He seemed for a moment able to look right into her, know her in a way that was uncluttered by actually knowing her. He seemed to have no information or misinformation, only a kind of photography, factless but true.

'Yes,' he said, 'you can.'

Which was how he came to spend the evening beneath the cheap stained-glass lamp of her dining room, its barroom red, its Schlitz-Tiffany light, and then to spend the night, and not leave.

* * *

Olena had never lived with a man before. 'Except my father,' she said, and Nick studied her eyes, the streak of blankness in them, when she said it. Though she had dated two different boys in college, they were the kind who liked to leave early, to eat breakfast without her at smoky greasy spoons, to sit at the counter with the large men in the blue windbreakers, read the paper, get their cups refilled.

She had never been with anyone who stayed. Anyone who'd moved in his box of tapes, his Ethan Allen chair.

Anyone who'd had lease problems at his old place.

'I'm trying to bring this thing together,' he said, holding her in the middle of the afternoon. 'My life, the campaign, my thing with you: I'm trying to get all my birds to land in the same yard.' Out the window, there was an afternoon moon, like a golf ball, pocked and stuck. She looked at the calcified egg of it, its coin face, its blue neighborhood of nothing. Then she looked at him. There was the pond life again in his eyes, and in the rest of his face a hesitant, warm stillness.

'Do you like making love to me?' she asked, at night, during a thunderstorm.

'Of course. Why do you ask?'

'Are you satisfied with me?'

He turned toward her, kissed her. 'Yes,' he said. 'I don't need a show.'

She was quiet for a long time. 'People are giving shows?'

The rain and wind rushed down the gutters, snapped the branches of the weak trees in the side yard.

He had her inexperience and self-esteem in mind. At the movies, at the beginning, he whispered, 'Twentieth Century-Fox. Baby, that's you.' During a slapstick part, in a library where card catalogs were upended and scattered wildly through the air, she broke into a pale, cold sweat, and he moved toward her, hid her head in his chest, saying, 'Don't look, don't look.' At the end, they would sit through the long credits – gaffer, best boy, key grip. 'That's what *we* need to get,' he said. 'A grip.'

'Yes,' she said. 'Also a *negative cutter.*'

Other times, he encouraged her to walk around the house naked. 'If you got it, do it.' He smiled, paused, feigned confusion. 'If you do it, have it. If you flaunt it, do it.'

'If you have it, got it,' she added.

'If you say it, mean it.' And he pulled her toward him like a dancing partner with soft shoes and the smiling mouth of love.

But too often she lay awake, wondering. There was something missing. Something wasn't happening to her, or was it to him? All through the summer, the thunderstorms set the sky on fire while she lay there, listening for the train sound of a tornado, which never came – though the lightning ripped open the night and lit the trees like things too suddenly remembered, then left them indecipherable again in the dark.

'You're not feeling anything, are you?' he finally said. 'What is wrong?'

'I'm not sure,' she said cryptically. 'The rainstorms are so loud in this part of the world.' The wind from a storm blew through the screens and sometimes caused the door to the bedroom to slam shut. 'I don't like a door to slam,' she whispered. 'It makes me think someone is mad.'

At the library, there were Romanian books coming in – Olena was to skim them, read them just enough to proffer a brief description for the catalog listing. It dismayed her that her Romanian was so weak, that it had seemed almost to vanish, a mere handkerchief in a stairwell, and that now, daily, another book arrived to reprimand her.

She missed her mother the most.

On her lunch break, she went to Nick's stand for a frozen yogurt. He looked tired, bedraggled, his hair like sprockets. 'You want the Sperry Cherry or the Lemon Bomber?' he asked. These were his joke names, the ones he threatened really to use someday.

'How about apple?' she said.

He cut up an apple and arranged it in a paper dish. He squeezed yogurt from a chrome machine. 'There's a fund-raiser tonight for the Teetlebaum campaign.'

'Oh,' she said. She had been to these fund-raisers before. At first she had liked them, glimpsing corners of the city she would never have seen otherwise, Nick leading her out into them, Nick knowing everyone, so that it seemed her life filled with possibility, with homefulness. But finally, she felt, such events were too full of dreary, glad-handing people speaking incessantly of their camping trips out west. They never really spoke *to* you. They spoke toward you. They spoke at you. They spoke near you, on you. They believed themselves crucial to the welfare of the community. But they seldom went to libraries. They didn't read books. 'At least they're *contributers to the community*,' said Nick. 'At least they're not sucking the blood of it.'

'Lapping,' she said.

'What?'

'Gnashing and lapping. Not sucking.'

He looked at her in a doubtful, worried way. 'I looked it up once,' she said.

'Whatever.' He scowled. 'At least they care. At least they're trying to give something back.'

'I'd rather live in Russia,' she said.

95

'I'll be back around ten or so,' he said.

'You don't want me to come?' Truth was she disliked Ken Teetlebaum. Perhaps Nick had figured this out. Though he had the support of the local leftover Left, there was something fatuous and vain about Ken. He tended to do little isometric leg exercises while you were talking to him. Often he took out a Woolworth photo of himself and showed it to people. 'Look at this,' he'd say. 'This was back when I had long hair, can you believe it?' And people would look and see a handsome teenaged boy who bore only a slight resemblance to the puffy Ken Teetlebaum of today. 'Don't I look like Eric Clapton?'

'Eric Clapton would never have sat in a Woolworth photo booth like some high school girl,' Olena had said once, in the caustic blurt that sometimes afflicts the shy. Ken had looked at her in a laughing, hurt sort of way, and after that he stopped showing the photo around when she was present.

'You can come, if you want to.' Nick reached up, smoothed his hair, and looked handsome again. 'Meet me there.'

The fund-raiser was in the upstairs room of a local restaurant called Dutch's. She paid ten dollars, went in, and ate a lot of raw cauliflower and hummus before she saw Nick back in a far corner, talking to a woman in jeans and a brown blazer. She was the sort of woman that Nick might twist around to look at in restaurants: fiery auburn hair cut bluntly in a pageboy. She had a pretty face, but the hair was too severe, too separate and tended to. Olena herself had long, disorganized hair, and she wore it pulled back messily in a clip. When she reached up to wave to Nick, and he looked away without acknowledging her, back toward the auburn pageboy, Olena kept her hand up and moved it back, to fuss with the clip.

She would never fit in here, she thought. Not among these jolly, activist-clerk types. She preferred the quiet poet-clerks of the library. They were delicate and territorial, intellectual, and physically unwell. They sat around at work, thinking up Tom Swifties: *I have to go to the hardware store, he said wrenchingly.*

Would you like a soda? he asked spritely.

They spent weekends at the Mayo Clinic. 'An amusement park for hypochondriacs,' said a cataloger named Sarah. 'A cross between Lourdes and *The New Price Is Right,*' said someone else named George. These were the people she liked: the kind you couldn't really live with.

She turned to head toward the ladies' room and bumped into Ken. He gave her a hug hello, and then whispered in her ear, 'You live with Nick. Help us think of an issue. I need another issue.'

'I'll get you one at the issue store,' she said, and pulled away as someone approached him with a heartily extended hand and a false, booming 'Here's the man of the hour.' In the bathroom, she stared at her own reflection: in an attempt at extroversion, she had worn a tunic with large slices of watermelon depicted on the front. What had she been thinking of?

She went into the stall and slid the bolt shut. She read the graffiti on the back of the door. *Anita loves David S.* Or: *Christ + Diane W.* It was good to see that even in a town like this, people could love one another.

'Who were you talking to?' she asked him later at home.

'Who? What do you mean?'

'The one with the plasticine hair.'

'Oh, Erin? She does look like she does something to her hair. It looks like she hennas it.'

'It looks like she tacks it against the wall and stands under-neath it.'

'She's head of the Bayre Corners Neighborhood Asso-ciation. Come September, we're really going to need her endorsement.'

Olena sighed, looked away.

'It's the democratic process,' said Nick.

'I'd rather have a king and queen,' she said.

The following Friday, the night of the Fish Fry Fund-raiser at the Labor Temple, was the night Nick slept with Erin of the Bayre Corners Neighborhood Association. He arrived back home at seven in the morning and confessed to Olena, who, when Nick hadn't come home, had downed half a packet of Dramamine to get to sleep.

'I'm sorry,' he said, his head in his hands. 'It's a sixties thing.'

'A sixties thing?' She was fuzzy, zonked from the Dramamine.

'You get all involved in a political event, and you find yourself sleeping together. She's from that era, too. It's also that, I don't know, she just seems to really care about her community. She's got this reaching, expressive side to her. I got caught up in that.' He was sitting down, leaning for-ward on his knees, talking to his shoes. The electric fan was blowing on him, moving his hair gently, like weeds in water.

'A sixties thing?' Olena repeated. 'A sixties thing, what is that – like "Easy to Be Hard"?' It was the song she remem-bered best. But now something switched off in her. The bones in her chest hurt. Even the room seemed changed – brighter and awful. Everything had fled, run away to become something else. She started to perspire under her arms and her face grew hot. 'You're a murderer,' she said.

'That's finally what you are. That's finally what you'll always be.' She began to weep so loudly that Nick got up, closed the windows. Then he sat down and held her – who else was there to hold her? – and she held him back.

He bought her a large garnet ring, a cough drop set in brass. He did the dishes ten straight days in a row. She had a tendency to go to bed right after supper and sleep, heavily, needing the escape. She had become afraid of going out – restaurants, stores, the tension in her shoulders, the fear gripping her face when she was there, as if people knew she was a foreigner and a fool – and for fifteen additional days he did the cooking and shopping. His car was always parked on the outside of the driveway, and hers was always in first, close, blocked in, as if to indicate who most belonged to the community, to the world, and who most belonged tucked in away from it, in a house. Perhaps in bed. Perhaps asleep.

'You need more life around you,' said Nick, cradling her, though she'd gone stiff and still. His face was plaintive and suntanned, the notes and varnish of a violin. 'You need a greater sense of life around you.' Outside, there was the old rot smell of rain coming.

'How have you managed to get a suntan when there's been so much rain?' she asked.

'It's summer,' he said. 'I work outside, remember?'

'There are no sleeve marks,' she said. 'Where are you going?'

She had become afraid of the community. It was her enemy. Other people, other women.

She had, without realizing it at the time, learned to follow Nick's gaze, learned to learn his lust, and when she did go out, to work at least, his desires remained memorized within her. She looked at the attractive women he would look at.

She turned to inspect the face of every pageboy haircut she saw from behind and passed in her car. She looked at them furtively or squarely – it didn't matter. She appraised their eyes and mouths and wondered about their bodies. She had become him: she longed for these women. But she was also herself, and so she despised them. She lusted after them, but she also wanted to beat them up.

A rapist.

She had become a rapist, driving to work in a car.

But for a while, it was the only way she could be.

She began to wear his clothes – a shirt, a pair of socks – to keep him next to her, to try to understand why he had done what he'd done. And in this new empathy, in this pants role, like an opera, she thought she understood what it was to make love to a woman, to open the hidden underside of her, like secret food, to thrust yourself up in her, her arch and thrash, like a puppet, to watch her later when she got up and walked around without you, oblivious to the injury you'd surely done her. How could you not love her, gratefully, marveling? She was so mysterious, so recovered, an unshared thought enlivening her eyes; you wanted to follow her forever.

A man in love. That was a man in love. So different from a woman.

A woman cleaned up the kitchen. A woman gave and hid, gave and hid, like someone with a May basket.

She made an appointment with a doctor. Her insurance covered her only if she went to the university hospital, and so she made an appointment there.

'I've made a doctor's appointment,' she said to Nick, but he had the water running in the tub and didn't hear her. 'To find out if there's anything wrong with me.'

When he got out, he approached her, nothing on but a towel, pulled her close to his chest, and lowered her to the floor, right there in the hall by the bathroom door. Something was swooping, back and forth in an arc above her. May Day, May Day. She froze.

'What was that?' She pushed him away.

'What?' He rolled over on his back and looked. Something was flying around in the stairwell – a bird. 'A bat,' he said.

'Oh my God,' cried Olena.

'The heat can bring them out in these old rental houses,' he said, stood, rewrapped his towel. 'Do you have a tennis racket?'

She showed him where it was. 'I've only played tennis once,' she said. 'Do you want to play tennis sometime?' But he proceeded to stalk the bat in the dark stairwell.

'Now don't get hysterical,' he said.

'I'm already hysterical.'

'Don't get – There!' he shouted, and she heard the *thwack* of the racket against the wall, and the soft drop of the bat to the landing.

She suddenly felt sick. 'Did you have to kill it?' she said.

'What did you want me to do?'

'I don't know. Capture it. Rough it up a little.' She felt guilty, as if her own loathing had brought about its death. 'What kind of bat is it?' She tiptoed up to look, to try to glimpse its monkey face, its cat teeth, its pterodactyl wings veined like beet leaves. 'What kind? Is it a fruit bat?'

'Looks pretty straight to me,' said Nick. With his fist, he tapped Olena's arm lightly, teasingly.

'Will you stop?'

'Though it *was* doing this whole astrology thing – I don't know. Maybe it's a zodiac bat.'

'Maybe it's a brown bat. It's not a vampire bat, is it?'

'I think you have to go to South America for those,' he said. 'Take your platform shoes!'

She sank down on the steps, pulled her robe tighter. She felt for the light switch and flicked it on. The bat, she could now see, was small and light-colored, its wings folded in like a packed tent, a mouse with backpacking equipment. It had a sweet face, like a deer, though blood drizzled from its head. It reminded her of a cat she'd seen once as a child, shot with a BB in the eye.

'I can't look anymore,' she said, and went back upstairs.

Nick appeared a half hour later, standing in the doorway. She was in bed, a book propped in her lap – a biography of a French feminist, which she was reading for the hairdo information.

'I had lunch with Erin today,' he said.

She stared at the page. Snoods. Turbans and snoods. You could go for days in a snood. 'Why?'

'A lot of different reasons. For Ken, mostly. She's still head of the neighborhood association, and he needs her endorsement. I just wanted to let you know. Listen, you've gotta cut me some slack.'

She grew hot in the face again. 'I've cut you some slack,' she said. 'I've cut you a whole forest of slack. The whole global slack forest has been cut for you.' She closed the book. 'I don't know why you cavort with these people. They're nothing but a bunch of clerks.'

He'd been trying to look pleasant, but now he winced a little. 'Oh, I see,' he said. 'Miss High-Minded. You whose father made his living off furs. Furs!' He took two steps toward her, then turned and paced back again. 'I can't believe I'm living with someone who grew up on the proceeds of tortured animals!'

She was quiet. This lunge at moral fastidiousness was

something she'd noticed a lot in the people around here. They were not good people. They were not kind. They played around and lied to their spouses. But they recycled their newspapers!

'Don't drag my father into this.'

'Look, I've spent years of my life working for peace and free expression. I've been in prison already. I've lived in a cage! I don't need to live in another one.'

'You and your free expression! You who can't listen to me for two minutes!'

'Listen to you what?'

'Listen to me when I' – and here she bit her lip a little – 'when I tell you that these people you care about, this hateful Erin what's-her-name, they're just small, awful, nothing people.'

'So they don't *read enough books*,' he said slowly. 'Who the fuck cares.'

The next day he was off to a meeting with Ken at the Senior Citizens Association. The host from *Jeopardy!* was going to be there, and Ken wanted to shake a few hands, sign up volunteers. The host from *Jeopardy!* was going to give a talk.

'I don't get it,' Olena said.

'I know.' He sighed, the pond life treading water in his eyes. 'But, well – it's the American way.' He grabbed up his keys, and the look that quickly passed over his face told her this: she wasn't pretty enough.

'I hate America,' she said.

Nonetheless, he called her at the library during a break. She'd been sitting in the back with Sarah, thinking up Tom Swifties, her brain ready to bleed from the ears, when the phone rang. 'You should see this,' he said. 'Some old geezer raises his hand, I call on him, and he stands up, and the first thing he says is, "I had my hand raised for ten whole minutes and you kept passing over me. I don't like to be passed over. You can't just pass over a guy like me, not at my age."'

She laughed, as he wanted her to.

This hot dog's awful, she said frankly.

'To appeal to the doctors, Ken's got all these signs up that say "Teetlebaum for tort reform."'

'Sounds like a Wallace Stevens poem,' she said.

'I don't know what I expected. But the swirl of this whole event has not felt right.'

She's a real dog, he said cattily.

She was quiet, deciding to let him do the work of this call.

'Do you realize that Ken's entire softball team just wrote a letter to *The Star*, calling him a loudmouth and a cheat?'

'Well,' she said, 'what can you expect from a bunch of grown men who pitch underhand?'

There was some silence. 'I care about us,' he said finally. 'I just want you to know that.'

'Okay,' she said.

'I know I'm just a pain in the ass to you,' he said. 'But you're an inspiration to me, you are.'

I like a good sled dog, she said huskily.

'Thank you for just – for saying that,' she said.

'I just sometimes wish you'd get involved in the community, help out with the campaign. Give of yourself. Connect a little with something.'

At the hospital, she got up on the table and pulled the paper gown tightly around her, her feet in the stirrups. The doctor took a plastic speculum out of a drawer. 'Anything particular seem to be the problem today?' asked the doctor.

'I just want you to look and tell me if there's anything wrong,' said Olena.

The doctor studied her carefully. 'There's a class of medical students outside. Do you mind if they come in?'

'Excuse me?'

'You know this is a teaching hospital,' she said. 'We hope that our patients won't mind contributing to the education of our medical students by allowing them in during an examination. It's a way of contributing to the larger medical community, if you will. But it's totally up to you. You can say no.'

Olena clutched at her paper gown. *There's never been an accident, she said recklessly.* 'How many of them are there?'

The doctor smiled quickly. 'Seven,' she said. 'Like dwarfs.'

'They'll come in and do what?'

The doctor was growing impatient and looked at her watch. 'They'll participate in the examination. It's a learning visit.'

Olena sank back down on the table. She didn't feel that she could offer herself up this way. *You're only average, he said meanly.*

'All right,' she said. 'Okay.'

Take a bow, he said sternly.

The doctor opened up the doorway and called a short way down the corridor. 'Class?'

They were young, more than half of them men, and they gathered around the examination table in a horseshoe shape, looking slightly ashamed, sorry for her, no doubt, the way art students sometimes felt sorry for the shivering model they were about to draw. The doctor pulled up a stool between Olena's feet and inserted the plastic speculum, the stiff, widening arms of it uncomfortable, embarrassing. 'Today we will be doing a routine pelvic examination,' she announced loudly, and then she got up again, went to a drawer, and passed out rubber gloves to everyone.

Olena went a little blind. A white light, starting at the center, spread to the black edges of her sight. One by one, the hands of the students entered her, or pressed on her abdomen, felt hungrily, innocently, for something to learn from her, in her.

She missed her mother the most.

'Next,' the doctor was saying. And then again. 'All right. Next?'

Olena missed her mother the most.

But it was her father's face that suddenly loomed before her now, his face at night in the doorway of her bedroom, coming to check on her before he went to bed, his bewildered face, horrified to find her lying there beneath the covers, touching herself and gasping, his whispered 'Nell? Are you okay?' and then his vanishing, closing the door loudly, to leave her there, finally forever; to die and leave her there feeling only her own sorrow and disgrace, which she would live in like a coat.

There were rubber fingers in her, moving, wriggling around, but not like the others. She sat up abruptly and the young student withdrew his hand, moved away. 'He didn't do it right,' she said to the doctor. She pointed at the student. 'He didn't do it correctly!'

'All right, then,' said the doctor, looking at Olena with concern and alarm. 'All right. You may all leave,' she said to the students.

The doctor herself found nothing. 'You are perfectly normal,' she said. But she suggested that Olena take vitamin B and listen quietly to music in the evening.

Olena staggered out through the hospital parking lot, not finding her car at first. When she found it, she strapped herself in tightly, as if she were something wild – an animal or a star.

She drove back to the library and sat at her desk. Everyone had gone home already. In the margins of her notepad she wrote, 'Alone as a book, alone as a desk, alone as a library, alone as a pencil, alone as a catalog, alone as a number, alone as a notepad.' Then she, too, left, went home, made herself tea. She felt separate from her body, felt herself dragging it up the stairs like a big handbag, its leathery hollowness something you could cut up and give away or stick things in. She lay between the sheets of her bed, sweating, perhaps from the tea. The world felt over to her, used up, off to one side. There were no more names to live by.

One should live closer. She had lost her place, as in a book.

One should live closer to where one's parents were buried.

Waiting for Nick's return, she felt herself grow dizzy, float up toward the ceiling, look down on the handbag. Tomorrow, she would get an organ donor's card, an eye donor's card, as many cards as she could get. She would show them all to Nick. 'Nick! Look at my cards!'

And when he didn't come home, she remained awake through the long night, through the muffled thud of a bird hurling itself against the window, through the thunder leaving and approaching like a voice, through the Frankenstein light of the storm. Over her house, in lieu of stars, she felt the bright heads of her mother and father, searching for her, their eyes beaming down from the sky.

Oh, there you are, they said. *Oh, there you are.*

But then they went away again, and she lay waiting, fist in her spine, for the grace and fatigue that would come, surely it must come, of having given so much to the world.

MARY ARNOLD

A MORNING IN
THE BODLEIAN
(1871)

TO Mrs. ARNOLD,

ON HER BIRTHDAY,

FROM

HER ELDEST GRAND-DAUGHTER AND HER
YOUNGEST GRANDSON.

———

Fox How, August 21st, 1871.

———

[Mary Arnold (1851–1920), grand-daughter of the famous Dr. Arnold of Rugby School, was seventeen years old when she proudly became the first female to gain access to the inner sanctuary of Oxford's Bodleian Library. For three years she studied there, providing herself with the university education which was still being denied to women.]

HOW MANY PEOPLE in England have ever been into the Bodleian? How many have ever read there, and how many even of the readers have ever dived into its depths or explored even a fraction of one of its departments? In the Summer Term at Oxford, down the centre passage of the library goes a ceaseless rustle of ladies' dresses; 'lionesses,' led by undergraduate escorts as strange to the place as themselves, glide past the studies or stand more than half-bored at the cases of manuscripts and autograph letters. Yet the giddiest and most ignorant among them must feel a little ashamed of the *ennui* which oppresses them. Surrounded by the thought of centuries, and face to face with those old parchments with their famous signatures and ghostly halo of associations, even the hard-riding undergraduate, even the girl fresh from one flirtation and already planning another, must feel a moment's sobering, a moment's sense of insignificance. But the visit and its conscience-prickings are but short-lived; half-an-hour is enough for most sightseers, and the Bodleian knows them no more. Sometimes as you stand at the catalogue-shelf you may see a more interesting group approaching – a little old parish clergyman, perhaps, with thin white hair and generally wise look, arrayed in a rusty Master's gown infinitely too long for him – he has just hired it, with the battered cap, regardless of fit. No matter: behind walk wife and daughter, much impressed by the new splendour of his appearance; besides, in the wife's heart, perhaps, – she has a shrewd kindly look, motherly eyes, a pleasant brow – there awakes a sweet momentary sympathy with her husband's youth, that youth which laid all its capabilities and crudities at her feet, to which her girlhood gave itself gladly, and which is now such a dream to both. Then you may see him, the small ancient man, with conscious gait and eyes twinkling under his spectacles, board a passing librarian, make his name and academical status known with modest dignity, and demand a book. It is a MS. of Wyclif's Sermons perhaps, or a superb St. Augustine; and tottering under its weight he takes it to some quiet resting-place where in the bosom of his family he details in an audible whisper his knowledge of its meaning. Gladly the Bodleian harbours such a simple reverend presence, and she closes her doors upon him with a benison.

Not less varied are the readers for whose present benefit these priceless stores are opened; readers of both sexes and of every age, from the freshman touched with a love for gay illuminations, to the spectacled bookworm whose mornings for forty weeks in the year have ever been consecrated to learning here. They come from all lands, for the Bodleian has treasures inaccessible elsewhere; its manuscripts and unique early printed books draw hungry seekers from across the sea. From Russia sometimes; of course from Germany; now and then an Italian may be here for whom Milan and the Vatican have not sufficed; or even an American scholar whom the

New World's inevitable emptiness sends to draw from one of the oldest storehouses of the old. Most typical of all is the German; a man still young probably, and yet with an air of age lent to him by his spectacles and his grey complexion and his colourless hair; a man of few words, and those guttural ones, of manners not the pleasantest, of dress not the most becoming; but patient in his obedience to his self-set task as his countrymen to their captains in the field. He may be single-minded, or he may be controversial and terribly militant; but whether or no he has an enemy to crush, he travels straight on, missing nothing relevant, sparing no pains and troubled by no vile illegibilities of fifteenth-century handwritings. He is editing Nonnus perhaps; he finds nothing tedious in those forty-eight books of Dionysiaca, where the tinsel and the dulness of *rococo* poetry is poorly redeemed by little gems of real observation and feeling; our German for the present thinks nothing of feeling or *rococo*; his business is to collate! Or it is a question of Athenian Economy, misjudged by Boeckh, or Lachmann's Lucretius has to be exploded, or Herr Tischendorf shown to be wrong on the text of St. John. Then his notes will be bitter enough, and he will exult in true Teutonic fashion at the slaughter of his enemy; and if his enemy's little helper perish with him, some poor Englishman who has ventured to adopt and support his reading, fresh joy is spread over the soul of our reader, Dr. Grausam, of Leipsic. But for all that he will not work more patiently; he will not, (for it is impossible,) be more absorbed in the papers before him, more utterly heedless of the whispering visitors that curiously rustle by.

Yet not all readers are foreigners – not all love for learning has died out of England. Practical we are for the most part, even in our higher education; if we do not learn book-keeping and the theory of the steam engine, we strive, most of us, to learn those things only which will fit us to play our part, our social part, in the world: to talk well, to write brilliantly, to philosophise cleverly at any and every crisis. But though this is the tendency of the higher education in England, and notably in Oxford, there are students left among us still. That old man in the study that you are passing, with his face buried in a folio of Plotinus, has learning enough to make even Dr. Grausam stare. Perhaps, if the paradox be allowed, he is too literally a student; too much bent on study, too little on realising study for the world's benefit. Endowments, ever good and evil, have had an evil effect on him; his rich fellowship has taken away one stimulus for public work, and his conscience has failed to supply him with another. So he has settled down to a life of mere luxury, not of the table but of the library, not of wines but of books. His wonderful receptive powers, his inexhaustible memory, his insatiable appetite, have made him a mine of knowledge in all its forms. Perhaps if he has a strong point where all are strong, it is the Neoplatonic philosophy; his keen perception, his imagination, his tranquil disregard of the world around him, have perhaps led him to an affinity with that strangest form of mysticism where eastern and western thought join hands. But if you have other sympathies he will satisfy them, supposing you to take him in one of those moments when he chooses to be generous of his learning; he will make Condé's campaigns with you, or Cabot's voyages; he will talk to you of Shakespeare and the First Folio, of the disputed lines in *Cymbeline*; he will teach you to

'– See two points in Hamlet's soul
Unseized by the Germans yet.'

Or passing back though the history of poetry, if you ask

whence Shakespeare drew his inspiration, he will roam with you by the canal sides in Venice, and will quote Ariosto to you and Bojardo, and so pass backward through Spanish Romance and Provençal love-song, and onward again through the Minnesäger to all that warp and woof of sentiment which they first taught Germany to weave. Yet with all this, part indolent, part cynical, part fastidious, he will not write, he never has written. He knows too many books. He has seen too many reputations made by charlatans, marred for students; too many histories written, admired, and superseded; too many classics revived by patient editors to fall again to death. The game is not worth the candle. It is better to sit still and enjoy.

Many others there are, very different from each other and from him; such as the student tradesman, who for the morning hours when business is light leaves his hosiery to an assistant and comes to compare charters and gather facts for a history of Herefordshire, among whose orchards he was born. He has had no teaching to speak of in his youth; but the historical impulse was strong in him, and Oxford awoke it into life; so he taught himself Latin enough to read a chronicle, and set to work, full of enthusiasm, certain of results. His neighbour, too, does good work; she too is enthusiastic, and with the enthusiasm which is the mother of patience. She wears spectacles; her nose is too *retroussé* for beauty, her colour too high; in the country she would be a prodigy, in Tyburnia she would be voted 'blue.' But she cares little for Tyburnia and much for beautiful things and great interests; and so she is studying Holbein here. She has to read much, to be often disappointed, before she can discover anything new; in the library, you would say, she has the habits of a bookworm. But in half-an-hour's talk you would find that the eyes behind those spectacles are deep as well as penetrating; her liveliness and her warmth would convince you that it is possible for a woman to be a student without being a pedant – without in fact ceasing to be a woman. You would find that the past is interesting to her because the present is so intensely real; that she handles knowledge purely as the instrument of feeling, and loves it only because by it feeling is deepened, widened and refined.

But the building itself, with its approaches, is as interesting as its inhabitants. Here it is, the low Tudor archway, the heavy oaken door swung back upon its hinges, and beyond it the stairs, cool in the utmost heat of summer, and pervaded with that mingled fragrance of books and old oak which is one of the most subtle and suggestive of scents. Pass up them, resting on the way, if you will, on the broad window seats, whence the quad is visible with its quaint mistaken tower of the Five Orders, and its memory-haunted Examination Schools. Here are portraits, John Balliol and Devorguila his wife, a pair of ancient Radicals, vigorous and unconventional, fit progenitors of the modern Balliol. Here are maps old and superseded, side by side with pictures of forgotten nobodies, – old worlds, and the inhabiters thereof. Yonder are the steps into the gallery, an enchanted place, long and spacious, hung with portaits old and new, – a marvellous Mary of Scots, from whose exquisite pale face sorrow has refined away the vanity and hardness of youth, – pranked out in no ruff, no peaked head-dress, no pearls, but shrouded in black folds of drapery, which suit with the long years of imprisonment behind, the inevitable death in front; a Cranmer, by Holbein, with full weak red lips; a Duns Scotus, gaunt and unkempt, representative of the fossil race of the Schoolmen; a solemn Lord Burleigh, riding solemnly upon a beast less than mule, more than ass, – strange and laughable conception. Here is Guy Fawkes' lantern, poor innocent accessory of a long-past crime, sole relic of many men and many passions; here is a chair made from the ship in which Sir Francis Drake sailed round the world, and as you touch it, the forests unfathomable and creeper-twined of the New World, spring up before you, and you catch in the offing the sails of the Spanish treasure-ship flying the pursuit of English hate. In a little octagonal chamber, lit by windows, over whose bright pure tints the becoming dimness of age has crept, stands the chest or strong box of Sir Thomas Bodley: it has a marvellous lock truly; puzzle out its intricacies of polished steel wrought here and there into mocking likenesses of leaves and flowers if you can, – the burglar of past centuries tried a shorter method, and in the bottom of the chest you may still see the square hole he cut, blessing the elaborate stupidity of owner and maker the while. In yonder case are the fruit-trenchers of Queen Elizabeth; they belong surely to the old age of the Virgin Queen, so cynical are the maxims, so bitter the would-be love poems inscribed upon them. It is a pleasant place, this gallery. At every turn, without effort or pain on our part, the Past floods in upon us, – the dry bones live, – the vast Library beneath our feet seems to take voice and speak from these faces, these varied relics from the holes and corners of bygone life.

But let us press on. This gallery after all is but full of symbols, – is but itself a great symbol; through that green door lies the reality.

A great cruciform space opens before you. Over your head a beamed and arched roof, the fire of whose bosses and blazonings time has long since sobered, and from whose painted squares speaks everywhere, and at all times, the prayer of medieval learning, 'Dominus illuminatio mea!' The eyes of Dr. Grausam of Leipsic rest upon it sometimes with the calm superiority proper to a disciple of Voltaire;

the English divine in yonder closed study, toiling over his Hebrew, notes it now and then with a vague feeling of refreshment, so subtly do the words recall the time of quiet cloisters and calm-faced monks busy with leaf-gold and paint and parchment. That is fifteenth century glass in those windows: match those fading blue, opal greens and lucid browns in modern work if you can. Here are cases like those in the gallery, – Queen Elizabeth's Latin exercises, her books, her gloves. They are large, these last, – it were hard to connect anything small and soft with the signing of those two death-warrants of Essex and Mary. On the other side is a letter of Archbishop Laud's, written the night before his execution; the fine slanting characters aptly represent a man in whom a fatal leaven of sentiment, a fatal poetry of nature fought obstinately against the drivings of common sense. Here is Monmouth's last humbling act of submission the day before his death, and so on, – a refined symbolic Chamber of Horrors which need detain us no longer. Beyond the cases you come to the Catalogue, the key to the great silent enigma around you; the new Catalogue is a great and thorough piece of work, as yet incomplete. Standing behind the librarian's chair you look down the nave of the library, honey-combed on either hand by studies open and closed, filled with various readers and confusion of many books. Ah! those studies! – let us open one of them. The latticed doors green-curtained fly open, and you pass into a tiny room, book-walled, jutting flaps ancient and dusty, on either hand, lit by an Elizabethan window through whose stone-framed panes the eye wanders to the green and reverend stillness of a college garden far beneath. As you slip into the chair set ready for you, a deep repose steals over you, – the repose not of indolence, but of possession; the product of time, work, and patient thought only. Literature has no guerdon for 'bread-students', to quote the expressive German phrase: let not the young man reading for his pass, the London copyist or the British Museum illuminator, hope to enter within the enchanted ring of her benignest influences; only to the silent ardour, the thirst, the disinterestedness of the true learner, is she prodigal of all good gifts. To him she beckons, in him she confides, till she has produced in him that wonderful many-sidedness, that universal human sympathy which stamps the true literary man, and which is more religious than any form of creed.

So far we have gone; so far all the world may go. Let us pass downwards, however; let us enter the *penetralia*, leaving the studies where the brown folios lie, whose very titles are a dead letter to us, *Pymander Mercurii Trismegisti*, *Rosscelus de Sacramentis VII*, *Ribera in Prophetas*, *Snepffius in Esaiam*; the mighty works of forgotten casuists, *Azorii Institt. Morales*, in two enormous volumes, the ponderous *Œuvres de Richeome*, and hundreds more. Downwards through that green door marked 'private', by stairs book-lined through a long room, where live maps innumerable, roll-maps, sheet-maps, bound-maps of every date and every size; past stands containing every report of every learned society throughout the world – a department which makes one hurry on, inwardly shivering: – through masses of periodicals, old and young, serious and trivial, from the *Quarterly* down to the *Lady's Magazine*, from *Punch* to the *Christian Remembrancer*, till we reach a room filled with strange folios, lettered with strange names, a room which faintly represents a literature once the noblest of the modern world, a room symbolised by the superb Koran lying open on yonder desk. In a small inner room are the Hebrew manuscripts; a German is working there, another in shirt-sleeves is here – strange people of innumerable tentacles, stretching all ways, from Genesis to the latest form of the needle-gun. Up the steps there is a mixed room, partly oriental, partly European: it need not detain us. But let us pause in the octagon of octagons, gem of these lower abodes. The rooms around and beyond may suggest labour and patience, may depress with the consciousness of immeasureable inferiority; this only suggests the cream of work, the flowers that bloom rarely and brightly on the steep hillsides of literature. Here is the sumptuousness of modern binding; the *Paléographies*, the *Voyages Pittoresques*, the *Antiquities* of this and that; all, in short, that is most princely and most lavish in modern culture. Then turn your hand a moment to these shelves so close and so inviting; pull them out, the little shining slender volumes, and pass, with mind attuned and sympathies awake, into the play-ground of the middle-ages. Petrarch, Boccaccio, Ariosto, Tasso, – copy after copy, edition after edition. Here is a *Decameron*, Venezia 1517. The name and date go strangely together. In a solemn upheaval time when Wittenberg theses were start- ling Europe, when Protestantism, with all its bare austere variations, was springing into being, this little book saw the light, glided into the world of the sixteenth century, whose public life wears so grim and earnest a look to posterity, and slipping from house to house, and hand to hand, woke laughter in Italian eyes, and fed the unquenched craving of the South for story-telling. Look at this annotated edition of Petrarch's sonnets, the sonnet, a gem, though scarcely of the first water, in a worthless setting of wire-spun commentary. At the time this was printed, Petrarch was a greater force in the world than Dante, – Europe was still young and childish, with youth's passion for grace, youth's shrinking from deep waters, and love for beautiful outsides. There is a Bojardo side by side with *Orlando Furioso*, – shadow and substance. And in that lowest shelf, a grim row of *Todten-tänzer* quaintly underlies these tales of love and war. All the characters in those haunts of pleasure are here reproduced, knight and maiden, monk and matron, but beside them all stands the inevitable spectre with scythe and hour-glass, and in the midst of its riot and festival, you see the Middle-Age standing still, with down-dropt eyes and hand on mouth, pondering for an instant the awful secret ringed by which it lives and laughs. Opposite are books of alchemy, interspersed with unintelligible cyphers, such books as Leonardo da Vinci may have studied in that withdrawn transition time of his. Ah! we must leave it, our room of rooms, carrying with us a summer picture of it, – calm bands of sunlight lying on the brown polish of the floor, and creeping along the book-lined angles, fit companion for all the jest and laughter, all the love and pathos, which dwell here embalmed.

We have stayed so long in the antichambers that we have no time to linger long in the Douce Library to which it leads. And yet the Douce Library is rich beyond all telling in MSS., Latin, French, and English; in early printed work, in the out-of-the-way corners of Elizabethan literature; in old stories of travel, quaintly illustrated and adorned. That centre-stand boasts four manuscripts of the Roman de la Rose, one with four half-page illustrations drawn in soft dove-like tints of grey, refreshing after the commoner reds and blues of the other three. *Lancelot du Lac*, *Reynaut et Isemgrim*, *Vie de Merlin*, *Vœu du Paon*, *Roman d'Alexandre* – there they stand, one after another, names of enchantment for all time. And by them is the shelf of 'Hours', not the least attractive of the books that surround you. Take out one of them, a small red ocatvo: *Heurs Gotique* the binder mysteriously calls it, but if you turn to the mutilated title-page, you will find that it is a book of Hours 'à l'usaige de Soissons'. The famous Simon Vostre is the printer, so the date must be 1510 or so;

on the wide margin of nearly every one of the 500 pages, are four exquisite woodcuts, all different, all intensely German. Dürer might have drawn them all, except that they are even quainter than his work – a priest admitting a company of veritable Nürembergers to celebration; Herodias' daughter watching the fall of John the Baptist's head; devils cast out and flying away on leathern wings; Dives and Lazarus, terribly specific; a double page, terribly dramatic, of 'David and Urie,' where Urie is in the forefront of the battle in grim earnest, and the Nüremberger-fashioned spear of an Ammonite lanz-knecht is entering deep into his side. Or, if you care more for illumination than for minute engraving, get the librarian's leave and spend an hour with the famous 'Ormesby Psalter,' the 'Salterium fratris Roberti de Ormes-by' as the inscription calls it, among the most magnificent of all the monk-works of the magnificent fourteenth century. Not even the treasures of San Marco at Florence, where Angelico's own hand is traceable on the precious missals, can show more brilliant colouring, more fertile design, more delicate leafwork, or fanciful grotesque, than the patient life-labour of the northern friar.

Who can pass out of such a building without a feeling of profound melancholy? The thought is almost too obvious to be dwelt upon; but it is overpowering and inevitable. These shelves of mighty folios, these cases of laboured manuscripts, these illuminated volumes of which each may represent a life – the first, dominant impression which they make cannot fail to be like that which a burial-ground leaves – a Hamlet-like sense of 'the pity of it'. Which is the sudden image, the dust of Alexander stopping a bunghole, or the brain and lifeblood of a hundred monks cumbering the shelves of the Bodleian? Not the former, perhaps, for Alexander's dust matters little where his work is considered, but these monks' work is in their books; to their books they sacrificed their lives, and gave themselves up as an offering to posterity. And posterity, over-burdened by its own concerns, passes them by without a look or a word! Here and there, of course, is a volume which has made a mark upon the world; but the mass are silent for ever, and zeal, industry, talent, for once that they have had permanent results, have a thousand times been sealed by failure. And yet men go on writing, writing; and books are born under the shadow of the great libraries just as children are born within sight of the tombs. It seems as though Nature's law were universal as well as rigid in its sphere – wide wastes of sand shut in the green oasis, many a seed falls among thorns or by the wayside, many a bud must be sacrificed before there comes the perfect flower, many a little life must exhaust itself in a useless book before the great book is made which is to remain a force for ever. And so we might as profitably murmur at the withered buds, at the seed that takes no root, at the stretch of desert, as at the unread folios. They are waste, it is true; but it is the waste that is thrown off by Humanity in its ceaseless process towards the fulfilment of its law.

[*In April 1872 Mary Arnold, not quite twenty-one, married an Oxford don and ever afterwards styled herself 'Mrs. Humphry Ward'. But in the Douce Library she had been quietly turning herself into a specialist in early Spanish history and literature, and after having three children she returned to the Bodleian for further research in her chosen field, becoming a noted scholar. Then she made a highly successful career as a novelist.*]

ELIZABETH TAYLOR

GIRL READING
(1961)

ETTA'S DESIRE WAS to belong. Sometimes she felt on the fringe of the family, at other times drawn headily into its very centre. At meal-times – those occasions of argument and hilarity, of thrust and counterstroke, bewildering to her at first – she was especially on her mettle, turning her head alertly from one to another as if watching a fast tennis match. She hoped soon to learn the art of riposte and already used, sometimes unthinkingly, family words and phrases; and had one or two privately treasured memories of even having made them laugh. They delighted in laughing and often did so scoffingly – 'at the expense of those less fortunate' as Etta's mother would sententiously have put it.

Etta and Sarah were school-friends. It was not the first time that Etta had stayed with the Lippmanns in the holidays. Everyone understood that the hospitality would not be returned, for Etta's mother, who was widowed, went out to work each day. Sarah had seen only the outside of the drab terrace house where her friend lived. She had persuaded her elder brother, David, to take her spying there one evening. They drove fifteen miles to Market Swanford and Sarah, with great curiosity, studied the street names until at last she discovered the house itself. No one was about. The street was quite deserted and the two rows of houses facing one another were blank and silent as if waiting for a hearse to appear. 'Do hurry!' Sarah urged her brother. It had been a most dangerous outing and she was thoroughly depressed by it. Curiosity now seemed a trivial sensation compared with the pity she was feeling for her friend's drab life and her shame at having confirmed her own suspicions of it. She was threatened by tears. 'Aren't you going in?' her brother asked in great surprise. 'Hurry, hurry,' she begged him. There had never been any question of her calling at that house.

'She must be very lonely there all through the holidays, poor Etta,' she thought, and could imagine hour after hour in the dark house. Bickerings with the daily help she had already heard of and – Etta trying to put on a brave face and make much of nothing – trips to the public library the highlight of the day, it seemed. No wonder that her holiday reading was always so carefully done, thought Sarah, whereas she herself could never snatch a moment for it except at night in bed.

Sarah had a lively conscience about the seriousness of her friend's private world. Having led her more than once into trouble, at school, she had always afterwards felt a disturbing sense of shame; for Etta's work was more important than her own could ever be, too important to be interrupted by escapades. Sacrifices had been made and scholarships must be won. Once – it was a year ago when they were fifteen and had less sense – Sarah had thought up some rough tomfoolery and Etta's blazer had been torn. She was still haunted by her friend's look of consternation. She had remembered too late, as always – the sacrifices that had been made, the widowed mother sitting year after year at her office desk, the holidays that were never taken and the contriving that had to be done.

Her own mother was so warm and worldly. If she had anxieties she kept them to herself, setting the pace of gaiety, up to date and party-loving. She was popular with her friends' husbands who, in their English way, thought of her comfortably as nearly as good company as a man and full of bright ways as well. Etta felt safer with her than with Mr. Lippmann, whose enquiries were often too probing; he touched nerves, his jocularity could be an embarrassment. The boys – Sarah's elder brothers – had their own means of communication which their mother unflaggingly strove to interpret and, on Etta's first visit, she had tried to do so for her, too.

She *was* motherly, although she looked otherwise, the girl decided. Lying in bed at night, in the room she shared with Sarah, Etta would listen to guests driving noisily away or to the Lippmanns returning, full of laughter, from some neighbour's house. Late night door-slamming in the country disturbed only the house's occupants, who all contributed to it. Etta imagined them pottering about downstairs – husband and wife, would hear bottles clinking, laughter, voices raised from room to room, good-night endearments to cats and dogs and at last Mrs. Lippmann's running footsteps on the stairs and the sound of her jingling bracelets coming nearer. Outside their door she would pause, listening, wondering if they were asleep already. They never were. 'Come in!' Sarah would shout, hoisting herself up out of the bed clothes on one elbow, her face turned expectantly towards the door, ready for laughter – for something amusing would surely have happened. Mrs. Lippmann, sitting on one of the beds, never failed them. When they were children, Sarah said, she brought back *petits fours* from parties; now she brought back *faux pas*. She specialised in little stories against herself – Mummy's Humiliations, Sarah named them – tactless things she had said, never-to-be-remedied remarks which sprang fatally from her lips. Mistakes in identity was her particular line, for she never remembered a face, she declared. Having kissed Sarah, she would bend over Etta to do the same. She smelt of scent and gin and cigarette smoke. After this they would go to sleep. The house would be completely quiet for several hours.

Etta's mother had always had doubts about the suitability of this *ménage*. She knew it only at second hand from her daughter, and Etta said very little about her visits and that little was only in reply to obviously resented questions. But she had a way of looking about her with boredom when she returned, as if she had made the transition unwillingly and incompletely. She hurt her mother – who wished only to do everything in the world for her, having no one else to please or protect.

'I should feel differently if we were able to return the hospitality,' she told Etta. The Lippmanns' generosity depressed her. She knew that it was despicable to feel jealous, left out, kept in the dark, but she tried to rationalise her feelings before Etta. 'I could take a few days off and invite Sarah here,' she suggested.

Etta was unable to hide her consternation and her expression deeply wounded her mother. 'I shouldn't know what to do with her,' she said.

'Couldn't you go for walks? There are the Public Gardens. And take her to the cinema one evening. What do you do at *her* home?'

'Oh, just fool about. Nothing much.' Some afternoons they just lay on their beds and ate sweets, keeping all the windows shut and the wireless on loud, and no one ever disturbed them or told them they ought to be out in the fresh air. Then they had to plan parties and make walnut fudge and deflea the dogs. Making fudge was the only one of these things she could imagine them doing in her own home and they could not do it all the time. As for the dreary Public Gardens, she could not herself endure the asphalt paths and the bandstand and the beds of salvias. She could imagine vividly how dejected Sarah would feel.

Early in these summer holidays, the usual letter had come from Mrs. Lippmann. Etta, returning from the library, found that the charwoman had gone early and locked her out. She rang the bell, but the sound died away and left an even more forbidding silence. All the street, where elderly people dozed in stuffy rooms, was quiet. She lifted the flap of the letter-box and called through it. No one stirred or came. She could just glimpse an envelope, lying face up on the doormat, addressed in Mrs. Lippmann's large, loopy, confident handwriting. The house-stuffiness wafted through the letter-box. She imagined the kitchen floor slowly drying, for there was a smell of soapy water. A tap was steadily dripping.

She leant against the door, waiting for her mother's return, in a sickness of impatience at the thought of the letter lying there inside. Once or twice, she lifted the flap and had another look at it.

Her mother came home at last, very tired. With an anxious air, she set about cooking supper, which Etta had promised to have ready. The letter was left among her parcels on the kitchen table, and not until they had finished their stewed rhubarb did she send Etta to fetch it. She opened it carefully with the bread knife and deepened the frown on her forehead in preparation for reading it. When she had, she gave Etta a summary of its contents and put forward her objections, her unnerving proposal.

'She wouldn't come,' Etta said. 'She wouldn't leave her dog.'

'But, my dear, she has to leave him when she goes back to school.'

'I know. That's the trouble. In the holidays she likes to be with him as much as possible, to make up for it.'

Mrs. Salkeld, who had similar wishes about her daughter, looked sad. 'It is too one-sided,' she gently explained. 'You must try to understand how I feel about it.'

'They're only too glad to have me. I keep Sarah company when they go out.'

They obviously went out a great deal and Mrs. Salkeld suspected that they were frivolous. She did not condemn them for that – they must lead their own lives, but those were in a world which Etta would never be able to afford the time or money to inhabit. 'Very well, Musetta,' she said, removing the girl further from her by using her full name – used only on formal and usually menacing occasions.

That night she wept a little from tiredness and depression – from disappointment, too, at the thought of returning in the evenings to the dark and empty house, just as she usually did, but when she had hoped for company. They were not healing tears she shed and they did nothing but add self-contempt to her other distresses.

A week later, Etta went the short distance by train to stay with the Lippmanns. Her happiness soon lost its edge of guilt, and once the train had rattled over the iron bridge that spanned the broad river, she felt safe in a different country. There seemed to be even a different weather, coming from a wider sky, and a riverside glare – for the curves of the railway line brought it close to the even more winding course of the river, whose silver loops could be glimpsed through the trees. There were islands and backwaters and a pale heron standing on a patch of mud.

Sarah was waiting at the little station and Etta stepped down on to the platform as if taking a footing into promised land. Over the station and the gravelly lane outside hung a noonday quiet. On one side were grazing meadows, on the other side the drive gateways of expensive houses. The

Gables was indeed gabled and so was its boat-house. It was also turreted and balconied. There was a great deal of woodwork painted glossy white, and a huge-leaved Virginia creeper covered much of the red-brick walls – in the front beds were the salvias and lobelias Etta had thought she hated. Towels and swim-suits hung over balcony rails and a pair of tennis-shoes had been put out on a window-sill to dry. Even though Mr. Lippmann and his son, David, went to London every day, the house always had – for Etta – a holiday atmosphere.

The hall door stood open and on the big round table were the stacks of new magazines which seemed to her the symbol of extravagance and luxury. At the back of the house, on the terrace overlooking the river, Mrs. Lippmann, wearing tight, lavender pants and a purple shirt, was drinking vodka with a neighbour who had called for a subscription to some charity. Etta was briefly enfolded in scented silk and tinkling bracelets and then released and introduced. Sarah gave her a red, syrupy drink and they sat down on the warm steps among the faded clumps of aubretia and rocked the ice cubes to and fro in their glasses, keeping their eyes narrowed to the sun.

Mrs. Lippmann gossiped, leaning back under a fringed chair-umbrella. She enjoyed exposing the frailties of her friends and family, although she would have been the first to hurry to their aid in trouble. Roger, who was seventeen, had been worse for drink the previous evening, she was saying. Faced with breakfast, his face had been a study of disgust which she now tried to mimic. And David could not eat, either; but from being in love. She raised her eyes to heaven most dramatically, to convey that great patience was demanded of her.

'He eats like a horse,' said Sarah. 'Etta, let's go upstairs.' She took Etta's empty glass and led her back across the lawn, seeming not to care that her mother would without doubt begin to talk about her the moment she had gone.

Rich and vinegary smells of food came from the kitchen as they crossed the hall. (There was a Hungarian cook to whom Mrs. Lippmann spoke in German and a Portuguese 'temporary' to whom she spoke in Spanish.) The food was an important part of the holiday to Etta, who had nowhere else eaten *Sauerkraut* or *Apfelstrudel* or cold fried fish, and she went into the dining-room each day with a sense of adventure and anticipation.

On this visit she was also looking forward to the opportunity of making a study of people in love – an opportunity she had not had before. While she unpacked, she questioned Sarah about David's Nora, as she thought of her; but Sarah would only say that she was quite a good sort with dark eyes and an enormous bust, and that as she was coming to dinner that evening, as she nearly always did, Etta would be able to judge for herself.

While they were out on the river all the afternoon – Sarah rowing her in a dinghy along the reedy backwater – Etta's head was full of love in books, even in those holiday set books Sarah never had time for – *Sense and Sensibility* this summer. She felt that she knew what to expect, and her perceptions were sharpened by the change of air and scene, and the disturbing smell of the river, which she snuffed up deeply as if she might be able to store it up in her lungs. 'Mother thinks it is polluted,' Sarah said when Etta lifted a streaming hand from trailing in the water and brought up some slippery weeds and held them to her nose. They laughed at the idea.

Etta, for dinner, put on the liberty silk they wore on Sunday evenings at school and Sarah at once brought out her own hated garment from the back of the cupboard where she had pushed it out of sight on the first day of the holidays. When they appeared downstairs, they looked unbelievably dowdy, Mrs. Lippmann thought, turning away for a moment because her eyes had suddenly pricked with tears at the sight of her kind daughter.

Mr. Lippmann and David returned from Lloyd's at half-past six and with them brought Nora – a large, calm girl with an air of brittle indifference towards her fiancé which disappointed but did not deceive Etta, who knew enough to remain undeceived by banter. To interpret from it the private tendernesses it hid was part of the mental exercise she was to be engaged in. After all, David would know better than to have his heart on his sleeve, especially in this *dégagé* family where nothing seemed half so funny as falling in love.

After dinner, Etta telephoned her mother, who had perhaps been waiting for the call, as the receiver was lifted immediately. Etta imagined her standing in the dark and narrow hall with its smell of umbrellas and furniture polish.

'I thought you would like to know I arrived safely.'

'What have you been doing?'

'Sarah and I went to the river. We have just finished dinner.' Spicy smells still hung about the house. Etta guessed that her mother would have had half a tin of sardines and put the other half by for her breakfast. She felt sad for her and guilty herself. Most of her thoughts about her mother were deformed by guilt.

'What have you been doing?' she asked.

'Oh, the usual,' her mother said brightly. 'I am just turn-ing the collars and cuffs of your winter blouses. By the way, don't forget to pay Mrs. Lippmann for the telephone call.'

'No. I shall have to go now. I just thought . . .'

'Yes, of course, dear. Well, have a lovely time.'

'We are going for a swim when our dinner has gone down.'

'Be careful of cramp, won't you? But I mustn't fuss from this distance. I know you are in good hands. Give my kind regards to Mrs. Lippmann and Sarah, will you, please. I must get back to your blouses.'

'I wish you wouldn't bother. You must be tired.'

'I am perfectly happy doing it,' Mrs. Salkeld said. But if that were so, it was unnecessary, Etta thought, for her to add, as she did: 'And someone has to do it.'

She went dully back to the others. Roger was strumming on a guitar, but he blushed and put it away when Etta came into the room.

As the days went quickly by, Etta thought that she was belonging more this time than ever before. Mr. Lippmann, a genial patriarch, often patted her head when passing, in confirmation of her existence, and Mrs. Lippmann let her run errands. Roger almost wistfully sought her company, while Sarah disdainfully discouraged him; for they had their own employments, she implied; her friend – 'my best friend', as she introduced Etta to lesser ones or adults – could hardly be expected to want the society of schoolboys. Although he was a year older than themselves, being a boy he was less sophisticated, she explained. She and Etta considered themselves to be rather worldly-wise – Etta having learnt from literature and Sarah from putting two and two together, her favourite pastime. Her parents seemed to her to behave with the innocence of children, unconscious of their motives, so continually betraying themselves to her experienced eye, when knowing more would have made them guarded. She had similarly put two and two together about Roger's behaviour to Etta, but she kept these conclusions to herself – partly from not wanting to make her friend feel self-conscious and partly – for she scorned self-deception – from what she recognised to be jealousy. She and Etta were very well as they were, she thought.

Etta herself was too much absorbed by the idea of love to ever think of being loved. In this house, she had her first chance of seeing it at first hand and she studied David and Nora with such passionate speculation that their loving seemed less their own than hers. At first, she admitted to herself that she was disappointed. Their behaviour fell short of what she required of them; they lacked a romantic attitude to one another and Nora was neither touching nor glorious – neither Viola nor Rosalind. In Etta's mind to be either was satisfactory; to be boisterous and complacent was not. Nora was simply a plump and genial girl with a large bust and a faint moustache. She could not be expected to inspire David with much gallantry and, in spite of all the red roses he brought her from London, he was not above telling her that she was getting fat. Gaily retaliatory, she would threaten him with the bouquet, waving it about his head, her huge engagement ring catching the light, flashing with different colours, her eyes flashing too.

Sometimes, there was what Etta's mother would have called 'horseplay', and Etta herself deplored the noise, the dishevelled romping. 'We know quite well what it's instead of,' said Sarah. 'But I sometimes wonder if *they* do. They would surely cut it out if they did.'

As intent as a bird-watcher, Etta observed them, but was puzzled that they behaved like birds, making such a display of their courtship, an absurd-looking frolic out of a serious matter. She waited in vain for a sigh or secret glance. At night, in the room she shared with Sarah, she wanted to talk about them more than Sarah, who felt that her own family was the last possible source of glamour or enlightenment. Discussing her bridesmaid's dress was the most she would be drawn into and that subject Etta felt was devoid of romance. She was not much interested in mere weddings and thought them rather banal and public celebrations. 'With an overskirt of embroidered net,' said Sarah in her decisive voice. 'How nice if you could be a bridesmaid, too; but she has all those awful Greenbaum cousins. As ugly as sin, but not to be left out.' Etta was inattentive to her. With all her studious nature she had set herself to study love and study it she would. She made the most of what the holiday offered and when the exponents were absent she fell back on the textbooks – *Tess of the D'Urbervilles* and *Wuthering Heights* at that time.

To Roger she seemed to fall constantly into the same pose, as she sat on the river bank, bare feet tucked sideways, one arm cradling a book, the other outstretched to pluck – as if to aid her concentration – at blades of grass. Her face remained pale, for it was always in shadow, bent over her book. Beside her, glistening with oil, Sarah spread out her body to the sun. She was content to lie for hour after hour with no object but to change the colour of her skin and with thoughts crossing her mind as seldom as clouds passed overhead – and in as desultory a way when they did so. Sometimes, she took a book out with her, but nothing happened to it except that it became smothered with oil. Etta, who found sunbathing boring and enervating, read steadily on – her straight, pale hair hanging forward as if to seclude her, to screen her from the curious eyes of passers-by – shaken by passions of the imagination as she was. Voices from boats came clearly across the water, but she did not heed them. People going languidly by in punts shaded their eyes and admired the scarlet geraniums and the greenness of the grass. When motor cruisers passed, their wash jogged against the mooring stage and swayed into the boat-house, whose lacy fretwork trimmings had just been repainted glossy white.

Sitting there, alone by the boat-house at the end of the grass bank, Roger read, too; but less diligently than Etta. Each time a boat went by, he looked up and watched it out of sight. A swan borne towards him on a wake, sitting neatly on top of its reflection, held his attention. Then his place on the page was lost. Anyhow, the sun fell too blindingly upon it. He would glance again at Etta and briefly, with distaste, at his indolent, spread-eagled sister, who had rolled over on to her stomach to give her shiny back, criss-crossed from the grass, its share of sunlight. So the afternoons passed, and they would never have such long ones in their lives again.

Evenings were more social. The terrace with its fringed umbrellas – symbols of gaiety to Etta – became the gathering place. Etta, listening intently, continued her study of love, and as intently Roger studied her and the very emotion which in those others so engrossed her.

'You look still too pale,' Mr. Lippmann told her one evening. He put his hands to her face and tilted it to the sun.

'You shan't leave us until there are roses in those cheeks.' He implied that only in his garden did sun and air give their full benefit. The thought was there and Etta shared it. 'Too much of a bookworm, I'm afraid,' he added and took one of her textbooks which she carried everywhere for safety, lest she should be left on her own for a few moments. '*Tess of the D'Urbervilles,*' read out Mr. Lippmann. 'Isn't it deep? Isn't it on the morbid side?' Roger was kicking rhythmically at a table leg in glum embarrassment. 'This won't do you any good at all, my dear little girl. This won't put the roses in your cheeks.'

'You are doing that,' his daughter told him – for Etta was blushing as she always did when Mr. Lippmann spoke to her.

'What's a nice book, Babs?' he asked his wife, as she came

out on to the terrace. 'Can't you find a nice story for this child?' The house must be full, he was sure, of wonderfully therapeutic novels if only he knew where to lay hands on them. 'Roger, you're our bookworm. Look out a nice story-book for your guest. This one won't do her eyes any good.' Buying books with small print was a false economy, he thought, and bound to land one in large bills from an eye specialist before long. 'A very short-sighted policy,' he explained genially when he had given them a little lecture to which no one listened.

His wife was trying to separate some slippery cubes of ice and Sarah sprawled in a cane chair with her eyes shut. She was making the most of the setting sun, as Etta was making the most of romance.

'We like the same books,' Roger said to his father. 'So she can choose as well as I could.'

Etta was just beginning to feel a sense of surprised gratitude, had half turned to look in his direction when the betrothed came through the French windows and claimed her attention.

'In time for a lovely drink,' Mrs. Lippmann said to Nora.

'She is too fat already,' said David.

Nora swung round and caught his wrists and held them threateningly. 'If you say that once more, I'll . . . I'll just . . .' He freed himself and pulled her close. She gasped and panted, but leant heavily against him. 'Promise!' she said.

'Promise what?'

'You won't ever say it again?'

He laughed at her mockingly.

They were less the centre of attention than they thought – Mr. Lippmann was smiling, but rather at the lovely evening and that the day in London was over; Mrs. Lippmann, impeded by the cardigan hanging over her shoulders, was mixing something in a glass jug and Sarah had her eyes closed against the evening sun. Only Etta, in some bewilderment, heeded them. Roger, who had his own ideas about love, turned his head scornfully.

Sarah opened her eyes for a moment and stared at Nora, in her mind measuring against her the wedding dress she had been designing. She is too fat for satin, she decided, shutting her eyes again and disregarding the bridal gown for the time being. She returned to thoughts of her own dress, adding a little of what she called 'back interest' (though lesser bridesmaids would no doubt obscure it from the congregation – or audience) in the form of long velvet ribbons in turquoise . . . or rose? She drew her brows together and with her eyes still shut said, 'All the colours of the rainbow aren't very many, are they?'

'Now, Etta dear, what will you have to drink?' asked Mrs. Lippmann.

Just as she was beginning to ask for some tomato juice, Mr. Lippmann interrupted. He interrupted a great deal, for there were a great many things to be put right, it seemed to him. 'Now, Mommy, you should give her a glass of sherry with an egg beaten up in it. Roger, run and fetch a nice egg and a whisk, too . . . all right, Babsie dear, I shall do it myself . . . don't worry, child,' he said, turning to Etta and seeing her look of alarm. 'It is no trouble to me. I shall do this for you every evening that you are here. We shall watch the roses growing in your cheeks, shan't we, Mommy?'

He prepared the drink with a great deal of clumsy fuss and sat back to watch her drinking it, smiling to himself, as if the roses were already blossoming. 'Good, good!' he murmured, nodding at her as she drained the glass. Every evening, she thought, hoping that he would forget; but horrible though the drink had been, it was also reassuring; their concern for her was reassuring. She preferred it to the cold anxiety of her mother hovering with pills and thermometer.

'Yes,' said Mr. Lippmann, 'we shall see. We shall see. I think your parents won't know you.' He puffed out his cheeks and sketched with a curving gesture the bosom she would soon have. He always forgot that her father was dead. It was quite fixed in his mind that he was simply a fellow who had obviously not made the grade; not everybody could. Roger bit his tongue hard, as if by doing so he could curb his father's. 'I must remind him again,' Sarah and her mother were both thinking.

The last day of the visit had an unexpected hazard as well as its own sadness, for Mrs. Salkeld had written to say that her employer would lend her his car for the afternoon. When she had made a business call for him in the neighbourhood she would arrive to fetch Etta at about four o'clock.

'She is really to leave us, Mommy?' asked Mr. Lippmann at breakfast, folding his newspaper and turning his attention on his family before hurrying to the station. He examined Etta's face and nodded. 'Next time you stay longer and we make rosy apples of these.' He patted her cheeks and ruffled her hair. 'You tell your Mommy and Dadda next time you stay a whole week.'

'She *has* stayed a whole week,' said Sarah.

'Then a fortnight, a month.'

He kissed his wife, made a gesture as if blessing them all, with his newspaper raised above his head, and went from the room at a trot. 'Thank goodness', thought Sarah, 'that he won't be here this afternoon to make kind enquiries about *her* husband.'

When she was alone with Etta, she said, 'I'm sorry about that mistake he keeps making.'

'I don't mind,' Etta said truthfully, 'I am only embarrassed because I know that you are.' That's *nothing*, she thought; but the day ahead was a different matter.

As time passed, Mrs. Lippmann also appeared to be suffering from tension. She went upstairs and changed her matador pants for a linen skirt. She tidied up the terrace and told Roger to take his bathing things off his window-sill. As soon as she had stubbed out a cigarette, she emptied and dusted the ash-tray. She was conscious that Sarah was trying to see her with another's eyes.

'Oh, do stop taking photographs,' Sarah said tetchily to Roger, who had been clicking away with his camera all morning. He obeyed her only because he feared to draw attention to his activities. He had just taken what he hoped would be a very beautiful study of Etta in a typical pose – sitting on the river bank with a book in her lap. She had lifted her eyes and was gazing across the water as if she were pondering whatever she had been reading. In fact, she had been arrested by thoughts of David and Nora and, although her eyes followed the print, the scene she saw did not correspond with the lines she read. She turned her head and looked at the willow trees on the far bank, the clumps of borage from which moorhens launched themselves. 'Perhaps next time that I see them, they'll be married and it will all be over,' she thought. The evening before, there had been a great deal of high-spirited sparring about between them. Offence meant and offence taken they assured one another. 'If you do that once more . . . I am absolutely serious,' cried Nora. 'You are trying not to laugh,' David said. 'I'm not. I am absolutely serious.' 'It will end in tears,' Roger had muttered contemptuously. Even good-tempered Mrs. Lippmann had looked down her long nose disapprovingly. And that was the last, Etta supposed, that she would see of love for a long time. She was left once again with books. She returned to the one she was reading.

Roger had flung himself on to the grass nearby, appearing to trip over a tussock of grass and collapse. He tried to think of some opening remark which might lead to a discussion of the book. In the end, he asked abruptly, 'Do you like that?' She sat brooding over it, chewing the side of her finger. She nodded without looking up and, with a similar automatic gesture, she waved away a persistent wasp. He leant forward and clapped his hands together smartly and was relieved to see the wasp drop dead into the grass, although he would rather it had stung him first. Etta, however, had not noticed this brave deed.

The day passed wretchedly for him; each hour was more filled with the doom of her departure than the last. He worked hard to conceal his feelings, in which no one took an interest. He knew that it was all he could do, although no good could come from his succeeding. He took a few more secret photographs from his bedroom window, and then he sat down and wrote a short letter to her, explaining his love.

At four o'clock, her mother came. He saw at once that Etta was nervous and he guessed that she tried to conceal her nervousness behind a much jauntier manner to her mother than was customary. It would be a bad hour, Roger decided.

His own mother, in spite of her linen skirt, was gawdy and exotic beside Mrs. Salkeld, who wore a navy-blue suit which looked as if it had been sponged and pressed a hundred times – a depressing process unknown to Mrs. Lippmann. The pink-rimmed spectacles that Mrs. Salkeld wore seemed to reflect a little colour on to her cheekbones, with the result that she looked slightly indignant about something or other. However, she smiled a great deal, and only Etta guessed what an effort it was to her to do so. Mrs. Lippmann gave her a chair where she might have a view of the river and she sat down, making a point of not looking round the room, and smoothed her gloves. Her jewellery was real but very small.

'If we have tea in the garden, the wasps get into Anna's rose-petal jam,' said Mrs. Lippmann. Etta was not at her best, she felt – not helping at all. She was aligning herself too staunchly with the Lippmanns, so that her mother seemed a stranger to her, as well. 'You see, I am at home here,' she implied, as she jumped up to fetch things or hand things round. She was a little daring in her familiarity.

Mrs. Salkeld had contrived the visit because she wanted to understand and hoped to approve of her daughter's friends. Seeing the lawns, the light reflected from the water, later this large, bright room, and the beautiful poppy-seed cake the Hungarian cook had made for tea, she understood completely and felt pained. She could see then, with Etta's eyes, their own dark, narrow house, and she thought of the lonely hours she spent there reading on days of imprisoning rain. The Lippmanns would even have better weather, she thought bitterly. The bitterness affected her enjoyment of the poppy-seed cake. She had, as puritanical people often have, a sweet tooth. She ate the cake with a casual air, determined not to praise.

'You are so kind to spare Etta to us,' said Mrs. Lippmann.

'*You* are kind to invite her,' Mrs. Salkeld replied, and then for Etta's sake, added: 'She loves to come to you.'

Etta looked self-consciously down at her feet.

'No, I don't smoke,' her mother said primly. 'Thank you.'

Mrs. Lippmann seemed to decide not to, either, but very soon her hand stole out and took a cigarette – while she was not looking, thought Roger, who was having some amusement from watching his mother on her best behaviour. Wherever she was, the shagreen cigarette case and the gold lighter were nearby. Ash-trays never were. He got up and fetched one before Etta could do so.

The girls' school was being discussed – one of the few topics the two mothers had in common. Mrs. Lippmann had never taken it seriously. She laughed at the uniform and despised the staff – an attitude she might at least have hidden from her daughter, Mrs. Salkeld felt. The tea-trolley was being wheeled away and her eyes followed the remains of the poppy-seed cake. She had planned a special supper for Etta to return to, but she felt now that it was no use. The things of the mind had left room for an echo. It sounded with every footstep or spoken word in that house where not enough was going on. She began to wonder if there were things of the heart and not the mind that Etta fastened upon so desperately when she was reading. Or was her desire to be in a different place? Lowood was a worse one – she could raise her eyes and look round her own room in relief; Pemberley was better and she would benefit from the change. 'But how can I help her?' she asked herself in anguish. 'What possible change – and radical it must be – can I ever find the strength to effect?' People had thought her wonderful to have made her own life and brought up her child alone. She had kept their heads above water and it had taken all her resources to do so.

Her lips began to refuse the sherry Mrs. Lippmann suggested and then, to her surprise and Etta's astonishment, she said 'yes' instead.

It was very early to have suggested it, Mrs. Lippmann thought, but it would seem to put an end to the afternoon. Conversation had been as hard work as she had anticipated and she longed for a dry martini to stop her from yawning, as she was sure it would; but something about Mrs. Salkeld seemed to discourage gin drinking.

'Mother, it isn't half-past five yet,' said Sarah.

'Darling, don't be rude to your mummy. I know perfectly well what the time is.' ('Who better?' she wondered.) 'And this isn't a public house, you know.'

She had flushed a little and was lighting another cigarette. Her bracelets jangled against the decanter as she handed Mrs. Salkeld her glass of sherry, saying, 'Young people are so stuffy,' with an air of complicity.

Etta, who had never seen her mother drinking sherry before, watched nervously, as if she might not know how to do it. Mrs. Salkeld – remembering the flavour from Christmas mornings many years ago and – more faintly – from her mother's party trifle – sipped cautiously. In an obscure way she was doing this for Etta's sake. 'It may speed her on her way,' thought Mrs. Lippmann, playing idly with her charm bracelet, having run out of conversation.

When Mrs. Salkeld rose to go, she looked round the room once more as if to fix it in her memory – the setting where she would imagine her daughter on future occasions.

'And come again soon, there's a darling girl,' said Mrs. Lippmann, putting her arm round Etta's shoulder as they walked towards the car. Etta, unused to but not ungrateful for embraces, leant awkwardly against her. Roger, staring at the gravel, came behind carrying the suitcase.

'I have wasted my return ticket,' Etta said.

'Well, that's not the end of the world,' her mother said briskly. She thought, but did not say, that perhaps they could claim the amount if they wrote to British Railways and explained.

Mrs. Lippmann's easy affection meant so much less than her own stiff endearments, but she resented it all the same and when she was begged, with enormous warmth, to visit them all again soon her smile was a prim twisting of her lips.

The air was bright with summer sounds, voices across the water and rooks up in the elm trees. Roger stood back listening in a dream to the good-byes and thank yous. Nor was *this* the end of the world, he told himself. Etta would come again and, better than that, they would also grow older and so be less at the mercy of circumstances. He would be in a position to command his life and turn occasions to his own advantage. Meanwhile, he had done what he could. None the less, he felt such dejection, such an overwhelming conviction that it was the end of the world after all, that he could not watch the car go down the drive, and he turned and walked quickly – rudely, off-handedly, his mother thought – back to the house.

Mrs. Salkeld, driving homewards in the lowering sun, knew that Etta had tears in her eyes. 'I'm glad you enjoyed yourself,' she said. Without waiting for an answer, she added: 'They are very charming people.' She had always suspected charm and rarely spoke of it, but in this case the adjective seemed called for.

Mr. Lippmann would be coming back from London about now, Etta was thinking. 'And David will bring Nora. They will all be on the terrace having drinks – dry martinis, not sherry.'

She was grateful to her mother about the sherry and understood that it had been an effort towards meeting Mrs. Lippmann's world half-way, and on the way back, she had not murmured one word of criticism – for their worldliness or extravagance or the vulgar opulence of their furnishings. She had even made a kind remark about them.

I might buy her a new dress, Mrs. Salkeld thought – something like the one Sarah was wearing. Though it does seem a criminal waste when she has all her good school clothes to wear out.

They had come on to the main road, and evening traffic streamed by. In the distance the gas holder looked pearl grey and the smoke from factories was pink in the sunset. They were nearly home. Etta, who had blinked her tears back from her eyes, took a sharp breath, almost a sigh.

Their own street with its tall houses was in shadow. 'I wish we had a cat,' said Etta, as she got out of the car and saw the next door tabby looking through the garden railings. She imagined burying her face in its warm fur, it loving only her. To her surprise, her mother said: 'Why not?' Briskly, she went up the steps and turned the key with its familiar grating sound in the lock. The house, with its smell – familiar, too – of floor polish and stuffiness, looked secretive. Mrs. Salkeld, hardly noticing this, hurried to the kitchen to put the casserole of chicken in the oven.

Etta carried her suitcase upstairs. On the dressing-table was a jar of marigolds. She was touched by this – just when she did not want to be touched. She turned her back on them and opened her case. On the top was the book she had left on the terrace. Roger had brought it to her at the last moment. Taking it now, she found a letter inside. Simply 'Etta' was written on the envelope.

Roger had felt that he had done all he was capable of and that was to write in the letter those things he could not have brought himself to say, even if he had had an opportunity. No love letter could have been less anticipated and Etta read it twice before she could realise that it was neither a joke nor a mistake. It was the most extraordinary happening of her life, the most incredible.

Her breathing grew slower and deeper as she sat staring before her, pondering her mounting sense of power. It was as if the whole Lippmann family – Nora as well – had proposed to her. To marry Roger – a long, long time ahead though she must wait to do so – would be the best possible way of belonging.

She got up stiffly – for her limbs now seemed too clumsy a part of her body with its fly-away heart and giddy head – she went over to the dressing-table and stared at herself in the glass. 'I am I,' she thought, but she could not believe it. She stared and stared, but could not take in the tantalising idea.

After a while, she began to unpack. The room was a place of transit, her temporary residence. When she had made it tidy, she went downstairs to thank her mother for the marigolds.

EVELYN WAUGH

THE MAN WHO
LIKED DICKENS
(1933)

ALTHOUGH MR. McMASTER had lived in Amazonas for nearly sixty years, no one except a few families of Shiriana Indians was aware of his existence. His house stood in a small savannah, one of those little patches of sand and grass that crop up occasionally in that neighbourhood, three miles or so across, bounded on all sides by forest.

The stream which watered it was not marked on any map; it ran through rapids, always dangerous and at most seasons of the year impassable, to join the upper waters of the River Uraricuera, whose course, though boldly delineated in every school atlas, is still largely conjectural. None of the inhabitants of the district, except Mr. McMaster, had ever heard of the republic of Colombia, Venezuela, Brazil or Bolivia, each of whom had at one time or another claimed its possession.

Mr. McMaster's house was larger than those of his neighbours, but similar in character – a palm thatch roof; breast high walls of mud and wattle, and a mud floor. He owned the dozen or so head of puny cattle which grazed in the savannah, a plantation of cassava, some banana and mango trees, a dog, and, unique in the neighbourhood, a single-barrelled, breech-loading shotgun. The few commodities which he employed from the outside world came to him through a long succession of traders, passed from hand to hand, bartered for in a dozen languages at the extreme end of one of the longest threads in the web of commerce that spreads from Manáos into the remote fastness of the forest.

One day while Mr. McMaster was engaged in filling some cartridges, a Shiriana came to him with the news that a white man was approaching through the forest, alone and very sick. He closed the cartridge and loaded his gun with it, put those that were finished into his pocket and set out in the direction indicated.

The man was already clear of the bush when Mr. Mc-Master reached him, sitting on the ground, clearly in a very bad way. He was without hat or boots, and his clothes were so torn that it was only by the dampness of his body that they adhered to it; his feet were cut and grossly swollen, every exposed surface of skin was scarred by insect and bat bites; his eyes were wild with fever. He was talking to himself in delirium, but stopped when Mr. McMaster approached and addressed him in English.

'I'm tired,' the man said; then: 'Can't go any farther. My name is Henty and I'm tired. Anderson died. That was a long time ago. I expect you think I'm very odd.'

'I think you are ill, my friend.'

'Just tired. It must be several months since I had anything to eat.'

Mr. McMaster hoisted him to his feet and, supporting him by the arm, led him across the hummocks of grass towards the farm.

'It is a very short way. When we get there I will give you something to make you better.'

'Jolly kind of you.' Presently he said: 'I say, you speak English. I'm English, too. My name is Henty.'

'Well, Mr. Henty, you aren't to bother about anything more. You're ill and you've had a rough journey. I'll take care of you.'

They went very slowly, but at length reached the house.

'Lie there in the hammock. I will fetch something for you.'

Mr. McMaster went into the back room of the house and dragged a tin canister from under a heap of skins. It was full of a mixture of dried leaf and bark. He took a handful and went outside to the fire. When he returned he put one hand behind Henty's head and held up the concoction of herbs in a calabash for him to drink. He sipped, shuddering slightly at the bitterness. At last he finished it. Mr. McMaster threw out the dregs on the floor. Henty lay back in the hammock sobbing quietly. Soon he fell into a deep sleep.

'Ill-fated' was the epithet applied by the press to the Anderson expedition to the Parima and upper Uraricuera region of Brazil. Every stage of the enterprise from the preliminary arrangements in London to its tragic dissolution in Amazonas was attacked by misfortune. It was due to one of the early setbacks that Paul Henty became connected with it.

He was not by nature an explorer; an even-tempered, good-looking young man of fastidious tastes and enviable possessions, unintellectual, but appreciative of fine architecture and the ballet, well travelled in the more accessible parts of the world, a collector though not a connoisseur, popular among hostesses, revered by his aunts. He was married to a lady of exceptional charm and beauty, and it was she who upset the good order of his life by confessing her affection for another man for the second time in the eight years of their marriage. The first occasion had been a short-lived infatuation with a tennis professional, the second was a captain in the Coldstream Guards, and more serious.

Henty's first thought under the shock of this revelation was to go out and dine alone. He was a member of four clubs, but at three of them he was liable to meet his wife's lover. Accordingly he chose one which he rarely frequented, a semi-intellectual company composed of publishers, barristers, and men of scholarship awaiting election to the Athenaeum.

Here, after dinner, he fell into conversation with Professor Anderson and first heard of the proposed expedition to Brazil. The particular misfortune that was retarding arrangements at that moment was the defalcation of the secretary with two-thirds of the expedition's capital. The principals were ready – Professor Anderson, Dr. Simmons the anthropologist, Mr. Necher the biologist, Mr. Brough the surveyor, wireless operator and mechanic – the scientific and sporting apparatus was packed up in crates ready to be embarked, the necessary facilities had been stamped and signed by the proper authorities, but unless twelve hundred pounds was forthcoming the whole thing would have to be abandoned.

Henty, as has been suggested, was a man of comfortable means; the expedition would last from nine months to a year; he could shut his country house – his wife, he reflected, would want to remain in London near her young man – and cover more than the sum required. There was a glamour about the whole journey which might, he felt, move even his wife's sympathies. There and then, over the club fire, he decided to accompany Professor Anderson.

When he went home that evening he announced to his wife: 'I have decided what I shall do.'

'Yes, darling?'

'You are certain that you no longer love me?'

'*Darling*, you *know*, I *adore* you.'

'But you are certain you love this guardsman, Tony whatever-his-name-is, more?'

'Oh, yes, *ever* so much more. Quite a different thing altogether.'

'Very well, then. I do not propose to do anything about a divorce for a year. You shall have time to think it over. I am leaving next week for the Uraricuera.'

'Golly, where's that?'

'I am not perfectly sure. Somewhere in Brazil, I think. It is unexplored. I shall be away a year.'

'But darling, how ordinary! Like people in books – big game, I mean, and all that.'

'You have obviously already discovered that I am a very ordinary person.'

'Now, Paul, don't be disagreeable – oh, there's the telephone. It's probably Tony. If it is, d'you mind terribly if I talk to him alone for a bit?'

But in the ten days of preparation that followed she showed greater tenderness, putting off her soldier twice in order to accompany Henty to the shops where he was choosing his equipment and insisting on his purchasing a worsted cummerbund. On his last evening she gave a supper party for him at the Embassy to which she allowed him to ask any of his friends he liked; he could think of no one except Professor Anderson, who looked oddly dressed, danced tirelessly and was something of a failure with everyone. Next day Mrs. Henty came with her husband to the boat train and presented him with a pale blue, extravagantly soft blanket, in a suede case of the same colour furnished with a zip fastener and monogram. She kissed him goodbye and said, 'Take care of yourself in wherever it is.'

Had she gone as far as Southampton she might have witnessed two dramatic passages. Mr. Brough got no farther than the gangway before he was arrested for debt – a matter of £32; the publicity given to the dangers of the expedition was responsible for the action. Henty settled the account.

The second difficulty was not to be overcome so easily. Mr.

Necher's mother was on the ship before them; she carried a missionary journal in which she had just read an account of the Brazilian forests. Nothing would induce her to permit her son's departure; she would remain on board until he came ashore with her. If necessary, she would sail with him, but go into those forests alone he should not. All argument was unavailing with the resolute old lady, who eventually, five minutes before the time of embarkation, bore her son off in triumph, leaving the company without a biologist.

Nor was Mr. Brough's adherence long maintained. The ship in which they were travelling was a cruising liner taking passengers on a round voyage. Mr. Brough had not been on board a week and had scarcely accustomed himself to the motion of the ship before he was engaged to be married; he was still engaged, although to a different lady, when they reached Manáos and refused all inducements to proceed farther, borrowing his return fare from Henty and arriving back in Southampton engaged to the lady of his first choice, whom he immediately married.

In Brazil the officials to whom their credentials were addressed were all out of power. While Henty and Professor Anderson negotiated with the new administrators, Dr. Simmons proceeded up river to Boa Vista where he established a base camp with the greater part of the stores. These were instantly commandeered by the revolutionary garrison, and he himself imprisoned for some days and subjected to various humiliations which so enraged him that, when released, he made promptly for the coast, stopping at Manáos only long enough to inform his colleagues that he insisted on leaving his case personally before the central authorities at Rio.

Thus, while they were still a month's journey from the start of their labours, Henty and Professor Anderson found themselves alone and deprived of the greater part of their supplies. The ignominy of immediate return was not to be borne. For a short time they considered the advisability of going into hiding for six months in Madeira or Tenerife, but even there detection seemed probable; there had been too many photographs in the illustrated papers before they left London. Accordingly, in low spirits, the two explorers at last set out alone for the Uraricuera with little hope of accomplishing anything of any value to anyone.

For seven weeks they paddled through green, humid tunnels of forest. They took a few snapshots of naked, misanthropic Indians; bottled some snakes and later lost them when their canoe capsized in the rapids; they over-taxed their digestions, imbibing nauseous intoxicants at native galas; they were robbed of the last of their sugar by a Guianese prospector. Finally, Professor Anderson fell ill with malignant malaria, chattered feebly for some days in his hammock, lapsed into coma and died, leaving Henty alone with a dozen Maku oarsmen, none of whom spoke a word of any language known to him. They reversed their course and drifted down stream with a minimum of provisions and no mutual confidence.

One day, a week or so after Professor Anderson's death, Henty awoke to find that his boys and his canoe had disappeared during the night, leaving him with only his hammock and pyjamas some two or three hundred miles from the nearest Brazilian habitation. Nature forbade him to remain where he was although there seemed little purpose in moving. He set himself to follow the course of the stream, at first in the hope of meeting a canoe. But presently the whole forest became peopled for him with frantic apparitions, for no conscious reason at all. He plodded on, now wading in the water, now scrambling through the bush.

Vaguely at the back of his mind he had always believed

that the jungle was a place full of food; that there was danger of snakes and savages and wild beasts, but not of starvation. But now he observed that this was far from being the case. The jungle consisted solely of immense tree trunks, embedded in a tangle of thorn and vine rope, all far from nutritious. On the first day he suffered hideously. Later he seemed anaesthetized and was chiefly embarrassed by the behaviour of the inhabitants who came out to meet him in footman's livery, carrying his dinner, and then irresponsibly disappeared or raised the covers of their dishes and revealed live tortoises. Many people who knew him in London appeared and ran round him with derisive cries, asking him questions to which he could not possibly know the answer. His wife came, too, and he was pleased to see her, assuming that she had got tired of her guardsman and was there to fetch him back; but she soon disappeared, like all the others.

It was then that he remembered that it was imperative for him to reach Manáos; he redoubled his energy, stumbling against boulders in the stream and getting caught up among the vines. 'But I mustn't waste my strength,' he reflected. Then, he forgot that, too, and was conscious of nothing more until he found himself lying in a hammock in Mr. McMaster's house.

His recovery was slow. At first, days of lucidity alternated with delirium; then his temperature dropped and he was conscious even when most ill. The days of fever grew less frequent, finally occurring in the normal system of the tropics, between long periods of comparative health. Mr. McMaster dosed him regularly with herbal remedies.

'It's very nasty,' said Henty, 'but it does do good.'

'There is medicine for everything in the forest,' said Mr. McMaster; 'to make you well and to make you ill. My mother was an Indian and she taught me many of them. I have learned others from time to time from my wives. There are plants to cure you and give you fever, to kill you and send you mad, to keep away snakes, to intoxicate fish so that you can pick them out of the water with your hands like fruit from a tree. There are medicines even I do not know. They say that it is possible to bring dead people to life after they have begun to stink, but I have not seen it done.'

'But surely you are English?'

'My father was – at least a Barbadian. He came to British Guiana as a missionary. He was married to a white woman but he left her in Guiana to look for gold. Then he took my mother. The Shiriana women are ugly but very devoted. I have had many. Most of the men and women living in this savannah are my children. That is why they obey – for that reason and because I have the gun. My father lived to a great age. It is not twenty years since he died. He was a man of education. Can you read?'

'Yes, of course.'

'It is not everyone who is so fortunate. I cannot.'

Henty laughed apologetically. 'But I suppose you haven't much opportunity here.'

'Oh yes, that is just it. I have a great many books. I will show you when you are better. Until five years ago there was an Englishman – at least a black man, but he was well educated in Georgetown. He died. He used to read to me every day until he died. You shall read to me when you are better.'

'I shall be delighted to.'

'Yes, you shall read to me,' Mr. McMaster repeated, nodding over the calabash.

During the early days of his convalescence Henty had little conversation with his host; he lay in the hammock staring up at the thatched roof and thinking about his wife, rehearsing over and over again different incidents in their life together, including her affairs with the tennis professional and the soldier. The days, exactly twelve hours each, passed without distinction. Mr. McMaster retired to sleep at sundown, leaving a little lamp burning – a hand-woven wick drooping from a pot of beef fat – to keep away vampire bats.

The first time that Henty left the house Mr. McMaster took him for a little stroll around the farm.

'I will show you the black man's grave,' he said, leading him to a mound between the mango trees. 'He was very kind to me. Every afternoon until he died, for two hours, he used to read to me. I think I will put up a cross – to commemorate his death and your arrival – a pretty idea. Do you believe in God?'

'I've never really thought about it much.'

'You are perfectly right. I have thought about it a *great* deal and I still do not know . . . Dickens did.'

'I suppose so.'

'Oh yes, it is apparent in all his books. You will see.'

That afternoon Mr. McMaster began the construction of a headpiece for the negro's grave. He worked with a large spokeshave in a wood so hard that it grated and rang like metal.

At last when Henty had passed six or seven consecutive days without fever, Mr. McMaster said, 'Now I think you are well enough to see the books.'

At one end of the hut there was a kind of loft formed by a rough platform erected up in the eaves of the roof. Mr. McMaster propped a ladder against it and mounted. Henty followed, still unsteady after his illness. Mr. McMaster sat on the platform and Henty stood at the top of the ladder looking over. There was a heap of small bundles there, tied up with rag, palm leaf and raw hide.

'It has been hard to keep out the worms and ants. Two are practically destroyed. But there is an oil the Indians know how to make that is useful.'

He unwrapped the nearest parcel and handed down a calf-bound book. It was an early American edition of *Bleak House*.

'It does not matter which we take first.'

'You are fond of Dickens?'

'Why, yes, of course. More than fond, far more. You see, they are the only books I have ever heard. My father used to read them and then later the black man . . . and now you. I have heard them all several times by now but I never get tired; there is always more to be learned and noticed, so many characters, so many changes of scene, so many words . . . I have all Dickens's books except those that the ants devoured. It takes a long time to read them all – more than two years.'

'Well,' said Henty lightly, 'they will well last out my visit.'

'Oh, I hope not. It is delightful to start again. Each time I think I find more to enjoy and admire.'

They took down the first volume of *Bleak House* and that afternoon Henty had his first reading.

He had always rather enjoyed reading aloud and in the first year of marriage had shared several books in this way with his wife, until one day, in one of her rare moments of confidence, she remarked that it was torture to her. Sometimes after that he had thought it might be agreeable to have children to read to. But Mr. McMaster was a unique audience.

The old man sat astride his hammock opposite Henty, fixing him throughout with his eyes, and following the words, soundlessly, with his lips. Often when a new character was introduced he would say, 'Repeat the name, I have forgotten him,' or, 'Yes, yes, I remember her well. She dies, poor woman.' He would frequently interrupt with questions; not as Henty would have imagined about the circumstances of the story – such things as the procedure of the Lord Chancellor's Court or the social conventions of the time, though they must have been unintelligible, did not concern him – but always about the characters. 'Now, why does she say that? Does she really mean it? Did she feel faint because of the heat of the fire or of something in that paper?' He laughed loudly at all the jokes and at some passages which did not seem humorous to Henty, asking him to repeat them two or three times; and later at the description of the sufferings of the outcasts in 'Tom-all-Alone's' tears ran down his cheeks into his beard. His comments on the story were usually simple. 'I think that Dedlock is a very proud man,' or, 'Mrs. Jellyby does not take enough care of her children.' Henty enjoyed the readings almost as much as he did.

At the end of the first day the old man said, 'You read beautifully, with a far better accent than the black man. And you explain better. It is almost as though my father were here again.' And always at the end of a session he thanked his guest courteously. 'I enjoyed that very much. It was an extremely distressing chapter. But, if I remember rightly, it will all turn out well.'

By the time that they were well into the second volume, however, the novelty of the old man's delight had begun to wane, and Henty was feeling strong enough to be restless. He touched more than once on the subject of his departure, asking about canoes and rains and the possibility of finding guides. But Mr. McMaster seemed obtuse and paid no attention to these hints.

One day, running his thumb through the pages of *Bleak House* that remained to be read, Henty said, 'We still have a lot to get through. I hope I shall be able to finish it before I go.'

'Oh yes,' said Mr. McMaster. 'Do not disturb yourself about that. You will have time to finish it, my friend.'

For the first time Henty noticed something slightly menacing in his host's manner. That evening at supper, a brief meal of farine and dried beef eaten just before sundown, Henty renewed the subject.

'You know, Mr. McMaster, the time has come when I must be thinking about getting back to civilization. I have already imposed myself on your hospitality for too long.'

Mr. McMaster bent over his plate, crunching mouthfuls of farine, but made no reply.

'How soon do you think I shall be able to get a boat? . . . I said how soon do you think I shall be able to get a boat? I appreciate all your kindness to me more than I can say, but . . .'

'My friend, any kindness I may have shown is amply repaid by your reading of Dickens. Do not let us mention the subject again.'

'Well, I'm very glad you have enjoyed it. I have, too. But I really must be thinking of getting back . . .'

'Yes,' said Mr. McMaster. 'The black man was like that. He thought of it all the time. But he died here . . .'

Twice during the next day Henty opened the subject but his host was evasive. Finally he said, 'Forgive me, Mr. McMaster, but I really must press the point. When can I get a boat?'

'There is no boat.'

'Well, the Indians can build one.'

'You must wait for the rains. There is not enough water in the river now.'

'How long will that be?'

'A month . . . two months . . .'

They had finished *Bleak House* and were nearing the end of *Dombey and Son* when the rain came.

'Now it is time to make preparations to go.'

'Oh, that is impossible. The Indians will not make a boat during the rainy season – it is one of their superstitions.'

'You might have told me.'

'Did I not mention it? I forgot.'

Next morning Henty went out alone while his host was busy, and, looking as aimless as he could, strolled across the savannah to the group of Indian houses. There were four or five Shirianas sitting in one of the doorways. They did not look up as he approached them. He addressed them in the few words of Maku he had acquired during the journey but they made no sign whether they understood him or not. Then he drew a sketch of a canoe in the sand, he went through some vague motions of carpentry, pointed from them to him, then made motions of giving something to them and scratched out the outlines of a gun and a hat and a few other recognizable articles of trade. One of the women giggled, but no one gave any sign of comprehension, and he went away unsatisfied.

At their midday meal Mr. McMaster said, 'Mr. Henty, the Indians tell me that you have been trying to speak with them. It is easier that you say anything you wish through me. You realize, do you not, that they would do nothing without my authority. They regard themselves, quite rightly in most cases, as my children.'

'Well, as a matter of fact, I was asking them about a canoe.'

'So they gave me to understand . . . and now if you have

finished your meal perhaps we might have another chapter. I am quite absorbed in the book.'

They finished *Dombey and Son*; nearly a year had passed since Henty had left England, and his gloomy foreboding of permanent exile became suddenly acute when, between the pages of *Martin Chuzzlewit*, he found a document written in pencil in irregular characters.

Year 1919

I James McMaster of Brazil do swear to Barnabas Washington of Georgetown that if he finish this book in fact Martin Chuzzlewit I will let him go away back as soon as finished.

There followed a heavy pencil *X*, and after it: *Mr. McMaster made this mark signed Barnabas Washington.*

'Mr. McMaster,' said Henty. 'I must speak frankly. You saved my life, and when I get back to civilization I will reward you to the best of my ability. I will give you anything within reason. But at present you are keeping me here against my will. I demand to be released.'

'But, my friend, what is keeping you? You are under no restraint. Go when you like.'

'You know very well that I can't get away without your help.'

'In that case you must humour an old man. Read me another chapter.'

'Mr. McMaster, I swear by anything you like that when I get to Manáos I will find someone to take my place. I will pay a man to read to you all day.'

'But I have no need of another man. You read so well.'

'I have read for the last time.'

'I hope not,' said Mr. McMaster politely.

That evening at supper only one plate of dried meat and farine was brought in and Mr. McMaster ate alone. Henty lay without speaking, staring at the thatch.

Next day at noon a single plate was put before Mr. McMaster, but with it lay his gun, cocked, on his knee, as he ate. Henty resumed the reading of *Martin Chuzzlewit* where it had been interrupted.

Weeks passed hopelessly. They read *Nicholas Nickleby* and *Little Dorrit* and *Oliver Twist*. Then a stranger arrived in the savannah, a half-caste prospector, one of that lonely order of men who wander for a lifetime through the forests, tracing the little streams, sifting the gravel and, ounce by ounce, filling the little leather sack of gold dust, more often than not dying of exposure and starvation with five hundred dollars' worth of gold hung around their necks. Mr. McMaster was vexed at his arrival, gave him farine and *passo* and sent him on his journey within an hour of his arrival, but in that hour Henty had time to scribble his name on a slip of paper and put it into the man's hand.

From now on there was hope. The days followed their unvarying routine; coffee at sunrise, a morning of inaction while Mr. McMaster pottered about on the business of the farm, farine and *passo* at noon, Dickens in the afternoon, farine and *passo* and sometimes some fruit for supper, silence from sunset to dawn with the small wick glowing in the beef fat and the palm thatch overhead dimly discernible; but Henty lived in quiet confidence and expectation.

Some time, this year or the next, the prospector would arrive at a Brazilian village with news of his discovery. The disasters to the Anderson expedition would not have passed unnoticed. Henty could imagine the headlines that must have appeared in the popular press; even now probably there were search parties working over the country he had crossed; any day English voices might sound over the savannah and a dozen friendly adventurers come crashing through the bush. Even as he was reading, while his lips mechanically followed the printed pages, his mind wandered away from his eager, crazy host opposite, and he began to narrate to himself incidents of his homecoming – the gradual re-encounters with civilization; he shaved and bought new clothes at Manáos, telegraphed for money, received wires of congratulation; he enjoyed the leisurely river journey to Belem, the big liner to Europe; savoured good claret and fresh meat and spring vegetables; he was shy at meeting his wife and uncertain how to address . . . '*Darling*, you've been much longer than you said. I quite thought you were lost . . .'

And then Mr. McMaster interrupted. 'May I trouble you to read that passage again? It is one I particularly enjoy.'

The weeks passed; there was no sign of rescue, but Henty endured the day for hope of what might happen on the morrow; he even felt a slight stirring of cordiality towards his gaoler and was therefore quite willing to join him when, one evening after a long conference with an Indian neighbour, he proposed a celebration.

'It is one of the local feast days,' he explained, 'and they have been making *piwari*. You may not like it, but you should try some. We will go across to this man's home to-night.'

Accordingly after supper they joined a party of Indians that were assembled round the fire in one of the huts at the other side of the savannah. They were singing in an apathetic, monotonous manner and passing a large calabash of liquid from mouth to mouth. Separate bowls were brought for Henty and Mr. McMaster, and they were given hammocks to sit in.

'You must drink it all without lowering the cup. That is the etiquette.'

Henty gulped the dark liquid, trying not to taste it. But it was not unpleasant, hard and muddy on the palate like most of the beverages he had been offered in Brazil, but with a flavour of honey and brown bread. He leant back in the hammock feeling unusually contented. Perhaps at that very moment the search party was in camp a few hours' journey from them. Meanwhile he was warm and drowsy. The cadence of song rose and fell interminably, liturgically. Another calabash of *piwari* was offered him and he handed it back empty. He lay full length watching the play of shadows on the thatch as the Shirianas began to dance. Then he shut his eyes and thought of England and his wife and fell asleep.

He awoke, still in the Indian hut, with the impression that he had outslept his usual hour. By the position of the sun he knew it was late afternoon. No one else was about. He looked for his watch and found to his surprise that it was not on his wrist. He had left it in the house, he supposed, before coming to the party.

'I must have been tight last night,' he reflected. 'Treacherous drink, that.' He had a headache and feared a recurrence of fever. He found when he set his feet to the ground that he stood with difficulty; his walk was unsteady and his mind confused as it had been during the first weeks of his convalescence. On the way across the savannah he was obliged to stop more than once, shutting his eyes and breathing deeply. When he reached the house he found Mr. McMaster sitting there.

'Ah, my friend, you are late for the reading this afternoon. There is scarcely another half hour of light. How do you feel?'

'Rotten. That drink doesn't seem to agree with me.'

'I will give you something to make you better. The forest has remedies for everything; to make you awake and to make you sleep.'

'You haven't seen my watch anywhere?'

'You have missed it?'

'Yes. I thought I was wearing it. I say, I've never slept so long.'

'Not since you were a baby. Do you know how long? Two days.'

'Nonsense. I can't have.'

'Yes, indeed. It is a long time. It is a pity because you missed our guests.'

'Guests?'

'Why, yes. I have been quite gay while you were asleep. Three men from outside. Englishmen. It is a pity you missed them. A pity for them, too, as they particularly wished to see you. But what could I do? You were so sound asleep. They had come all the way to find you, so – I thought you would not mind – as you could not greet them yourself I gave them a little souvenir, your watch. They wanted something to take home to your wife who is offering a great reward for news of you. They were very pleased with it. And they took some photographs of the little cross I put up to commemorate your coming. They were pleased with that, too. They were very easily pleased. But I do not suppose they will visit us again, our life here is so retired . . . no pleasures except reading . . . I do not suppose we shall ever have visitors again . . . well, well, I will get you some medicine to make you feel better. Your head aches, does it not . . . We will not have any Dickens to-day . . . but to-morrow, and the day after that, and the day after that. Let us read *Little Dorrit* again. There are passages in that book I can never hear without the temptation to weep.'

JULIO CORTÁZAR

CONTINUITY
OF PARKS
(1956)

Translated by Paul Blackburn

HE HAD BEGUN to read the novel a few days before. He had put it down because of some urgent business conferences, opened it again on his way back to the estate by train; he permitted himself a slowly growing interest in the plot, in the characterisations. That afternoon, after writing a letter giving his power of attorney and discussing a matter of joint ownership with the manager of his estate, he returned to the book in the tranquillity of his study which looked out upon the park with its oaks. Sprawled in his favorite armchair, its back toward the door – even the possibility of an intrusion would have irritated him, had he thought of it – he let his left hand caress repeatedly the green velvet upholstery and set to reading the final chapters. He remembered effortlessly the names and his mental image of the characters; the novel spread its glamour over him almost at once. He tasted the almost perverse pleasure of disengaging himself line by line from the things around him, and at the same time feeling his head rest comfortably on the green velvet of the chair with its high back, sensing that the cigarettes rested within reach of his hand, that beyond the great windows the air of afternoon danced under the oak trees in the park. Word by word, licked up by the sordid dilemma of the hero and heroine, letting himself be absorbed to the point where the images settled down and took on color and movement, he was witness to the final encounter in the mountain cabin. The woman arrived first, apprehensive; now the lover came in, his face cut by the backlash of a branch. Admirably, she stanched the blood with her kisses, but he rebuffed her caresses, he had not come to perform again the ceremonies of a secret passion, protected by a world of dry leaves and furtive paths through the forest. The dagger warmed itself against his chest, and underneath liberty pounded, hidden close. A lustful, panting dialogue raced down the pages like a rivulet of snakes, and one felt it had all been decided from eternity. Even to those caresses which writhed about the lover's body, as though wishing to keep him there, to dissuade him from it; they sketched abominably the frame of that other body it was necessary to destroy. Nothing had been forgotten: alibis, unforeseen hazards, possible mistakes. From this hour on, each instant had its use minutely assigned. The cold-blooded, twice-gone-over re-examination of the details was barely broken off so that a hand could caress a cheek. It was beginning to get dark.

Not looking at one another now, rigidly fixed upon the task which awaited them, they separated at the cabin door. She was to follow the trail that led north. On the path leading in the opposite direction, he turned for a moment to watch her running, her hair loosened and flying. He ran in turn, crouching among the trees and hedges until, in the yellowish fog of dusk, he could distinguish the avenue of trees which led up to the house. The dogs were not supposed to bark, they did not bark. The estate manager would not be there at this hour, and he was not there. He went up the three porch steps and entered. The woman's words reached him over the thudding of blood in his ears: first a blue chamber, then a hall, then a carpeted stairway. At the top, two doors. No one in the first room, no one in the second. The door of the salon, and then, the knife in hand, the light from the great windows, the high back of an armchair covered in green velvet, the head of the man in the chair reading a novel.

ALI SMITH

THE EX-WIFE
(2015)

AT FIRST I thought it was just that you really liked books, just that you were someone who really loved your work. I thought it was just more evidence of your passionate and sensitive nature.

At first I was quite charmed by it. It was charming. She was charming.

But here are three instances of what it was like for me.

1: I'd be deep asleep, in the place where all the healing happens, the place all the serious newspapers talk about in their health pages as crucial because that's where the things that fray or need patched in our daily lives get physically and mentally attended to and if we don't attend to them something irreparable will happen. Then something would wake me. It'd be you, suddenly sitting straight up in the bed so all the covers would be off both of us, then it'd be you not there, I mean I'd come to myself and the covers would be off me, I'd open my eyes into a blur of dark, put my hand out and feel the place going cold where you should be. Then a light would come on somewhere in the house. Then a small noise would be happening. I'd get up. I'd blur my way downstairs, one hand on the wall. I'd blur into the front room, or the kitchen, or the study. You'd be sitting at the table. There'd be a too-high pile of books on it. Even in the blur I'd be able to see that that pile was going to topple any moment. You'd be sitting beyond it, looking through a book. Your eyes would be distant, as if closed and open at the

179

same time. I'd stand there for a bit. You'd not look up. What's going on? I'd say. It'd come out sounding blurry. Nothing, you'd say, I just need to know whether Wing was actually the original kitten of Charlie Chaplin. To know what? I'd say. In a letter to Woolf somewhere, you'd say. There's a kind of family tree, and I know Athenaeum is one of the kittens that Charlie Chaplin gave birth to. But there's another one and I'm pretty sure it's not Wing or at least not called Wing in this particular reference and I need to know what its name is and whether it's another name for Wing, or whether Wing was actually another cat altogether or maybe even another name for Charlie Chaplin. You're looking up her cats now? I'd say. Now? What the fuck time is it? I need to know, you'd say. Why exactly do you need to know this? I'd say. Because I realized I don't know it, you'd say. In what context could it possibly be useful? I'd say. I'll just be another minute, you'd say. I know pretty much where to look, it'll just take a minute. You'd pull another book out of the pile and catch the pile, shunt it back together with your elbow, wait till it was definitely not going to fall, and open the book at the index at the back. I'd go up to bed. I'd lie there unable to sleep. When you'd come up again two and a half hours later I'd be pretending not to be awake. You'd sigh back into bed and lie down next to me. Immediately you'd be asleep. But for me the windowblind would be edged with something far too bright. What would that noise be now? Birds.

2: We'd be talking about something really important, well, important to me at least. We'd be talking, for instance, about what happened to me at work, how everybody's running really scared about the cuts. I'd tell you what had happened in the office that day. And you'd say, God, you know that's exactly like in psychology. And I'd say, what in psychology, like manic depression or passive aggression?

And you'd say, no, not psychology, I don't mean psychology, I mean pictures, it's exactly like in pictures, and I'd say, pictures of what? and you'd say, well, what happens is, this woman, she's a bit past it though she used to be a good singer, she got a medal for it, but now she's more middle-aged and she's trying to get a job as an extra in films so she can pay her rent, and the first thing Mansfield does is, like, the story opens and this woman is lying in bed in a rented room and she's got no rent. Oh, right, Mansfield, I'd say. Yeah, you'd say, and she wakes up and she's cold and she thinks it's maybe because she hasn't eaten properly, so then it's like a pageant of images crosses the ceiling in front of her, pictures of hot dinners sort of marching over the ceiling, and then she thinks she'd like some breakfast and then on the ceiling it's a pageant of images of big breakfasts, it's brilliant really when you consider what it's doing, it's a story about the fantasy of nourishment and what happens when that fantasy hits, like, reality, she even uses the word nourishing at one point I think. It's a fantastic critique of cinema actually. Yeah, I'd say, but I'm struggling to make the link between you telling me the plot of a short story and Johnston email-bullying me at work. Are you saying I'm a bit past it? No, you'd say, listen, if you read it you'd see, it's obvious, I'll go and get it for you. No, don't, I'd say. It's okay, really. I can sort it out for myself. I don't need to talk about it to anybody. But you'd be on your way to the shelf, and it's got this really lovely little throwaway phrase, you'd be saying, I can't remember it exactly but it kind of goes, something *fell, sepulchral*, she's so brilliant, that so-simple word fell with the word sepulchral after it, wait, it's here somewhere, I'll look it up. Look up the word sepulchral for me while you're at it, would you? I'd say. You know what sepulchral means, you'd say. Yeah, obviously, I'd say, everyone knows what sepulchral means.

Well, everyone will one day, you'd say. Ha ha, yes, I'd say. Too true. And I'd have to tell myself to remember to look up what it meant later. I myself am not very interested in books, or words. When we were first together you used to tell me it was a relief, to be with me, because I wasn't.

3: There was the day I came home from work and I found you sitting holding a glossy book, and the cardboard envelope from Amazon still on the floor. The book was open on your knee, one page black, one page white. On the black page there was a picture of a twined thick piece of hair. On the white page there was another picture of a coiled palmful of hair, darker, and a black and white picture of a woman, a girl. You were crying, and it was about the most ridiculous thing I could think of, in the real world with all its awful things to really cry about. The thing is, I never imagined her in colour before, you said. The book you were holding was called Traces of a Writer. It was full of pictures of what was left of your favourite writer after she died, pictures of a brooch, a little knife, bits of fabric, a little pair of scissors, a chess set, things like that. This was the day I first called her your ex-wife. I said, it's like living with an extra person in our relationship. It's like there's always someone else. I meant it as a joke. But you were off on to the next page. You said, look, look, what's this little leather thing? It's called the fairy purse. Look. It's a purse, for a sovereign. She gave it to her friend when they were schoolgirls, her friend that stayed with her all through her life, you know. It's a bit weird, though, looking at this private stuff, isn't it? I said. You'd stopped crying. It's a bit necro, no? I said. You wiped at the sides of your eyes. It says here there's a message inside it, a note, you said. It says here it's never been taken out because it's too fragile, but that it says on it, 'Katie and Ida's fairy purse'. How do they know it says that, if they haven't ever taken

182

it out? I said. And what if your ex-wife doesn't want people looking at her private stuff? I don't know that I'd want the general public always to be reading my letters or looking at my private writings, even if they did have research grant money to do it and they could give looking at old bits of rubbish left behind by a dead person a grandiose name like The Memory Meme And Materiology In Katherine Mansfield's Metaphorical Landscape. Stop pretending you're stupid, you said, why do you always pretend you're stupid, why do you always pretend to be less than you are, and why do you always use my passion for what I'm working on against me to duck responsibility in our relationship? Ha! I said, I do know some stuff, actually. I can read Wikipedia as well as the next person, actually, and if she's your ex-wife, then which does that make you, the vain incompetent who was always letting her down and who sold everything after she was dead and made a fortune out of it, or that poor woman she kept calling the Mountain? Because whichever one of those you are, that makes me the other, and I'm not playing that kind of weirdo role-play thank you very much. She was cruel, your ex-wife. She was a piece of work, all right. It was shortly after that that you threw the glossy book at the shelf and four of the little cups we'd bought in Mexico broke. Then I went over to the shelf, took the fifth cup, held it up above the fireplace and dropped it, and we both watched it break. It wasn't long after that particular day that you and I split up.

Not long after that, I remembered, and looked up the meaning. Something fell. Sepulchral.

I was walking through the park, through the bit where the fountains and the bushes are all laid out neatly. It was dusk and I was coming home from a meeting. It had been quite a tough meeting. I had had to lay off three people, most of a whole team, and we'd been told that Google Translate was basically going to be used to replace our report copywriting in all the sub-Saharan countries. I was a bit fed up. On top of this, I'd gone into the park to get a bit of space from the traffic and the people on the pavements, but I was still feeling crowded even here in the park, as if someone was walking a little too close to me. Someone *was* walking a little too close to me. There was a definite feeling of boundary-trespass in it. Then this voice, close to my ear, said: *To think one can speak with someone who really knew Tchekhov.*

I stepped to the side, turned like you do when you want to signal to people to back off.

I've no change, I said, I've no money at all to spare and there's no point in asking me.

Indecent, she said and shook her head. *We must never speak of ourselves to* anybody: *they come crashing in like cows into a garden.*

Look, I said –

How did Dostoievsky know, she interrupted me, *about that extraordinary vindictiveness, that relish for bitter laughter that comes over women in pain?*

What? I said because she had stopped me in my tracks, was standing right in front of me now blocking my way, and because it was the first time I had realized quite how in pain I was. I was actually in physical pain, walking through the park, without you.

Supposing, she said, *one's bones were not bone but liquid light.*

It was a dead person stopping me on my path, young and wiry and alarmingly lively, alarmingly bright at the eyes.

Back off, I said. I mean it. I don't know who you are, but I know who you are.

She laughed. She turned on her heel in a little dance, like I was the dead person, compared to her.

I shall be obliged, she said, *if the contents of this book are regarded as my private property.*

Then she threw me a little look.

Yes! I said. Yes exactly! Because that's what I was always saying!

I am thinking over my philosophy, she said. *The defeat of the personal. And let us be honest. How much do we know of Tchekhov from his letters. Was that all? Of course not. Don't you suppose he had a whole longing life of which there is hardly a word?*

That's what I told her, over and over! I said.

This is the moment which, after all, we live for, she said, *the moment of direct feeling when we are most ourselves and least personal.*

You've no idea, I said. I mean, one night it was even the genealogy of your cats, for God sake.

She flung her arms into the air and shouted at the sky.

Robert Louis Stevenson is a literary vagrant! she shouted.

Then she burst out laughing. I joined in.

Whatever it was she was laughing about, it was contagious.

Fiction, she said when she'd stopped laughing, *is impossible but enables us to reach what is relatively truth.*

Okay, I said, yeah, I think that's fair, I mean, if people are reading your stories and enjoying or understanding and analysing them as stories and everything. That's different. But people who were born, like, decades after you died, writing about pictures of your scissors.

I sat down on a bench. She sat down next to me with a thump and huffed a breath out loud like a teenage girl. She turned towards me nodding, confidential, like we were such friends.

What the writer does is not so much to solve the question, but to put the question. There must be the question put. That seems to me a very nice dividing line between the true and the false writer.

Then she stood up on the bench. She laughed, then got her balance. She spoke generally, to the trees in the park.

As I see it, she said, *the whole stream of English literature is trickling out in little innumerable marsh trickles. There is no gathering together, no fire, no impetus, absolutely no passion!*

She waved her arm at the bushes behind us, and her other arm at the pond in front of us.

This new bracken is like HG Wells dream flowers, like strings of Beads, she said. *The sky in the water is like white swans in a blue mirror.*

She was right. The sky in the water *did* look like she said. The bloom on the bracken behind us *was* like beads, *did* look strange, like made up in a dream. But while I was looking at this, off she went. When I looked back there was nobody else on the bench and though the park was full of people it was like there was nobody left in it either.

I don't know who you are but I know who you are.

The way it was impossible haunted me.

That night I sat down in front of my computer and wrote you an email. It was the third email I'd sent you since we broke up. The first one had been fifteen pages long when I printed it out; it was mostly mundane lists of things: kitchenware, DVDs, things you'd done that'd made me furious. The second one said: Please also return the three Kate Rusby CDs, the hat that belonged to my father, the picture frame which I bought and paid the whole amount for in Habitat and have a receipt for, the TV Digibox, the food processor which I bought and paid the whole amount for in Dixons and have the receipt for, and the kitchen bin which I still can't believe you took. I will record any other items I find missing as I find them missing.

You had sent me none, not even one saying you wanted those precious books back.

This time I typed in your address (I had to do it by hand and from memory because I'd deleted you off my system) and I wrote in the subject box: not about the Kate Rusby CDs etc please read.

Then in the body of the email I wrote: Please write back telling me one single thing you think I should know about the life of the writer K Mansfield.

I pressed send, then I went to bed.

I saw the light come round the edge of the windowblind. I heard the waking of the birds.

I logged on before I left for work, and under the subject heading *one thing* you had sent me this:

Mansfield was close good friends with the writer DH Lawrence, but it was a very rocky friendship, it blew hot and cold, and there were times in their lives when neither of them could stand the other. Once, when they'd had one of their most serious fallings-out and Mansfield was full of fury at him, she was sitting in a tea room with some friends and they overheard two or three people talking about one of Lawrence's books, a collection of poems called Amores. One of them was holding it up and they were all being most disparaging about it. She herself had just been being most disparaging about Lawrence to her friends, before they went to tea. But seeing these other people be it, she leaned over and asked politely, sweetly, might she just have a look at that book they were talking about for a moment. Then she stood up and simply left the tea room, taking the book with her. The people sat there waiting for her to come back. She didn't come back.

I read this three times before I left for work. At work I read it too many times to count. I wasn't sure what it meant, but I liked it. I sat in my mid-morning break and thought about how like you it was to use the words *most disparaging.* Most disparaging. Most disparaging. *Blew hot and cold.* I sat in my lunch break. I loved the last sentence, but all the same it worried me. *She didn't come back.*

Wasn't it Santayana who said: every artist holds a lunatic in leash? I was back in the park with what was left of the life of your favourite writer, whose five volumes of letters and whose big thick journal I had removed from the book box by the front door when you were busy loading the van, and the space left by which I had filled with my Stieg Larsson Girl With The Dragon Tattoo books, which I knew you hated, and which I had disguised by placing all those volumes of that book Pilgrimage on top of.

I went most evenings after work now to the park, before I got the bus home. I went at lunchtimes too.

James makes me ashamed for real artists. He's a pompazoon. Who was James? I didn't care. I never knew what she was talking about, but I loved it. She was so much herself, and she was different every time, could change her air like the horse can change colour in The Wizard Of Oz. It crossed my mind to ask her, did she know what The Wizard Of Oz was. Maybe the book. She'd definitely died before the film. Strange to think she never knew Judy Garland or the tune of Somewhere Over the Rainbow, or that song about the munchkins. I wondered if anybody in your work circles had ever written a paper about that. What would it be called?

Ultra-Modern Future-Memory: A Study Of Things That Happened After My Ex-Wife's Ex-Wife Died And How They Feature In The Work Of My Ex-Wife's Ex-Wife.

What makes Lawrence a real writer is his passion. Without passion one writes in the air or on the sands of the seashore. Oh, I know about you and Lawrence, I said, because a friend of mine told me a story about that. But she was off like a butterfly on to the next flowerhead. *Nathaniel Hawthorne – he is with Tolstoi the only novelist of the soul. He is concerned with what is abnormal. His people are dreams, sometimes faintly conscious that they dream.* Right, I said. I get that. Right. *The intensity of an action is its truth. Is a thing the expression of an individuality?* No, I said. Well, maybe sometimes it is. Sometimes yes and sometimes no. *Maupassant – his abundant vitality. Great artists are those who can make men see their particular illusion.* I like that, I said, looking her right in the eyes. She did have extraordinarily clear and piercing eyes. *I want to remember,* she said, *how the light fades from a room – and one fades with it.*

And one what? I said. Fades, did you say?

The sky is grey – it's like living inside a pearl today, she said.

She said such beautiful things that often they left me with nothing to say. She leaned forward on the table, shook her head, held her face in her hands.

I have been feeling lately a horrible sense of indifference, she said.

Indifferent? I said. You? No way.

A very bad feeling, she said. *Neither hot nor cold; lukewarm.* Doesn't sound at all like you, I said.

Nearly all people swing in with the tide, she said, *and out with the tide again like heavy seaweed. And they seem to take a kind of pride in denying Life.*

Yes, I said. Much better to be hot or cold, like you and

your friend, what's his name. The delivery man. DHL.

Mentioning him to her was usually a good way to get her up and talking and excited. But she placed her hands on the edge of the table in fists that were little and bony.

I woke up early this morning, she said, *and when I opened the shutters the full round sun was just risen. I began to repeat that verse of Shakespeare's; lo here the gentle lark weary of rest, and I bounded back into bed. The bound made me cough. I spat – it tasted strange – it was bright red blood.*

I felt myself go pale.

You what? I said.

Since then I've gone on spitting each time I cough a little more, she said.

No, I said.

Perhaps it's going to gallop – who knows – she said, *and I shan't have my work written. That's what matters . . . unbearable . . . 'scraps', 'bits' . . . nothing real finished.*

I saw then how ill she looked, and how thin, and how far too young. I had to look away in case she saw, by looking at me, what I was seeing.

I began reading the songs in Twelfth Night in bed this morning early, she said.

Right, Twelfth Night, right, yes, I said.

Mark it, Cesario, it is old and plain. The spinsters and the knitters in the sun. And the free maids that weave their thread with bones. Do use to chant it – it is silly sooth. And dallies with the innocence of love. Like the old age, she said.

She saw how close to tears I was.

Come away, come away death, etc, she said.

Then she gave me a sly look from under her fringe.

I could make the girls cry when I read Dickens in the sewing class, she said.

* * *

And here it fell. Sepulchral.

That's the actual real line from the story you were telling me about once. I've read the story now. I've read all her stories, from the one at the start of the book where the girl is in the emptied house and the little birds flick from branch to branch, to the one at the end of her life about the poor bird in a cage, and that one about the fly that gets all inked. *Oh, the times when she had walked upside down on the ceiling, up, up glittering panes floated on a lake of light, flashed through a shining beam!*

I sat down in front of my computer in what was once our house and I typed the word WING into the subject heading. Then I wrote this.

Hello.

I wanted to tell you that I found out a thing that might be of use to you, well a couple of things, well three things altogether.

1: I was speaking to a lady from New Zealand at work because of our New Zealand contract and I told her I was reading your ex-wife and she told me an amazing story, and then she sent me a newspaper clipping, and this is what it says in short, that your ex-wife maybe was actually given birth to in a hot-air balloon. Yes I know it sounds unlikely and like I'm lying but I have the newspaper to prove it and I knew it would interest you. It says in it that her mother was pregnant with her and on the day your ex-wife was born she had actually booked to go up above Wellington in a balloon with a man called Mr. Montgolf who was charging five shillings a shot. Anyway on 15 October 1888 a newspaper called The Dominion reported that the flight the day before took 'much longer than expected because of the medical condition of one of its female occupants . . . fortunately this young woman had recovered by the time the balloon landed'. Which means, the paper implies, that your ex-wife might have been born with both feet off the ground.

2: You know the story you told me about, the one with the word sepulchral in it? The one about the past-it lady who goes to act as an extra in films. Can you remember, I wonder, that there is a moment when she is filling in a form to see if she is the right sort of extra and it says, 'Can you aviate – high-dive – drive a car – buck-jump-shoot?' And you know how your ex-wife also did quite a lot of extra-work in films in the war years and once even caught a quite bad cold from doing a long shoot in evening dress in January? Well, I went looking for whether there was any chance of seeing her on any of these films, so far I have been unsuccessful. But I have discovered, by chance, that in the mid-1920s loads of those films, hundreds and hundreds of them made by the British film industry in the earlier years, were melted down and used to make the resin that was painted on the wings of aeroplanes to make them weather resistant. So now when you think of your ex-wife it is possible to think of those pictures of her moving as maybe really on the wing.

Also I remember that one of the things you were working on was a book by her friend and rival Virginia Woolf about a plane that all the people in London look up and see, that's writing words in the sky above them, and I remember you gave a paper about it somewhere. Well, I have deduced that because they started coating the wings of planes in or before 1924 with melted films, it is perfectly possible that the wings of the plane all those people are craning their necks and looking up at in Virginia Woolf's famous novel which if I am right is the one that was published in 1925, could actually be coated in melted-down moving pictures of your ex-wife. It is funny to me too because I have a sense that Virginia Woolf always thought your ex-wife a bit flighty.

3: Finally did you know that it is now possible to fly from Auckland to Sydney in your ex-wife? There is a new generation Boeing 737 that Qantas use whose features include a 12 seat business class and 156 seat economy, with individual state of the art Panasonic in-flight entertainment-on-demand systems in both business and economy, ergonomic cushions and adjustable headrests and a choice on board of New Zealand or Australian wines. The plane is called The Katherine Mansfield.

It all really makes me think of the thing she says where she says: 'Your wife won't have a tomb – she'll have at most a butterfly fanning its wings on her grave and then off.'

You might say I have been thinking of you a bit.

I very much hope you are well.

I didn't send that flight email in the end. I looked at my language and couldn't. I knew I'd got punctuation and things wrong, and was embarrassed at the words I'd used when I looked back at it later after a glass of wine, which is usually when embarrassment disappears and it's easier to press send. Those are some of the reasons I didn't send it.

The main one, though, was that I didn't want you to think I was trying to know more about something you knew about than you did. Also, I was worried that maybe you really wouldn't know these things. I realized I really didn't want to know more about what you knew about than you.

Which is all a roundabout way of saying I didn't want to trespass on what was yours.

Everything in life that we really accept undergoes a change.
So suffering must become love.
That is the mystery.

In the end what I did was this. The next time I was in London, I went to find the house your ex-wife had lived in for, well I didn't know if it was for longest, but I knew it was for happiest.

I stood outside it and I thought about how close it was to the Heath, and how much that must have pleased her cats. I worried about what an uphill climb it must have been to get to the house from the nearest Tube, for somebody not very well. I thought about how she wrote to this address from a cold house in Italy. She wrote imagining coming home and kissing its gate and door, and about how she imagined the cat going up the stairs, it was how she pictured home, and I think the word she used is *lopping, Wing come lopping up*. There's a big locked gate on it, too high to see over and you can't see in, though there is a blue plaque on it saying it is your ex-wife's house and that her husband lived there too. (The plaque doesn't mention the Mountain.) But I took a photo of the outside of it on my phone, and then I took a close-up of the brick of the whitewashed wall of it, where ivy or some plant with tiny splayed-out roots has grown over the place and someone has repeatedly stripped it back. Some of it, delicate, is preserved forever under the whitewash, and some of it has kept on growing new roots on top of the whitewash.

When I got home that night I keyed in your address above an email and sent you that photo of the wall and the plantlife without saying where it was of, or telling you anything about it.

Then I put the books I had stolen from you back on the shelf you'd kept them on in the study, and I shut the door. And then I went and got on with it, the rest of my life.

ISAAC BABEL

THE PUBLIC
LIBRARY
(1916)

Translated by Peter Constantine

ONE FEELS RIGHT away that this is the kingdom of books. People working at the library commune with books, with the life reflected in them, and so become almost reflections of real-life human beings.

Even the cloakroom attendants – not brown-haired, not blond, but something in between – are mysteriously quiet, filled with contemplative composure.

At home on Saturday evenings they might well drink methylated spirits and give their wives long, drawn-out beatings, but at the library their comportment is staid, circumspect, and hazily somber.

And then there is the cloakroom attendant who draws. In his eyes there is a gentle melancholy. Once every two weeks, as he helps a fat man in a black vest out of his coat, he mumbles, 'Nikolai Sergeyevich approves of my drawings, and Konstantin Vasilevich also approves of them. . . . In the first thing I was originating . . . but I have no idea, no idea where to go!'

The fat man listens. He is a reporter, a married man, gluttonous and overworked. Once every two weeks he goes to the library to rest. He reads about court cases, painstakingly copies out onto a piece of paper the plan of the house where the murder took place, is very pleased, and forgets that he is married and overworked.

The reporter listens to the attendant with fearful bewilderment, and wonders how to handle such a man. Do you give him a ten-kopeck coin on your way out? He might be offended – he's an artist. Then again, if you don't he might also be offended – after all, he's a cloakroom attendant.

In the reading room are the more elevated staff members, the librarians. Some, the 'conspicuous ones,' possess some starkly pronounced physical defect. One has twisted fingers, another has a head that lolled to the side and stayed there. They are badly dressed, and emaciated in the extreme. They look as if they are fanatically possessed by an idea unknown to the world.

Gogol would have described them well!

The 'inconspicuous' librarians show the beginnings of bald patches, wear clean gray suits, have a certain candor in their eyes, and a painful slowness in their movements. They are forever chewing something, moving their jaws, even though they have nothing in their mouths. They talk in a practiced whisper. In short, they have been ruined by books, by being forbidden from enjoying a throaty yawn.

Now that our country is at war, the public has changed. There are fewer students. There are very few students. Once in a blue moon you might see a student painlessly perishing in a corner. He's a 'white-ticketer,' exempt from service. He wears a pince-nez and has a delicate limp. But then there is also the student on state scholarship. This student is pudgy, with a drooping mustache, tired of life, a man prone to contemplation: he reads a bit, thinks about something a bit, studies the patterns on the lampshades, and nods off over a book. He has to finish his studies, join the army, but – why hurry? Everything in good time.

A former student returns to the library in the figure of a wounded officer with a black sling. His wound is healing. He is young and rosy. He has dined and taken a walk along the Nevsky Prospekt. The Nevsky Prospekt is already lit.

The late edition of the *Stock Exchange News* has already set off on its triumphal march around town. Grapes lying on millet are displayed in the store window at Eliseyev's. It is still too early to make the social rounds. The officer goes to the public library for old times' sake, stretches out his long legs beneath the table where he is sitting, and reads *Apollon*. It's somewhat boring. A female student is sitting opposite him. She is studying anatomy, and is copying a picture of a stomach into her notebook. It looks like she might be of Kalugan origin – large-faced, large-boned, rosy, dedicated, and robust. If she has a lover, that would be perfect – she's good material for love.

Beside her is a picturesque tableau, an immutable feature of every public library in the Russian Empire: a sleeping Jew. He is worn out. His hair is a fiery black. His cheeks are sunken. There are bumps on his forehead. His mouth is half open. He is wheezing. Where he is from, nobody knows. Whether he has a residence permit or not, nobody knows. He reads every day. He also sleeps every day. There is a terrible, ineradicable weariness in his face, almost madness. A martyr to books – a distinct, indomitable Jewish martyr.

Near the librarians' desk sits a large, broad-chested woman in a gray blouse reading with rapturous interest. She is one of those people who suddenly speaks with unexpected loudness in the library, candidly and ecstatically overwhelmed by a passage in the book, and who, filled with delight, begins discussing it with her neighbors. She is reading because she is trying to find out how to make soap at home. She is about forty-five years old. Is she sane? Quite a few people have asked themselves that.

There is one more typical library habitué: the thin little colonel in a loose jacket, wide pants, and extremely well-polished boots. He has tiny feet. His whiskers are the color of cigar ash. He smears them with a wax that gives them a whole spectrum of dark gray shades. In his day he was so devoid of talent that he didn't manage to work his way up to the rank of colonel so that he could retire a major general. Since his retirement he ceaselessly pesters the gardener, the maid, and his grandson. At the age of seventy-three he has taken it into his head to write a history of his regiment.

He writes. He is surrounded by piles of books. He is the librarians' favorite. He greets them with exquisite civility. He no longer gets on his family's nerves. The maid gladly polishes his boots to a maximal shine.

Many more people of every kind come to the public library. More than one could describe. There is also the tattered reader who does nothing but write a luxuriant monograph on ballet. His face: a tragic edition of Hauptmann's. His body: insignificant.

There are, of course, also bureaucrats riffling through piles of *The Russian Invalid* and the *Government Herald*. There are the young provincials, ablaze as they read.

It is evening. The reading room grows dark. The immobile figures sitting at the tables are a mix of fatigue, thirst for knowledge, ambition.

Outside the wide windows soft snow is drifting. Nearby, on the Nevsky Prospekt, life is blossoming. Far away, in the Carpathian Mountains, blood is flowing.

C'est la vie.

ELIZABETH McCRACKEN

JULIET
(1998)

WE CALLED THE bunny that lived in the children's room Kaspar, as in Kaspar Hauser, but the children who came to torment and visit it thought we meant the friendly ghost. That might have made sense had the rabbit been white, but it was dun-colored. It cowered in the corner of its cage while children stuck their fingers through the wire; they sang, *Bunny, bunny, bunny rabbit*; they cried when their mothers informed them it was time to go, they'd see Bunny next time. Bunny, we suspected, prayed nightly to become a ghost. It never got out, never saw sunlight; it was never given a carrot or a chance to hop; it indulged in no lapine pleasures at all. Mostly, it shook or slept, was careless about its hygiene. Mornings, it ripped its newsprint bedding in strips and drew them into its mouth in damp pleats, chewing and swallowing by inches. The children's librarian said this was normal, but we thought the bunny was trying to overdose, using the materials nearby.

The six finches, on the other hand, seemed happy in their communal cage; and if the fish were unhappy, we couldn't tell. Maybe they wept in the terrible privacy of their tank. The occasional dog would slip in through the exit, wanting to find its owner, and one woman brought her cat, left it crying like a baby in the vestibule while she returned a video. 'I am in a hurry,' she told the circulation desk. 'My cat is waiting for me.' Also, once, a man found a wounded bird outside the library and brought it to the reference desk for identification. When he opened his hand to indicate the peculiarities of its markings, the bird took a notion to live after all and flew to the highest corner of the balcony, up by the replica Parthenon frieze that girdled the reading room. The bird stayed there for days, setting off the motion detectors at night. It never got close enough to the reference desk to identify.

That was it for wildlife, unless you counted the children themselves, often wild: not the toddlers, who couldn't bear to leave the bunny's side, but the ten- and eleven-year-olds who threw books off the balcony or slung their skinny legs on the tables or slipped whatever they wished, like a bad joke, into the book drop. The book drop was a door set in the library façade that opened like an oven and dropped its contents into a closet in the circulation office. Snow in the winter, firecrackers in the summer, uncapped bottles of Coke year-round. One weekend, a passing man employed the book drop for a public urinal, and several books were destroyed. 'Urine is sterile,' the head of circulation explained to her staff as she dropped a sodden *Garfield Rounds Out* into a wastebasket, but it was clear nobody believed this perfectly scientific fact, including her.

It was on this day, a Monday, that we first saw Juliet.

She was a young woman, late twenties we thought, with long, loose dark hair. Her clothes were white, and at first we thought she was in uniform, a nurse, perhaps – she had a sort of nursey look to her, sweet and determined and recently divorced. Or maybe she was from an unfamiliar order of nuns, because in our library we did get the occasional Sister. But it turned out she just wore white that day. Maybe she wasn't wearing white, maybe we just remember that now because in the picture we saw so often, later, she wore white. At any rate, there was something forsaken and hopeful about her. She stood patiently at the front desk, waiting for assistance. In front of her, a man filled out an application for a card. On the line marked OCCUPATION, he filled in EMPLOYEE.

She clutched a book in her hand in such a way that it looked like a knife she was prepared to use on herself, which was one of the reasons we ended up calling her Juliet. That, and her habit of leaning on the rail of the balcony that ran around the reading room, looking up instead of down, into the cloudy green of the skylight. Her book had that pebbly leatherette navy-blue grain usually found on diaries and giveaway Bibles. *Are you returning that?* somebody asked her.

'No,' she said. 'No. It's mine. I just was never in here before, and I was wondering what you could tell me.'

The departments were pointed out to her – audiovisual this way, children's the other, adult library upstairs. She was offered a brochure.

'May I get a card?'

Was she a resident of the town? Yes. Had she had a card with us before? No. Did she have proof of address and a photo ID?

'Not with me,' she said. 'Next time, then. For now, I'll just look around.'

We had regulars, of course, and they were demanding. People wanted not just books but attention and advice and, in the case of one widower, the occasional rear end to pat affectionately. We got teenagers who came daily to read or nap or use the Internet away from their parents; mothers and their toddlers and their tiny trails of cheese crackers. We had two transgendered patrons that we knew of, one now a radical lesbian who came in with her girlfriend and wore a T-shirt that said, BECAUSE I'M THE TOP, THAT'S WHY, who liked to gab and gossip; the other the shy and girlish and bangled Janice, whom we'd first known as Jonathan, winner three years in a row of the junior high science fair, under both names one of our most regular regulars. There was a woman with no eyebrows who never said a word and a pleasant, paranoid old lady who occasionally, sweetly, accused us of poisoning her. There were the screamers, mostly businessmen who believed they could threaten our jobs and could not understand why we humble city employees weren't frightened. One blond man – his face as ruddy and pitted as a basketball – screamed, 'Where's the guy who wouldn't let my son take out books?' The guy in question was outside, obliviously smoking a cigarette, and though the matter was resolved, clearly what the man really wanted was to punch someone.

The man's son, who looked just like him, though with a beautiful complexion, hadn't seemed at all disturbed or surprised by the delinquency of his library card. He was a quiet kid who had to lick his lips several times to get his mouth to work, and then he'd said only, 'OK.' It turned out he'd been checking out books for his grandfather, anyhow; the clerk at the desk told his father the kid should just bring in his grandfather's card.

We got asked for love advice and job applications, the whereabouts of relatives. 'Did you see a girl?' a kid would ask, and the head of circulation would answer wearily, 'I've seen lots of girls.' One man called because he wanted to know whether his daughter, whom he had not seen in five years, had a library card she'd used recently.

'I'd like to see her again,' he said when he was told library records were confidential. 'I think maybe she tried to contact me a few years ago.'

When somebody like this called – for instance, the woman who wanted to know how to stop having bad thoughts

– the circulation desk happily sent the person to reference, because, after all, it sounded like a job for a professional librarian.

Juliet surprised us, coming back every day, clean, starched. Usually, the people who showed up like that looked slightly worse every visit. She never did get that library card, but many of our most beloved patrons never did. She favored the children's room. She became special friends with the children's librarian, a young woman who said everything as if she were reading a story, as if the end of her sentence contained a wonderful surprise: a beggar revealed to be a lost prince, a talkative young bear no longer afraid of the dark. The children's librarian had no friends at the library. She wore peasant skirts and thick-soled shoes and pendants on long black strings. Juliet smiled, listened to the librarian's stories, consoled her the day the Harriet Tubman impersonator failed to show up for the Black History Month program. Once a week, they ate lunch together in the park in front of the building, at one of the concrete tables with an inlaid chessboard. Frequently, Juliet talked to the rabbit. The bunny eyed her with its usual unhappiness, another grubby pair of hands reaching into the cage. Human flesh gave our neurotic bunny the willies.

In this the rabbit was not so different from the head of reference, who had been cranky for so long his bad mood had turned to superstition, a primitive who believed that the requests for addresses and statistics from the reference collection were akin to soul stealing. He was particularly suspicious of Juliet. Too sunny, that one, and the way she said hello, every single time: she wanted something. She was formulating an immense, subtly impossible, demanding, deadly reference question, one that would begin in the almanacs kept at the desk and then lead to encyclopedias, newspaper articles, and finally some now-unknown reference book kept in the basement, some cursed volume that turned its opener to dust. Even then, there would be no answer.

'I don't trust her,' said the head of reference. 'She wants something.'

The other librarians bumped into one another behind the reference desk, trying to intercept patrons before they got to the head of reference, who claimed to be ignorant of any subject that sounded vaguely scientific.

We heard the big news slowly. There had been a murder. A woman. A woman from our town, killed in her own house. A woman stabbed ten times, twenty, sixty-three. It was as if the police were taking forever to examine the body and called up the local gossips to report: we found five more wounds in the last hour. You could see the cops, turning the body over and over, looking for what was neither evidence nor cause of death – she'd died after her poor body had caught the knife only a few times – one officer with a pencil and white pad, making hash marks. The final count was ninety-six.

A murder. We hoped for two things: that we did not know the victim and that the murderer did. *Please*, we prayed, though we never said those prayers aloud, *let it be a husband, a boyfriend*. We wanted to read in the paper: *Last week, she filed for a restraining order*. Hadn't every murdered woman? None of the library staff had ever asked for a restraining order, except the assistant director, who'd filed one against his sister. That was entirely different.

And then, on the evening news, we saw her picture: Juliet.

It wasn't the usual blurry victim snapshot, the kind that makes it seem as if the last thing the person did, before hauling off and getting killed, was to indulge an elderly uncle with a camera. Juliet's picture – the one that appeared on all the newscasts, on the covers of all the papers – was clear and sharp and pretty. Her hair was done. She was wearing a white strapless gown. Depending on how the paper or channel cropped the picture, you could see the shoulder of her date, wearing a white jacket and black bow tie. He was still alive; you didn't need to see any more of him. He wasn't a suspect.

Her name was Suzanne Cunningham. She was thirty-four. She was, in fact, divorced (we'd suspected) and had three children (we'd had no idea). The oldest, a boy, was fifteen; the two girls were twelve and thirteen. The children's librarian had known all of this, of course, but would not answer questions. In fact, she had taken several days off work around the time of the murder, and we made a few dark jokes about how suspicious that seemed. Oh, that sweetness and light and arts-and-crafts stuff, that didn't fool us. She must be a sadist. Look how she treats that poor rabbit.

We didn't believe our jokes, but we needed them. Our town was near a big city, but it wasn't the big city. The famous names of murderers and murdered women – they often shared the same name, of course – were featured in the metropolitan paper, not ours. We had never seen the faces close up or walked by the houses.

The only thing the children's librarian said, when she came in to ask the director for the rest of the week off, was, *She knew. She knew someone was after her.*

One of the reference librarians confirmed it: Suzanne Cunningham had once asked for a book that would tell her how to keep people out of her house. *Burglars?* the librarian had asked. *Anyone*, Suzanne Cunningham answered. *I think someone has been sneaking into my house.* So the librarian had found a crime-prevention book, which Suzanne Cunningham smiled at and set down on a table without reading.

That made us feel better – a boyfriend, surely, or even her ex-husband – but we wondered why the newspapers didn't say so. The book she carried: it must be a diary – it must have clues. We wondered why she hadn't called the police. Someone sneaks into your house, you have to be worried, don't you?

Maybe not. Maybe you don't know that someone has been there – you just suspect. Nothing is broken or rearranged; no pets have been menaced. There's just the lingering, careless presence of someone who doesn't know how the house works. The back door has to be closed with both a knee and a shoulder; the kitchen faucets must be turned off with a wrench; mud must be knocked from shoes and the portable phone doesn't always want to hang up and the fridge door will float open if you aren't careful. And then one day, when the kids are with their father – thank God, as it turns out – you come home and surprise him in your kitchen. Maybe you've known all along who it was.

And maybe he even has a crush on you. That's the thing about crushes – sometimes they fly below the radar, the way in high school, when someone told you a boy had a crush, you could tell by the way he ignored you. The way he ignored you meant everything. A terrible word, crush – you could die from crushing, from having one, anyhow; you remember listening to music that meant the world to you and nothing, you were quite sure, to your beloved. Who knows what teenagers listen to today; your own boy plays music that you can't imagine swooning to; your own boy is friends with this boy, who is now in your kitchen, licking his lips nervously to oil up his mouth. You know everything about this kid: a neighborhood babysitter, sixteen years old but enormous, big enough to gently swing a laughing five-year-old over his head without fear; an altar boy who goes to the library to pick up books for his grandfather, in his pocket the grandfather's faultless library card; a part-time drugstore clerk; a good boy who loves his parents, whose parents love him.

What you don't know is that he has a knife, and that you have frightened him.

Ninety-six times, though. We couldn't imagine it. We tried it ourselves, started to hit our own knees softly, ninety-six times. We gave up, we got tired, we made ourselves sick.

Four days later, they made the arrest. The accused was the blond boy whose father had come in screaming. Another library patron. We all knew him, too: Tommy Mason. The Masons were a big, famous family in our town. Tommy Mason's grandfather had been mayor once, back in the 1950s.

An altar boy, a good boy, a boy with a library card. Could such a boy possibly be guilty? He lived across the street from the dead woman. He had shoveled her walk in the winter; his sisters had sold her Girl Scout cookies. He was good friends with Suzanne Cunningham's oldest child, Kevin. Kevin Cunningham had found his mother's body.

Within twenty-four hours, every library staff member who knew how had looked up the accused's library record. Tommy Mason's card was still delinquent, told us nothing: a single book called *Soap Science*, no doubt for school. We looked at the record for the book daily – the title, the author (Bell), the publication date (1993), the due date (May 4, two years ago). We wanted to know something. These were the only facts we had.

We weren't supposed to do that, of course. We were supposed to be bound by ethics and privacy, but it felt as if we could break them, the way that cannibalism, in certain extreme cases, is acceptable.

He was put in jail, and nothing could persuade the judge

– also a patron, as it happened – to let him out on bail. Reports came down from the neighborhood and on the TV news. Mr. and Mrs. Mason let themselves be interviewed in their kitchen. They swore that it was impossible, that time would prove them right. Ask anyone in the neighborhood: Tom was the best kid. He wasn't even interested in girls – why would he kill one? The Masons' hands were woven together on the kitchen tabletop; their fingers were the same pink, their hands a solid knot. Mr. Mason was calm and reasonable. We wondered whether Tommy Mason was taking the fall for him. We remembered the screaming father, bright red with the idea we'd denied Tommy Mason anything; surely he turned that anger on his family.

The papers interviewed neighbors. *Such a nice boy. There was something about him. He didn't have a temper. You know, he was off – he didn't have what you'd call emotions. He was shy. He was a loner. He was a daydreamer. Sometimes he stared through people's windows.*

Really, there was no prior proof other than vague gossip. He really was, or had been, a good kid, and who knew? The book Juliet had carried was discovered in her living room; it contained only sketches of her children. Maybe Tommy Mason's parents – and some of the people on the street, who'd already lost one neighbor – were right. Maybe Tommy Mason was innocent and the two men he said he'd seen fleeing the scene were at large, dreaming of their perfect crime. A single perfect crime: the woman was not raped, the house was not robbed, the door had not been tampered with.

There were two bloody fingerprints, Tommy Mason's, in the cellar. Bloody, but not his blood. The police said that, and we believed them.

Tommy Mason stayed in jail, and people stopped believing

he hadn't done it. Of course he'd done it. TV reporters were no longer interested in his parents' version of the story. One day, at a community picnic in the park, a Little League coach began his remarks, 'With all the troubles in our neighborhood in past months . . .' and one of Tommy Mason's sisters was there. She went home to tell Mrs. Mason, who returned and stood at the edge of the baseball field. Mrs. Mason was a small woman to have had such a big son, and she looked smaller, cut into diamonds by the chain link of the backstop. 'You'll be sorry!' she screamed. She curled her fingers into the fence. 'You'll see, my Tommy never did it! You'll see, you assholes!' Some people wondered whether they should go to her, say something comforting. But she scared them, rattling the backstop. Maybe she'd start climbing up it. People walked the other way. They waited for her to stop.

And perhaps she never will stop. What can you do? Your son, your only boy – whether he killed somebody or not, though he didn't – is lost to you. He never could have killed anyone. He never even liked horror movies. He was always respectful. He believes in God. And if – though he didn't! – if he did kill her, that's one life gone already. Your child used to live in your house, and he has been taken from you, and all you can hope for is that eventually he will be returned. He will already be ruined. The best you can hope for is your ruined boy back in your house.

Tommy Mason – no matter what – has no doubt already been ruined. The newspapers refer to the Tommy Mason Case, not the Suzanne Cunningham Murder. In fifty years, neighborhood kids will choose kickball teams with rhymes about Tommy Mason, not knowing exactly who that was. Tommy Mason had a knife / Tommy Mason took a life / How. Many. Times. Did. He. Stab. YOU.

You better be good, or Tommy Mason will get you.

The children's librarian was inconsolable. Her mind wandered; her story times made no sense; she forgot the words to 'The Wheels on the Bus.' She also forgot to feed the rabbit, who died a week later. The cage had to be covered with cloth so the children wouldn't peep in. The rabbit lay in state all morning, till someone from the DPW could come and haul it away.

'You know,' said the children's librarian to the head of cataloging that day, 'she told me, "I've had a good life. If I died tomorrow, I'd have no regrets." ' The head of cataloging stared, thinking, *That rabbit said no such thing.*

'Suzanne,' said the children's librarian. 'I don't care about the rabbit. I'm talking about Suzanne.'

Which, when the news made its way around the library, struck us as stupid. She had children who grieved for her – isn't that regret enough? How could sunny Suzanne, sunny Juliet, with her book and her dark hair and her three beloved and loving children, think that if she had to die tomorrow, she wouldn't mind? We thought perhaps she had lost her life through carelessness and underappraisal. We wouldn't be so free with our own lives. The difference is, no one has ever wanted ours.

Did he love her? We had encyclopedias of criminals, anthologies of love poems, textbooks on abnormal psychology. All useless. The newspaper articles said that he admitted nothing, including love. 'He's scared,' said his lawyer. We never heard him speak, and maybe we never would.

The bitter head of reference read newspaper articles, sick that he'd ever distrusted Juliet. At night, he had dreams of Suzanne Cunningham standing on the reading-room balcony. He saw himself presenting her things, back issues of magazines, rare tax forms, the best-reviewed books. Anything to win her back.

The bunny was dead. Perhaps the children's librarian had killed it, but she claimed the rabbit was simply old, and she was the only one who knew anything about rabbits. That day with the bunny beneath its cloth, we thought we should have a funeral behind the library, out by the staff parking. We could turn it into something educational and useful, a children's program on death. Didn't parents always bury pets with a small lecture, a made-up eulogy, a somber taps played on a hand held to the mouth like a trumpet? Maybe –

'It's a fucking rabbit,' said the children's librarian, in full hearing of Preschool Arts and Crafts. 'It doesn't stand for anything.' Then she sighed. 'I'll miss Jessica,' she said.

Jessica? She must have meant Juliet.

'Jessica,' she said. 'Jessica Rabbit.'

Tommy Mason had three sisters who looked like him, all of whom seemed to be about the same age, twins or Irish twins or a combination of both. They were tall and blond and had beautiful skin with rosy, radishy cheeks, red with white beneath. They started coming back to the library with the grandfather's card. He still needed books.

For a while, they rotated duty. Then one started coming in week after week. She was a thin girl, the oldest Mason kid, someone said. Perhaps twenty years old. Pretty, like Juliet – like Suzanne – but pale, a mirror image. They could have been allegorical pictures in an old painting, or sisters on a soap opera, even though Suzanne Cunningham had been years older. Tommy Mason's sister carried the grandfather's library card and never spoke to anyone.

Somehow, we loved her. She seemed brave; she nodded when we nodded at her. We almost forgot who she was, the same way we almost forgot that Janice had ever been a nervous young man with a robot obsession and a faint, endearing mustache. She had become herself.

Ours had been a fine building until the mid-1970s, when it had the misfortune of being introduced to the wrong sort of architect. He knocked down the grand marble staircases that had led from the entrance to the reading room, and sealed off the first floor from the upstairs; he installed coarse brick walls and staircases that were only staircases, only transportation. It was possible for the people who worked in the first-floor departments – children's, circulation – to go days without seeing their upstairs colleagues.

So the day the children's librarian went up to reference and ran into Tommy Mason's sister might have been the first day the two had met at all. Circulation knew the Mason girl well; reference saw her as she deliberated among the mysteries. The children's librarian rarely left her room, its puppets, its jigsaw puzzles. Somebody else had taken over feeding the finches and the fish.

She recognized Tommy Mason's sister from news reports or neighborhood gossip. She stared for a while, confirmed the identity with the head of reference. No harm in answering, he thought.

Tommy Mason's sister was in the mysteries, because that's what her grandfather still read. Maybe he needed to read them especially now, to know that murders happened in this way: someone was killed, and there were clues and an explanation, and at the very end a madman or bitter wife was led away, and nobody but the murderer wept. She looked at the books, at the skull-and-crossbones stickers the cataloging department stuck on the spines of mysteries. She selected three and tucked them close to her chest and was halfway across the floor to the stairs when the children's librarian stepped in front of her and said, 'I knew her, you know.'

Tommy Mason's sister looked towards the ground. That was where she always looked. The children's librarian tried to lower herself into eyeshot.

'I knew the woman your brother murdered.' And then, in her storytelling voice, the calm one that explained that Rosetta Stone was a thing and not a person and wasn't that wonderful, she said, 'Your brother's a monster. A freak.'

Everyone watched the two of them, the children's librarian with her tough, tiny soldier's shoes, Tommy Mason's sister dressed the way all the library teenagers dressed: baggy pants, sneakers, a hooded warm-up jacket – ready, the way they all were, for an escape. Except she didn't. She stood there, and then she turned away and walked to a table. The children's librarian went downstairs. She gave her footsteps extra echo. Tommy Mason's sister sat and began to cry.

It didn't look serious at first, and people tried to give her privacy. She held the books to her as if they were a compress for her heart, and tears slid down her face and onto the table, which was itself carved with hearts, declarations of love and being: CK WAS HERE. WANDA + BILLY. We didn't know anything about her. We didn't even know her first name.

She stayed there for an hour. The reference librarians didn't know what to do. One of them approached her, said, 'Dear, can I call somebody?' The girl didn't move. Her tears were so regular they seemed mechanical, manufactured inside her for this purpose: to darken the wooden table in front of her, to pave the carved grooves of graffiti.

The head of reference called down to the children's room. 'I don't care,' he said into the phone. 'You come up here.' The other librarians thought that this was like asking the snake that bit you to come suck out the venom.

You could tell the children's librarian expected to be chewed out. She figured that the girl she'd accused was long gone, that her matter-of-fact words were just one more thing that the Masons would discuss, outraged, over dinner. But there the girl was.

So, then. The children's librarian sat at the table. Such a clumsy young woman, really. She whispered something to the crying girl. She reached to touch the girl's elbow. The elbow stayed put.

I didn't, said the children's librarian.

No response.

I'm lost –

– for words, – without her.

A dead person is lost property. You know this. Still, you've been searching for what was taken. You know – you've been schooled in this fact – that what you owned will never be returned to you. But you're still owed something. You can't eat lunch with your friend, her fingers marking chess moves across the board. You can't hear those same fingers on a computer keyboard or feel them on your shoulder at a time you need them. People take their hands with them, no matter where they go.

Surely there is happiness somewhere in the world. And God will forgive you if, for a moment, you labor under the common misconception that happiness is created – you'd swear one of the students has done a science-fair project on this – when two unhappy people collide and one of them makes the other unhappier. It's steam, it's energy. It works: you feel something rise in you. But it doesn't last.

The children's librarian began to cry, too. Not like Tommy Mason's sister, beautiful in her sorrow, but like one of the toddlers refused longer visiting hours with the bunny. She rearranged her features into something terrible. When she caught her breath, you could hear it, you would think it hurt. Nobody felt sorry for her. Then she left the table and walked up the stairs to the balcony to watch what would happen. As she passed the reference desk, she said, 'Call her family.'

They had to find the phone number by looking up Tommy Mason's library record. His card was still delinquent.

'Is this Mr. Mason?' the head of reference asked. That sounded frightening. He tried, 'Your daughter –' but that was worse. Then he said, 'This is the library –' as if the building were calling. 'This is the library, Mr. Mason. Your daughter is fine, she's here, but I think you better pick her up.'

The entire family arrived, and the father with his florid face sat next to her at the table. *Sarah*, he said, *don't you want to go home? Let's go home, Sarah*, and then the mother and sisters said it, too: *Let's go home, Sarah*. They stayed there awhile, and we wondered whether they'd ever leave. Maybe they'd move in. There were worse places for a troubled family to live. We had plenty of books and magazines. We had a candy machine downstairs. They could move into the religion section in the corner, a quiet, untouched neighborhood with a window. They could string up a curtain and never be bothered. A nice cul-de-sac far from the chaos of the cookbooks, the SAT guides.

They did not look up to see the children's librarian on the dull staircase. Sarah did not direct them there.

The Masons bundled Sarah up in their eight bare arms, the devoted family octopus, and led her out the door. She was a child who could be rescued. She could be taken home and given a meal and put to bed; they could slip the puffy sneakers she wore off her feet. In the morning, the sneakers would still be there where she'd left them, waiting for her to put them on and pull the laces tight and live the rest of her life.

The books in her arms set the alarm off on the way out. No one stopped her.

Up on the balcony stairs, the children's librarian stopped crying. She didn't move. The few patrons there stepped around her, because there was only the one staircase. The head of reference went to her. He sat down; he set his hand on her shoulder to steady himself.

'You've done a terrible thing,' he said, and she nodded. Then he took her hand, the way he wished he had taken Juliet's hand, or Sarah's – or a dozen sad girls he'd known before but never discussed. 'Everyone does,' he said.

'Not everyone,' said the children's librarian.

'You just know that you have, that's all.'

The Masons would have been home by then. We thought we could feel the door of the house, closing behind them.

It's been months since Sarah left us, more months since Juliet died. The Masons gave up and moved to another city nearby; Tommy Mason hasn't even gone on trial yet, though they've decided that when he does, it will be as a juvenile and not as an adult. He's in the news every now and then. The family goes to another library, in a town where the grandfather was never a mayor and Mason is an unremarkable name and their blond looks don't mean anything. But they don't know that their library is in our computer network. Their new library is a relative of ours, which means we can look their cards up on the computer if we want to, we can renew their books and erase their fines and wonder if they ever think about us.

The children's librarian is living with her cruel thing. We have forgiven her. We go into the children's room. She is silent behind the desk cutting out Santa Clauses or Easter eggs or autumn leaves, which children will cover with cotton balls and glitter. We talk to the finches, those filthy creatures.

We imagine opening the cage and telling them to go ahead
– it wouldn't be the first time – they should go ahead and fly.
Even though we don't open the door, we tell them anyhow.
Stranger things, we tell them, have happened.

MAX BEERBOHM

ENOCH SOAMES
(1916)

WHEN A BOOK about the literature of the eighteen-nineties was given by Mr. Holbrook Jackson to the world, I looked eagerly in the index for SOAMES, ENOCH. I had feared he would not be there. He was not there. But everybody else was. Many writers whom I had quite forgotten, or remembered but faintly, lived again for me, they and their work, in Mr. Holbrook Jackson's pages. The book was as thorough as it was brilliantly written. And thus the omission found by me was an all the deadlier record of poor Soames' failure to impress himself on his decade.

I daresay I am the only person who noticed the omission. Soames had failed so piteously as all that! Nor is there a counterpoise in the thought that if he had had some measure of success he might have passed, like those others, out of my mind, to return only at the historian's beck. It is true that had his gifts, such as they were, been acknowledged in his lifetime, he would never have made the bargain I saw him make – that strange bargain whose results have kept him always in the foreground of my memory. But it is from those very results that the full piteousness of him glares out.

Not my compassion, however, impels me to write of him. For his sake, poor fellow, I should be inclined to keep my pen out of the ink. It is ill to deride the dead. And how can I write about Enoch Soames without making him ridiculous? Or rather, how am I to hush up the horrid fact that he *was* ridiculous? I shall not be able to do that. Yet, sooner or later, write about him I must. You will see, in due course, that I have no option. And I may as well get the thing done now.

In the Summer Term of '93 a bolt from the blue flashed down on Oxford. It drove deep, it hurtlingly embedded itself in the soil. Dons and undergraduates stood around, rather pale, discussing nothing but it. Whence came it, this meteorite? From Paris. Its name? Will Rothenstein. Its aim? To do a series of twenty-four portraits in lithograph. These were to be published from the Bodley Head, London. The matter was urgent. Already the Warden of A, and the Master of B, and the Regius Professor of C, had meekly 'sat'. Dignified and doddering old men, who had never consented to sit to any one, could not withstand this dynamic little stranger. He did not sue: he invited; he did not invite: he commanded. He was twenty-one years old. He wore spectacles that flashed more than any other pair ever seen. He was a wit. He was brimful of ideas. He knew Whistler. He knew Edmond de Goncourt. He knew everyone in Paris. He knew them all by heart. He was Paris in Oxford. It was whispered that, so soon as he had polished off his selection of dons, he was going to include a few undergraduates. It was a proud day for me when I – I – was included. I liked Rothenstein not less than I feared him; and there arose between us a friendship that has grown ever warmer, and been more and more valued by me, with every passing year.

At the end of Term he settled in – or rather, meteoritically into – London. It was to him I owed my first knowledge of that forever enchanting little world-in-itself, Chelsea, and my first acquaintance with Walter Sickert and other august elders who dwelt there. It was Rothenstein that took me to see, in Cambridge Street, Pimlico, a young man whose drawings were already famous among the few – Aubrey Beardsley, by name. With Rothenstein I paid my first visit to the Bodley Head. By him I was inducted into another haunt of intellect and daring, the domino room of the Café Royal.

There, on that October evening – there, in that exuberant vista of gilding and crimson velvet set amidst all those opposing mirrors and upholding caryatids, with fumes of tobacco ever rising to the painted and pagan ceiling, and with the hum of presumably cynical conversation broken into so sharply now and again by the clatter of dominoes shuffled on marble tables, I drew a deep breath, and 'This indeed,' said I to myself, 'is life!'

It was the hour before dinner. We drank vermouth. Those who knew Rothenstein were pointing him out to those who knew him only by name. Men were constantly coming in through the swing-doors and wandering slowly up and down in search of vacant tables, or of tables occupied by friends. One of these rovers interested me because I was sure he wanted to catch Rothenstein's eye. He had twice passed our table, with a hesitating look; but Rothenstein, in the thick of a disquisition on Puvis de Chavannes, had not seen him. He was a stooping, shambling person, rather tall, very pale, with longish and brownish hair. He had a thin vague beard – or rather, he had a chin on which a large number of hairs weakly curled and clustered to cover its retreat. He was an odd-looking person; but in the 'nineties odd apparitions were more frequent, I think, than they are now. The young writers of that era – and I was sure this man was a writer – strove earnestly to be distinct in aspect. This man had striven unsuccessfully. He wore a soft black hat of clerical kind but of Bohemian intention, and a grey waterproof cape which, perhaps because it was waterproof, failed to be romantic.

I decided that 'dim' was the *mot juste* for him. I had already essayed to write, and was immensely keen on the *mot juste*, that Holy Grail of the period.

The dim man was now again approaching our table, and this time he made up his mind to pause in front of it. 'You don't remember me,' he said in a toneless voice.

Rothenstein brightly focused him. 'Yes, I do,' he replied after a moment, with pride rather than effusion – pride in a retentive memory. 'Edwin Soames.'

'Enoch Soames,' said Enoch.

'Enoch Soames,' repeated Rothenstein in a tone implying that it was enough to have hit on the surname. 'We met in Paris two or three times when you were living there. We met at the Café Groche.'

'And I came to your studio once.'

'Oh yes; I was sorry I was out.'

'But you were in. You showed me some of your paintings, you know. . . . I hear you're in Chelsea now.'

'Yes.'

I almost wondered that Mr. Soames did not, after this monosyllable, pass along. He stood patiently there, rather like a dumb animal, rather like a donkey looking over a gate. A sad figure, his. It occurred to me that 'hungry' was perhaps the *mot juste* for him; but – hungry for what? He looked as if he had little appetite for anything. I was sorry for him; and Rothenstein, though he had not invited him to Chelsea, did ask him to sit down and have something to drink.

Seated, he was more self-assertive. He flung back the wings of his cape with a gesture which – had not those wings been waterproof – might have seemed to hurl defiance at things in general. And he ordered an absinthe. '*Je me tiens toujours fidèle*', he told Rothenstein, '*à la sorcière glauque.*'

'It is bad for you,' said Rothenstein drily.

'Nothing is bad for one,' answered Soames. '*Dans ce monde il n'y a ni de bien ni de mal.*'

'Nothing good and nothing bad? How do you mean?'

'I explained it all in the preface to *Negations*.'

'*Negations?*'

'Yes; I gave you a copy of it.'

'Oh yes, of course. But did you explain – for instance – that there was no such thing as bad or good grammar?'

'N-no,' said Soames. 'Of course in Art there is the good and the evil. But in Life – no.' He was rolling a cigarette. He had weak white hands, not well washed, and with finger-tips much stained by nicotine. 'In Life there are illusions of good and evil, but' – his voice trailed away to a murmur in which the words 'vieux jeu' and 'rococo' were faintly audible. I think he felt he was not doing himself justice, and feared that Rothenstein was going to point out fallacies. Anyway, he cleared his throat and said, '*Parlons d'autre chose.*'

It occurs to you that he was a fool? It didn't to me. I was young, and had not the clarity of judgement that Rothen-stein already had. Soames was quite five or six years older than either of us. Also, he had written a book.

It was wonderful to have written a book.

If Rothenstein had not been there, I should have revered Soames. Even as it was, I respected him. And I was very near indeed to reverence when he said he had another book coming out soon. I asked if I might ask what kind of book it was to be.

'My poems,' he answered. Rothenstein asked if this was to be the title of the book. The poet meditated on this sugges-tion, but said he rather thought of giving the book no title at all. 'If a book is good in itself –' he murmured, waving his cigarette.

Rothenstein objected that absence of title might be bad

for the sale of a book. 'If,' he urged, 'I went into a bookseller's and said simply "Have you got?" or "Have you a copy of?" how would they know what I wanted?'

'Oh, of course I should have my name on the cover,' Soames answered earnestly. 'And I rather want', he added, looking hard at Rothenstein, 'to have a drawing of myself as frontispiece.' Rothenstein admitted that this was a capital idea, and mentioned that he was going into the country and would be there for some time. He then looked at his watch, exclaimed at the hour, paid the waiter, and went away with me to dinner. Soames remained at his post of fidelity to the glaucous witch.

'Why were you so determined not to draw him?' I asked.

'Draw him? Him? How can one draw a man who doesn't exist?'

'He is dim,' I admitted. But my *mot juste* fell flat. Rothenstein repeated that Soames was non-existent.

Still, Soames had written a book. I asked if Rothenstein had read *Negations*. He said he had looked into it, 'but,' he added crisply, 'I don't profess to know anything about writing.' A reservation very characteristic of the period! Painters would not then allow that any one outside their own order had a right to any opinion about painting. This law (graven on the tablets brought down by Whistler from the summit of Fujiyama) imposed certain limitations. If other arts than painting were not utterly unintelligible to all but the men who practised them, the law tottered – the Monroe Doctrine, as it were, did not hold good. Therefore no painter would offer an opinion of a book without warning you at any rate that his opinion was worthless. No one is a better judge of literature than Rothenstein; but it wouldn't have done to tell him so in those days; and I knew that I must form an unaided judgement on *Negations*.

Not to buy a book of which I had met the author face to face would have been for me in those days an impossible act of self-denial. When I returned to Oxford for the Christmas Term I had duly secured *Negations*. I used to keep it lying carelessly on the table in my room, and whenever a friend took it up and asked what it was about I would say 'Oh, it's rather a remarkable book. It's by a man whom I know.' Just 'what it was about' I never was able to say. Head or tail was just what I hadn't made of that slim green volume. I found in the preface no clue to the exiguous labyrinth of contents, and in that labyrinth nothing to explain the preface.

Lean near to life. Lean very near – nearer.
Life is web, and therein nor warp nor woof is, but web only.
It is for this I am Catholick in church and in thought, yet do let swift Mood weave there what the shuttle of Mood wills.

These were the opening phrases of the preface, but those which followed were less easy to understand. Then came 'Stark: A *Conte*', about a midinette who, so far as I could gather, murdered, or was about to murder, a mannequin. It seemed to me like a story by Catule Mendès in which the translator had either skipped or cut out every alternate sentence. Next, a dialogue between Pan and St. Ursula – lacking, I rather felt, in 'snap'. Next, some aphorisms (entitled ἀφορίσματα). Throughout, in fact, there was a great variety of form; and the forms had evidently been wrought with much care. It was rather the substance that eluded me. Was there, I wondered, any substance at all? It did now occur to me: suppose Enoch Soames was a fool! Up cropped a rival hypothesis: suppose *I* was! I inclined to give Soames the benefit of the doubt. I had read *L'Après-midi d'un Faune* without extracting a glimmer of meaning. Yet Mallarmé – of course – was a Master. How was I to know that Soames wasn't another? There was a sort of music in his prose, not indeed arresting, but perhaps, I thought, haunting, and laden perhaps with meanings as deep as Mallarmé's own. I awaited his poems with an open mind.

And I looked forward to them with positive impatience after I had had a second meeting with him. This was on an evening in January. Going into the aforesaid domino room, I passed a table at which sat a pale man with an open book before him. He looked from his book to me, and I looked back over my shoulder with a vague sense that I ought to have recognised him. I returned to pay my respects. After exchanging a few words, I said with a glance to the open book, 'I see I am interrupting you,' and was about to pass on, but 'I prefer', Soames replied in his toneless voice, 'to be interrupted,' and I obeyed his gesture that I should sit down.

I asked him if he often read here. 'Yes; things of this kind I read here,' he answered, indicating the title of his book – *The Poems of Shelley.*

'Anything that you really' – and I was going to say 'admire?' But I cautiously left my sentence unfinished, and was glad that I had done so, for he said, with unwonted emphasis, 'Anything second-rate.'

I had read little of Shelley, but 'Of course,' I murmured, 'he's very uneven.'

'I should have thought evenness was just what was wrong with him. A deadly evenness. That's why I read him here. The noise of this place breaks the rhythm. He's tolerable here.' Soames took up the book and glanced through the pages. He laughed. Soames' laugh was a short, single and mirthless sound from the throat, unaccompanied by any movement of the face or brightening of the eyes. 'What a period!' he uttered, laying the book down. And 'What a country!' he added.

I asked rather nervously if he didn't think Keats had more or less held his own against the drawbacks of time and place. He admitted that there were 'passages in Keats', but did not specify them. Of 'the older men', as he called them, he seemed to like only Milton. 'Milton', he said, 'wasn't senti-mental.' Also, 'Milton had a dark insight.' And again, 'I can always read Milton in the reading-room.'

'The reading-room?'

'Of the British Museum. I go there every day.'

'You do? I've only been there once. I'm afraid I found it rather a depressing place. It – it seemed to sap one's vitality.'

'It does. That's why I go there. The lower one's vitality, the more sensitive one is to great art. I live near the Museum. I have rooms in Dyott Street.'

'And you go round to the reading-room to read Milton?'

'Usually Milton.' He looked at me. 'It was Milton', he certificatively added, 'who converted me to Diabolism.'

'Diabolism? Oh yes? Really?' said I, with that vague dis-comfort and that intense desire to be polite which one feels when a man speaks of his own religion. 'You – worship the Devil?'

Soames shook his head. 'It's not exactly worship,' he qual-ified, sipping his absinthe. 'It's more a matter of trusting and encouraging.'

'Ah, yes. . . . But I had rather gathered from the preface to *Negations* that you were a – a Catholic.'

'*Je l'étais à cette époque.* Perhaps I still am. Yes, I'm a Catholic Diabolist.'

This profession he made in an almost cursory tone. I could see that what was upmost in his mind was the fact that I had read *Negations*. His pale eyes had for the first time

233

gleamed. I felt as one who is about to be examined, *viva voce*, on the very subject in which he is shakiest. I hastily asked him how soon his poems were to be published. 'Next week,' he told me.

'And are they to be published without a title?'

'No, I found a title, at last. But I shan't tell you what it is,' as though I had been so impertinent as to inquire. 'I am not sure that it wholly satisfies me. But it is the best I can find. It does suggest something of the quality of the poems. . . . Strange growths, natural and wild; yet exquisite,' he added, 'and many-hued, and full of poisons.'

I asked him what he thought of Baudelaire. He uttered the snort that was his laugh, and 'Baudelaire', he said, 'was a *bourgeois malgré lui.*' France had had only one poet: Villon; 'and two-thirds of Villon were sheer journalism.' Verlaine was 'an *épicier malgré lui.*' Altogether, rather to my surprise, he rated French literature lower than English. There were 'passages' in Villiers de l'Isle-Adam. But 'I', he summed up, 'owe nothing to France.' He nodded at me. 'You'll see,' he predicted.

I did not, when the time came, quite see that. I thought the author of *Fungoids* did – unconsciously, no doubt – owe something to the young Parisian decadents, or to the young English ones who owed something to *them*. I still think so. The little book – bought by me in Oxford – lies before me as I write. Its pale grey buckram cover and silver lettering have not worn well. Nor have its contents. Through these, with a melancholy interest, I have again been looking. They are not much. But at the time of their publication I had a vague suspicion that they *might* be. I suppose it's my capacity for faith, not poor Soames' work, that is weaker than it once was. . . .

Thou art, who has not been!
    Pale tunes irresolute
    And traceries of old sounds
    Blown from a rotted flute
Mingle with noise of cymbals rouged with rust,
Nor not strange forms and epicene
    Lie bleeding in the dust,
      Being wounded with wounds.
      For this it is
    That is thy counterpart
      Of age-long mockeries
      Thou has not been nor art!

There seemed to me a certain inconsistency as between the first and last lines of this. I tried, with bent brows, to resolve the discord. But I did not take my failure as wholly incompatible with a meaning in Soames' mind. Might it not rather indicate the depth of his meaning? As for the craftsmanship, 'rouged with rust' seemed to me a fine stroke, and 'nor not' instead of 'and' had a curious felicity. I wondered who the Young Woman was, and what she had made of it all. I sadly suspect that Soames could not have made more of it than she. Yet, even now, if one doesn't try to make any sense at all of the poem, and reads it just for the sound, there is a certain grace of cadence. Soames was an artist – in so far as he was anything, poor fellow!

It seemed to me, when first I read *Fungoids*, that, oddly enough, the Diabolistic side of him was the best. Diabolism seemed to be a cheerful, even a wholesome, influence in his life.

Round and round the shutter'd Square
I stroll'd with the Devil's arm in mine.
No sound but the scrape of his hoofs was there
And the ring of his laughter and mine.
    We had drunk black wine.

I scream'd 'I will race you, Master!'
'What matter,' he shriek'd, 'to-night
Which of us runs the faster?
There is nothing to fear to-night
    In the foul moon's light!'

Then I look'd him in the eyes,
And I laugh'd full shrill at the lie he told
And the gnawing fear he would fain disguise.
It was true, what I'd time and again been told:
    He was old – old.

There was, I felt, quite a swing about that first stanza –
a joyous and rollicking note of comradeship. The second
was slightly hysterical perhaps. But I liked the third: it was
so bracingly unorthodox, even according to the tenets of
Soames' peculiar sect in the faith. Not much 'trusting and
encouraging' here! Soames triumphantly exposing the Devil
as a liar, and laughing 'full shrill', cut a quite heartening
figure, I thought – then! Now, in the light of what befell,
none of his poems depresses me so much as 'Nocturne'.

I looked out for what the metropolitan reviewers would
have to say. They seemed to fall into two classes: those who
had little to say and those who had nothing. The second
class was the larger, and the words of the first were cold;
insomuch that

was the sole lure offered in advertisements by Soames' publisher. I had hoped that when next I met the poet I could congratulate him on having made a stir; for I fancied he was not so sure of his intrinsic greatness as he seemed. I was but able to say, rather coarsely, when next I did see him, that I hoped *Fungoids* was 'selling splendidly'. He looked at me across his glass of absinthe and asked if I had bought a copy. His publisher had told him that three had been sold. I laughed, as at a jest.

'You don't suppose I *care*, do you?' he said, with something like a snarl. I disclaimed the notion. He added that he was not a tradesman. I said mildly that I wasn't, either, and murmured that an artist who gave truly new and great things to the world had always to wait long for recognition. He said he cared not a sou for recognition. I agreed that the act of creation was its own reward.

His moroseness might have alienated me if I had regarded myself as a nobody. But ah! hadn't both John Lane and Aubrey Beardsley suggested that I should write an essay for the great new venture that was afoot – *The Yellow Book*? And hadn't Henry Harland, as editor, accepted my essay? And wasn't it to be in the very first number? At Oxford I was still *in statu pupillari*. In London I regarded myself as very much indeed a graduate now – one whom no Soames could ruffle. Partly to show off, partly in sheer good-will, I told Soames he ought to contribute to *The Yellow Book*. He uttered from the throat a sound of scorn for that publication.

Nevertheless, I did, a day or two later, tentatively ask Harland if he knew anything of the work of a man called Enoch Soames. Harland paused in the midst of his characteristic stride around the room, threw up his hands towards the ceiling, and groaned aloud: he had often met 'that absurd creature' in Paris, and this very morning had received some poems in manuscript from him.

'Has he *no* talent?' he asked.

'He has an income. He's all right.' Harland was the most joyous of men and most generous of critics, and he hated to talk of anything about which he couldn't be enthusiastic. So I dropped the subject of Soames. The news that Soames had an income did take the edge off solicitude. I learned afterwards that he was the son of an unsuccessful and deceased bookseller in Preston, but had inherited an annuity of £300 from a married aunt, and had no surviving relatives of any kind. Materially, then, he was 'all right'. But there was still a spiritual pathos about him, sharpened for me now by the possibility that even the praises of *The Preston Telegraph* might not have been forthcoming had he not been the son of a Preston man. He had a sort of weak doggedness which I could not but admire. Neither he nor his work received the slightest encouragement; but he persisted in behaving as a personage: always he kept his dingy little flag flying. Wherever congregated the *jeunes féroces* of the arts, in whatever Soho restaurant they had just discovered, in whatever music-hall they were most frequenting, there was Soames in the midst of them, or rather on the fringe of them, a dim but inevitable figure. He never sought to propitiate his fellow-writers, never bated a jot of his arrogance about his own work or of his contempt of theirs. To the painters he was respectful, even humble; but for the poets and prosaists of *The Yellow Book*, and later of *The Savoy*, he had never a word but of scorn. He wasn't resented. It didn't occur to anybody that he or his Catholic Diabolism mattered. When, in the autumn of '96, he brought out (at his own expense, this time) a third book, his last book, nobody said a word for or against it. I meant, but forgot, to buy it. I never saw it, and am ashamed to say I don't even remember what it was called. But I did, at the time of its publication, say to Rothenstein that I thought poor old Soames was really a rather tragic figure, and that I believed he would literally die for want of recognition. Rothenstein scoffed. He said I was trying to get credit for a kind heart which I didn't possess; and perhaps this was so. But at the private view of the New English Art Club, a few weeks later, I beheld a pastel portrait of 'Enoch Soames, Esq.'. It was very like him, and very like Rothenstein to have done it. Soames was standing near it, in his soft hat and his waterproof cape, all through the afternoon. Anybody who knew him would have recognised the portrait at a glance, but nobody who didn't know him would have recognised the portrait from its bystander: it 'existed' so much more than he; it was bound to. Also, it had not that expression of faint happiness which on this day was discernible, yes, in Soames' countenance. Fame had breathed on him. Twice again in the course of the month I went to the New English, and on both occasions Soames himself was on view there. Looking back, I regard the close of that exhibition as having been virtually the close of his career. He had felt the breath of Fame against his cheek – so late, for such a little while; and at its withdrawal he gave in, gave up, gave out. He, who had never looked strong or well, looked ghastly now – a shadow of the shade he had once been. He still frequented the domino room, but, having lost all wish to excite curiosity, he no longer read books there. 'You read only at the Museum now?' asked I, with attempted cheerfulness. He said he never went there now. 'No absinthe there,' he muttered. It was the sort of thing that in the old days he would have said for effect; but it carried conviction now. Absinthe, erst but a point in the 'personality' he had striven so hard to build up, was solace and necessity now. He no longer called it *la sorcière glauque.* He had shed away all his French phrases. He had become a plain, unvarnished, Preston man.

Failure, if it be a plain, unvarnished, complete failure, and even though it be a squalid failure, has always a certain dignity. I avoided Soames because he made me feel rather vulgar. John Lane had published, by this time, two little books of mine, and they had had a pleasant little success of esteem. I was a – slight but definite – 'personality'. Frank Harris had engaged me to kick up my heels in *The Saturday Review,* Alfred Harmsworth was letting me do likewise in *The Daily Mail,* I was just what Soames wasn't. And he shamed my gloss. Had I known that he really and firmly believed in the greatness of what he as an artist had achieved, I might not have shunned him. No man who hasn't lost his vanity can be held to have altogether failed. Soames' dignity was an illusion of mine. One day in the first week of June, 1897, that illusion went. But on the evening of that day Soames went too.

I had been out most of the morning, and, as it was too late to reach home in time for luncheon, I sought 'the Vingtième'. This little place – Restaurant du Vingtième Siècle, to give it its full title – had been discovered in '96 by the poets and prosaists, but had now been more or less abandoned in favour of some later find. I don't think it lived long enough to justify its name; but at that time it still was, in Greek Street, a few doors from Soho Square, and almost opposite to that house where, in the first years of the century, a little girl, and with her a boy named De Quincey, made nightly encampment in darkness and hunger among dust and rats and old legal parchments. The Vingtième was but a small whitewashed room, leading out into the street at one end and into a kitchen at the other. The proprietor and cook was a Frenchman, known to us as Monsieur Vingtième; the waiters were his two daughters, Rose and Berthe; and the food, according to faith, was good. The tables were so narrow, and were set so close together, that there was space for twelve of them, six jutting from either wall.

Only the two nearest to the door, as I went in, were occupied. On one side sat a tall, flashy, rather Mephistophelian man whom I had seen from time to time in the domino room and elsewhere. On the other side sat Soames. They made a queer contrast in that sunlit room – Soames sitting haggard in that hat and cape which nowhere at any season had I seen him doff, and this other, this keenly vital man, at sight of whom I more than ever wondered whether he were a diamond merchant, a conjurer, or the head of a private detective agency. I was sure Soames didn't want my company; but I asked, as it would have seemed brutal not to, whether I might join him, and took the chair opposite to his. He was smoking a cigarette, with an untasted salmi of something on his plate and a half-empty bottle of Sauterne before him; and he was quite silent. I said that the preparations for the Jubilee made London impossible. (I rather liked them, really.) I professed a wish to go right away till the whole thing was over. In vain did I attune myself to his gloom. He seemed not to hear me nor even to see me. I felt that his behaviour made me ridiculous in the eyes of the other man. The gangway between the two rows of tables at the Vingtième was hardly more than two feet wide (Rose and Berthe, in their ministrations, had always to edge past each other, quarrelling in whispers as they did so), and any one at the table abreast of yours was practically at yours. I thought our neighbour was amused at my failure to interest Soames, and so, as I could not explain to him that my insistence was merely charitable, I became silent. Without turning my head, I had him well within my range of vision. I hoped I looked less vulgar than he in contrast with Soames. I was sure he was not an Englishman, but what *was* his nationality? Though his jet-black hair was *en brosse*, I did not think he was French. To Berthe, who waited on him, he spoke French fluently, but with a hardly native idiom and accent. I gathered that this was his first visit to the Vingtième; but Berthe was offhand in her manner to him: he had not made a good impression. His eyes were handsome, but – like the Vingtième's tables – too narrow and set too close together. His nose was predatory, and the points of his moustache, waxed up beyond his nostrils, gave a fixity to his smile. Decidedly, he was sinister. And my sense of discomfort in his presence was intensified by the scarlet waistcoat which tightly, and so unseasonably in June, sheathed his ample chest. This waistcoat wasn't wrong merely because of the heat, either. It was somehow all wrong in itself. It wouldn't have done on Christmas morning. It would have struck a jarring note at the first night of 'Hernani'. I was trying to account for its wrongness when Soames suddenly and strangely broke silence. 'A hundred years hence!' he murmured, as in a trance.

'We shall not be here!' I briskly but fatuously added.

'We shall not be here. No,' he droned, 'but the Museum will still be just where it is. And the reading-room, just where it is. And people will be able to go and read there.' He inhaled sharply, and a spasm as of actual pain contorted his features.

I wondered what train of thought poor Soames had been following. He did not enlighten me when he said, after a long pause, 'You think I haven't minded.'

'Minded what, Soames?'

'Neglect. Failure.'

'*Failure?*' I said heartily. 'Failure?' I repeated vaguely. 'Neglect – yes, perhaps; but that's quite another matter. Of course you haven't been – appreciated. But what then? Any artist who – who gives –' What I wanted to say was, 'Any artist who gives truly new and great things to the world has always to wait long for recognition'; but the flattery would not out: in the face of his misery, a misery so genuine and so unmasked, my lips would not say the words.

And then – he said them for me. I flushed. 'That's what you were going to say, isn't it?' he asked.

'How did you know?'

'It's what you said to me three years ago, when *Fungoids* was published.' I flushed the more. I need not have done so at all, for 'It's the only important thing I ever heard you say,' he continued. 'And I've never forgotten it. It's a true thing. It's a horrible truth. But – d'you remember what I answered? I said "I don't care a sou for recognition." And you believed me. You've gone on believing I'm above that sort of thing. You're shallow. What should *you* know of the feelings of a man like me? You imagine that a great artist's faith in himself and in the verdict of posterity is enough to keep him happy. . . . You've never guessed at the bitterness and loneliness, the' – his voice broke; but presently he resumed, speaking with a force that I had never known in him. 'Posterity! What use is it to *me*? A dead man doesn't know that people are visiting his grave – visiting his birthplace – putting up tablets to him – unveiling statues of him. A dead man can't read the books that are written about him. A hundred years hence! Think of it! If I could come back to life *then* – just for a few hours – and go to the reading-room, and *read*! Or better still: if I could be projected, now, at this moment, into that future, into that reading-room, just for this one afternoon! I'd sell myself body and soul to the devil, for that! Think of the pages and pages in the catalogue: "SOAMES, ENOCH" endlessly – endless editions, commentaries, prolegomena, biographies' – but here he was interrupted by a sudden loud creak of the chair at the next table. Our neighbour had half risen from his place. He was leaning towards us, apologetically intrusive.

'Excuse – permit me,' he said softly. 'I have been unable not to hear. Might I take a liberty? In this little *restaurant-sans-façon*' – he spread wide his hands – 'might I, as the phrase is, "cut in"?'

I could but signify our acquiescence. Berthe had appeared at the kitchen door, thinking the stranger wanted his bill. He waved her away with his cigar, and in another moment had seated himself beside me, commanding a full view of Soames.

'Though not an Englishman,' he explained, 'I know my London well, Mr. Soames. Your name and fame – Mr. Beerbohm's too – very known to me. Your point is: who am *I*?' He glanced quickly over his shoulder, and in a lowered voice said, 'I am the Devil.'

I couldn't help it: I laughed. I tried not to, I knew there was nothing to laugh at, my rudeness shamed me, but – I laughed with increasing volume. The Devil's quiet dignity, the surprise and disgust of his raised eyebrows, did but the more dissolve me. I rocked to and fro, I lay back aching. I behaved deplorably.

'I am a gentleman, and,' he said with intense emphasis, 'I thought I was in the company of *gentlemen*.'

'Don't!' I gasped faintly. 'Oh, don't!'

'Curious, *nicht wahr*?' I heard him say to Soames. 'There is a type of person to whom the very mention of my name is – oh-so-awfully-funny! In your theatres the dullest *comédien* needs only to say "The Devil!" and right away they give him "the loud laugh that speaks the vacant mind". Is it not so?'

I had now just breath enough to offer my apologies. He accepted them, but coldly, and readdressed himself to Soames.

'I am a man of business,' he said, 'and always I would put things through "right now", as they say in the States. You are a poet. *Les affaires* – you detest them. So be it. But with me you will deal, eh? What you have said just now gives me furiously to hope.'

Soames had not moved, except to light a fresh cigarette. He sat crouched forward, with his elbows squared on the table, and his head just above the level of his hands, staring up at the Devil. 'Go on,' he nodded. I had no remnant of laughter in me now.

'It will be the more pleasant, our little deal,' the Devil went on, 'because you are – I mistake not? – a Diabolist.'

'A Catholic Diabolist,' said Soames.

The Devil accepted the reservation genially. 'You wish', he resumed, 'to visit now – this afternoon as-ever-is – the reading-room of the British Museum, yes? but of a hundred years hence, yes? *Parfaitement*. Time – an illusion. Past and future – they are as ever-present as the present, or at any rate only what you call "just-round-the-corner". I switch you on to any date. I project you – pouf! You wish to be in the reading-room just as it will be on the afternoon of June 3rd, 1997? You wish to find yourself standing in that room, just past the swing-doors, this very minute, yes? and to stay there till closing time? Am I right?'

Soames nodded.

The Devil looked at his watch. 'Ten past two,' he said. 'Closing time in summer same then as now: seven o'clock. That will give you almost five hours. At seven o'clock – pouf! – you find yourself again here, sitting at this table. I am dining to-night *dans le monde – dans le higlif.* That concludes my present visit to your great city. I come and fetch you here, Mr. Soames, on my way home.'

'Home?' I echoed.

'Be it never so humble!' said the Devil lightly.

'All right,' said Soames.

'Soames!' I entreated. But my friend moved not a muscle.

The Devil had made as though to stretch forth his hand across the table and touch Soames' forearm; but he paused in his gesture.

'A hundred years hence, as now,' he smiled, 'no smoking allowed in the reading-room. You would better therefore –'

Soames removed the cigarette from his mouth and dropped it into his glass of Sauterne.

'Soames!' again I cried. 'Can't you' – but the Devil had now stretched forth his hand across the table. He brought it slowly down on – the table-cloth. Soames's chair was empty. His cigarette floated sodden in his wine-glass. There was no other trace of him.

For a few moments the Devil let his hand rest where it lay, gazing at me out of the corners of his eyes, vulgarly triumphant.

A shudder shook me. With an effort I controlled myself and rose from my chair. 'Very clever,' I said condescendingly. 'But – *The Time Machine* is a delightful book, don't you think? So entirely original!'

'You are pleased to sneer,' said the Devil, who had also risen, 'but it is one thing to write about a not possible machine; it is a quite other thing to be a Supernatural Power.' All the same, I had scored.

Berthe had come forth at the sound of our rising. I explained to her that Mr. Soames had been called away, and that both he and I would be dining here. It was not until

I was out in the open air that I began to feel giddy. I have but the haziest recollection of what I did, where I wandered, in the glaring sunshine of that endless afternoon. I remember the sound of carpenters' hammers all along Piccadilly, and the bare chaotic look of the half-erected 'stands'. Was it in the Green Park or in Kensington Gardens or *where* was it that I sat on a chair beneath a tree, trying to read an evening paper? There was a phrase in the leading article that went on repeating itself in my fagged mind – 'Little is hidden from this august Lady full of the garnered wisdom of sixty years of Sovereignty.' I remember wildly conceiving a letter (to reach Windsor by express messenger told to await answer):

'MADAM, – Well knowing that your Majesty is full of the garnered wisdom of sixty years of Sovereignty, I venture to ask your advice in the following delicate matter. Mr. Enoch Soames, whose poems you may or may not know,' . . .

Was there *no* way of helping him – saving him? A bargain was a bargain, and I was the last man to aid or abet any one in wriggling out of a reasonable obligation. I wouldn't have lifted a little finger to save Faust. But poor Soames! – doomed to pay without respite an eternal price for nothing but a fruitless search and a bitter disillusioning. . . .

Odd and uncanny it seemed to me that he, Soames, in the flesh, in the waterproof cape, was at this moment living in the last decade of the next century, poring over books not yet written, and seeing and seen by men not yet born. Uncannier and odder still that to-night and evermore he would be in Hell. Assuredly, truth was stranger than fiction.

Endless that afternoon was. Almost I wished I had gone with Soames – not indeed to stay in the reading-room, but to sally forth for a brisk sight-seeing walk around a new

London. I wandered restlessly out of the Park I had sat in. Vainly I tried to imagine myself an ardent tourist from the eighteenth century. Intolerable was the strain of the slow-passing and empty minutes. Long before seven o'clock I was back at the Vingtième.

I sat there just where I had sat for luncheon. Air came in listlessly through the open door behind me. Now and again Rose or Berthe appeared for a moment. I told them I would not order any dinner until Mr. Soames came. A hurdy-gurdy began to play, abruptly drowning the noise of a quarrel between some Frenchmen further up the street. Whenever the tune was changed I heard the quarrel still raging. I had bought another evening paper on my way. I unfolded it. My eyes gazed ever away from it to the clock over the kitchen door. . . .

Five minutes, now, to the hour! I remembered that clocks in restaurants are kept five minutes fast. I concentrated my eyes on the paper. I vowed I would not look away from it again. I held it upright, at its full width, close to my face, so that I had no view of anything but it. . . . Rather a tremulous sheet? Only because of the draught, I told myself.

My arms gradually became stiff; they ached, but I could not drop them – now. I had a suspicion, I had a certainty. Well, what then? . . . What else had I come for? Yet I held tight that barrier of newspaper. Only the sound of Berthe's brisk footstep from the kitchen enabled me, forced me, to drop it, and to utter:

'What shall we have to eat, Soames?'

'*Il est souffrant, ce pauvre Monsieur Soames?*' asked Berthe.

'He's only – tired.' I asked her to get some wine – Burgundy – and whatever food might be ready. Soames sat crouched forward against the table, exactly as when last I had seen him. It was as though he had never moved – he who had moved so unimaginably far. Once or twice in the afternoon it had for an instant occurred to me that perhaps his journey was not to be fruitless – that perhaps we had all been wrong in our estimate of the works of Enoch Soames. That we had been horribly right was horribly clear from the look of him. But 'Don't be discouraged,' I falteringly said. 'Perhaps it's only that you – didn't leave enough time. Two, three centuries hence, perhaps –'

'Yes,' his voice came. 'I've thought of that.'

'And now – now for the more immediate future! Where are you going to hide? How would it be if you caught the Paris express from Charing Cross? Almost an hour to spare. Don't go on to Paris. Stop at Calais. Live in Calais. He'd never think of looking for you in Calais.'

'It's like my luck', he said, 'to spend my last hours on earth with an ass.' But I was not offended. 'And a treacherous ass,' he strangely added, tossing across to me a crumpled bit of paper which he had been holding in his hand. I glanced at the writing on it – some sort of gibberish, apparently. I laid it impatiently aside.

'Come, Soames! pull yourself together! This isn't a mere matter of life and death. It's a question of eternal torment, mind you! You don't mean to say you're going to wait limply here till the Devil comes to fetch you?'

'I can't do anything else. I've no choice.'

'Come! This is "trusting and encouraging" with a vengeance! This is Diabolism run mad!' I filled his glass with wine. 'Surely, now that you've *seen* the brute –'

'It's no good abusing him.'

'You must admit there's nothing Miltonic about him, Soames.'

'I don't say he's not rather different from what I expected.'

'He's a vulgarian, he's a swell-mobsman, he's the sort of

249

man who hangs about the corridors of trains going to the Riviera and steals ladies' jewel-cases. Imagine eternal torment presided over by *him*!'

'You don't suppose I look forward to it, do you?'

'Then why not slip quietly out of the way?'

Again and again I filled his glass, and always, mechanically, he emptied it; but the wine kindled no spark of enterprise in him. He did not eat, and I myself ate hardly at all. I did not in my heart believe that any dash for freedom could save him. The chase would be swift, the capture certain. But better anything than this passive, meek, miserable waiting. I told Soames that for the honour of the human race he ought to make some show of resistance. He asked what the human race had ever done for him. 'Besides,' he said, 'can't you understand that I'm in his power? You saw him touch me, didn't you? There's an end of it. I've no will. I'm sealed.'

I made a gesture of despair. He went on repeating the word 'sealed'. I began to realise that the wine had clouded his brain. No wonder! Foodless he had gone into futurity, foodless he still was. I urged him to eat at any rate some bread. It was maddening to think that he, who had so much to tell, might tell nothing. 'How was it all,' I asked, 'yonder? Come! Tell me your adventures.'

'They'd make first-rate "copy", wouldn't they?'

'I'm awfully sorry for you, Soames, and I make all possible allowances; but what earthly right have you to insinuate that I should make "copy", as you call it, out of you?'

The poor fellow pressed his hands to his forehead. 'I don't know,' he said. 'I had some reason, I'm sure. . . . I'll try to remember.'

'That's right. Try to remember everything. Eat a little more bread. What did the reading-room look like?'

'Much as usual,' he at length muttered.

'Many people there?'

'Usual sort of number.'

'What did they look like?'

Soames tried to visualise them. 'They all,' he presently remembered, 'looked very like one another.'

My mind took a fearsome leap. 'All dressed in Jaeger?'

'Yes, I think so. Greyish-yellowish stuff.'

'A sort of uniform?' He nodded. 'With a number on it, perhaps? – a number on a large disc of metal sewn on to the left sleeve? DKF 78,910 – that sort of thing?' It was even so. 'And all of them – men and women alike – looking very well-cared-for? very Utopian? and smelling rather strongly of carbolic? and all of them quite hairless?' I was right every time. Soames was only not sure whether the men and women were hairless or shorn. 'I hadn't time to look at them very closely,' he explained.

'No, of course not. But –'

'They stared at *me*, I can tell you. I attracted a great deal of attention.' At last he had done that! 'I think I rather scared them. They moved away whenever I came near. They followed me about at a distance, wherever I went. The men at the round desk in the middle seemed to have a sort of panic whenever I went to make inquiries.'

'What did you do when you arrived?'

Well, he had gone straight to the catalogue, of course – to the S volumes, and had stood long before SN–SOF, unable to take this volume out of the shelf, because his heart was beating so. . . . At first, he said, he wasn't disappointed – he only thought there was some new arrangement. He went to the middle desk and asked where the catalogue of *twentieth*-century books was kept. He gathered that there was still only one catalogue. Again he looked up his name, stared at the three little pasted slips he had known so well. Then he went and sat down for a long time. . . .

'And then,' he droned, 'I looked up the *Dictionary of National Biography* and some encyclopaedias. . . . I went back to the middle desk and asked what was the best modern book on late nineteenth-century literature. They told me Mr. T. K. Nupton's book was considered the best. I looked it up in the catalogue and filled in a form for it. It was brought to me. My name wasn't in the index, but – Yes!' he said with a sudden change of tone. 'That's what I'd forgotten. Where's that bit of paper? Give it me back.'

I, too, had forgotten that cryptic screed. I found it fallen on the floor, and handed it to him.

He smoothed it out, nodding and smiling at me disagreeably. 'I found myself glancing through Nupton's book,' he resumed. 'Not very easy reading. Some sort of phonetic spelling. . . . All the modern books I saw were phonetic.'

'Then I don't want to hear any more, Soames, please.'

'The proper names seemed all to be spelt in the old way. But for that, I mightn't have noticed my own name.'

'Your own name? Really? Soames, I'm *very* glad.'

'And yours.'

'No!'

'I thought I should find you waiting here to-night. So I took the trouble to copy out the passage. Read it.'

I snatched the paper. Soames' handwriting was characteristically dim. It, and the noisome spelling, and my excitement, made me all the slower to grasp what T. K. Nupton was driving at.

The document lies before me at this moment. Strange that the words I here copy out for you were copied out for me by poor Soames just seventy-eight years hence. . . .

From p. 234 of 'Inglish Littracher 1890–1900', bi T. K. Nupton, published bi th Stait, 1992:

'Fr. egzarmpl, a riter ov th time, naimd Max Beer-bohm, hoo woz stil alive in th twentieth senchri, rote a stauri in wich e pautraid an immajnari karrakter kauld "Enoch Soames" – a thurd-rait poit hoo beleevz imself a grate jeneus and maix a bargin with th Devvl in auder ter no wot poster-riti thinx ov im! It is a sumwot labud sattire but not without vallu az showing hou seriusli the yung men ov th aiteen-ninetiz took themselvz. Nou that the littreri professhn has bin auganized az a department of publik servis, our riters hav found their levvl an hav lernt ter doo their duti without thort ov th morro. "Th laibrer iz werthi ov hiz hire", an that iz aul. Thank hevvn we hav no Enoch Soameses amung us to-dai!'

I found that by murmuring the words aloud (a device which I commend to my reader) I was able to master them, little by little. The clearer they became, the greater was my bewilderment, my distress and horror. The whole thing was a nightmare. Afar, the great grisly background of what was in store for the poor dear art of letters; here, at the table, fixing on me a gaze that made me hot all over, the poor fellow whom – whom evidently . . . but no: whatever down-grade my character might take in coming years, I should never be such a brute as to –

Again I examined the screed. 'Immajnari' – but here Soames was, no more imaginary, alas! than I. And 'labud' – what on earth was that? (To this day, I have never made out that word.) 'It's all very – baffling,' I at length stammered.

Soames said nothing, but cruelly did not cease to look at me.

'Are you sure,' I temporised, 'quite sure you copied the thing out correctly?'

'Quite.'

'Well, then it's this wretched Nupton who must have made – must be going to make – some idiotic mistake. . . . Look here, Soames! you know me better than to suppose that I . . . After all, the name "Max Beerbohm" is not at all an uncommon one, and there must be several Enoch Soameses running around – or rather, "Enoch Soames" is a name that might occur to any one writing a story. And I don't write stories: I'm an essayist, an observer, a recorder. . . . I admit that it's an extraordinary coincidence. But you must see –'

'I see the whole thing,' said Soames quietly. And he added, with a touch of his old manner, but with more dignity than I had ever known in him, '*Parlons d'autre chose.*'

I accepted that suggestion very promptly. I returned straight to the more immediate future. I spent most of the long evening in renewed appeals to Soames to slip away and seek refuge somewhere. I remember saying at last that if indeed I was destined to write about him, the supposed 'stauri' had better have at least a happy ending. Soames repeated those last three words in a tone of intense scorn. 'In Life and in Art,' he said, 'all that matters is an *inevitable* ending.'

'But,' I urged, more hopefully than I felt, 'an ending that can be avoided *isn't* inevitable.'

'You aren't an artist,' he rasped. 'And you're so hopelessly not an artist that, so far from being able to imagine a thing and make it seem true, you're going to make even a true thing seem as if you'd made it up. You're a miserable bungler. And it's like my luck.'

I protested that the miserable bungler was not I – was not going to be I – but T. K. Nupton; and we had a rather heated argument, in the thick of which it suddenly seemed to me that Soames saw he was in the wrong: he had quite physically cowered. But I wondered why – and now I guessed with a cold throb just why – he stared so, past me. The bringer of that 'inevitable ending' filled the doorway.

I managed to turn in my chair and to say, not without a semblance of lightness, 'Aha, come in!' Dread was indeed rather blunted in me by his looking so absurdly like a villain in a melodrama. The sheen of his tilted hat and of his shirt-front, the repeated twists he was giving to his moustache, and most of all the magnificence of his sneer, gave token that he was there only to be foiled.

He was at our table in a stride. 'I am sorry', he sneered witheringly, 'to break up your pleasant party, but –'

'You don't: you complete it,' I assured him. 'Mr. Soames and I want to have a little talk with you. Won't you sit? Mr. Soames got nothing – frankly nothing – by his journey this afternoon. We don't wish to say that the whole thing was a swindle – a common swindle. On the contrary, we believe you meant well. But of course the bargain, such as it was, is off.'

The Devil gave no verbal answer. He merely looked at Soames and pointed with rigid forefinger to the door. Soames was wretchedly rising from his chair when, with a desperate quick gesture, I swept together two dinner-knives that were on the table, and laid their blades across each other. The Devil stepped sharp back against the table behind him, averting his face and shuddering.

'You are not superstitious!' he hissed.

'Not at all,' I smiled.

'Soames!' he said as to an underling, but without turning his face, 'put those knives straight!'

With an inhibitive gesture to my friend, 'Mr. Soames',

I said emphatically to the Devil, 'is a *Catholic* Diabolist'; but my poor friend did the Devil's bidding, not mine; and now, with his master's eyes again fixed on him, he arose, he shuffled past me. I tried to speak. It was he that spoke. 'Try,' was the prayer he threw back at me as the Devil pushed him roughly out through the door, '*try* to make them know that I did exist!'

In another instant I too was through that door. I stood staring all ways – up the street, across it, down it. There was moonlight and lamplight, but there was not Soames nor that other.

Dazed, I stood there. Dazed, I turned back, at length, into the little room; and I suppose I paid Berthe or Rose for my dinner and luncheon, and for Soames': I hope so, for I never went to the Vingtième again. Ever since that night I have avoided Greek Street altogether. And for years I did not set foot even in Soho Square, because on that same night it was there that I paced and loitered, long and long, with some such dull sense of hope as a man has in not straying far from the place where he has lost something. . . . 'Round and round the shutter'd Square' – that line came back to me on my lonely beat, and with it the whole stanza, ringing in my brain and bearing in on me how tragically different from the happy scene imagined by him was the poet's actual experience of that prince in whom of all princes we should put not our trust.

But – strange how the mind of an essayist, be it never so stricken, roves and ranges! – I remember pausing before a wide doorstep and wondering if perchance it was on this very one that the young De Quincey lay ill and faint while poor Ann flew as fast as her feet would carry her to Oxford Street, the 'stony-hearted stepmother' of them both, and came back bearing that 'glass of port wine and spices' but for which he might, so he thought, actually have died. Was this the very doorstep that the old De Quincey used to revisit in homage? I pondered Ann's fate, the cause of her sudden vanishing from the ken of her boy-friend; and presently I blamed myself for letting the past over-ride the present. Poor vanished Soames!

And for myself, too, I began to be troubled. What had I better do? Would there be a hue and cry – Mysterious Disappearance of an Author, and all that? He had last been seen lunching and dining in my company. Hadn't I better get a hansom and drive straight to Scotland Yard? . . . They would think I was a lunatic. After all, I reassured myself, London was a very large place, and one very dim figure might easily drop out of it unobserved – now especially, in the blinding glare of the near Jubilee. Better say nothing at all, I thought.

And I was right. Soames' disappearance made no stir at all. He was utterly forgotten before any one, so far as I am aware, noticed that he was no longer hanging around. Now and again some poet or prosaist may have said to another, 'What has become of that man Soames?' but I never heard any such question asked. The solicitor through whom he was paid his annuity may be presumed to have made inquiries, but no echo of these resounded. There was something rather ghastly to me in the general unconsciousness that Soames had existed, and more than once I caught myself wondering whether Nupton, that babe unborn, were going to be right in thinking him a figment of my brain.

In that extract from Nupton's repulsive book there is one point which perhaps puzzles you. How is it that the author, though I have here mentioned him by name and have quoted the exact words he is going to write, is not going to grasp the obvious corollary that I have invented nothing? The answer can be but this: Nupton will not have read the later passages of this memoir. Such lack of thoroughness is a serious fault in any one who undertakes to do scholar's work. And I hope these words will meet the eye of some contemporary rival to Nupton and be the undoing of Nupton.

I like to think that some time between 1992 and 1997 somebody will have looked up this memoir, and will have forced on the world his inevitable and startling conclusions. And I have reasons for believing that this will be so. You realise that the reading-room into which Soames was projected by the Devil was in all respects precisely as it will be on the afternoon of June 3rd, 1997. You realise, therefore, that on that afternoon, when it comes round, there the self-same crowd will be, and there Soames too will be, punctually, he and they doing precisely what they did before. Recall now Soames' account of the sensation he made. You may say that the mere difference of his costume was enough to make him sensational in that uniformed crowd. You wouldn't say so if you had ever seen him. I assure you that in no period could Soames be anything but dim. The fact that people are going to stare at him, and follow him around, and seem afraid of him, can be explained only on the hypothesis that they will somehow have been prepared for his ghostly visitation. They will have been awfully waiting to see whether he really would come. And when he does come the effect will of course be – awful.

An authentic, guaranteed, proven ghost, but – only a ghost, alas! Only that. In his first visit, Soames was a creature of flesh and blood, whereas the creatures into whose midst he was projected were but ghosts, I take it – solid, palpable, vocal, but unconscious and automatic ghosts, in a building that was itself an illusion. Next time, that building and those creatures will be real. It is of Soames that there will be but the semblance. I wish I could think him destined to revisit the world actually, physically, consciously. I wish he had this one brief escape, this one small treat, to look forward to. I never forget him for long. He is where he is, and forever. The more rigid moralists among you may say he has only himself to blame. For my part, I think he has been very hardly used. It is well that vanity should be chastened; and Enoch Soames' vanity was, I admit, above the average, and called for special treatment. But there was no need for vindictiveness. You say he contracted to pay the price he is paying; yes; but I maintain that he was induced to do so by fraud. Well-informed in all things, the Devil must have known that my friend would gain nothing by his visit to futurity. The whole thing was a very shabby trick. The more I think of it, the more detestable the Devil seems to me.

Of him I have caught sight several times, here and there, since that day at the Vingtième. Only once, however, have I seen him at close quarters. This was in Paris. I was walking, one afternoon, along the Rue d'Antin, when I saw him advancing from the opposite direction – over-dressed as ever, and swinging an ebony cane, and altogether behaving as though the whole pavement belonged to him. At thought of Enoch Soames and the myriads of other sufferers eternally in this brute's dominion, a great cold wrath filled me, and I drew myself up to my full height. But – well, one is so used to nodding and smiling in the street to anybody one knows, that the action becomes almost independent of oneself: to prevent it requires a very sharp effort and great presence of mind. I was miserably aware, as I passed the Devil, that I nodded and smiled to him. And my shame was the deeper and hotter because he, if you please, stared straight at me with the utmost haughtiness.

To be cut – deliberately cut – by *him*! I was, I still am, furious at having had that happen to me.

JORGE LUIS BORGES

THE LIBRARY
OF BABEL
(1941)

Translated by Anthony Kerrigan

By this art you may contemplate the
variation of the 23 letters . . .

The Anatomy of Melancholy,
Part 2, Sect. II, Mem. IV.

THE UNIVERSE (which others call the Library) is composed
of an indefinite, perhaps an infinite, number of hexagonal
galleries, with enormous ventilation shafts in the middle,
encircled by very low railings. From any hexagon the upper
or lower stories are visible, interminably. The distribution of
the galleries is invariable. Twenty shelves – five long shelves
per side – cover all sides except two; their height, which is
that of each floor, scarcely exceeds that of an average librarian. One of the free sides gives upon a narrow entrance way,
which leads to another gallery, identical to the first and to all
the others. To the left and to the right of the entrance way are
two miniature rooms. One allows standing room for sleeping; the other, the satisfaction of fecal necessities. Through
this section passes the spiral staircase, which plunges down
into the abyss and rises up to the heights. In the entrance
way hangs a mirror, which faithfully duplicates appearances.
People are in the habit of inferring from this mirror that
the Library is not infinite (if it really were, why this illusory
duplication?); I prefer to dream that the polished surfaces
feign and promise infinity. . . .

Light comes from some spherical fruits called by the name of lamps. There are two, running transversally, in each hexagon. The light they emit is insufficient, incessant.

Like all men of the Library, I have travelled in my youth. I have journeyed in search of a book, perhaps of the catalogue of catalogues; now that my eyes can scarcely decipher what I write, I am preparing to die a few leagues from the hexagon in which I was born. Once dead, there will not lack pious hands to hurl me over the banister; my sepulchre shall be the unfathomable air: my body will sink lengthily and will corrupt and dissolve in the wind engendered by the fall, which is infinite. I affirm that the Library is interminable. The idealists argue that the hexagonal halls are a necessary form of absolute space or, at least, of our intuition of space. They contend that a triangular or pentagonal hall is inconceivable. (The mystics claim that to them ecstasy reveals a round chamber containing a great book with a continuous back circling the walls of the room; but their testimony is suspect; their words, obscure. That cyclical book is God.) Let it suffice me, for the time being, to repeat the classic dictum: *The Library is a sphere whose consummate centre is any hexagon, and whose circumference is inaccessible.*

Five shelves correspond to each one of the walls of each hexagon; each shelf contains thirty-two books of a uniform format; each book is made up of four hundred and ten pages; each page, of forty lines; each line, of some eighty black letters. There are also letters on the spine of each book; these letters do not indicate or prefigure what the pages will say. I know that such a lack of relevance, at one time, seemed mysterious. Before summarizing the solution (whose disclosure, despite its tragic implications, is perhaps the capital fact of this history), I want to recall certain axioms.

The first: The Library exists *ab aeterno*. No reasonable

mind can doubt this truth, whose immediate corollary is the future eternity of the world. Man, the imperfect librarian, may be the work of chance or of malevolent demiurges; the universe, with its elegant endowment of shelves, of enigmatic volumes, of indefatigable ladders for the voyager, and of privies for the seated librarian, can only be the work of a god. In order to perceive the distance which exists between the divine and the human, it is enough to compare the rude tremulous symbols which my fallible hand scribbles on the end pages of a book with the organic letters inside: exact, delicate, intensely black, inimitably symmetric.

The second: *The number of orthographic symbols is twenty-five.* * This bit of evidence permitted the formulation, three hundred years ago, of a general theory of the Library and the satisfactory resolution of the problem which no conjecture had yet made clear: the formless and chaotic nature of almost all books. One of these books, which my father saw in a hexagon of the circuit number fifteen ninety-four, was composed of the letters MCV perversely repeated from the first line to the last. Another, very much consulted in this zone, is a mere labyrinth of letters, but on the next-to-the-last page, one may read *O Time your pyramids.* As is well-known: for one reasonable line or one straightforward note there are leagues of insensate cacophony, of verbal farragoes and incoherencies. (I know of a wild region whose librarians repudiate the vain superstitious custom of seeking any sense in books and compare it to looking for meaning

---

* The original manuscript of the present note does not contain digits or capital letters. The punctuation is limited to the comma and the period. These two signs, plus the space sign, and the twenty-two letters of the alphabet, make up the twenty-five sufficient symbols enumerated by the unknown author.

in dreams or in the chaotic lines of one's hands. . . . They admit that the inventors of writing imitated the twenty-five natural symbols, but they maintain that this application is accidental and that books in themselves mean nothing. This opinion – we shall see – is not altogether false.)

For a long time it was believed that these impenetrable books belonged to past or remote languages. It is true that the most ancient men, the first librarians, made use of a language quite different from the one we speak today; it is true that some miles to the right the language is dialectical and that ninety stories up it is incomprehensible. All this, I repeat, is true; but four hundred and ten pages of unvarying MCVs do not correspond to any language, however dialectical or rudimentary it might be. Some librarians insinuated that each letter could influence the next, and that the value of MCV on the third line of page 71 was not the same as that of the same series in another position on another page; but this vague thesis did not prosper. Still other men thought in terms of cryptographs; this conjecture has come to be universally accepted, though not in the sense in which it was formulated by its inventors.

Five hundred years ago, the chief of an upper hexagon* came upon a book as confusing as all the rest but which contained nearly two pages of homogeneous lines. He showed his find to an ambulant decipherer, who told him the lines were written in Portuguese. Others told him they were in Yiddish. In less than a century the nature of the language was

* Formerly, for each three hexagons there was one man. Suicide and pulmonary diseases have destroyed this proportion. My memory recalls scenes of unspeakable melancholy: there have been many nights when I have ventured down corridors and polished staircases without encountering a single librarian.

finally established: it was a Samoyed-Lithuanian dialect of Guaraní, with classical Arabic inflections. The contents were also deciphered: notions of combinational analysis, illustrated by examples of variations with unlimited repetition. These examples made it possible for a librarian of genius to discover the fundamental law of the Library. This thinker observed that all the books, however diverse, are made up of uniform elements: the period, the comma, the space, the twenty-two letters of the alphabet. He also adduced a circumstance confirmed by all travellers: *There are not, in the whole vast Library, two identical books.* From all these incontrovertible premises he deduced that the Library is total and that its shelves contain all the possible combinations of the twenty-odd orthographic symbols (whose number, though vast, is not infinite); that is, everything which can be expressed, in all languages. Everything is there: the minute history of the future, the autobiographies of the archangels, the faithful catalogue of the Library, thousands and thousands of false catalogues, a demonstration of the fallacy of these catalogues, a demonstration of the fallacy of the true catalogue, the Gnostic gospel of Basilides, the commentary on this gospel, the commentary on the commentary of this gospel, the veridical account of your death, a version of each book in all languages, the interpolations of every book in all books.

When it was proclaimed that the Library comprised all books, the first impression was one of extravagant joy. All men felt themselves lords of a secret, intact treasure. There was no personal or universal problem whose eloquent solution did not exist – in some hexagon. The universe was justified, the universe suddenly expanded to the limitless dimensions of hope. At that time there was much talk of the Vindications: books of apology and prophecy, which vindicated for all time the actions of every man in the world and established a store of prodigious arcana for the future. Thousands of covetous persons abandoned their dear natal hexagons and crowded up the stairs, urged on by the vain aim of finding their Vindication. These pilgrims disputed in the narrow corridors, hurled dark maledictions, strangled each other on the divine stairways, flung the deceitful books to the bottom of the tunnels, and died as they were thrown into space by men from remote regions. Some went mad. . . .

The Vindications do exist. I have myself seen two of these books, which were concerned with future people, people who were perhaps not imaginary. But the searchers did not remember that the calculable possibility of a man's finding his own book, or some perfidious variation of his own book, is close to zero.

The clarification of the basic mysteries of humanity – the origin of the Library and of time – was also expected. It is credible that those grave mysteries can be explained in words: if the language of the philosophers does not suffice, the multiform Library will have produced the unexpected language required and the necessary vocabularies and gram-mars for this language.

It is now four centuries since men have been wearying the hexagons. . . .

There are official searchers, *inquisitors*. I have observed them carrying out their functions: they are always exhaust-ed. They speak of a staircase without steps where they were almost killed. They speak of galleries and stairs with the local librarian. From time to time they will pick up the nearest book and leaf through its pages, in search of infamous words. Obviously, no one expects to discover anything.

The uncommon hope was followed, naturally enough, by deep depression. The certainty that some shelf in some hexagon contained precious books and that these books were inaccessible seemed almost intolerable. A blasphemous sect suggested that all searches be given up and that men everywhere shuffle letters and symbols until they succeeded in composing, by means of an improbable stroke of luck, the canonical books. The authorities found themselves obliged to issue severe orders. The sect disappeared, but in my child-hood I still saw old men who would hide out in the privies for long periods of time, and, with metal discs in a forbidden dicebox, feebly mimic the divine disorder.

Other men, inversely, thought that the primary task was to eliminate useless works. They would invade the hexagons, exhibiting credentials which were not always false, skim through a volume with annoyance, and then condemn entire bookshelves to destruction: their ascetic, hygienic fury is responsible for the senseless loss of millions of books. Their name is execrated; but those who mourn the 'treasures' destroyed by this frenzy overlook two notorious facts. One: the Library is so enormous that any reduction undertaken by humans is infinitesimal. Two: each book is unique, irreplaceable, but (inasmuch as the Library is total) there are always several hundreds of thousands of imperfect facsimiles – of works which differ only by one letter or one comma. Contrary to public opinion, I dare suppose that the consequences of the depredations committed by the Purifi-ers have been exaggerated by the horror which these fanatics provoked. They were spurred by the delirium of storming the books in the Crimson Hexagon: books of a smaller than ordinary format, omnipotent, illustrated, magical.

We know, too, of another superstition of that time: the Man of the Book. In some shelf of some hexagon, men rea-soned, there must exist a book which is the cipher and perfect compendium of *all the rest*: some librarian has perused it, and it is analogous to a god. Vestiges of the worship of that remote functionary still persist in the language of this zone. Many pilgrimages have sought Him out. For a century they trod the most diverse routes in vain. How to locate the secret hexagon which harboured it? Someone proposed a regressive approach: in order to locate book A, first consult book B which will indicate the location of A; in order to locate book B, first consult book C, and so on ad infinitum. . . .

I have squandered and consumed my years in adventures of this type. To me, it does not seem unlikely that on some shelf of the universe there lies a total book.* I pray the unknown gods that some man – even if only one man, and though it may have been thousands of years ago! – may have examined and read it. If honour and wisdom and happiness are not for me, let them be for others. May heaven exist, though my place be in hell. Let me be outraged and annihilated, but may Thy enormous Library be justified, for one instant, in one being.

The impious assert that absurdities are the norm in the Library and that anything reasonable (even humble and pure coherence) is an almost miraculous exception. They speak (I know) of 'the febrile Library, whose hazardous volumes run the constant risk of being changed into others and in which everything is affirmed, denied, and confused as by a divinity in delirium.' These words, which not only denounce disorder but exemplify it as well, manifestly demonstrate the bad taste of the speakers and their desperate ignorance. Actually, the Library includes all verbal

---

* I repeat: it is enough that a book be possible for it to exist. Only the impossible is excluded. For example: no book is also a stairway, though doubtless there are books that discuss and deny and demonstrate this possibility and others whose structure corresponds to that of a stairway.

structures, all the variations allowed by the twenty-five orthographic symbols, but it does not permit of one absolute absurdity. It is pointless to observe that the best book in the numerous hexagons under my administration is entitled *Combed Clap of Thunder*, or that another is called *The Plaster Cramp*; and still another *Axaxaxas Mlö*. Such propositions as are contained in these titles, at first sight incoherent, doubtless yield a cryptographic or allegorical justification. Since they are verbal, these justifications already figure, *ex hypothesi*, in the Library. I cannot combine certain letters, as *dhcmrlchtdj*, which the divine Library has not already foreseen in combination, and which in one of its secret languages does not encompass some terrible meaning. No one can articulate a syllable which is not full of tenderness and fear, and which is not, in one of those languages, the powerful name of some god. To speak is to fall into tautologies. This useless and wordy epistle itself already exists in one of the thirty volumes of the five shelves in one of the uncountable hexagons – and so does its refutation. (And *n* number of possible languages make use of the same vocabulary; in some of them, the symbol *library* admits of the correct definition *ubiquitous and everlasting system of hexagonal galleries*, but *library* is *bread* or *pyramid* or anything else, and the seven words which define it possess another value. You who read me, are you sure you understand my language?)

Methodical writing distracts me from the present condition of men. But the certainty that everything has been already written nullifies or makes phantoms of us all. I know of districts where the youth prostrate themselves before books and barbarously kiss the pages, though they do not know how to make out a single letter. Epidemics, heretical disagreements, the pilgrimages which inevitably degenerate into banditry, have decimated the population.

I believe I have mentioned the suicides, more frequent each year. Perhaps I am deceived by old age and fear, but I suspect that the human species – the unique human species – is on the road to extinction, while the Library will last on forever: illuminated, solitary, infinite, perfectly immovable, filled with precious volumes, useless, incorruptible, secret.

Infinite I have just written. I have not interpolated this adjective merely from rhetorical habit. It is not illogical, I say, to think that the world is infinite. Those who judge it to be limited postulate that in remote places the corridors and stairs and hexagons could inconceivably cease – a manifest absurdity. Those who imagined it to be limitless forget that the possible number of books is limited. I dare insinuate the following solution to this ancient problem: *The Library is limitless and periodic*. If an eternal voyager were to traverse it in any direction, he would find, after many centuries, that the same volumes are repeated in the same disorder (which, repeated, would constitute an order: Order itself). My solitude rejoices in this elegant hope.*

* Letizia Alvarez de Toledo has observed that the vast Library is useless. Strictly speaking, *one single volume* should suffice: a single volume of ordinary format, printed in nine or ten type body, and consisting of an infinite number of infinitely thin pages. (At the beginning of the seventeenth century, Cavalieri said that any solid body is the superposition of an infinite number of planes.) This silky vade mecum would scarcely be handy: each apparent leaf of the book would divide into other analogous leaves. The inconceivable central leaf would have no reverse.

THE PLEASURE
OF BOOKS

That perfect Tranquillity of Life, which is nowhere to be
found but in Retreat, a faithful Friend, and a good Library.

APHRA BEHN, *The Lucky Mistake: A New Novel* (1689)

MICHEL DE MONTAIGNE

From *Essays*, Book III

OF THREE KINDS OF ASSOCIATION

[*The first two being 'rare and exquisite friendships' and 'the
company of well-bred and beautiful women'.*]

...ASSOCIATION WITH BOOKS, which is the third kind,
is much more certain and more our own. It yields the other
advantages to the first two, but it has for its share the constancy and ease of its service. It is at my side throughout
my course, and accompanies me everywhere. It consoles
me in old age and in solitude. It relieves me of the weight
of a tedious idleness, and releases me at any time from
disagreeable company. It dulls the pangs of sorrow, unless
they are extreme and overpowering. To be diverted from a
troublesome idea, I need only have recourse to books: they
easily turn my thoughts to themselves and steal away the
others. And yet they do not rebel at seeing that I seek them
out only for want of those other pleasures, that are more
real, lively, and natural; they always receive me with the same
expression.

He may well go on foot, they say, who leads his horse
by the bridle. And our James, king of Naples and Sicily,
who, handsome, young, and healthy, had himself carried
around the country on a stretcher, lying on a wretched
feather pillow, dressed in a gown of gray cloth with a cap
to match, meanwhile followed by great regal pomp, litters,
hand-led horses of all sorts, gentlemen and officers, showed
an austerity still weak and wavering. The sick man is not to

be pitied who has a cure up his sleeve. In the practice and application of this maxim, which is very true, lies all the fruit I reap from books. Actually I use them scarcely any more than those who do not know them at all. I enjoy them, as misers enjoy treasures, because I know that I can enjoy them when I please; my soul takes its fill of contentment from this right of possession.

I do not travel without books, either in peace or in war. However, many days will pass, and even some months, without my using them. I'll do it soon, I say, or tomorrow, or when I please. Time flies and is gone, meanwhile, without hurting me. For I cannot tell you what ease and repose I find when I reflect that they are at my side to give me pleasure at my own time, and when I recognize how much assistance they bring to my life. It is the best provision I have found for this human journey, and I am extremely sorry for men of understanding who do not have it. I sooner accept any other kind of amusement, however trivial, because this one cannot fail me.

When at home, I turn aside a little more often to my library, from which at one sweep I command a view of my household. I am over the entrance, and see below me my garden, my farmyard, my courtyard, and into most of the parts of my house. There I leaf through now one book, now another, without order and without plan, by disconnected fragments. One moment I muse, another moment I set down or dictate, walking back and forth, these fancies of mine that you see here.

It is on the third floor of a tower; the first is my chapel, the second a bedroom and dressing room, where I often sleep in order to be alone. Above it is a great wardrobe. In the past it was the most useless place in my house. In my library I spend most of the days of my life, and most of the hours of the day. I am never there at night. Adjoining it is a rather elegant little room, in which a fire may be laid in winter, very pleasantly lighted by a window. And if I feared the trouble no more than the expense, the trouble that drives me from all business, I could easily add on to each side a gallery a hundred paces long and twelve wide, on the same level, having found all the walls raised, for another purpose, to the necessary height. Every place of retirement requires a place to walk. My thoughts fall asleep if I make them sit down. My mind will not budge unless my legs move it. Those who study without a book are all in the same boat.

The shape of my library is round, the only flat side being the part needed for my table and chair; and curving round me it presents at a glance all my books, arranged in five rows of shelves on all sides. It offers rich and free views in three directions, and sixteen paces of free space in diameter.

In winter I am not there so continually; for my house is perched on a little hill, as its name indicates, and contains no room more exposed to the winds than this one, which I like for being a little hard to reach and out of the way, for the benefit of the exercise as much as to keep the crowd away. There is my throne. I try to make my authority over it absolute, and to withdraw this one corner from all society, conjugal, filial, and civil. Everywhere else I have only a verbal authority, essentially divided. Sorry the man, to my mind, who has not in his own home a place to be all by himself, to pay his court privately to himself, to hide! Ambition pays its servants well by keeping them ever on display, like a statue in a market place. *Great fortune is great slavery* [Seneca]. Even their privy is not private. I have found nothing so harsh in the austere life that our monks practice as this that I observe in the orders of these men, a rule to be perpetually in company, and to have numbers of others present for any action whatsoever. I find it measurably more endurable to be always alone than never to be able to be alone.

If anyone tells me that it is degrading the Muses to use them only as a plaything and a pastime, he does not know, as I do, the value of pleasure, play, and pastime. I would almost say that any other aim is ridiculous. I live from day to day, and, without wishing to be disrespectful, I live only for myself; my purposes go no further.

In my youth I studied for ostentation; later, a little to gain wisdom; now, for recreation; never for gain. As for the vain and spendthrift fancy I had for that sort of furniture, not just to supply my needs, but to go three steps beyond, for the purpose of lining and decorating my walls, I have given it up long ago.

Books have many charming qualities for those who know how to choose them. But no blessing without a drawback: it is a pleasure that is no clearer or purer than the others; it has its disadvantages, and very weighty ones. The mind is exercised in books, but the body, whose care I have not forgotten either, remains meanwhile inactive, droops and grieves. I know of no excess more harmful to me, or more to be avoided in my declining years.

Those are my three favorite and particular occupations. I will not speak of those that I owe the world out of civic duty.

Translated by Donald M. Frame

SAMUEL PEPYS

From the *Diary*

15th October 1660. Office all the morning. My wife and I by water; I landed her at Whitefriars, she went to my father's to dinner, it being my father's wedding day, there being a very great dinner, and only the Fenners and Joyces there. This morning Mr. Carew was hanged and quartered at Charing Cross; but his quarters, by a great favour, are not to be hanged up. I was forced to go to my Lord's to get him to meet the officers of the Navy this afternoon, and so could not go along with her, but I missed my Lord, who was this day upon the bench at the Sessions house. So I dined there, and went to White Hall, where I met with Sir W. Batten and Pen, who with the Comptroller, Treasurer, and Mr. Coventry (at his chamber) made up a list of such ships as are fit to be kept out for the winter guard, and the rest to be paid off by the Parliament when they can get money, which I doubt will not be a great while. That done, I took coach, and called my wife at my father's, and so homewards, calling at Thos. Pepys the turner's for some things that we wanted. And so home, where I fell to read *The Fruitless Precaution* (a book formerly recommended by Dr. Clerke at sea to me), which I read in bed till I had made an end of it, and do find it the best writ tale that ever I read in my life . . .

10th December 1663 . . . Hence to St. Paul's Church Yard, to my bookseller's, and having gained this day in the office by my stationer's bill to the King about 40*s*. or 3*l*., I did here sit two or three hours calling for twenty books to lay this money out upon, and found myself at a great loss where to choose, and do see how my nature would gladly return to laying out money in this trade. I could not tell whether to lay out my money for books of pleasure, as plays, which my nature was most earnest in; but at last, after seeing Chaucer, Dugdale's *History of Paul's*, Stowe's *London*, Gesner, *History of Trent*, besides Shakespeare, Johnson, and Beamont's plays, I at last chose Dr. Fuller's *Worthys*, *the Cabbala or Collections of Letters of State*, and a little book, *Delices de Hollande*, with another little book or two, all of good use or serious pleasure; and *Hudibras*, both parts, the book now in greatest fashion for drollery, though I cannot, I confess, see enough where the wit lies. My mind being thus settled, I went by link home, and so to my office, and to read in Rushworth; and so home to supper and to bed. . . .

5th November 1665 (Lord's day). Up, and after being trimmed, by boat to the Cockpitt, where I heard the Duke of Albemarle's chaplain make a simple sermon: among other things, reproaching the imperfection of humane learning, he cried: 'All our physicians cannot tell what an ague is, and all our arithmetique is not able to number the days of a man;' which, God knows, is not the fault of arithmetique, but that our understandings reach not the thing.

To dinner, where a great deal of silly discourse, but the worst is I hear that the plague increases much at Lambeth, St. Martin's and Westminster, and fear it will all over the city. Thence I to the Swan, thinking to have seen Sarah but she was at church, and so I by water to Deptford, and there made a visit to Mr. Evelyn, who, among other things, showed me most excellent painting in little; in distemper, Indian incke, water colours: graveing; and, above all, the whole secret of mezzo-tinto, and the manner of it, which is very pretty, and good things done with it. He read to me very much also of his discourse, he hath been many years and now is about, about Guardenage; which will be a most noble and pleasant piece. He read me part of a play or two of his making, very good, but not as he conceits them, I think, to be. He showed me his *Hortus Hyemalis*; leaves laid up in a book of several plants kept dry, which preserve colour, however, and look very finely, better than any Herball. In fine, a most excellent person he is, and must be allowed a little for a little conceitedness; but he may well be so, being a man so much above others. He read me, though with too much gusto, some little poems of his own, that were not transcendant, yet one or two very pretty epigrams; among others, of a lady looking in at a grate, and being pecked at by an eagle that was there. Here comes in, in the middle of our discourse Captain Cocke, as drunk as a dogg . . .

27th December 1665. Up, and with Cocke, by coach to London, there home to my wife, and angry about her desiring a maid yet, before the plague is quite over. It seems Mercer is troubled that she hath not one under her, but I will not venture my family by increasing it before it be safe. Thence about many businesses, particularly with Sir W. Warren on the 'Change, and he and I dined together and settled our Tangier matters, wherein I get above 200*l.* presently. We dined together at the Pope's Head to do this, and thence to the goldsmiths, I to examine the state of my matters there too, and so with him to my house, but my wife was gone abroad to Mrs. Mercer's, so we took boat, and it being dark and the thaw having broke the ice, but not carried it quite away, the boat did pass through so much of it all along, and that with the crackling and noise that it made me fearful indeed. So I forced the watermen to land us on Redriffe side, and so walked together till Sir W. Warren and

I parted near his house and thence I walked quite over the fields home by light of linke, one of my watermen carrying it, and I reading by the light of it, it being a very fine, clear, dry night. . . .

LADY MARY WORTLEY MONTAGU

ON THE READING OF NOVELS

To the Countess of Bute.

Sept. 30, 1757.

MY DEAR CHILD, – Lord Bute has been so obliging as to let me know your safe delivery, and the birth of another daughter; may she be as meritorious in your eyes as you are in mine! I can wish nothing better to you both, though I have some reproaches to make you. Daughter! daughter! don't call names; you are always abusing my pleasures, which is what no mortal will bear. Trash, lumber, sad stuff, are the titles you give to my favourite amusement. If I called a white staff a stick of wood, a gold key gilded brass, and the ensigns of illustrious orders coloured strings, this may be philosophically true, but would be very ill received. We have all our playthings: happy are they that can be contented with those they can obtain: those hours are spent in the wisest manner, that can easiest shade the ills of life, and are least productive of ill consequences. I think my time better employed in reading the adventures of imaginary people, than the Duchess of Marlborough's, who passed the latter years of her life in paddling with her will, and contriving schemes of plaguing some, and extracting praise from others, to no purpose; eternally disappointed, and eternally fretting. The active scenes are over at my age. I indulge, with all the art I can, my taste for reading. If I would confine it to valuable books, they are almost as rare as valuable men. I must be content with what I can find. As I approach a second childhood, I endeavour to enter in the pleasures of it. Your youngest son is, perhaps, at this very moment riding on a poker with great delight, not at all regretting that it is not a gold one, and much less wishing it an Arabian horse, which he would not know how to manage. I am reading an idle tale, not expecting wit or truth in it, and am very glad it is not metaphysics to puzzle my judgment, or history to mislead my opinion. He fortifies his health by exercise; I calm my cares by oblivion. The methods may appear low to busy people; but, if he improves his strength, and I forget my infirmities, we attain very desirable ends. I shall be much pleased if you would send your letters in Mr. Pitt's packet.

I have not heard from your father of a long time. I hope he is well, because you do not mention him.

I am ever, dear child, your most affectionate mother.

My compliments to Lord Bute, and blessing to all yours.

ALAN BENNETT

From

THE UNCOMMON READER

(2006)

AT WINDSOR IT was the evening of the state banquet and as the president of France took his place beside Her Majesty, the royal family formed up behind and the procession slowly moved off and through into the Waterloo Chamber.

'Now that I have you to myself,' said the Queen, smiling to left and right as they glided through the glittering throng, 'I've been longing to ask you about the writer Jean Genet.'

'Ah,' said the president. 'Oui.'

The 'Marseillaise' and the national anthem made for a pause in the proceedings, but when they had taken their seats Her Majesty turned to the president and resumed.

'Homosexual and jailbird, was he nevertheless as bad as he was painted? Or, more to the point' – and she took up her soup spoon – 'was he as good?'

Unbriefed on the subject of the glabrous playwright and novelist, the president looked wildly about for his minister of culture. But she was being addressed by the Archbishop of Canterbury.

'Jean Genet,' said the Queen again, helpfully. 'Vous le connaissez?'

'Bien sûr,' said the president.

'Il m'intéresse,' said the Queen.

'Vraiment?' The president put down his spoon. It was going to be a long evening.

* * *

It was the dogs' fault. They were snobs and ordinarily, having been in the garden, would have gone up the front steps, where a footman generally opened them the door. Today, though, for some reason they careered along the terrace, barking their heads off, and scampered down the steps again and round the end along the side of the house, where she could hear them yapping at something in one of the yards.

It was the City of Westminster travelling library, a large removal-like van parked next to the bins outside one of the kitchen doors. This wasn't a part of the palace she saw much of, and she had certainly never seen the library there before, nor presumably had the dogs, hence the din, so having failed in her attempt to calm them down she went up the little steps of the van in order to apologise.

The driver was sitting with his back to her, sticking a label on a book, the only seeming borrower a thin ginger-haired boy in white overalls crouched in the aisle reading. Neither of them took any notice of the new arrival, so she coughed and said, 'I'm sorry about this awful racket,' whereupon the driver got up so suddenly he banged his head on the Reference section and the boy in the aisle scrambled to his feet and upset Photography & Fashion.

She put her head out of the door. 'Shut up this minute, you silly creatures' – which, as had been the move's intention, gave the driver/librarian time to compose himself and the boy to pick up the books.

'One has never seen you here before, Mr. . . .'

'Hutchings, Your Majesty. Every Wednesday, ma'am.'

'Really? I never knew that. Have you come far?'

'Only from Westminster, ma'am.'

'And you are . . . ?'

'Norman, ma'am. Seakins.'

'And where do you work?'

'In the kitchen, ma'am.'

'Oh. Do you have much time for reading?'

'Not really, ma'am.'

'I'm the same. Though now that one is here I suppose one ought to borrow a book.'

Mr. Hutchings smiled helpfully.

'Is there anything you would recommend?'

'What does Your Majesty like?'

The Queen hesitated, because to tell the truth she wasn't sure. She'd never taken much interest in reading. She read, of course, as one did, but liking books was something she left to other people. It was a hobby and it was in the nature of her job that she didn't have hobbies. Jogging, growing roses, chess or rock-climbing, cake decoration, model aeroplanes. No. Hobbies involved preferences and preferences had to be avoided; preferences excluded people. One had no preferences. Her job was to take an interest, not to be interested herself. And besides, reading wasn't doing. She was a doer. So she gazed round the book-lined van and played for time. 'Is one allowed to borrow a book? One doesn't have a ticket?'

'No problem,' said Mr. Hutchings.

'One is a pensioner,' said the Queen, not that she was sure that made any difference.

'Ma'am can borrow up to six books.'

'Six? Heavens!'

Meanwhile the ginger-haired young man had made his choice and given his book to the librarian to stamp. Still playing for time, the Queen picked it up.

'What have you chosen, Mr. Seakins?' expecting it to be, well, she wasn't sure what she expected, but it wasn't what it was. 'Oh. Cecil Beaton. Did you know him?'

'No, ma'am.'

'No, of course not. You'd be too young. He always used to be round here, snapping away. And a bit of a tartar. Stand here, stand there. Snap, snap. So there's a book about him now?'

'Several, ma'am.'

'Really? I suppose everyone gets written about sooner or later.'

She riffled through it. 'There's probably a picture of me in it somewhere. Oh yes. That one. Of course, he wasn't just a photographer. He designed, too. *Oklahoma*, things like that.'

'I think it was *My Fair Lady*, ma'am.'

'Oh, was it?' said the Queen, unused to being contradicted.

'Where did you say you worked?' She put the book back in the boy's big red hands.

'In the kitchens, ma'am.'

She had still not solved her problem, knowing that if she left without a book it would seem to Mr. Hutchings that the library was somehow lacking. Then on a shelf of rather worn-looking volumes she saw a name she remembered. 'Ivy Compton-Burnett! I can read that.' She took the book out and gave it to Mr. Hutchings to stamp.

'What a treat!' She hugged it unconvincingly before opening it. 'Oh. The last time it was taken out was in 1989.'

'She's not a popular author, ma'am.'

'Why, I wonder? I made her a dame.'

Mr. Hutchings refrained from saying that this wasn't necessarily the road to the public's heart.

The Queen looked at the photograph on the back of the jacket. 'Yes. I remember that hair, a roll like a pie-crust that went right round her head.' She smiled and Mr. Hutchings knew that the visit was over. 'Goodbye.'

He inclined his head as they had told him at the library to

do should this eventuality ever arise, and the Queen went off in the direction of the garden with the dogs madly barking again, while Norman, bearing his Cecil Beaton, skirted a chef lounging by the bins having a cigarette and went back to the kitchens.

Shutting up the van and driving away, Mr. Hutchings reflected that a novel by Ivy Compton-Burnett would take some reading. He had never got very far with her himself and thought, rightly, that borrowing the book had just been a polite gesture. Still, it was one that he appreciated and as more than a courtesy. The council was always threatening to cut back on the library and the patronage of so distinguished a borrower (or customer as the council preferred to call it) would do him no harm.

'We have a travelling library,' the Queen said to her husband that evening. 'Comes every Wednesday.'

'Jolly good. Wonders never cease.'

'You remember *Oklahoma*?'

'Yes. We saw it when we were engaged.' Extraordinary to think of it, the dashing blond boy he had been.

'Was that Cecil Beaton?' said the Queen.

'No idea. Never liked the fellow. Green shoes.'

'Smelled delicious.'

'What's that?'

'A book. I borrowed it.'

'Dead, I suppose.'

'Who?'

'The Beaton fellow.'

'Oh yes. Everybody's dead.'

'Good show, though.'

And he went off to bed glumly singing 'Oh, what a beautiful morning' as the Queen opened her book.

* * *

291

The following week she had intended to give the book to a lady-in-waiting to return, but finding herself taken captive by her private secretary and forced to go through the diary in far greater detail than she thought necessary, she was able to cut off discussion of a tour round a road-research laboratory by suddenly declaring that it was Wednesday and she had to go to change her book at the travelling library. Her private secretary, Sir Kevin Scatchard, an over-conscientious New Zealander of whom great things were expected, was left to gather up his papers and wonder why ma'am needed a travelling library when she had several of the stationary kind of her own.

Minus the dogs this visit was somewhat calmer, though once again Norman was the only borrower.

'How did you find it, ma'am?' asked Mr. Hutchings.

'Dame Ivy? A little dry. And everybody talks the same way, did you notice that?'

'To tell you the truth, ma'am, I never got through more than a few pages. How far did Your Majesty get?'

'Oh, to the end. Once I start a book I finish it. That was the way one was brought up. Books, bread and butter, mashed potato – one finishes what's on one's plate. That's always been my philosophy.'

'There was actually no need to have brought the book back, ma'am. We're downsizing and all the books on that shelf are free.'

'You mean, I can have it?' She clutched the book to her. 'I'm glad I came. Good afternoon, Mr. Seakins. More Cecil Beaton?'

Norman showed her the book he was looking at, this time something on David Hockney. She leafed through it, gazing unperturbed at young men's bottoms hauled out of Californian swimming-pools or lying together on unmade beds.

'Some of them,' she said, 'some of them don't seem altogether finished. This one is quite definitely smudged.'

'I think that was his style then, ma'am,' said Norman. 'He's actually quite a good draughtsman.'

The Queen looked at Norman again. 'You work in the kitchens?'

'Yes, ma'am.'

She hadn't really intended to take out another book, but decided that now she was here it was perhaps easier to do it than not, though, regarding what book to choose, she felt as baffled as she had done the previous week. The truth was she didn't really want a book at all and certainly not another Ivy Compton-Burnett, which was too hard going altogether. So it was lucky that this time her eye happened to fall on a reissued volume of Nancy Mitford's *The Pursuit of Love.* She picked it up. 'Now. Didn't her sister marry the Mosley man?'

Mr. Hutchings said he believed she did.

'And the mother-in-law of another sister was my mistress of the robes?'

'I don't know about that, ma'am.'

'Then of course there was the rather sad sister who had the fling with Hitler. And one became a Communist. And I think there was another besides. But this is Nancy?'

'Yes, ma'am.'

'Good.'

Novels seldom came as well connected as this and the Queen felt correspondingly reassured, so it was with some confidence that she gave the book to Mr. Hutchings to be stamped.

The Pursuit of Love turned out to be a fortunate choice and in its way a momentous one. Had Her Majesty gone for another duff read, an early George Eliot, say, or a late Henry James, novice reader that she was she might have been put off reading for good and there would be no story to tell. Books, she would have thought, were work.

As it was, with this one she soon became engrossed and, passing her bedroom that night clutching his hot-water bottle, the duke heard her laugh out loud. He put his head round the door. 'All right, old girl?'

'Of course. I'm reading.'

'Again?' And he went off, shaking his head.

The next morning she had a little sniffle and, having no engagements, stayed in bed saying she felt she might be getting flu. This was uncharacteristic and also not true; it was actually so that she could get on with her book.

'The Queen has a slight cold' was what the nation was told, but what it was not told, and what the Queen herself did not know, was that this was only the first of a series of accommodations, some of them far-reaching, that her reading was going to involve.

The following day the Queen had one of her regular sessions with her private secretary, with as one of the items on the agenda what these days is called human resources.

'In my day,' she had told him, 'it was called personnel.' Although actually it wasn't. It was called 'the servants'. She mentioned this, too, knowing it would provoke a reaction.

'That could be misconstrued, ma'am,' said Sir Kevin. 'One's aim is always to give the public no cause for offence. "Servants" sends the wrong message.'

'Human resources', said the Queen, 'sends no message at all. At least not to me. However, since we're on the subject of human resources, there is one human resource currently working in the kitchens whom I would like promoted, or at any rate brought upstairs.'

Sir Kevin had never heard of Seakins but on consulting several underlings Norman was eventually located.

'I cannot understand', said Her Majesty, 'what he is doing in the kitchen in the first place. He's obviously a young man of some intelligence.'

'Not dolly enough,' said the equerry, though to the private secretary not to the Queen. 'Thin, ginger-haired. Have a heart.'

'Madam seems to like him,' said Sir Kevin. 'She wants him on her floor.'

Thus it was that Norman found himself emancipated from washing dishes and fitted (with some difficulty) into a page's uniform and brought into waiting, where one of his first jobs was predictably to do with the library.

Not free the following Wednesday (gymnastics in Nuneaton), the Queen gave Norman her Nancy Mitford to return, telling him that there was apparently a sequel and she wanted to read that too, plus anything else besides he thought she might fancy.

This commission caused him some anxiety. Well read up to a point, he was largely self-taught, his reading tending to be determined by whether an author was gay or not. Fairly wide remit though this was, it did narrow things down a bit, particularly when choosing a book for someone else, and the more so when that someone else happened to be the Queen.

Nor was Mr. Hutchings much help, except that when he mentioned dogs as a subject that might interest Her Majesty it reminded Norman of something he had read that could fit the bill, J. R. Ackerley's novel *My Dog Tulip*. Mr. Hutchings was dubious, pointing out that it was a gay book.

'Is it?' said Norman innocently. 'I didn't realise that. She'll think it's just about the dog.'

He took the books up to the Queen's floor and, having been told to make himself as scarce as possible, when the duke came by hid behind a boulle cabinet.

'Saw this extraordinary creature this afternoon,' HRH reported later. 'Ginger-stick-in-waiting.'

'That would be Norman,' said the Queen. 'I met him in the travelling library. He used to work in the kitchen.'

'I can see why,' said the duke.

'He's very intelligent,' said the Queen.

'He'll have to be,' said the duke. 'Looking like that.'

'Tulip,' said the Queen to Norman later. 'Funny name for a dog.'

'It's supposed to be fiction, ma'am, only the author did have a dog in life, an Alsatian.' (He didn't tell her its name was Queenie.) 'So it's really disguised autobiography.'

'Oh,' said the Queen. 'Why disguise it?'

Norman thought she would find out when she read the book, but he didn't say so.

'None of his friends liked the dog, ma'am.'

'One knows that feeling very well,' said the Queen, and Norman nodded solemnly, the royal dogs being generally unpopular. The Queen smiled. What a find Norman was. She knew that she inhibited, made people shy, and few of the servants behaved like themselves. Oddity though he was, Norman was himself and seemed incapable of being anything else. That was very rare.

The Queen, though, might have been less pleased had she known that Norman was unaffected by her because she seemed to him so ancient, her royalty obliterated by her seniority. Queen she might be but she was also an old lady, and since Norman's introduction to the world of work had been via an old people's home on Tyneside old ladies held no terrors for him. To Norman she was his employer, but her age made her as much patient as Queen and in both capacities to be humoured, though this was, it's true, before he woke up to how sharp she was and how much wasted.

She was also intensely conventional and when she had started to read she thought perhaps she ought to do some of it at least in the place set aside for the purpose, namely the palace library. But though it was called the library and was indeed lined with books, a book was seldom if ever read there. Ultimatums were delivered here, lines drawn, prayer books compiled and marriages decided upon, but should one want to curl up with a book the library was not the place. It was not easy even to lay hands on something to read, as on the open shelves, so called, the books were sequestered behind locked and gilded grilles. Many of them were price-less, which was another discouragement. No, if reading was to be done it were better done in a place not set aside for it. The Queen thought that there might be a lesson there and she went back upstairs.

Having finished the Nancy Mitford sequel, *Love in a Cold Climate*, the Queen was delighted to see she had written others, and though some of them seemed to be history she put them on her (newly started) reading list, which she kept in her desk. Meanwhile she got on with Norman's choice, *My Dog Tulip* by J. R. Ackerley. (Had she met him? She thought not.) She enjoyed the book if only because, as Norman had said, the dog in question seemed even more of a handful than hers and just about as unpopular. Seeing that Ackerley had written an autobiography, she sent Norman down to the London Library to borrow it. Patron of the London Library, she had seldom set foot in it and neither, of course, had Norman, but he came back full of wonder and excitement at how old-fashioned it was, saying it was the sort of library he had only read about in books and had thought confined to the past. He had wandered through its labyrinthine stacks marvelling that these were all books that he (or rather She) could borrow at will. So infectious was his enthusiasm that next time, the Queen thought, she might accompany him.

She read Ackerley's account of himself, unsurprised to find that, being a homosexual, he had worked for the BBC, though feeling also that he had had a sad life. His dog intrigued her, though she was disconcerted by the almost veterinary intimacies with which he indulged the creature. She was also surprised that the Guards seemed to be as readily available as the book made out and at such a reasonable tariff. She would have liked to have known more about this; but though she had equerries who were in the Guards she hardly felt able to ask.

E. M. Forster figured in the book, with whom she remembered spending an awkward half-hour when she invested him with the CH. Mouse-like and shy, he had said little and in such a small voice she had found him almost impossible to communicate with. Still, he was a bit of a dark horse. Sitting there with his hands pressed together like something out of *Alice in Wonderland*, he gave no hint of what he was thinking, and so she was pleasantly surprised to find on reading his biography that he had said afterwards that had she been a boy he would have fallen in love with her.

Of course he couldn't actually have said this to her face, she realised that, but the more she read the more she regretted how she intimidated people and wished that writers in particular had the courage to say what they later wrote down. What she was finding also was how one book led to another, doors kept opening wherever she turned and the days weren't long enough for the reading she wanted to do.

But there was regret, too, and mortification at the many opportunities she had missed. As a child she had met Masefield and Walter de la Mare; nothing much she could have said to them, but she had met T. S. Eliot, too, and there was Priestley and Philip Larkin and even Ted Hughes, to whom she'd taken a bit of a shine but who remained nonplussed in her presence. And it was because she had at that time read so little of what they had written that she could not find anything to say and they, of course, had not said much of interest to her. What a waste.

She made the mistake of mentioning this to Sir Kevin.

'But ma'am must have been briefed, surely?'

'Of course,' said the Queen, 'but briefing is not reading. In fact it is the antithesis of reading. Briefing is terse, factual and to the point. Reading is untidy, discursive and perpetually inviting. Briefing closes down a subject, reading opens it up.'

'I wonder whether I can bring Your Majesty back to the visit to the shoe factory,' said Sir Kevin.

'Next time,' said the Queen shortly. 'Where did I put my book?' . . .

So in due course Her Majesty went to Wales and to Scotland and to Lancashire and the West Country in that unremitting round of nationwide perambulation that is the lot of the monarch. The Queen must meet her people, however awkward and tongue-tied such meetings might turn out to be. Though it was here that her staff could help.

To get round the occasional speechlessness of her subjects when confronted with their sovereign the equerries would sometimes proffer handy hints as to possible conversations.

'Her Majesty may well ask you if you have had far to come. Have your answer ready and then possibly go on to say whether you came by train or by car. She may then ask you where you have left the car and whether the traffic was busier here than in – where did you say you came from? – Andover. The Queen, you see, is interested in all aspects of the nation's life, so she will sometimes talk about how difficult it is to park in London these days, which could take you on to a discussion of any parking problems you might have in Basingstoke.'

'Andover, actually, though Basingstoke's a nightmare too.'

'Quite so. But you get the idea? Small talk.'

Mundane though these conversations might be they had the merit of being predictable and above all brief, affording Her Majesty plenty of opportunities to cut the exchange short. The encounters ran smoothly and to a schedule, the Queen seemed interested and her subjects were seldom at a loss, and that perhaps the most eagerly anticipated conversation of their lives had only amounted to a discussion of the coned-off sections of the M6 hardly mattered. They had met the Queen and she had spoken to them and everyone got away on time.

So routine had such exchanges become that the equerries now scarcely bothered to invigilate them, hovering on the outskirts of the gathering always with a helpful if condescending smile. So it was only when it became plain that the tongue-tied quotient was increasing and that more and more of her subjects were at a loss when talking to Her Majesty that the staff began to eavesdrop on what was (or was not) being said.

It transpired that with no prior notification to her attendants the Queen had abandoned her long-standing lines of inquiry – length of service, distance travelled, place of origin – and had embarked on a new conversational gambit, namely, 'What are you reading at the moment?' To this very few of Her Majesty's loyal subjects had a ready answer (though one did try: 'The Bible?'). Hence the awkward pauses which the Queen tended to fill by saying, 'I'm reading . . .', sometimes even fishing in her handbag and giving them a glimpse of the lucky volume. Unsurprisingly the audiences got longer and more ragged, with a growing number of her loving subjects going away regretting that they had not performed well and feeling, too, that the monarch had somehow bowled them a googly.

Off duty, Piers, Tristram, Giles and Elspeth, all the Queen's devoted servants, compare notes: 'What are you reading? I mean, what sort of question is that? Most people, poor dears, aren't reading anything. Except if they say that, madam roots in her handbag, fetches out some volume she's just finished and makes them a present of it.'

'Which they promptly sell on eBay.'

'Quite. And have you been on a royal visit recently?' one of the ladies-in-waiting chips in. 'Because the word has got round. Whereas once upon a time the dear people would fetch along the odd daffodil or a bunch of mouldy old prim-roses which Her Majesty then passed back to us bringing up the rear, nowadays they fetch along books they're reading, or, wait for it, even writing, and if you're unlucky enough to be in attendance you practically need a trolley. If I'd wanted to cart books around I'd have got a job in Hatchards. I'm afraid Her Majesty is getting to be what is known as a handful.'

Still, the equerries accommodated, and disgruntled though they were at having to vary their routine, in the light of the Queen's new predilection her attendants reluctantly changed tack and in their pre-presentation warm-up now suggested that while Her Majesty might, as of old, still inquire as to how far the presentee had come and by what means, these days she was more likely to ask what the person was currently reading.

At this most people looked blank (and sometimes panic-stricken) but, nothing daunted, the equerries came up with a list of suggestions. Though this meant that the Queen came away with a disproportionate notion of the popularity of Andy McNab and the near universal affection for Joanna Trollope, no matter; at least embarrassment had been avoided. And once the answers had been supplied the audiences were back on track and finished on the dot as they used to do, the only hold-ups when, as seldom, one of her subjects confessed to a fondness for Virginia Woolf or Dickens, both of which provoked a lively (and lengthy) discussion. There were many who hoped for a similar meeting of minds by saying they were reading Harry Potter, but to this the Queen (who had no time for fantasy) invariably said briskly, 'Yes. One is saving that for a rainy day,' and passed swiftly on.

Seeing her almost daily meant that Sir Kevin was able to nag the Queen about what was now almost an obsession and to devise different approaches. 'I was wondering, ma'am, if we could somehow factor in your reading.' Once she would have let this pass, but one effect of reading had been to diminish the Queen's tolerance for jargon (which had always been low).

'Factor it in? What does that mean?'

'I'm just kicking the tyres on this one, ma'am, but it would help if we were able to put out a press release saying that, apart from English literature, Your Majesty was also reading ethnic classics.'

'Which ethnic classics did you have in mind, Sir Kevin? The Kama Sutra?'

Sir Kevin sighed.

'I am reading Vikram Seth at the moment. Would he count?'

Though the private secretary had never heard of him he thought he sounded right.

'Salman Rushdie?'

'Probably not, ma'am.'

'I don't see', said the Queen, 'why there is any need for a press release at all. Why should the public care what I am reading? The Queen reads. That is all they need to know. "So what?" I imagine the general response.'

'To read is to withdraw. To make oneself unavailable. One would feel easier about it', said Sir Kevin, 'if the pursuit itself were less . . . selfish.'

'Selfish?'

'Perhaps I should say solipsistic.'

'Perhaps you should.'

Sir Kevin plunged on. 'Were we able to harness your reading to some larger purpose – the literacy of the nation as a whole, for instance, the improvement of reading standards among the young . . .'

'One reads for pleasure,' said the Queen. 'It is not a public duty.'

'Perhaps', said Sir Kevin, 'it should be.'

'Bloody cheek,' said the duke when she told him that night.

MAXIM GORKY

THE ICON-PAINTERS

From

IN THE WORLD
(1916)

Translated by Gertrude M. Foakes

THE ICON-PAINTING workshop occupied two rooms in a large house partly built of stone. One room had three windows overlooking the yard and one overlooking the garden; the other room had one window overlooking the garden and another facing the street. These windows were small and square, and their panes, irisated by age, unwillingly admitted the pale, diffused light of the winter days. Both rooms were closely packed with tables, and at every table sat the bent figures of icon-painters. From the ceilings were suspended glass balls full of water, which reflected the light from the lamps and threw it upon the square surfaces of the icons in white cold rays.

It was hot and stifling in the workshop. Here worked about twenty men, icon-painters, from Palekh, Kholia, and Mstir. They all sat down in cotton overalls with unfastened collars. They had drawers made of ticking, and were barefooted, or wore sandals. Over their heads stretched, like a blue veil, the smoke of cheap tobacco, and there was a thick smell of size, varnish, and rotten eggs. The melancholy Vlandimirski song flowed slowly, like resin:

How depraved the people have now become;
The boy ruined the girl, and cared not who knew.

They sang other melancholy songs, but this was the one they sang most often. Its long-drawn-out movement did not hinder one from thinking, did not impede the movement of the fine brush, made of weasel hair, over the surface of the icons, as it painted in the lines of the figure, and laid upon the emaciated faces of the saints the fine lines of suffering. By the windows the chaser, Golovev, plied his small hammer. He was a drunken old man with an enormous blue nose. The lazy stream of song was punctuated by the ceaseless dry tap of the hammer; it was like a worm gnawing at a tree. Some evil genius had divided the work into a long series of actions, bereft of beauty and incapable of arousing any love for the business, or interest in it. The squinting joiner, Panphil, ill-natured and malicious, brought the pieces of cypress and lilac-wood of different sizes, which he had planed and glued; the consumptive lad, Davidov, laid the colors on; his comrade, Sorokin, painted in the inscription; Milyashin outlined the design from the original with a pencil; old Golovev gilded it, and embossed the pattern in gold; the finishers drew the landscape, and the clothes of the figures; and then they were stood with faces or hands against the wall, waiting for the work of the face-painter.

It was very weird to see a large icon intended for an icon-astasis, or the doors of the altar, standing against the wall without face, hands, or feet, – just the sacerdotal vestments, or the armor, and the short garments of archangels. These variously painted tablets suggested death. That which should have put life into them was absent, but it seemed as if it had been there, and had miraculously disappeared, leaving only its heavy vestments behind.

When the features had been painted in by the face-painter, the icon was handed to the workman, who filled in the design of the chaser. A different workman had to do the lettering, and the varnish was put on by the head workman himself, Ivan Larionovich, a quiet man. He had a gray face; his beard, too, was gray, the hair fine and silky; his gray eyes were peculiarly deep and sad. He had a pleasant smile, but one could not smile at him. He made one feel awkward, somehow. He looked like the image of Simon Stolpnik, just as lean and emaciated, and his motionless eyes looked far away in the same abstracted manner, through people and walls.

Some days after I entered the workshop, the banner-worker, a Cossack of the Don, named Kapendiukhin, a handsome, mighty fellow, arrived in a state of intoxication. With clenched teeth and his gentle, womanish eyes blinking, he began to smash up everything with his iron fist, without uttering a word. Of medium height and well built, he cast himself on the workroom like a cat chasing rats in a cellar. The others lost their presence of mind, and hid themselves away in the corners, calling out to one another:

'Knock him down!'

The face-painter, Evgen Sitanov, was successful in stunning the maddened creature by hitting him on the head with a small stool. The Cossack subsided on the floor, and was immediately held down and tied up with towels, which he began to bite and tear with the teeth of a wild beast. This infuriated Evgen. He jumped on the table, and with his hands pressed close to his sides, prepared to jump on the Cossack. Tall and stout as he was, he would have inevitably crushed the breast-bone of Kapendiukhin by his leap, but at that moment Larionovich appeared on the scene in cap and overcoat, shook his finger at Sitanov, and said to the workmen in a quiet and business-like tone:

'Carry him into the vestibule, and leave him there till he is sober.'

They dragged the Cossack out of the workshop, set the chairs and tables straight, and once again set to work, letting fall short remarks on the strength of their comrade, prophesying that he would one day be killed by some one in a quarrel.

'It would be a difficult matter to kill him,' said Sitanov very calmly, as if he were speaking of a business which he understood very well. . . .

My duties in the workshop were not complicated. In the morning when they were all asleep, I had to prepare the samovar for the men, and while they drank tea in the kitchen, Pavl and I swept and dusted the workshop, set out red, yellow, or white paints, and then I went to the shop. In the evening I had to grind up colors and 'watch' the work. At first I watched with great interest, but I soon realized that all the men who were engaged on this handicraft which was divided up into so many processes, disliked it, and suffered from a torturing boredom.

The evenings were free. I used to tell them stories about life on the steamer and different stories out of books, and without noticing how it came about, I soon held a peculiar position in the workshop as story-teller and reader.

I soon found out that all these people knew less than I did; almost all of them had been stuck in the narrow cage of workshop life since their childhood, and were still in it. Of all the occupants of the workshop, only Jikharev had been in Moscow, of which he spoke suggestively and frowningly:

'Moscow does not believe in tears; there they know which side their bread is buttered.'

None of the rest had been farther than Shuya, or Vladimir. When mention was made of Kazan, they asked me:

'Are there many Russians there? Are there any churches?'

For them, Perm was in Siberia, and they would not believe that Siberia was beyond the Urals.

'Sandres come from the Urals; and sturgeon – where are they found? Where do they get them? From the Caspian Sea? That means that the Urals are on the sea!'

Sometimes I thought that they were laughing at me when they declared that England was on the other side of the Atlantic, and that Bonaparte belonged by birth to a noble family of Kalonga. When I told them stories of what I had seen, they hardly believed me, but they all loved terrible tales intermixed with history. Even the men of mature years evidently preferred imagination to the truth. I could see very well that the more improbable the events, the more fantastic the story, the more attentively they listened to me. On the whole, reality did not interest them, and they all gazed dreamily into the future, not wishing to see the poverty and hideousness of the present.

This astonished me so much the more, inasmuch as I had felt keenly enough the contradiction existing between life and books. Here before me were living people, and in books there were none like them – no Smouri, stoker Yaakov, fugitive Aleksander Vassiliev, Jikharev, or washerwoman Natalia.

In Davidov's trunk a torn copy of Golitzinski's stories was found – 'Ivan Vuijigin,' 'The Bulgar,' 'A Volume of Baron Brambeuss.' I read all these aloud to them, and they were delighted. Larionovich said:

'Reading prevents quarrels and noise; it is a good thing!'

I began to look about diligently for books, found them, and read almost every evening. Those were pleasant evenings. It was as quiet as night in the workshop; the glass balls hung over the tables like white cold stars, their rays lighting up shaggy and bald heads. I saw round me at the table, calm, thoughtful faces; now and again an exclamation of praise of the author, or hero was heard. They were attentive and benign, quite unlike themselves. I liked them very much at those times, and they also behaved well to me. I felt that I was in my right place.

'When we have books it is like spring with us; when the winter frames are taken out and for the first time we can open the windows as we like,' said Sitanov one day.

It was hard to find books. We could not afford to subscribe to a library, but I managed to get them somehow, asking for them wherever I went, as a charity. One day the second officer of the fire brigade gave me the first volume of 'Lermontov,' and it was from this that I felt the power of poetry, and its mighty influence over people. I remember even now how, at the first lines of 'The Demon,' Sitanov looked first at the book and then at my face, laid down his brush on the table, and, embracing his knee with his long arms, rocked to and fro, smiling.

'Not so much noise, brothers,' said Larionovich, and also laying aside his work, he went to Sitanov's table where I was reading. The poem stirred me painfully and sweetly; my voice was broken; I could hardly read the lines. Tears poured from my eyes. But what moved me still more was the dull, cautious movement of the workmen. In the workshop everything seemed to be diverted from its usual course – drawn to me as if I had been a magnet. When I had finished the first part, almost all of them were standing round the table, closely pressing against one another, embracing one another, frowning and laughing.

'Go on reading,' said Jikharev, bending my head over the book.

When I had finished reading, he took the book, looked at the title, put it under his arm, and said:

'We must read this again! We will read it to-morrow! I will hide the book away.'

He went away, locked 'Lermontov' in his drawer, and

returned to his work. It was quiet in the workshop; the men stole back to their tables. Sitanov went to the window, pressed his forehead against the glass, and stood there as if frozen. Jikharev, again laying down his brush, said in a stern voice:

'Well, such is life; slaves of God – yes – ah!'

He shrugged his shoulders, hid his face, and went on:

'I can draw the devil himself; black and rough, with wings of red flame, with red lead, but the face, hands, and feet – these should be bluish-white, like snow on a moonlight night.'

Until close upon supper-time he revolved about on his stool, restless and unlike himself, drumming with his fingers and talking unintelligibly of the devil, of women and Eve, of paradise, and of the sins of holy men.

'That is all true!' he declared. 'If the saints sinned with sinful women, then of course the devil may sin with a pure soul.'

They listened to him in silence; probably, like me, they had no desire to speak. They worked unwillingly, looking all the time at their watches, and as soon as it struck ten, they put away their work altogether.

Sitanov and Jikharev went out to the yard, and I went with them. There, gazing at the stars, Sitanov said:

> 'Like a wandering caravan
> Thrown into space, it shone.'

'You did not make that up yourself!'

'I can never remember words,' said Jikharev, shivering in the bitter cold. 'I can't remember anything; but he, I see – It is an amazing thing – a man who actually pities the devil! He has made you sorry for him, hasn't he?"

'He has,' agreed Sitanov.

'There, that is a real man!' exclaimed Jikharev reminiscently. In the vestibule he warned me: 'You, Maxim, don't speak to any one in the shop about that book, for of course it is a forbidden one.'

I rejoiced; this must be one of the books of which the priest had spoken to me in the confessional.

We supped languidly, without the usual noise and talk, as if something important had occurred and we could not keep from thinking about it, and after supper, when we were going to bed, Jikharev said to me, as he drew forth the book:

'Come, read it once more!'

Several men rose from their beds, came to the table, and sat themselves round it, undressed as they were, with their legs crossed.

And again when I had finished reading, Jikharev said, strumming his fingers on the table:

'That is a living picture of him! Ach, devil, devil – that's how he is, brothers, eh?'

Sitanov leaned over my shoulder, read something, and laughed, as he said:

'I shall copy that into my own note-book.'

Jikharev stood up and carried the book to his own table, but he turned back and said in an offended, shaky voice:

'We live like blind puppies – to what end we do not know. We are not necessary either to God or the devil! How are we slaves of the Lord? The Jehovah of slaves and the Lord Himself speaks with them! With Moses, too! He even gave Moses a name; it means "This is mine" – a man of God. And we – what are we?'

He shut up the book and began to dress himself, asking Sitanov:

'Are you coming to the tavern?'

'I shall go to my own tavern,' answered Sitanov softly.

When they had gone out, I lay down on the floor by the door, beside Pavl Odintzov. He tossed about for a long time, snored, and suddenly began to weep quietly.

'What is the matter with you?'

'I am sick with pity for all of them,' he said. 'This is the fourth year of my life with them, and I know all about them.'

I also was sorry for these people. We did not go to sleep for a long time, but talked about them in whispers, finding goodness, good traits in each one of them, and also something which increased our childish pity.

I was very friendly with Pavl Odintzov. They made a good workman of him in the end, but it did not last long; before the end of three years he had begun to drink wildly, later on I met him in rags on the Khitrov market-place in Moscow, and not long ago I heard that he had died of typhoid. It is painful to remember how many good people in my life I have seen senselessly ruined. People of all nations wear themselves out, and to ruin themselves comes naturally, but nowhere do they wear themselves out so terribly quickly, so senselessly, as in our own Russia.

CHARLES LAMB

TWO ESSAYS OF ELIA
(1822, 1820)

DETACHED THOUGHTS ON BOOKS
AND READING

To mind the inside of a book is to entertain one's self with the forced product of another man's brain. Now I think a man of quality and breeding may be much amused with the natural sprouts of his own. – *Lord Foppington, in the Relapse.*

AN INGENIOUS ACQUAINTANCE of my own was so much struck with this bright sally of his Lordship, that he has left off reading altogether, to the great improvement of his originality. At the hazard of losing some credit on this head, I must confess that I dedicate no inconsiderable portion of my time to other people's thoughts. I dream away my life in others' speculations. I love to lose myself in other men's minds. When I am not walking, I am reading; I cannot sit and think. Books think for me.

I have no repugnances. Shaftesbury is not too genteel for me, nor Jonathan Wild too low. I can read anything which I call *a book*. There are things in that shape which I cannot allow for such.

In this catalogue of *books which are no books – biblia a-biblia* – I reckon Court Calendars, Directories, Pocket-Books, Draught Boards, bound and lettered on the back, Scientific Treatises, Almanacks, Statutes at Large: the works of Hume, Gibbon, Robertson, Beattie, Soame Jenyns, and generally, all those volumes which 'no gentleman's library should be without:' the Histories of Flavius Josephus (that learned Jew), and Paley's Moral Philosophy. With these exceptions, I can read almost anything. I bless my stars for a taste so catholic, so unexcluding.

I confess that it moves my spleen to see these *things in books' clothing* perched upon shelves, like false saints, usurpers of true shrines, intruders into the sanctuary, thrusting out the legitimate occupants. To reach down a well-bound semblance of a volume, and hope it some kind-hearted play-book, then, opening what 'seem its leaves,' to come bolt upon a withering Population Essay. To expect a Steele, or a Farquhar, and find – Adam Smith. To view a well-arranged assortment of block-headed Encyclopaedias (Anglicanas or Metropolitanas) set out in an array of russia, or morocco, when a tithe of that good leather would comfortably re-clothe my shivering folios; would renovate Paracelsus himself, and enable old Raymund Lully to look like himself again in the world. I never see these impostors, but I long to strip them, to warm my ragged veterans in their spoils.

To be strong-backed and neat-bound is the desideratum of a volume. Magnificence comes after. This, when it can be afforded, is not to be lavished upon all kinds of books indiscriminately. I would not dress a set of Magazines, for instance, in full suit. The dishabille, or half-binding (with russia backs ever) is *our* costume. A Shakespeare, or a Milton (unless the first editions), it were mere fopperty to trick out in gay apparel. The possession of them confers no distinction. The exterior of them (the things themselves being so common), strange to say, raises no sweet emotions, no tickling sense of property in the owner. Thomson's Seasons, again, looks best (I maintain it) a little torn, and dog's-eared. How beautiful to a genuine lover of reading are the sullied leaves, and worn-out appearance, nay the very odour (beyond russia), if we would not forget kind feelings in fastidiousness, of an old 'Circulating Library' Tom Jones, or

Vicar of Wakefield! How they speak of the thousand thumbs that have turned over their pages with delight! – of the lone sempstress, whom they may have cheered (milliner, or harder-working mantua-maker) after her long day's needle-toil, running far into midnight, when she has snatched an hour, ill spared from sleep, to steep her cares, as in some Lethean cup, in spelling out their enchanting contents! Who would have them a whit less soiled? What better condition could we desire to see them in?

In some respects the better a book is, the less it demands from binding. Fielding, Smollett, Sterne, and all that class of perpetually self-reproductive volumes – Great Nature's Stereotypes – we see them individually perish with less regret, because we know the copies of them to be 'eterne.' But where a book is at once both good and rare – where the individual is almost the species, and when *that* perishes,

> We know not where is that Promethean torch
> That can its light relumine –

such a book, for instance, as the Life of the Duke of Newcastle, by his Duchess – no casket is rich enough, no casing sufficiently durable, to honour and keep safe such a jewel.

Not only rare volumes of this description, which seem hopeless ever to be reprinted; but old editions of writers, such as Sir Philip Sydney, Bishop Taylor, Milton in his prose works, Fuller – of whom we *have* reprints, yet the books themselves, though they go about, and are talked of here and there, we know, have not endenizened themselves (nor possibly ever will) in the national heart, so as to become stock books – it is good to possess these in durable and costly covers. I do not care for a First Folio of Shakespeare. I rather prefer the common editions of Rowe and Tonson, without notes, and with *plates*, which, being so execrably bad, serve as maps, or modest remembrancers, to the text; and without pretending to any supposable emulation with it, are so much better than the Shakespeare gallery *engravings*, which *did*. I have a community of feeling with my countrymen about his Plays, and I like those editions of him best, which have been oftenest tumbled about and handled. – On the contrary, I cannot read Beaumont and Fletcher but in Folio. The Octavo editions are painful to look at. I have no sympathy with them. If they were as much read as the current editions of the other poet, I should prefer them in that shape to the older one. I do not know a more heartless sight than the reprint of the Anatomy of Melancholy. What need was there of unearthing the bones of that fantastic old great man, to expose them in a winding-sheet of the newest fashion to modern censure? what hapless stationer could dream of Burton ever becoming popular? – The wretched Malone could not do worse, when he bribed the sexton of Stratford church to let him whitewash the painted effigy of old Shakespeare, which stood there, in rude but lively fashion depicted, to the very colour of the cheek, the eye, the eyebrow, hair, the very dress he used to wear – the only authentic testimony we had, however imperfect, of these curious parts and parcels of him. They covered him over with a coat of white paint. By———, if I had been a justice of peace for Warwickshire, I would have clapt both commentator and sexton fast in the stocks, for a pair of meddling sacrilegious varlets.

I think I see them at their work – these sapient trouble-tombs.

Shall I be thought fantastical, if I confess, that the names of some of our poets sound sweeter, and have a finer relish to the ear – to mine, at least – than that of Milton or of Shakespeare? It may be, that the latter are more staled and rung upon in common discourse. The sweetest names, and which carry a perfume in the mention, are, Kit Marlowe, Drayton, Drummond of Hawthornden, and Cowley.

Much depends upon *when* and *where* you read a book. In the five or six impatient minutes, before the dinner is quite ready, who would think of taking up the Fairy Queen for a stop-gap, or a volume of Bishop Andrewes' sermons?

Milton almost requires a solemn service of music to be played before you enter upon him. But he brings his music, to which, who listens, had need bring docile thoughts, and purged ears.

Winter evenings – the world shut out – with less of ceremony the gentle Shakespeare enters. At such a season, the Tempest, or his own Winter's Tale –

These two poets you cannot avoid reading aloud – to yourself, or (as it chances) to some single person listening. More than one – and it degenerates into an audience.

Books of quick interest, that hurry on for incidents, are for the eye to glide over only. It will not do to read them out. I could never listen to even the better kind of modern novels without extreme irksomeness.

A newspaper, read out, is intolerable. In some of the Bank offices it is the custom (to save so much individual time) for one of the clerks – who is the best scholar – to commence upon the Times, or the Chronicle, and recite its entire contents aloud, *pro bono publico*. With every advantage of lungs and elocution, the effect is singularly vapid. In barbers' shops and public-houses a fellow will get up and spell out a paragraph, which he communicates as some discovery. Another follows with *his* selection. So the entire journal transpires at length by piece-meal. Seldom-readers are slow readers, and, without this expedient, no one in the company would probably ever travel through the contents of a whole paper.

Newspapers always excite curiosity. No one ever lays one down without a feeling of disappointment.

What an eternal time that gentleman in black, at Nando's, keeps the paper! I am sick of hearing the waiter bawling out incessantly, 'The Chronicle is in hand, Sir.'

Coming into an inn at night – having ordered your supper – what can be more delightful than to find lying in the window-seat, left there time out of mind by the carelessness of some former guest – two or three numbers of the old Town and Country Magazine, with its amusing *tête-à-tête* pictures – 'The Royal Lover and Lady G——;' 'The Melting Platonic and the old Beau,' – and such-like antiquated scandal? Would you exchange it – at that time, and in that place – for a better book?

Poor Tobin, who latterly fell blind, did not regret it so much for the weightier kinds of reading – the Paradise Lost, or Comus, he could have *read* to him – but he missed the pleasure of skimming over with his own eye a magazine, or a light pamphlet.

I should not care to be caught in the serious avenues of some cathedral alone, and reading *Candide*.

I do not remember a more whimsical surprise than having been once detected – by a familiar damsel – reclined at my ease upon the grass, on Primrose Hill (her Cythera), reading *Pamela*. There was nothing in the book to make a man seriously ashamed at the exposure; but as she seated herself down by me, and seemed determined to read in company, I could have wished it had been – any other book. We read on very sociably for a few pages; and, not finding the author much to her taste, she got up, and – went away. Gentle casuist, I leave it to thee to conjecture, whether the blush (for there was one between us) was the property of the nymph or the swain in this dilemma. From me you shall never get the secret.

I am not much a friend to out-of-doors reading. I cannot settle my spirits to it. I knew a Unitarian minister, who was generally to be seen upon Snow-hill (as yet Skinner's-street *was not*), between the hours of ten and eleven in the morning, studying a volume of Lardner. I own this to have been a strain of abstraction beyond my reach. I used to admire how he sidled along, keeping clear of secular contacts. An illiterate encounter with a porter's knot, or a bread-basket, would have quickly put to flight all the theology I am master of, and have left me worse than indifferent to the five points.

There is a class of street-readers, whom I can never contemplate without affection – the poor gentry, who, not having wherewithal to buy or hire a book, filch a little learning at the open stalls – the owner, with his hard eye, casting envious looks at them all the while, and thinking when they will have done. Venturing tenderly, page after page, expecting every moment when he shall interpose his interdict, and yet unable to deny themselves the gratification, they 'snatch a fearful joy.' Martin B——, in this way, by daily fragments, got through two volumes of Clarissa, when the stall-keeper damped his laudable ambition, by asking him (it was in his younger days) whether he meant to purchase the work. M. declares, that under no circumstance in his life did he ever peruse a book with half the satisfaction which he took in those uneasy snatches. A quaint poetess of our day has moralised upon this subject in two very touching but homely stanzas.

I saw a boy with eager eye
Open a book upon a stall,
And read, as he'd devour it all;
Which when the stall-man did espy,
Soon to the boy I heard him call,

'You Sir, you never buy a book,
Therefore in one you shall not look.'
The boy pass'd slowly on, and with a sigh
He wish'd he never had been taught to read,
Then of the old churl's books he should have had
   no need.

Of sufferings the poor have many,
Which never can the rich annoy:
I soon perceived another boy,
Who look'd as if he had not any
Food, for that day at least – enjoy
The sight of cold meat in a tavern larder.
This boy's case, then thought I, is surely harder,
Thus hungry, longing, thus without a penny,
Beholding choice of dainty-dressed meat:
No wonder if he wish he ne'er had learn'd to eat.

From THE TWO RACES OF MEN

The human species, according to the best theory I can form of it, is composed of two distinct races, *the men who borrow, and the men who lend*. . . .

To one like Elia, whose treasures are rather cased in leather covers than closed in iron coffers, there is a class of alienators more formidable than that which I have touched upon; I mean your *borrowers of books* – those mutilators of collections, spoilers of the symmetry of shelves, and creators of odd volumes. There is Comberbatch,* matchless in his depredations!

That foul gap in the bottom shelf facing you, like a great eye-tooth knocked out – (you are now with me in my little back study in Bloomsbury, reader!) – with the huge Switzer-like tomes on each side (like the Guildhall giants, in their reformed posture, guardant of nothing) once held the tallest of my folios, *Opera Bonaventuræ*, choice and massy divinity, to which its two supporters (school divinity also, but of a lesser calibre, – Bellarmine, and Holy Thomas), showed but as dwarfs, – itself an Ascapart! – *that* Comberbatch abstracted upon the faith of a theory he holds, which is more easy, I confess, for me to suffer by than to refute, namely, that 'the title to property in a book (my Bonaventure, for instance), is in exact ratio to the claimant's powers of understanding and appreciating the same.' Should he

* The poet Samuel Taylor Coleridge.

go on acting upon this theory, which of our shelves is safe?

The slight vacuum in the left-hand case – two shelves from the ceiling – scarcely distinguishable but by the quick eye of a loser – was whilom the commodious resting-place of Brown on Urn Burial. C. will hardly allege that he knows more about that treatise than I do, who introduced it to him, and was, indeed, the first (of the moderns) to discover its beauties – but so have I known a foolish lover to praise his mistress in the presence of a rival more qualified to carry her off than himself. Just below, Dodsley's dramas want their fourth volume, where Vittoria Corombona is. The remainder nine are as distasteful as Priam's refuse sons, when the Fates *borrowed* Hector. Here stood the Anatomy of Melancholy, in sober state. There loitered the Complete Angler; quiet as in life, by some stream side. In yonder nook, John Buncle, a widower-volume, with 'eyes closed,' mourns his ravished mate.

One justice I must do my friend, that if he sometimes, like the sea, sweeps away a treasure, at another time, sea-like, he throws up as rich an equivalent to match it. I have a small under-collection of this nature (my friend's gatherings in his various calls,) picked up, he has forgotten at what odd places, and deposited with as little memory at mine. I take in these orphans, the twice-deserted. These proselytes of the gate are welcome as the true Hebrews. There they stand in conjunction; natives, and naturalized. The latter seem as little disposed to inquire out their true lineage as I am. – I charge no warehouse-room for these deodands, nor shall ever put myself to the ungentlemanly trouble of advertising a sale of them to pay expenses.

To lose a volume to C. carries some sense and meaning in it. You are sure that he will make one hearty meal on your viands, if he can give no account of the platter after it. But

what moved thee, wayward, spiteful K.,* to be so importu-
nate to carry off with thee, in spite of tears and adjurations
to thee to forbear, the Letters of that princely woman, the
thrice noble Margaret Newcastle? – knowing at the time,
and knowing that I knew also, thou most assuredly wouldst
never turn over one leaf of the illustrious folio: – what but
the mere spirit of contradiction, and childish love of getting
the better of thy friend? – Then, worst cut of all! to transport
it with thee to the Gallican land –

Unworthy land to harbour such a sweetness,
A virtue in which all ennobling thoughts dwelt,
Pure thoughts, kind thoughts, high thoughts, her sex's
  wonder!

– hadst thou not thy play-books, and books of jests and
fancies, about thee, to keep thee merry, even as thou keepest
all companies with thy quips and mirthful tales? Child of
the Green-room, it was unkindly done of thee. Thy wife,
too, that part-French, better-part Englishwoman! – that *she*
could fix upon no other treatise to bear away, in kindly
token of remembering us, than the works of Fulke Greville,
Lord Brook – of which no Frenchman, nor woman of
France, Italy, or England, was ever by nature constituted to
comprehend a tittle! – *Was there not Zimmerman on Solitude?*
Reader, if haply thou art blessed with a moderate collection, be shy of showing it; or if thy heart over-floweth to
lend them, lend thy books; but let it be to such a one as
S. T. C. – he will return them (generally anticipating the
time appointed) with usury; enriched with annotations
tripling their value. I have had experience. Many are these
precious MSS. of his – (in *matter* oftentimes, and almost in

* The dramatist James Kenney.

quantity not unfrequently, vying with the originals) in no very clerkly hand – legible in my Daniel; in old Burton; in Sir Thomas Browne; and those abstruser cogitations of the Greville, now, alas! wandering in Pagan lands. – I counsel thee, shut not thy heart, nor thy library, against S. T. C.

COLETTE

MY MOTHER AND THE BOOKS

From

CLAUDINE'S HOUSE
(1922)

Translated by Una Vicenza Troubridge
and Enid McLeod

THROUGH THE OPEN top of its shade, the lamp cast its beams upon a wall entirely corrugated by the backs of books, all bound. The opposite wall was yellow, the dirty yellow of the paper-backed volumes, read, re-read and in tatters. A few 'Translated from the English' – price, one franc twenty-five – gave a scarlet note to the lowest shelf.

Halfway up, Musset, Voltaire and the Gospels gleamed in their leaf-brown sheepskin. Littré, Larousse and Bec-querel displayed bulging backs like black tortoises, while d'Orbigny, pulled to pieces by the irreverent adoration of four children, scattered its pages blazoned with dahlias, parrots, pink-fringed jellyfish and duck-billed platypi.

Camille Flammarion, in gold-starred blue, contained the yellow planets, the chalk-white frozen craters of the moon, and Saturn rolling within his orbit like an iridescent pearl.

Two solid earth-coloured partitions held together Elisée Reclus, Voltaire in marbled boards, Balzac in black, and Shakespeare in olive-green.

After all these years, I have only to shut my eyes to see once more those walls faced with books. In those days I could find them in the dark. I never took a lamp when I went at night to choose one, it was enough to feel my way, as though on the keyboard of a piano, along the shelves. Lost, stolen or strayed, I could catalogue them to-day. Almost every one of them had been there before my birth.

There was a time, before I learned to read, when I would

curl up into a ball, like a dog in its kennel, between two volumes of Larousse. Labiche and Daudet wormed their way early into my happy childhood, condescending teachers who played with a familiar pupil. Mérimée came along with them, seductive and severe, dazzling my eight years at times with an incomprehensible light. *Les Misérables* also, yes, *Les Misérables* – in spite of Gavroche; but that was a case of a reasoned passion which lived to weather coldness and long infidelities. No love lost between me and Dumas, save that the *Collier de la Reine* glittered for a few nights in my dreams upon the doomed neck of Jeanne de la Motte. Neither the enthusiasm of my brothers nor the disapproving surprise of my parents could persuade me to take an interest in the Musketeers.

There was never any question of my taste in children's books. Enamoured of the Princess in her chariot, dreaming beneath an attenuated crescent moon, and of Beauty sleeping in the wood surrounded by her prostrate pages; in love with Lord Puss in his gigantic funnel boots, I searched vainly in Perrault's text for the velvet blacks, the flash of silver, the ruins, the knights, the elegant little hooves of the horses of Gustave Doré; after a couple of pages I returned, disappointed, to Doré himself. I read the story of the Hind and that of Beauty only in Walter Crane's pure, fresh illustrations. The large characters of his text linked up picture with picture like the plain pieces of net connecting the patterns in lace. But not a single word ever passed the barrier that I erected against them. What becomes in later life of that tremendous determination not to know, that quiet strength expended on avoidance and rejection?

Books, books, books. It was not that I read so many. I read and re-read the same ones. But all of them were necessary to me. Their presence, their smell, the letters of their titles and the texture of their leather bindings. Perhaps those most hermetically sealed were the dearest. I have long forgotten the name of the author of a scarlet-clad Encyclopedia, but the alphabetical references marked upon each volume have remained for me an indelible and magic word: *Aphbicécla-diggalbymaroidphorebstevanzy.* And how I loved the Guizot whose ornate green and gold was never opened! And the inviolate *Voyage d'Anacharsis!* If the *Histoire du Consulat et de l'Empire* ever found its way to the Quais, I wager that a label would proudly proclaim its condition as 'mint'.

The twenty-odd volumes of Saint-Simon replaced each other nightly at my mother's bedside; their pages provided her with endlessly renewed pleasure, and she thought it strange that at eight years old I should sometimes fail to share in her enjoyment.

'Why don't you read Saint-Simon?' she would ask me. 'I can't understand why children are so slow in learning to appreciate really interesting books!'

Beautiful books that I used to read, beautiful books that I left unread, warm covering of the walls of my home, variegated tapestry whose hidden design rejoiced my initiated eyes. It was from them I learned, long before the age for love, that love is complicated, tyrannical and even burdensome, since my mother grudged the prominence they gave it.

'It's a great bore – all the love in these books,' she used to say. 'In life, my poor Minet-Chéri, folk have other fish to fry. Did none of these lovesick people you read of have children to rear or a garden to care for? Judge for yourself, Minet-Chéri, have you or your brothers ever heard me harp on love as they do in books? And yet I think I ought to know something about it, having had two husbands and four children!'

If I bent over the fascinating abysses of terror that opened

335

in many a romance, there swarmed there plenty of classically white ghosts, sorcerers, shadows and malevolent monsters, but the denizens of that world could never climb up my long plaits to get at me, because a few magic words kept them at bay.

'Have you been reading that ghost story, Minet-Chéri? It's a lovely story, isn't it? I can't imagine anything lovelier than the description of the ghost wandering by moonlight in the churchyard. The part, you know, where the author says that the moonlight shone right through the ghost and that it cast no shadow on the grass. A ghost must be a wonderful thing to see. I only wish I could see one; I should call you at once if I did. Unfortunately, they don't exist. But if I could become a ghost after my death, I certainly should, to please you and myself too. And have you read that idiotic story about a dead woman's revenge? I ask you, did you ever hear such rubbish! What would be the use of dying if one didn't gain more sense by it? No, my child, the dead are a peaceful company. I don't fall out with my living neighbours, and I'll undertake to keep on good terms with the dead ones!'

I hardly know what literary coldness, healthy on the whole, protected me from romantic delirium, and caused me – a little later, when I sampled certain books of time-honoured and supposedly infallible seductiveness – to be critical when I should by rights have fallen an intoxicated victim. There again I was perhaps influenced by my mother, whose innate innocence made her inclined to deny evil, even when her curiosity led her to seek it out, and to consider it, jumbled up with good, with wondering eyes.

'This one? Oh, this isn't a harmful book, Minet-Chéri,' she would say. 'Yes, I know there's one scene, one chapter . . . But it's only a novel. Nowadays writers sometimes run short of ideas, you know. You might have waited a year or two before reading it, perhaps. But after all, Minet-Chéri, you must learn to use your judgement. You've got enough sense to keep it to yourself if you understand too much, and perhaps there are no such things as harmful books.'

Nevertheless, there were those that my father locked away in his thuya-wood desk. But chiefly it was the author's name that he locked away.

'I fail to see the use of these children reading Zola!'

Zola bored him, and rather than seek in his pages for reasons that would explain why he allowed or forbade us to read him, he placed upon the index a vast, complete Zola, periodically increased by further yellow deposits.

'Mother, why aren't I allowed to read Zola?'

Her grey eyes, so unskilled at dissimulation, revealed their perplexity.

'It's quite true there are certain Zola's that I would rather you didn't read.'

'Then let me have the ones that aren't "certain".'

She gave me *La Faute de l'Abbé Mouret*, *Le Docteur Pascal* and *Germinal*, but I, wounded at the mistrust that locked away from me a corner of that house where all doors were open, where cats came and went by night and the cellar and larder were mysteriously depleted, was determined to have the others. I got them. Although she may be ashamed of it later, a girl of fourteen has no difficulty, and no credit, in deceiving two trustful parents. I went out into the garden with my first pilfered book. Like several others by Zola it contained a rather insipid story of heredity, in which an amiable and healthy woman gives up her beloved cousin to a sickly friend, and all of it might well have been written by Ohnet, God knows, had the puny wife not known the joy of bringing a child into the world. She produced it suddenly, with a blunt, crude wealth of detail, an anatomical analysis, a dwelling on the colour, odour, contortions and cries, wherein I recognised nothing of my quite country-bred experience. I felt credulous, terrified, threatened in my dawning femininity. The matings of browsing cattle, of tom cats covering their females like jungle beasts, the simple, almost austere precision of the farmers' wives discussing their virgin heifer or their daughter in labour, I summoned them all to my rescue. But above all I invoked the exorcising voice.

'When you came into the world, my last born, Minet-Chéri, I suffered for three days and two nights. When I was carrying you I was as big as a house. Three days seems a long time. The beasts put us to shame, we women who can no longer bear our children joyfully. But I've never regretted my suffering. They do say that children like you, who have been carried so high in the womb and have taken so long to come down into the daylight, are always the children that are most loved, because they have lain so near their mother's heart and have been so unwilling to leave her.'

Vainly I hoped that the gentle words of exorcism, hastily summoned, would sing in my ears, where a metallic reverberation was deafening me. Beneath my eyes other words painted the flesh split open, the excrement, the polluted blood. I managed to raise my head, and saw a bluish garden and smoke-coloured walls wavering strangely under a sky turned yellow. I collapsed on the grass, prostrate and limp like one of those little leverets that the poachers bring, fresh killed, into the kitchen.

When I regained consciousness, the sky was blue once more, and I lay at the feet of my mother, who was rubbing my nose with eau de Cologne.

'Are you better, Minet-Chéri?'

'Yes. I can't think what came over me.'

The grey eyes, gradually reassured, dwelt on mine.

'I think I know what it was. A smart little rap on the knuckles from Above.'

I remained pale and troubled and my mother misunderstood:

'There, there now. There's nothing so terrible as all that in the birth of a child, nothing terrible at all. It's much more beautiful in real life. The suffering is so quickly forgotten, you'll see! The proof that all women forget is that it is only men – and what business was it of Zola's, anyway? – who write stories about it.'

SAKI

FOREWARNED
(1919)

ALETHIA DEBCHANCE SAT in a corner of an otherwise empty railway carriage, more or less at ease as regarded body, but in some trepidation as to mind. She had embarked on a social adventure of no little magnitude as compared with the accustomed seclusion and stagnation of her past life. At the age of twenty-eight she could look back on nothing more eventful than the daily round of her existence in her aunt's house at Webblehinton, a hamlet four and a half miles distant from a country town and about a quarter of a century removed from modern times. Their neighbours had been elderly and few, not much given to social intercourse, but helpful or politely sympathetic in times of illness. Newspapers of the ordinary kind were a rarity; those that Alethia saw regularly were devoted exclusively either to religion or to poultry, and the world of politics was to her an unheeded unexplored region. Her ideas on life in general had been acquired through the medium of popular respectable novel-writers, and modified or emphasised by such knowledge as her aunt, the vicar, and her aunt's housekeeper had put at her disposal. And now, in her twenty-ninth year, her aunt's death had left her, well provided for as regards income, but somewhat isolated in the matter of kith and kin and human companionship. She had some cousins who were on terms of friendly, though infrequent, correspondence with her, but as they lived permanently in Ceylon, a locality about which she knew little, beyond the assurance contained in the missionary hymn that the human element there was vile, they were not of much immediate use to her. Other cousins she also possessed, more distant as regards relationship, but not quite so geographically remote, seeing that they lived somewhere in the Midlands. She could hardly remember ever having met them, but once or twice in the course of the last three or four years they had expressed a polite wish that she should pay them a visit; they had probably not been unduly depressed by the fact that her aunt's failing health had prevented her from accepting their invitation. The note of condolence that had arrived on the occasion of her aunt's death had included a vague hope that Alethia would find time in the near future to spend a few days with her cousins, and after much deliberation and many hesitations she had written to propose herself as a guest for a definite date some weeks ahead. The family, she reflected with relief, was not a large one; the two daughters were married and away, there was only old Mrs. Bludward and her son Robert at home. Mrs. Bludward was something of an invalid, and Robert was a young man who had been at Oxford and was going into Parliament. Further than that Alethia's information did not go; her imagination, founded on her extensive knowledge of the people one met in novels, had to supply the gaps. The mother was not difficult to place; she would either be an ultra-amiable old lady, bearing her feeble health with uncomplaining fortitude, and having a kind word for the gardener's boy and a sunny smile for the chance visitor, or else she would be cold and peevish, with eyes that pierced you like a gimlet, and an unreasoning idolatry of her son. Alethia's imagination rather inclined her to the latter view. Robert was more of a problem. There were three dominant types of manhood to be taken into consideration in working out his classification; there was Hugo, who was strong, good, and beautiful, a rare type and not very often met with; there was Sir Jasper, who was utterly vile and absolutely unscrupulous, and there was Nevil, who was not really bad at heart, but had a weak mouth and usually required the life-work of two good women to keep him from ultimate disaster. It was probable, Alethia considered, that Robert came into the last category, in which case she was certain to enjoy the companionship of one or two excellent women, and might possibly catch glimpses of undesirable adventuresses or come face to face with reckless admiration-seeking married women. It was altogether an exciting prospect, this sudden venture into an unexplored world of unknown human beings, and Alethia rather wished that she could have taken the vicar with her; she was not, however, rich or important enough to travel with a chaplain, as the Marquis of Moystoncleugh always did in the novel she had just been reading, so she recognised that such a proceeding was out of the question.

The train which carried Alethia towards her destination was a local one, with the wayside station habit strongly developed. At most of the stations no one seemed to want to get into the train or to leave it, but at one there were several market folk on the platform, and two men, of the farmer or small cattle-dealer class, entered Alethia's carriage. Apparently they had just foregathered, after a day's business, and their conversation consisted of a rapid exchange of short friendly inquiries as to health, family, stock, and so forth, and some grumbling remarks on the weather. Suddenly, however, their talk took a dramatically interesting turn, and Alethia listened with wide-eyed attention.

'What do you think of Mister Robert Bludward, eh?'

There was a certain scornful ring in his question.

'Robert Bludward? An out-an'-out rotter, that's what he is. Ought to be ashamed to look any decent man in the face.

Send him to Parliament to represent us – not much! He'd rob a poor man of his last shilling, he would.'

'Ah, that he would. Tells a pack of lies to get our votes, that's all that he's after, damn him. Did you see the way the *Argus* showed him up this week? Properly exposed him, hip and thigh, I tell you.'

And so on they ran, in their withering indictment. There could be no doubt that it was Alethia's cousin and prospective host to whom they were referring; the allusion to a Parliamentary candidature settled that. What could Robert Bludward have done, what manner of man could he be, that people should speak of him with such obvious reprobation?

'He was hissed down at Shoalford yesterday,' said one of the speakers

Hissed! Had it come to that? There was something dramatically biblical in the idea of Robert Bludward's neighbours and acquaintances hissing him for very scorn. Lord Hereward Stranglath had been hissed, now Alethia came to think of it, in the eighth chapter of *Matterby Towers*, while in the act of opening a Wesleyan bazaar, because he was suspected (unjustly as it turned out afterwards) of having beaten the German governess to death. And in *Tainted Guineas* Roper Squenderby had been deservedly hissed, on the steps of the Jockey Club, for having handed a rival owner a forged telegram, containing false news of his mother's death, just before the start for an important race, thereby ensuring the withdrawal of his rival's horse. In placid Saxon-blooded England people did not demonstrate their feelings lightly and without some strong compelling cause. What manner of evildoer was Robert Bludward?

The train stopped at another small station, and the two men got out. One of them left behind him a copy of the *Argus*, the local paper to which he had made reference.

Alethia pounced on it, in the expectation of finding a cultured literary endorsement of the censure which these rough farming men had expressed in their homely, honest way. She had not far to look; 'Mr. Robert Bludward, Swanker,' was the title of one of the principal articles in the paper. She did not exactly know what a swanker was, probably it referred to some unspeakable form of cruelty, but she read enough in the first few sentences of the article to discover that her cousin Robert, the man at whose house she was about to stay, was an unscrupulous, unprincipled character, of a low order of intelligence, yet cunning withal, and that he and his associates were responsible for most of the misery, disease, poverty, and ignorance with which the country was afflicted; never, except in one or two of the denunciatory Psalms, which she had always supposed to have been written in a spirit of exaggerated Oriental imagery, had she read such an indictment of a human being. And this monster was going to meet her at Derrelton Station in a few short minutes. She would know him at once; he would have the dark beetling brows, the quick, furtive glance, the sneering, unsavoury smile that always characterised the Sir Jaspers of this world. It was too late to escape; she must force herself to meet him with outward calm.

It was a considerable shock to her to find that Robert was fair, with a snub nose, merry eye, and rather a schoolboy manner. 'A serpent in duckling's plumage,' was her private comment; merciful chance had revealed him to her in his true colours.

As they drove away from the station a dissipated-looking man of the labouring class waved his hat in friendly salute. 'Good luck to you, Mr. Bludward,' he shouted; 'you'll come out on top! We'll break old Chobham's neck for him.'

'Who was that man?' asked Alethia quickly.

'Oh, one of my supporters,' laughed Robert; 'a bit of a poacher and a bit of a pub-loafer, but he's on the right side.'

So these were the sort of associates that Robert Bludward consorted with, thought Alethia.

'Who is the person he referred to as old Chobham?' she asked.

'Sir John Chobham, the man who is opposing me,' answered Robert; 'that is his house away there among the trees on the right.'

So there was an upright man, possibly a very Hugo in character, who was thwarting and defying the evildoer in his nefarious career, and there was a dastardly plot afoot to break his neck! Possibly the attempt would be made within the next few hours. He must certainly be warned. Alethia remembered how Lady Sylvia Broomgate, in *Nightshade Court*, had pretended to be bolted with by her horse up to the front door of a threatened county magnate, and had whispered a warning in his ear which saved him from being the victim of foul murder. She wondered if there was a quiet pony in the stables on which she would be allowed to ride out alone. The chances were that she would be watched. Robert would come spurring after her and seize her bridle just as she was turning in at Sir John's gates.

A group of men that they passed in a village street gave them no very friendly looks, and Alethia thought she heard a furtive hiss; a moment later they came upon an errand boy riding a bicycle. He had the frank open countenance, neatly brushed hair and tidy clothes that betoken a clear conscience and a good mother. He stared straight at the occupants of the car, and, after he had passed them, sang in his clear, boyish voice:

'We'll hang Bobby Bludward on the sour apple tree.'

Robert merely laughed. That was how he took the scorn

and condemnation of his fellow-men. He had goaded them to desperation with his shameless depravity till they spoke openly of putting him to a violent death, and he laughed.

Mrs. Bludward proved to be of the type that Alethia had suspected, thin-lipped, cold-eyed, and obviously devoted to her worthless son. From her no help was to be expected. Alethia locked her door that night, and placed such ramparts of furniture against it that the maid had great difficulty in breaking in with the early tea in the morning.

After breakfast Alethia, on the pretext of going to look at an outlying rose-garden, slipped away to the village through which they had passed on the previous evening. She remembered that Robert had pointed out to her a public reading-room, and here she considered it possible that she might meet Sir John Chobham, or some one who knew him well and would carry a message to him. The room was empty when she entered it; a *Graphic*, twelve days old, a yet older copy of *Punch*, and one or two local papers lay upon the central table; the other tables were stacked for the most part with chess and draughts-boards, and wooden boxes of chessmen and dominoes. Listlessly she picked up one of the papers, the *Sentinel*, and glanced at its contents. Suddenly she started, and began to read with breathless attention a prominently printed article, headed 'A Little Limelight on Sir John Chobham.' The colour ebbed away from her face, a look of frightened despair crept into her eyes. Never, in any novel that she had read, had a defenceless young woman been confronted with a situation like this. Sir John, the Hugo of her imagination, was, if anything, rather more depraved and despicable than Robert Bludward. He was mean, evasive, callously indifferent to his country's interests, a cheat, a man who habitually broke his word, and who was responsible, with his associates, for most of the poverty, misery, crime, and national degradation with which the country was afflicted. He was also a candidate for Parliament, it seemed, and as there was only one seat in this particular locality, it was obvious that the success of either Robert or Sir John would mean a check to the ambitions of the other, hence, no doubt, the rivalry and enmity between these otherwise kindred souls. One was seeking to have his enemy done to death, the other was apparently trying to stir up his supporters to an act of 'Lynch law.' All this in order that there might be an unopposed election, that one or other of the candidates might go into Parliament with honeyed eloquence on his lips and blood on his heart. Were men really so vile?

'I must go back to Webblehinton at once,' Alethia informed her astonished hostess at lunch time; 'I have had a telegram. A friend is very seriously ill and I have been sent for.'

It was dreadful to have to concoct lies, but it would be more dreadful to have to spend another night under that roof.

Alethia reads novels now with even greater appreciation than before. She has been herself in the world outside Webblehinton, the world where the great dramas of sin and villainy are played unceasingly. She had come unscathed through it, but what might have happened if she had gone unsuspectingly to visit Sir John Chobham and warn him of his danger? What indeed! She had been saved by the fearless outspokenness of the local Press.

ITALO CALVINO

From

IF ON A WINTER'S
NIGHT A TRAVELER
(1979)

Translated by William Weaver

AT THIS POINT they throw open the discussion. Events, characters, settings, impressions are thrust aside, to make room for the general concepts.

'The polymorphic-perverse sexuality . . .'

'The laws of a market economy . . .'

'The homologies of the signifying structures . . .'

'Deviation and institutions . . .'

'Castration . . .'

Only you have remained suspended there, you and Ludmilla, while nobody else thinks of continuing the reading.

You move closer to Lotaria, reach out one hand toward the loose sheets in front of her, and ask, 'May I?'; you try to gain possession of the novel. But it is not a book: it is one signature that has been torn out. Where is the rest?

'Excuse me, I was looking for the other pages, the rest,' you say.

'The rest? . . . Oh, there's enough material here to discuss for a month. Aren't you satisfied?'

'I didn't mean to discuss; I wanted to read . . .' you say.

'Listen, there are so many study groups, and the Erulo-Altaic Department had only one copy, so we've divided it up; the division caused some argument, the book came to pieces, but I really believe I captured the best part.'

* * *

Seated at a café table, you sum up the situation, you and Ludmilla. 'To recapitulate: *Without fear of wind or vertigo* is not *Leaning from the steep slope*, which, in turn, is not *Outside the town of Malbork*, which is quite different from *If on a winter's night a traveler*. The only thing we can do is go to the source of all this confusion.'

'Yes. It's the publishing house that subjected us to these frustrations, so it's the publishing house that owes us satisfaction. We must go and ask them.'

'If Ahti and Viljandi are the same person?'

'First of all, ask about *If on a winter's night a traveler*, make them give us a complete copy, and also a complete copy of *Outside the town of Malbork*. I mean copies of the novels we began to read, thinking they had that title; and then, if their real titles and authors are different, the publishers must tell us and explain the mystery behind these pages that move from one volume to another.'

'And in this way,' you add, 'perhaps we will find a trail that will lead us to *Leaning from the steep slope*, unfinished or completed, whichever it may be . . .'

'I must admit,' Ludmilla says, 'that when I heard the rest had been found, I allowed my hopes to rise.'

'. . . and also to *Without fear of wind or vertigo*, which is the one I'd be impatient to go on with now. . . .'

'Yes, me, too, though I have to say it isn't my ideal novel. . . .'

Here we go again. The minute you think you're on the right track, you promptly find yourself blocked by a switch: in your reading, in the search for the lost book, in the identification of Ludmilla's tastes.

'The novel I would most like to read at this moment,' Ludmilla explains, 'should have as its driving force only the desire to narrate, to pile stories upon stories, without trying

354

to impose a philosophy of life on you, simply allowing you to observe its own growth, like a tree, an entangling, as if of branches and leaves. . . .'

On this point you are in immediate agreement with her; putting behind you pages lacerated by intellectual analyses, you dream of rediscovering a condition of natural reading, innocent, primitive. . . .

'We must find again the thread that has been lost,' you say. 'Let's go to the publishers' right now.'

And she says, 'There's no need for both of us to confront them. You go and then report.'

You're hurt. This hunt excites you because you're pursuing it with her, because the two of you can experience it together and discuss it as you are experiencing it. Now, just when you thought you had reached an accord with her, an intimacy, not so much because now you also call each other *tu*, but because you feel like a pair of accomplices in an enterprise that perhaps nobody else can understand.

'Why don't you want to come?'

'On principle.'

'What do you mean?'

'There's a boundary line: on one side are those who make books, on the other those who read them. I want to remain one of those who read them, so I take care always to remain on my side of the line. Otherwise, the unsullied pleasure of reading ends, or at least is transformed into something else, which is not what I want. This boundary line is tentative, it tends to get erased: the world of those who deal with books professionally is more and more crowded and tends to become one with the world of readers. Of course, readers are also growing more numerous, but it would seem that those who use books to produce other books are increasing more than those who just like to read books and nothing else.

I know that if I cross that boundary, even as an exception, by chance, I risk being mixed up in this advancing tide; that's why I refuse to set foot inside a publishing house, even for a few minutes.'

'What about me, then?' you reply.

'I don't know about you. Decide for yourself. Everybody reacts in a different way.'

There's no making this woman change her mind. You will carry out the expedition by yourself, and you and she will meet here again, in this café, at six.

'You've come about your manuscript? It's with the reader; no, I'm getting that wrong, it's been read, very interesting, of course, now I remember! Remarkable sense of language, heartfelt denunciation, didn't you receive our letter? We're very sorry to have to tell you, in the letter it's all explained, we sent it some time ago, the mail is so slow these days, you'll receive it of course, our list is overloaded, unfavorable economic situation. Ah, you see? You've received it. And what else did it say? Thanking you for having allowed us to read it, we will return it promptly. Ah, you've come to collect the manuscript? No, we haven't found it, do just be patient a bit longer, it'll turn up, nothing is ever lost here, only today we found a manuscript we'd been looking for these past ten years, oh, not another ten years, we'll find yours sooner, at least let's hope so, we have so many manuscripts, piles this high, if you like we'll show them to you, of course you want your own, not somebody else's, that's obvious, I mean we preserve so many manuscripts we don't care a fig about, we'd hardly throw away yours which means so much to us, no, not to publish it, it means so much for us to give it back to you.'

The speaker is a little man, shrunken and bent, who seems to shrink and bend more and more every time anyone calls him, tugs at his sleeve, presents a problem to him, empties a pile of proofs into his arms. 'Mr. Cavedagna!' 'Look, Mr. Cavedagna!' 'We'll ask Mr. Cavedagna!' And every time, he concentrates on the query of the latest interlocutor, his eyes staring, his chin quivering, his neck twisting in the effort to keep pending and in plain view all the other unresolved queries, with the mournful patience of overnervous people and the ultrasonic nervousness of overpatient people.

When you came into the main office of the publishing firm and explained to the doormen the problem of the wrongly bound books you would like to exchange, first they told you to go to Administration; then, when you added that it wasn't only the exchange of books that interested you but also an explanation of what had happened, they sent you to Production; and when you made it clear that what mattered to you was the continuation of the story of the interrupted novels, 'Then you'd better speak with our Mr. Cavedagna,' they concluded. 'Have a seat in the waiting room; some others are already in there; your turn will come.'

And so, making your way among the other visitors, you heard Mr. Cavedagna begin several times the story of the manuscript that couldn't be found, each time addressing different people, yourself included, and each time being interrupted before realizing his mistake, by visitors or by other editors and employees. You realize at once that Mr. Cavedagna is that person indispensable to every firm's staff, on whose shoulders his colleagues tend instinctively to unload all the most complex and tricky jobs. Just as you are about to speak to him, someone arrives bearing a production schedule for the next five years to be brought up to date, or an index of names in which all the page numbers must be changed, or an edition of Dostoyevsky that has to be reset from beginning to end because every time it reads Maria now it should read Mar'ja and every time it says Pyotr it has to be corrected to Pëtr. He listens to everybody, though always tormented by the thought of having broken off the conversation with a previous postulant, and as soon as he can he tries to appease the more impatient, assuring them he hasn't forgotten them, he is keeping their problem in mind. 'We much admired the atmosphere of fantasy. . . .' ('What?' says a historian of Trotskyite splinter groups in New Zealand, with a jolt.) 'Perhaps you should tone down some of the scatological images. . . .' ('What are you talking about?' protests a specialist in the macroeconomy of the oligopolises.)

Suddenly Mr. Cavedagna disappears. The corridors of the publishing house are full of snares: drama cooperatives from psychiatric hospitals roam through them, groups devoted to group analysis, feminist commandos. Mr. Cavedagna, at every step, risks being captured, besieged, swamped.

You have turned up here at a time when those hanging around publishing houses are no longer aspiring poets or novelists, as in the past, would-be poetesses or lady writers; this is the moment (in the history of Western culture) when self-realization on paper is sought not so much by isolated individuals as by collectives: study seminars, working parties, research teams, as if intellectual labor were too dismaying to be faced alone. The figure of the author has become plural and moves always in a group, because nobody can be delegated to represent anybody: four ex-convicts of whom one is an escapee, three former patients with their male nurse and the male nurse's manuscript. Or else there are pairs, not necessarily but tendentially husband and wife, as if the shared life of a couple had no greater consolation than the production of manuscripts.

Each of these characters has asked to speak with the person in charge of a certain department or the expert in a certain area, but they all end up being shown in to Mr. Cavedagna. Waves of talk from which surface the vocabularies of the most specialized and most exclusive disciplines and schools are poured over this elderly editor, whom at first glance you defined as 'a little man, shrunken and bent,' not because he is more of a little man, more shrunken, more bent than so many others, or because the words 'little man, shrunken and bent' are part of his way of expressing himself, but because he seems to have come from a world where they still – no: he seems to have emerged from a book where you still encounter – you've got it: he seems to have come from a world in which they still read books where you encounter 'little men, shrunken and bent.'

Without allowing himself to be distracted, he lets the array of problems flow over his bald pate, he shakes his head, and he tries to confine the question to its more practical aspects: 'But couldn't you, forgive me for asking, include the footnotes in the body of the text, and perhaps condense the text a bit, and even – the decision is yours – turn it into a footnote?'

'I'm a reader, only a reader, not an author,' you hasten to declare, like a man rushing to the aid of somebody about to make a misstep.

'Oh, really? Good, good! I'm delighted!' And the glance he gives you really is a look of friendliness and gratitude. 'I'm so pleased. I come across fewer and fewer readers. . . .'

He is overcome by a confidential urge: he lets himself be carried away; he forgets his other tasks; he takes you aside. 'I've been working for years and years for this publisher . . . so many books pass through my hands . . . but can I say that I read? This isn't what I call reading. . . . In my village there were few books, but I used to read, yes, in those days I did read. . . . I keep thinking that when I retire I'll go back to my village and take up reading again, as before. Every now and then I set a book aside, I'll read this when I retire, I tell myself; but then I think that it won't be the same thing any more. . . . Last night I had a dream, I was in my village, in the chicken coop of our house, I was looking, looking for something in the chicken coop, in the basket where the hens lay their eggs, and what did I find? A book, one of the books I read when I was a boy, a cheap edition, the pages tattered, the black-and-white engravings all colored, by me, with crayons . . . You know? As a boy, in order to read, I would hide in the chicken coop. . . .'

You start to explain to him the reason for your visit. He understands at once, and doesn't even let you continue: 'You, too! The mixed-up signatures, we know all about it, the books that begin and don't continue, the entire recent production of the firm is in turmoil, you've no idea. We can't make head or tail of it any more, my dear sir.'

In his arms he has a pile of galleys; he sets them down gently, as if the slightest jolt could upset the order of the printed letters. 'A publishing house is a fragile organism, dear sir,' he says. 'If at any point something goes askew, then the disorder spreads, chaos opens beneath our feet. Forgive me, won't you? When I think about it I have an attack of vertigo.' And he covers his eyes, as if pursued by the sight of billions of pages, lines, words, whirling in a dust storm.

'Come, come, Mr. Cavedagna, don't take it like this.' Now it's your job to console him. 'It was just a reader's simple curiosity, my question. . . . But if there's nothing you can tell me . . .'

'What I know, I'll tell you gladly,' the editor says. 'Listen. It all began when a young man turned up in the office, claiming to be a translator from the whatsitsname, from the youknowwhat. . . .'

'Polish?'

'No, no, Polish indeed! A difficult language, one not many people know . . .'

'Cimmerian?'

'Not Cimmerian. Farther on. What do you call it? This person passed himself off as an extraordinary polyglot, there was no language he didn't know, even whatchamacallit, Cimbrian, yes, Cimbrian. He brings us a book written in that language, a great big novel, very thick, whatsitsname, the *Traveler*, no, the *Traveler* is by the other one, *Outside the town* . . .'

'By Tazio Bazakbal?'

'No, not Bazakbal, this was the *Steep slope*, by whosit. . . .'

'Ahti?'

'Bravo, the very one. Ukko Ahti.'

'But . . . I beg your pardon: isn't Ukko Ahti a Cimmerian author?'

'Well, to be sure, he was Cimmerian before, Ahti was; but you know what happened, during the war, after the war, the boundary adjustments, the Iron Curtain, the fact is that now there is Cimbria where Cimmeria used to be, and Cimmeria has shifted farther on. And so Cimmerian literature was also taken over by the Cimbrians, as part of their war reparations. . . .'

'This is the thesis of Professor Galligani, which Professor Uzzi-Tuzii rejects. . . .'

'Oh, you can imagine the rivalry at the university between departments, two competing chairs, two professors who can't stand the sight of each other, imagine Uzzi-Tuzii admitting that the masterpiece of his language has to be read in the language of his colleague. . . .'

'The fact remains,' you insist, 'that *Leaning from the steep slope* is an unfinished novel, or, rather, barely begun. . . . I saw the original. . . .'

'*Leaning* . . . Now, don't get me mixed up, it's a title that sounds similar but isn't the same, it's something with *Vertigo*, yes, it's the *Vertigo* of Viljandi.'

'*Without fear of wind or vertigo*? Tell me: has it been translated? Have you published it?'

'Wait. The translator, a certain Ermes Marana, seemed a young man with all the proper credentials: he hands in a sample of the translation, we schedule the title, he is punctual in delivering the pages of the translation, a hundred at a time, he pockets the payments, we begin to pass the translation on to the printer, to have it set, in order to save time. . . . And then, in correcting the proofs, we notice some misconstructions, some oddities. . . . We send for Marana, we ask him some questions, he becomes confused, contradicts himself. . . . We press him, we open the original text in front of him and request him to translate a bit orally. . . . He confesses he doesn't know a single word of Cimbrian!'

'And what about the translation he turned in to you?'

'He had put the proper names in Cimbrian, no, in Cimmerian, I can't remember, but the text he had translated was from another novel. . . .'

'What novel?'

'What novel? we ask him. And he says: A Polish novel (there's your Polish!) by Tazio Bazakbal . . .'

'*Outside the town of Malbork* . . .'

'Exactly. But wait a minute. That's what he said, and for the moment we believed him; the book was already on the presses. We stop everything, change the title page, the cover. It was a big setback for us, but in any case, with one title or another, by one author or the other, the novel was there, translated, set, printed. . . . We calculated that all this to-ing and fro-ing with the print shop, the bindery, the replacement of all the first signatures with the wrong title page – in other words, it created a confusion that spread to all the new books we had in stock, whole runs had to be scrapped, volumes already distributed had to be recalled from the booksellers. . . .'

'There's one thing I don't understand: what novel are you talking about now? The one with the station or the one with the boy leaving the farm? Or – ?'

'Bear with me. What I've told you is only the beginning. Because by now, as is only natural, we no longer trust this gentleman, and we want to see the picture clearly, compare the translation with the original. And what do we discover next? It wasn't the Bazakbal, either, it was a novel translated from the French, a book by an almost unknown Belgian author, Bertrand Vandervelde, entitled . . . Wait: I'll show you.'

Cavedagna goes out, and when he reappears he hands you a little bundle of photocopies. 'Here, it's called *Looks down in the gathering shadow*. We have here the French text of the first pages. You can see with your own eyes, judge for yourself what a swindle! Ermes Marana translated this trashy novel, word by word, and passed it off to us as Cimmerian, Cimbrian, Polish. . . .'

You leaf through the photocopies and from the first glance you realize that this *Regarde en bas dans l'épaisseur des ombres* by Bertrand Vandervelde has nothing in common with any of the four novels you have had to give up reading. You would like to inform Cavedagna at once, but he is producing a paper attached to the file, which he insists on showing you: 'You want to see what Marana had the nerve to reply when we charged him with this fraud? This is his letter. . . .' And he points out a paragraph for you to read.

363

'What does the name of an author on the jacket matter? Let us move forward in thought to three thousand years from now. Who knows which books from our period will be saved, and who knows which authors' names will be remembered? Some books will remain famous but will be considered anonymous works, as for us the epic of Gilgamesh; other authors' names will still be well known, but none of their works will survive, as was the case with Socrates; or perhaps all the surviving books will be attributed to a single, mysterious author, like Homer.'

'Did you ever hear such reasoning?' Cavedagna exclaims; then he adds, 'And he might even be right, that's the rub. . . .'

He shakes his head, as if seized by a private thought; he chuckles slightly, and sighs slightly. This thought of his, you, Reader, can perhaps read on his brow. For many years Cavedagna has followed books as they are made, bit by bit, he sees books be born and die every day, and yet the true books for him remain others, those of the time when for him they were like messages from other worlds. And so it is with authors: he deals with them every day, he knows their fixations, indecisions, susceptibilities, egocentricities, and yet the true authors remain those who for him were only a name on a jacket, a word that was part of the title, authors who had the same reality as their characters, as the places mentioned in the books, who existed and didn't exist at the same time, like those characters and those countries. The author was an invisible point from which the books came, a void traveled by ghosts, an underground tunnel that put other worlds in communication with the chicken coop of his boyhood. . . .

Somebody calls him. He hesitates a moment, undecided whether to take back the photocopies or to leave them with you. 'Mind you, this is an important document; it can't leave

364

these offices, it's the corpus delicti, there could be a trial for plagiarism. If you want to examine it, sit down here at this desk, and remember to give it back to me, even if I forget it, it would be a disaster if it were lost. . . .'

You could tell him it didn't matter, this isn't the novel you were looking for, but partly because you rather like its opening, and partly because Mr. Cavedagna, more and more worried, has been swept away by the whirlwind of his publishing activities, there is nothing for you to do but start reading *Looks down in the gathering shadow.*

TEFFI

MY FIRST
TOLSTOY
(1920)

Translated by Anne Marie Jackson

I REMEMBER ... I'm nine years old.

I'm reading *Childhood and Boyhood* by Tolstoy. Over and over again.

Everything in this book is clear to me.

Volodya, Nikolenka and Lyubochka are all living with me; they're all just like me and my brothers and sisters. And their home in Moscow with their grandmother is our Moscow home; when I read about their drawing room, morning room or classroom, I don't have to imagine anything – these are all our own rooms.

I know Natalya Savishna, too. She's our old Avdotya Matveyevna, Grandmother's former serf. She too has a trunk with pictures glued to the top. Only she's not as good-natured as Natalya Savishna. She likes to grumble. 'Nor was there anything in nature he ever wished to praise.' So my older brother used to sum her up, quoting from Pushkin's 'The Demon'.

Nevertheless, the resemblance is so pronounced that every time I read about Natalya Savishna, I picture Avdotya Matveyevna.

Every one of these people is near and dear to me.

Even the grandmother – peering with stern, questioning eyes from under the ruching of her cap, a bottle of eau de Cologne on the little table beside her chair – even the grandmother is near and dear to me.

The only alien element is the tutor, Saint-Jérôme, whom

369

Nikolenka and I both hate. Oh, how I hate him! I hate him even more and longer than Nikolenka himself, it seems, because Nikolenka eventually buries the hatchet, but I go on hating him for the rest of my life.

Childhood and Boyhood became part of my own childhood and girlhood, merging with it seamlessly, as though I wasn't just reading but truly living it.

But what pierced my heart in its first flowering, what pierced it like a red arrow was another work by Tolstoy – *War and Peace*.

I remember . . .

I'm thirteen years old.

Every evening, at the expense of my homework, I'm reading one and the same book over and over again – *War and Peace*.

I'm in love with Prince Andrei Bolkonsky. I hate Natasha, first because I'm jealous, second because she betrayed him.

'You know what?' I tell my sister. 'I think Tolstoy got it wrong when he was writing about her. How could anyone possibly like her? How could they? Her braid was "thin and short", her lips were puffy. No, I don't think anyone could have liked her. And if Prince Andrei was going to marry her, it was because he felt sorry for her.'

It also bothered me that Prince Andrei always shrieked when he was angry. I thought Tolstoy had got it wrong here, too. I felt certain the Prince didn't shriek.

And so every evening I was reading *War and Peace*.

The pages leading up to the death of Prince Andrei were torture to me.

I think I always nursed a little hope of some miracle. I must have done, because each time he lay dying I felt overcome by the same despair.

Lying in bed at night, I would try to save him. I would make him throw himself to the ground along with everyone else when the grenade was about to explode. Why couldn't just one soldier think to push him out of harm's way? That's what I'd have done. I'd have pushed him out of the way all right.

Then I would have sent him the very best doctors and surgeons of the time.

Every week I would read that he was dying, and I would hope and pray for a miracle. I would hope and pray that maybe this time he wouldn't die.

But he did. He really did! He did die!

A living person dies once, but Prince Andrei was dying forever, forever.

My heart ached. I couldn't do my homework. And in the morning . . . Well, you know what it's like in the morning when you haven't done your homework!

Finally, I hit upon an idea. I decided to go and see Tolstoy and ask him to save Prince Andrei. I would even allow him to marry the Prince to Natasha. Yes, I was even prepared to agree to that – anything to save him from dying!

I asked my governess whether a writer could change something in a work he had already published. She said she thought he probably could – sometimes in later editions, writers made amendments.

I conferred with my sister. She said that when you called on a writer you had to bring a small photograph of him and ask him to autograph it, or else he wouldn't even talk to you. Then she said that writers didn't talk to juveniles anyway.

It was very intimidating.

Gradually I worked out where Tolstoy lived. People were telling me different things – one person said he lived in

Khamovniki, another said he'd left Moscow, and someone else said he would be leaving any day now.

I bought the photograph and started to think about what to say. I was afraid I might just start crying. I didn't let anyone in the house know about my plans – they would have laughed at me.

Finally, I took the plunge. Some relatives had come for a visit and the household was a flurry of activity – it seemed a good moment. I asked my elderly nanny to walk me 'to a friend's house to do some homework' and we set off.

Tolstoy was at home. The few minutes I spent waiting in his foyer were too short to orchestrate a getaway. And with my nanny there it would have been awkward.

I remember a stout lady humming as she walked by. I certainly wasn't expecting that. She walked by entirely naturally. She wasn't afraid, and she was even humming. I had thought everyone in Tolstoy's house would walk on tiptoe and speak in whispers.

Finally *he* appeared. He was shorter than I'd expected. He looked at Nanny, then at me. I held out the photograph and, too scared to be able to pronounce my 'R's, I mumbled, 'Would you pwease sign your photogwaph?'

He took it out of my hand and went into the next room.

At this point I understood that I couldn't possibly ask him for anything and that I'd never dare say why I'd come. With my 'pwease' and 'photogwaph' I had brought shame on myself. Never, in his eyes, would I be able to redeem myself. Only by the grace of God would I get out of here in one piece.

He came back and gave me the photograph. I curtsied.

'What can I do for you, madam?' he asked Nanny.

'Nothing, sir, I'm here with the young lady, that's all.'

Later on, lying in bed, I remembered my 'pwease' and 'photogwaph' and cried into my pillow.

At school I had a rival named Yulenka Arsheva. She, too, was in love with Prince Andrei, but so passionately that the whole class knew about it. She, too, was angry with Natasha Rostova and she, too, could not believe that the Prince shrieked.

I was taking great care to hide my own feelings. Whenever Yulenka grew agitated, I tried to keep my distance and not listen to her so that I wouldn't betray myself.

And then, one day, during literature class, our teacher was analysing various literary characters. When he came to Prince Bolkonsky, the class turned as one to Yulenka. There she sat, red faced, a strained smile on her lips and her ears so suffused with blood that they even looked swollen.

Their names were now linked. Their romance evoked mockery, curiosity, censure, intense personal involvement – the whole gamut of attitudes with which society always responds to any romance.

I alone did not smile – I alone, with my secret, 'illicit' feeling, did not acknowledge Yulenka or even dare look at her.

In the evening I sat down to read about his death. But now I read without hope. I was no longer praying for a miracle.

I read with feelings of grief and suffering, but without protest. I lowered my head in submission, kissed the book and closed it.

There once was a life. It was lived out and it finished.

FAY WELDON

LILY BART'S HAT SHOP
(1992)

IT IS SAID that Gustave Flaubert wove his novel *Madame Bovary* around a press cutting he read in a local newspaper – the sorry tale of a provincial doctor's wife who, unable to face the consequences of debt and adultery, took poison and committed suicide. It is my belief that gloom, and a passion to punish the frivolous Madame Bovary for the vulgarity of her sins, clouded the great writer's judgement. He was reading about attempted suicide, not suicide. The story has come down to me through members of my own family, that though in shame and desperation Emma did indeed cram arsenic into her pretty mouth, Justin the apprentice had wisely taken the precaution of liberally mixing the stuff with sugar and she survived. Black bile poured out of her mouth, true: her limbs for a time were mottled brown, the desecration of her marriage vows took visible and outward form – but there God and Flaubert's punishment ended – Emma lived. And if man's punishment came hot upon the Almighty's – poor pretty Emma went to prison for two years for her sin – to attempt suicide was at the time both a mortal and a criminal offence – there came an end to that too, and fortunately before she had altogether lost her looks.

My grandfather taught Emma's great grandchild the violin at the New York conservatoire, which is how I happen to know the truth of the matter. Perhaps the story has become garbled through the generations, for certainly the timescale is a little strange: but the fictional universe has its own rules as it brushes up against our own. I am happy enough to accept the family version.

Flaubert, having dismissed Emma to the grave, in an elaborate coffin which her husband Charles could ill afford, chose to visit unmitigated disaster on the whole Bovary family. The debts Emma had incurred in life had to be met by Charles in what remained of his, and he was left in penury. His eventual discovery of Emma's love letters to Leon and Rodolphe upset him dreadfully – the maid Felicite having already badly damaged his faith in human nature by stealing all Emma's clothes and running off with them – and the poor man died of grief. Emma's little girl Berthe, orphaned, went to live with her grandmother, and on the old woman's death ended up working in a cotton mill, and that was the end of the Bovarys.

The version handed down by my family is far more benign. After poor Emma went to prison in Rouen, Charles visited her weekly for a time – but dressed in drab as she was, her hair pulled back and greasy, her skin still blotchy from the effects of arsenic – his adoration for her quickly waned, and his visits became infrequent and then ceased. The servant Felicite, far from stealing Emma's clothes, simply wore them around the house to keep Charles happy, and was very soon replacing Emma in her master's bed. There is some reason to believe that Felicite's affair with Charles had been going on secretly for some years, and under Emma's nose. Charles had more or less pushed Leon and Rodolphe into Emma's arms and this is a sure sign of a guilty man. But perhaps it was no bad thing. Felicite made a gift of her considerable savings to Charles and financial disaster was replaced by prosperity. Under the girl's solicitous care little Berthe bloomed and was happy. Nor was the village unduly censorious.

Although Charles found Emma plain and unappealing,

the Prison Governor at Rouen did not. Much moved by Emma's plight, he allowed her many special privileges. She ate and slept in his quarters and having a gift for sewing and a love of fabric was kept more than busy embroidering his fine uniforms. Word of Charles's involvement with Felicite having come to Emma, she did not hesitate to accept the Governor's offer when her prison term was up, of a boat fare to New York. He was after all a married man.

In New York Emma quickly found work in Lily Bart's Hat Shop. Lily Bart, you may remember from the Edith Wharton novel *The House of Mirth* – most eloquently filmed in Hollywood, starring the delectable Scully from *The X-Files* – was the unfortunate young woman whose single act of sexual indiscretion in High Society led to her downfall. Cast out from decent company and reduced to penury, Lily, according to Wharton, was obliged to take work in a millinery shop but soon died from sheer despond.

My family assure me that Wharton's desire for a pointed tragedy must have got the better of her – the truth, and Wharton knew it well enough, was that Lily, though she could not sew for peanuts, was good at figures and soon took over the business: far from fading away she flourished, as did the hat shop. All the rich dowagers of New York flocked to its doors to buy, as did all the tragic heroines of literature, to work.

Customers would find themselves welcomed by none other than the lovely Anna Karenina from Moscow, who had escaped her author in the nick of time, saved herself from the iron wheels of the suicide train and bought a passage to the new world. Norah Krogstad from Norway, allowed by the forward thinking playwright Ibsen to flee from home rather than destroy herself, found the miracle came true in New York. Earning as much as man she could be at one with man. Effie Brieff from Prussia, spared the fate of social obloquy, made an excellent seamstress and quickly regained her health and youthful high spirits.

Pretty little Emma Bovary was more than happy in this company, and many were the tales of love and loss and new determination that were exchanged amongst the women, and many an account of the villainy of men. All were especially fond of Emma, who, being a most imaginative milliner found great favour with the customers, some of whom, being the wives of meat barons, scarcely knew how to arrange a scarf let alone fix a hat.

There was some small trouble amongst the workforce when on one occasion Mr. Rochester came round to buy a grey bonnet, untrimmed, for his wife Jane Eyre, and Emma was found alone in the back room with him, choosing scarlet ribbons. But Emma, reminded that Rochester had in all probability murdered his first wife by pushing her off a roof, agreed not to pursue the matter. Instead, the better to keep her mind off the delights off illicit love, she remembered her role as mother and sent for little Berthe. Charles and Felicite, now having twin sons of their own, were happy enough to see the girl go: she was too like her mother for comfort. Berthe showed considerable musical talent, was enrolled in the New York conservatoire, and within the year had married Lord Henry Ashton of Lammermoor, a baritone. It is thanks to Berthe and Henry's eldest daughter, a chatty little thing, to whom my grandfather taught the violin, that I come to know so much about Lily Bart's Hat Shop.

JASPER FFORDE

WUTHERING HEIGHTS

From

THE WELL OF LOST PLOTS

(2003)

[Thursday Next and mentor Miss Havisham at Jurisfiction – 'the policing agency that works inside books' – do some routine peace-keeping in Emily Brontë's novel.]

IT WAS SNOWING when we arrived and the wind whipped the flakes into something akin to a large cloud of excitable winter midges. The house was a lot smaller than I imagined but no less shabby, even under the softening cloak of snow; the shutters hung askew and only the faintest glimmer of light showed from within. It was clear we were visiting the house not in the good days of old Mr. Earnshaw but in the tenure of Mr. Heathcliff, whose barbaric hold over the house seemed to be reflected in the dour and windswept abode that we approached.

Our feet crunched on the fresh snow as we arrived at the front door and rapped upon the gnarled wood. It was answered, after a very long pause, by an old and sinewy man who looked at us both in turn with a sour expression before recognition dawned across his tired features and he launched into an excited gabble:

'It's bonny behaviour, lurking amang t' fields, after twelve o' t' night, wi' that fahl, flaysome divil of a gipsy, Heathcliff! They think I'm blind; but I'm noan: nowt ut t' soart! – I seed young Linton boath coming and going, and I seed YAH, yah gooid-fur-nowt, slatternly witch! nip up and bolt into th' house, t' minute yah heard t' maister's horse-fit clatter up t' road!'

'Never mind all that!' exclaimed Miss Havisham, to whom patience was an alien concept. 'Let us in, Joseph, or you'll be feeling my boot upon your trousers!'

He grumbled but opened the door anyway. We stepped in amongst a swirl of snowflakes and tramped our feet upon the mat as the door was latched behind us.

'What did he say?' I asked as Joseph carried on muttering to himself under his breath.

'I have absolutely no idea,' replied Miss Havisham, shaking the snow from her faded bridal veil. 'In fact, *nobody* does. Come, you are to meet the others. For the rage counselling session, we insist that every major character within *Heights* attends.'

There was no introductory lobby or passage to the room. The front door opened into a large family sitting room where six people were clustered around the hearth. One of the men rose politely and inclined his head in greeting. This, I learned later, was Edgar Linton, husband of Catherine Earnshaw, who sat next to him on the wooden settle and glowered meditatively into the fire. Next to them was a dissolute-looking man who appeared to be asleep, or drunk, or quite possibly both. It was clear that they were waiting for us, and equally clear from the lack of enthusiasm that counselling wasn't high on their list of priorities – or interests.

'Good evening, everyone,' said Miss Havisham, 'and I'd like to thank you all for attending this Jurisfiction Rage Counselling session.'

She sounded almost friendly; it was quite out of character and I wondered how long she could keep it up.

'This is Miss Next, who will be observing this evening's session,' she went on. 'Now, I want us all to join hands and create a circle of trust to welcome her to the group. Where's Heathcliff?'

'I have no idea where that scoundrel might be!' declaimed Linton angrily. 'Face down in a bog for all I care – the devil may take him and not before time!'

'Oh!' cried Catherine, withdrawing her hand from Edgar's. 'Why do you hate him so? He, who loved me more than you ever could –!'

'Now, now,' interrupted Havisham in a soothing tone. 'Remember what we said last week about name-calling? Edgar, I think you should apologise to Catherine for calling Heathcliff a scoundrel, and Catherine, you did promise last week not to mention how much you were in love with Heathcliff in front of your husband.'

They grumbled their apologies.

'Heathcliff is due here any moment,' said another servant, who I assumed was Nelly Dean. 'His agent said he had to do some publicity. Can we not start without him?'

Miss Havisham looked at her watch.

'We could get past the introductions, I suppose,' she replied, obviously keen to finish this up and go home. 'Perhaps we could introduce ourselves to Miss Next and sum up our feelings at the same time. Edgar, would you mind?'

'Me? Oh, very well. My name is Edgar Linton, true owner of Thrushcross Grange, and I hate and despise Heathcliff because no matter what I do, my wife Catherine is still in love with him.'

'My name is Hindley Earnshaw,' slurred the drunk, 'old Mr. Earnshaw's eldest son. I hate and despise Heathcliff because my father preferred Heathcliff to me, and later, because that scoundrel cheated me out of my birthright.'

'That was very good, Hindley,' said Miss Havisham, 'not one single swear word. I think we're making good progress. Who's next?'

'I am Hareton Earnshaw,' said a sullen-looking youth

who stared at the table as he spoke and clearly resented these gatherings more than most, 'son of Hindley and Frances. I hate and despise Heathcliff because he treats me as little more than a dog – and it's not as though I did anything against him, neither; he punishes me because my *father* treated him like a servant.'

'I am Isabella,' announced a good-looking woman, 'sister of Edgar. I hate and despise Heathcliff because he lied to me, abused me, beat me and tried to kill me. Then, after I was dead, he stole our son and used him to gain control of the Linton inheritance.'

'Lot of rage in *that* one,' whispered Miss Havisham. 'Do you see a pattern beginning to emerge?'

'That they don't much care for Heathcliff?' I whispered back.

'Does it show that badly?' she replied, a little crestfallen that her counselling didn't seem to be working as well as she'd hoped.

'I am Catherine Linton,' said a confident and headstrong young girl of perhaps no more than sixteen, 'daughter of Edgar and Catherine. I hate and despise Heathcliff because he kept me prisoner for five days away from my dying father to force me to marry Linton – solely to gain the title of Thrushcross Grange, the true Linton residence.'

'I am Linton,' announced a very sickly looking child, coughing into a pocket handkerchief, 'son of Heathcliff and Isabella. I hate and despise Heathcliff because he took away the only possible happiness I might have known, and let me die a captive, a pawn in his struggle for ultimate revenge.'

'Hear, hear,' murmured Catherine Linton.

'I am Catherine Earnshaw,' said the last woman, who looked around at the small group disdainfully, 'and I *love* Heathcliff more than life itself!'

The group groaned audibly, several members shook their heads sadly and the younger Catherine did the 'fingers down throat' gesture.

'None of you know him the way I do, and if you had treated him with kindness instead of hatred none of this would have happened!'

'Deceitful harlot!' yelled Hindley, leaping to his feet. 'If you hadn't decided to marry Edgar for power and position, Heathcliff might have been half reasonable – no, you brought all this on yourself, you selfish little minx!'

There was applause at this, despite Havisham's attempts to keep order.

'He is a *real* man,' continued Catherine, amid a barracking from the group, 'a Byronic hero who transcends moral and social law; my love for Heathcliff resembles the eternal rocks. Group, I *am* Heathcliff! He's always, always in my mind: not as a pleasure, any more than I am always a pleasure to myself, but as my own being!'

Isabella thumped the table and waved her finger angrily at Catherine.

'A *real* man would love and cherish the one he married,' she shouted, 'not throw a carving knife at her and use and abuse all those around him in a never-ending quest for ultimate revenge for some perceived slight of twenty years ago! So what if Hindley treated him badly? A good Christian man would forgive him and learn to live in peace!'

'Ah!' said the young Catherine, also jumping up and yelling to be heard above the uproar of accusations and pent-up frustrations. 'There we have the nub of the problem. Heathcliff is as far from Christian as one can be; a devil in human form who seeks to ruin all those about him!'

'I agree with Catherine,' said Linton weakly. 'The man is wicked and rotten to the core!'

'Come outside and say that!' yelled the elder Catherine, brandishing a fist.

'You would have him catch a chill and die, I suppose?' replied the younger Catherine defiantly, glaring at the mother who had died giving birth to her. 'It was your haughty spoilt airs that got us into this whole stupid mess in the first place! If you loved him as much as you claim, why didn't you just marry him and have done with it?'

'CAN WE HAVE SOME ORDER PLEASE!' yelled Miss Havisham so loudly that the whole group jumped. They looked a bit sheepish and sat down, grumbling slightly.

'Thank you. Now, all this yelling is *not* going to help, and if we are to do anything about the rage inside *Wuthering Heights* we are going to have to act like civilised human beings and discuss our feelings sensibly.'

'Hear, hear,' said a voice from the shadows. The group fell silent and turned in the direction of the newcomer, who stepped into the light accompanied by two minders and someone who looked like his agent. The newcomer was dark, swarthy and extremely handsome. Up until meeting him I had never comprehended why the characters in *Wuthering Heights* behaved in the sometimes irrational ways that they did; but after witnessing the glowering good looks, the piercing dark eyes, I understood. Heathcliff had an almost electrifying charisma; he could have charmed a cobra into a knot.

'Heathcliff!' cried Catherine, leaping into his arms and hugging him tightly. 'Oh, Heathcliff, my darling, how much I've missed you!'

'Bah!' cried Edgar, swishing his cane through the air in anger. 'Put down my wife immediately or I swear to God I shall –'

'Shall what? enquired Heathcliff. 'You gutless popinjay!

My dog has more valour in its pizzle than you possess in your entire body! And Linton, you weakling, what did you say about me being "wicked and rotten"?'

'Nothing,' said Linton quietly.

'Mr. Heathcliff,' said Miss Havisham sternly, 'it doesn't pay to be late for these sessions, nor to aggravate your co-characters.'

'The devil take your sessions, Miss Havisham,' he said angrily. 'Who is the star of this novel? Who do the readers expect to see when they pick up this book? Me. Who has won the "Most Troubled Romantic Lead" at the Book World Awards seventy-seven times in a row? Me. All me. Without me, *Heights* is a tediously overlong provincial potboiler of insignificant interest. I am the star of this book and do as I please, my lady, and you can take that to the Bellman, the Council, or all the way to the Great Panjandrum for all I care!'

He pulled a signed glossy photo of himself from his breast pocket and passed it to me with a wink. The odd thing was, I actually *recognised* him. He had been acting with great success in Hollywood under the name of Buck Stallion, which probably explained where he got his money from; he could have bought Thrushcross Grange and Wuthering Heights three times over on his salary.

'The Council of Genres has decreed that you *will* attend the sessions, Heathcliff,' said Havisham coldly. 'If this book is to survive we have to control the emotions within it; as it is the novel is three times more barbaric than when first penned – left to its own devices it won't be long before murder and mayhem start to take over completely. Remember what happened to that once gentle comedy of manners, *Titus Andronicus*? It's now the daftest, most cannibalistic bloodfest in the whole of Shakespeare. *Heights* will go the same way unless you can all somehow contain your anger and resentment!'

'I don't want to be made into a pie!' moaned Linton.

'Brave speech,' replied Heathcliff sardonically, *very* brave.' He leaned closer to Miss Havisham, who stood her ground defiantly. 'Let me "share" something with your little group. *Wuthering Heights* and all who live within her may go to the devil for all I care. It has served its purpose as I honed the delicate art of treachery and revenge – but I'm now bigger than this book and bigger than all of you. There are better novels waiting for me out there, that know how to properly service a character of my depth!'

There was a gasp from the assembled characters as this new intelligence sank in. Without Heathcliff there would be no book – and in consequence, none of them, either.

'You wouldn't make it into *Spot's Birthday* without the Council's permission,' growled Havisham. 'Try and leave *Heights* and we'll make you wish you'd never been written!'

Heathcliff laughed.

'Nonsense! The Council has urgent need of characters such as I; leaving me stuck in the classics where I am only ever read by bored English students is a waste of one of the finest romantic leads ever written. Mark my words, the Council will do whatever it takes to attract a greater readership – a transfer will not be opposed by them or anyone else, I can assure you of *that*!'

'What about us?' wailed Linton, coughing and on the verge of tears. 'We'll be reduced to text!'

'Best thing for all of you!' growled Heathcliff. 'And I'll be there at the shoreline, ready to rejoice at your last strangled cry as you dip beneath the waves!'

'And me?' asked Catherine.

'You will come with me.' Heathcliff smiled, softening.

'You and I will live again in a modern novel, without all these trappings of Victorian rectitude; I thought we could reside in a spy thriller somewhere, and have a boxer puppy with one ear that goes down –'

There was a loud detonation and the front door exploded inwards in a cloud of wood splinters and dust. Havisham instantly pushed Heathcliff to the ground and laid herself across him, yelling:

'Take cover!'

She fired her small derringer as a masked man jumped through the smoking doorway firing a machine gun. Havisham's bullet struck home and the figure crumpled in a heap. One of Heathcliff's two minders took rounds in the neck and chest from the first assailant but the second minder pulled out his own sub-machine gun and opened up as more assassins ran in. Linton fainted on the spot, quickly followed by Isabella and Edgar. At least it stopped them screaming. I drew my gun and fired along with the minder and Havisham as another masked figure came through the door; we got him but one of his bullets caught the second bodyguard in the head, and he dropped lifeless to the flags. I crawled across to Havisham and also laid myself across Heathcliff, who whimpered:

'Help me! Don't let them kill me! I don't want to die!'

'Shut up!' yelled Havisham, and Heathcliff was instantly quiet. I looked around. His agent was cowering under a briefcase and the rest of the cast were hiding beneath the oak table. There was a pause.

'What's going on?' I hissed.

'ProCath attack,' murmured Havisham, reloading her pistol in the sudden quiet. 'Support of the young Catherine and hatred of Heathcliff run deep in the BookWorld; usually it's only a lone gunman – I've never seen anything this well coordinated before. I'm going to jump out with Heathcliff; I'll be back for you straight away.'

She mumbled a few words but nothing happened. She tried them again out loud but still nothing.

'The devil take them!' she muttered, pulling her mobile footnoterphone from the folds of her wedding dress. 'They must be using a textual sieve.'

'What's a textual sieve?'

'I don't know – it's never fully explained.'

She looked at the mobile footnoterphone and shook it despairingly.

'Blast! No signal. Where's the nearest footnoterphone?'

'In the kitchen,' replied Nelly Dean, 'next to the bread basket.'

'We have to get word to the Bellman. Thursday, I want you to go to the kitchen –'

But she never got to finish her sentence as a barrage of machine-gun fire struck the house, decimating the windows and shutters; the curtains danced as they were shredded, the plaster erupting off the wall as the shots slammed into it. We kept our heads down as Catherine screamed, Linton woke up only to faint again, Hindley took a swig from a hip flask and Heathcliff convulsed with fear beneath us. After about ten minutes the firing stopped. Dust hung lazily in the air and we were covered with plaster, shards of glass and wood chips.

'Havisham!' said a voice on a bullhorn from outside. 'We wish you no harm! Just surrender Heathcliff and we'll leave you alone!'

'No!' cried the older Catherine, who had crawled across to us and was trying to clasp Heathcliff's head in her hands. 'Heathcliff, don't leave me!'

'I have no intention of doing any such thing,' he said in

a muffled voice, nose pressed hard into the flags by myself and Havisham's combined weight. 'Havisham, I hope you remember your orders.'

'Send out Heathcliff and we will spare you and your apprentice!' yelled the bullhorn again. 'Stand in our way and you'll both be terminated!'

'Do they mean it?' I asked.

'Oh, yes,' replied Havisham grimly. 'A group of ProCaths attempted to hijack Madame Bovary last year to force the Council to relinquish Heathcliff.'

'What happened?'

'The ones who survived were reduced to text,' replied Havisham, 'but it hasn't stopped the ProCath movement. Do you think you can get to the footnoterphone?'

'Sure – I mean, yes, Miss Havisham.'

I crawled towards the kitchen.

'We'll give you two minutes,' said the voice on the bullhorn again. 'After that, we're coming in.'

'I have a better deal,' yelled Havisham.

There was a pause.

'And that is?' spoke the bullhorn.

'Leave now and I will be merciful when I find you.'

'I think,' replied the voice on the bullhorn, 'that we'll stick to *my* plan. You have one minute forty-five seconds.'

I reached the doorway of the kitchen, which was as devastated as the living room. Flour and beans from broken storage jars were strewn across the floor and a flurry of snowflakes were blowing in through the windows. I found the footnoterphone; it had been riddled with machine-gun fire. I cursed and crawled rapidly back towards the living room. I caught Havisham's eye and shook my head. She signalled for me to look out the back way and I did, going into the darkness of the pantry to peer out. I could see two

393

of them, sitting in the snow, weapons ready. I dashed back to Havisham.

'How does it look?'

'Two at the back that I can see.'

'And at least three at the front,' she added. 'I'm open to suggestions.'

'How about giving them Heathcliff?' came a chorus of voices.

'*Other* than that?'

'I can try and get behind them,' I muttered, 'if you keep them pinned down –'

I was interrupted by an unearthly cry of terror from outside, followed by a sort of crunching noise, then another cry and sporadic machine-gun fire. There was a large thump and another shot, then a cry, then the ProCaths at the back started to open fire, too; but not at the house – at some unseen menace. Havisham and I exchanged looks and shrugged as a man came running into the house in panic; he was still holding his pistol, and because of that, his fate was sealed. Havisham fired two shots into him and he fell stone dead next to us, a look of abject terror on his face. There were a few more gunshots, another agonised cry, then silence. I shivered, and got up to peer cautiously from the door. There was nothing outside except the soft snow, disturbed occasionally by foot marks.

We found only one body, tossed on to the roof of the barn, but there was a great deal of blood, and what looked like the paw tracks of something very large and feline. I was staring at the dinner-plate-sized footprint slowly being obscured by the falling snow when Havisham laid her hand on my shoulder.

'Big Martin,' she said softly. 'He must have been following you.'

'Is he still?' I asked, understandably concerned.

'Who knows?' replied Miss Havisham. 'Big Martin is a law unto himself. Come back inside.'

We returned to where the cast were dusting themselves down. Joseph was muttering to himself and trying to block the windows up with blankets.

'Well,' said Miss Havisham, clapping her hands together, 'that was an exciting session, wasn't it?'

'I am still leaving this appalling book,' retorted Heathcliff, who was back on full obnoxious form again.

'No you're *not*,' replied Havisham.

'You just try and stop –'

Miss Havisham, who was fed up with pussyfooting around and hated men like Heathcliff with a vengeance, grasped him by the collar and pinned his head to the table with a well-placed gun barrel pressed painfully into his neck.

'Listen here,' she said, her voice quavering with anger, 'to me, you are worthless scum. Thank your lucky stars I am loyal to Jurisfiction. Many others in my place would have handed you over. I could kill you now and no one would be any the wiser.'

Heathcliff looked at me imploringly.

'I was outside when I heard the shot,' I told him.

'So were we!' exclaimed the rest of the cast eagerly, excepting Catherine Earnshaw, who simply scowled.

'Perhaps I *should* do it!' growled Havisham again. 'Perhaps it would be a mercy. I could make it look like an accident – !'

'No!' cried Heathcliff in a contrite tone. 'I've changed my mind. I'm going to stay right here and just be plain old Mr. Heathcliff for ever and ever.'

Havisham stared at him and slowly released her grasp.

'Right,' she said, switching her pistol to safe and regaining her breath, 'I think that pretty much concludes this session of Jurisfiction Rage Counselling. What did we learn?'

The co-characters all stared at her, dumbstruck.

'Good. Same time next week, everyone?'

HELENE HANFF

From

84 CHARING CROSS ROAD
(1970)

14 East 95th St.
New York City

Marks & Co.
84, Charing Cross Road
London, W.C. 2
England

Gentlemen:

Your ad in the *Saturday Review of Literature* says that you specialize in out-of-print books. The phrase 'antiquarian book-sellers' scares me somewhat, as I equate 'antique' with expensive. I am a poor writer with an antiquarian taste in books and all the things I want are impossible to get over here except in very expensive rare editions, or in Barnes & Noble's grimy, marked-up schoolboy copies.

I enclose a list of my most pressing problems. If you have clean secondhand copies of any of the books on the list, for no more than $5.00 each, will you consider this a purchase order and send them to me?

Very truly yours,

Helene Hanff
(Miss) Helene Hanff

MARKS & CO., Booksellers

84, Charing Cross Road
London, W.C. 2

25th OCTOBER, 1949

Miss Helene Hanff
14 East 95th Street
New York 28, New York
U.S.A.

Dear Madam,

In reply to your letter of October 5th, we have managed
to clear up two thirds of your problem. The three Hazlitt
essays you want are contained in the Nonesuch Press edition
of his *Selected Essays* and the Stevenson is found in *Virginibus
Puerisque*. We are sending nice copies of both these by Book
Post and we trust they will arrive safely in due course and
that you will be pleased with them. Our invoice is enclosed
with the books.

The Leigh Hunt essays are not going to be so easy but we
will see if we can find an attractive volume with them all in.
We haven't the Latin Bible you describe but we have a Latin
New Testament, also a Greek New Testament, ordinary
modern editions in cloth binding. Would you like these?

Yours faithfully,

FPD
For MARKS & CO.

14 East 95th St.
New York City

Marks & Co.
84, Charing Cross Road
London, W.C. 2
England

Gentlemen:

The books arrived safely, the Stevenson is so fine it embarrasses my orange-crate bookshelves, I'm almost afraid to handle such soft vellum and heavy cream-colored pages. Being used to the dead-white paper and stiff cardboardy covers of American books, I never knew a book could be such a joy to the touch.

A Britisher whose girl lives upstairs translated the £1/17/6 for me and says I owe you $5.30 for the two books. I hope he got it right. I enclose a $5 bill and a single, please use the 70c toward the price of the New Testaments, both of which I want.

Will you please translate your prices hereafter? I don't add too well in plain American, I haven't a prayer of ever mastering bilingual arithmetic.

Yours,

Helene Hanff

I hope 'madam' doesn't mean over there what it does here.

MARKS & CO., Booksellers
84, Charing Cross Road
London, W.C. 2

9TH NOVEMBER, 1949

Miss Helene Hanff
14 East 95th Street
New York 28, New York
U.S.A.

Dear Miss Hanff,

Your six dollars arrived safely, but we should feel very much easier if you would send your remittances by postal money order in future, as this would be quite a bit safer for you than entrusting dollar bills to the mails.

We are very happy you liked the Stevenson so much. We have sent off the New Testaments, with an invoice listing the amount due in both pounds and dollars, and we hope you will be pleased with them.

Yours faithfully,

FPD
For MARKS & CO.

WHAT KIND OF A BLACK PROTESTANT BIBLE
IS THIS?

Kindly inform the Church of England they have loused
up the most beautiful prose ever written, whoever told them
to tinker with the Vulgate Latin? They'll burn for it, you
mark my words.

It's nothing to me, I'm Jewish myself. But I have a Catholic
sister-in-law, a Methodist sister-in-law, a whole raft of Pres-
byterian cousins (through my Great-Uncle Abraham who
converted) and an aunt who's a Christian Science healer,
and I like to think *none* of them would countenance this
Anglican Latin Bible if they knew it existed. (As it happens,
they don't know Latin existed.)

Well, the hell with it. I've been using my Latin teacher's
Vulgate, what I imagine I'll do is just not give it back till you
find me one of my own.

I enclose $4 to cover the $3.88 due you, buy yourself a cup
of coffee with the 12c. There's no post office near here and
I am not running all the way down to Rockefeller Plaza to
stand in line for a $3.88 money order. If I wait till I get down
there for something else, I won't have the $3.88 any more.
I have implicit faith in the U.S. Airmail and His Majesty's
Postal Service.

Have you got a copy of Landor's *Imaginary Conversations*?
I think there are several volumes, the one I want is the one
with the Greek conversations. If it contains a dialogue
between Aesop and Rhodope, that'll be the volume I want.

Helene Hanff

MARKS & CO., Booksellers
84, Charing Cross Road
London, W.C. 2

26th NOVEMBER, 1949

Miss Helene Hanff
14 East 95th Street
New York 28, New York
U.S.A.

Dear Miss Hanff,

Your four dollars arrived safely and we have credited the 12 cents to your account.

We happen to have in stock Volume II of the Works & Life of Walter Savage Landor which contains the Greek dialogues including the one mentioned in your letter, as well as the Roman dialogues. It is an old edition published in 1876, not very handsome but well bound and a good clean copy, and we are sending it off to you today with invoice enclosed.

I am sorry we made the mistake with the Latin Bible and will try to find a Vulgate for you. Not forgetting Leigh Hunt.

Yours faithfully,

FPD
For MARKS & CO.

14 East 95th St.
New York City

Sir:

(It feels witless to keep writing 'Gentlemen' when the same solitary soul is obviously taking care of everything for me.)

Savage Landor arrived safely and promptly fell open to a Roman dialogue where two cities had just been destroyed by war and everybody was being crucified and begging passing Roman soldiers to run them through and end the agony. It'll be a relief to turn to Aesop and Rhodope where all you have to worry about is a famine. I do love secondhand books that open to the page some previous owner read oftenest. The day Hazlitt came he opened to 'I hate to read new books,' and I hollered 'Comrade!' to whoever owned it before me.

I enclose a dollar which Brian (British boy friend of Kay upstairs) says will cover the /8/ I owe you, you forgot to translate it.

Now then. Brian told me you are all rationed to 2 ounces of meat per family per week and one egg per person per month and I am simply appalled. He has a catalogue from a British firm here which flies food from Denmark to his mother, so I am sending a small Christmas present to Marks & Co. I hope there will be enough to go round, he says the Charing Cross Road bookshops are 'all quite small.'

I'm sending it c/o you, FPD, whoever you are.

Noel.

Helene Hanff

14 East 95th St.

DECEMBER 9, 1949

FPD! CRISIS!

I sent that package off. The chief item in it was a 6-pound ham, I figured you could take it to a butcher and get it sliced up so everybody would have some to take home.

But I just noticed on your last invoice it says, 'B. Marks. M. Cohen.' Props.

ARE THEY KOSHER? I could rush a tongue over.

ADVISE PLEASE!

Helene Hanff

MARKS & CO., Booksellers
84, Charing Cross Road
London, W.C. 2

20TH DECEMBER, 1949

Miss Helene Hanff
14 East 95th Street
New York 28, New York
U.S.A.

Dear Miss Hanff,

Just a note to let you know that your gift parcel arrived safely today and the contents have been shared out between the staff. Mr. Marks and Mr. Cohen insisted that we divide it up among ourselves and not include 'the bosses.' I should just like to add that everything in the parcel was something that we either never see or can only be had through the black market. It was extremely kind and generous of you to think of us in this way and we are all extremely grateful.

We all wish to express our thanks and send our greetings and best wishes for 1950.

Yours faithfully,

Frank Doel
For MARKS & CO.

14 East 95th St.

MARCH 25, 1950

Frank Doel, what are you DOING over there, you are not doing ANYthing, you are just sitting AROUND.

Where is Leigh Hunt? Where is the *Oxford Verse*? Where is the Vulgate and dear goofy John Henry, I thought they'd be such nice uplifting reading for Lent and NOTHING do you send me.

you leave me sitting here writing long margin notes in library books that don't belong to me, some day they'll find out i did it and take my library card away.

I have made arrangements with the Easter bunny to bring you an Egg, he will get over there and find you have died of Inertia.

I require a book of love poems with spring coming on. *No Keats* or *Shelley*, send me poets who can make love without slobbering – Wyatt or Jonson or somebody, use your own judgment. Just a nice book preferably small enough to stick in a slacks pocket and take to Central Park.

Well, don't just sit there! Go find it! i swear i don't know how that shop keeps going.

MARKS & CO., Booksellers
84, Charing Cross Road
London, W.C. 2

7TH APRIL, 1950

Dear Miss Hanff,

Please don't let Frank know I'm writing this but every time I send you a bill I've been dying to slip in a little note and he might not think it quite proper of me. That sounds stuffy and he's not, he's quite nice really, very nice in fact, it's just that he does rather look on you as his private correspondent as all your letters and parcels are addressed to him. But I just thought I would write to you on my own.

We all love your letters and try to imagine what you must be like. I've decided you're young and very sophisticated and smart-looking. Old Mr. Martin thinks you must be quite studious-looking in spite of your wonderful sense of humor. Why don't you send us a snapshot? We should love to have it.

If you're curious about Frank, he's in his late thirties, quite nice-looking, married to a very sweet Irish girl, I believe she's his second wife.

Everyone was so grateful for the parcel. My little ones (girl 5, boy 4) were in Heaven – with the raisins and egg I was actually able to make them a cake!

I do hope you don't mind my writing. Please don't mention it when you write to Frank.

With best wishes,

Cecily Farr

P.S. I shall put my home address on the back of this in case you should ever want anything sent you from London.

C.F.

14 East 95th St.

APRIL 10, 1950

Dear Cecily –

And a *very* bad cess to Old Mr. Martin, tell him I'm so unstudious I never even went to college. I just happen to have peculiar taste in books, thanks to a Cambridge professor named Quiller-Couch, known as Q, whom I fell over in a library when I was 17. And I'm about as smart-looking as a Broadway panhandler. I live in moth-eaten sweaters and wool slacks, they don't give us any heat here in the daytime. It's a 5-story brownstone and all the other tenants go out to work at 9 A.M. and don't come home till 6 – and why should the landlord heat the building for one small script-reader/ writer working at home on the ground floor?

Poor Frank, I give him such a hard time, I'm always bawling him out for something. I'm only teasing, but I know he'll take me seriously. I keep trying to puncture that proper British reserve, if he gets ulcers I did it.

Please write and tell me about London, I live for the day when I step off the boat-train and feel its dirty sidewalks under my feet. I want to walk up Berkeley Square and down Wimpole Street and stand in St. Paul's where John Donne preached and sit on the step Elizabeth sat on when she refused to enter the Tower, and like that. A newspaper man I know, who was stationed in London during the war, says tourists go to England with preconceived notions, so they always find exactly what they go looking for. I told him I'd go looking for the England of English literature, and he said:

'Then it's there.'

Regards –

Helene Hanff

MARKS & CO., Booksellers
84, Charing Cross Road
London, W.C. 2

20TH SEPTEMBER, 1950

Miss Helene Hanff
14 East 95th Street
New York 28, New York
U.S.A.

Dear Miss Hanff,

It is such a long time since we wrote to you I hope you do not think we have forgotten all about your wants.

Anyway, we now have in stock the *Oxford Book of English Verse*, printed on India paper, original blue cloth binding, 1905, inscription in ink on the flyleaf but a good secondhand copy, price $2.00 We thought we had better quote before sending, in case you have already purchased a copy.

Some time ago you asked us for Newman's *Idea of a University*. Would you be interested in a copy of the first edition? We have just purchased one, particulars as follows:

NEWMAN (JOHN HENRY, D.D.) Discourses on the Scope and Nature of University Education, Addressed to the Catholics of Dublin. First edition, 8vo. calf, Dublin, 1852. A few pages a little age-stained and spotted but a good copy in a sound binding.   Price – $6.00

In case you would like them, we will put both books on one side until you have time to reply.

> With kind regards,
> Yours faithfully,
>
> *Frank Doel*
> For MARKS & CO.

he has a first edition of Newman's *University* for six bucks, do i want it, he asks innocently.

Dear Frank:

Yes, I want it. I won't be fit to live with myself. I've never cared about first editions per se, but a first edition of THAT book —!

oh my.

i can just see it.

Send the *Oxford Verse*, too, please. Never wonder if I've found something somewhere else, I don't look anywhere else any more. Why should I run all the way down to 17th St. to buy dirty, badly made books when I can buy clean, beautiful ones from you without leaving the typewriter? From where I sit, London's a lot closer than 17th Street.

Enclosed please God please find $8. Did I tell you about Brian's lawsuit? He buys physics tomes from a technical book-shop in London, he's not sloppy and haphazard like me, he bought an expensive set and went down to Rockefeller Plaza and stood in line and got a money order and cabled it or whatever you do with it, he's a businessman, he does things right.

the money order got lost in transit.

Up His Majesty's Postal Service!

HH

am sending very small parcel to celebrate first edition, Overseas Associates finally sent me my own catalogue.

OCTOBER 15, 1950

WELL!!!

All I have to say to YOU, Frank Doel, is we live in depraved, destructive and degenerate times when a book-shop – a BOOKSHOP – starts tearing up beautiful old books to use as wrapping paper. I said to John Henry when he stepped out of it:

'Would you believe a thing like that, Your Eminence?' and he said he wouldn't. You tore that book up in the middle of a major battle and I don't even know which war it was.

The Newman arrived almost a week ago and I'm just beginning to recover. I keep it on the table with me all day, every now and then I stop typing and reach over and touch it. Not because it's a first edition; I just never saw a book so beautiful. I feel vaguely guilty about owning it. All that gleaming leather and gold stamping and beautiful type belongs in the pine-panelled library of an English country home; it wants to be read by the fire in a gentleman's leather easy chair – not on a secondhand studio couch in a one-room hovel in a broken-down brownstone front.

I want the Q anthology. I'm not sure how much it was, I lost your last letter. I think it was about two bucks, I'll enclose two singles, if I owe you more let me know.

Why don't you wrap it in pages LCXII and LCXIII so I can at least find out who won the battle and what war it was?

HH

P.S. Have you got Sam Pepys' diary over there? I need him for long winter evenings.

MARKS & CO., Booksellers
84, Charing Cross Road
London, W.C. 2

Miss Helene Hanff
14 East 95th Street
New York 28, New York
U.S.A.

Dear Miss Hanff,

I am sorry for the delay in answering your letter but I have been away out of town for a week or so and am now busy trying to catch up on my correspondence.

First of all, please don't worry about us using old books such as Clarendon's Rebellion for wrapping. In this particular case they were just two odd volumes with the covers detached and nobody in their right senses would have given us a shilling for them.

The Quiller-Couch anthology, *The Pilgrim's Way*, has been sent to you by Book Post. The balance due was $1.85 so your $2 more than covered it. We haven't a copy of Pepys' *Diary* in stock at the moment but shall look out for one for you.

With kind wishes,
Yours faithfully,

F. Doel
For MARKS & CO.

MARKS & CO., Booksellers
84, Charing Cross Road
London, W.C. 2

2ND FEBRUARY, 1951

Miss Helene Hanff
14 East 95th Street
New York 28, New York
U.S.A.

Dear Miss Hanff,

We are glad you liked the 'Q' anthology. We have no copy of the *Oxford Book of English Prose* in stock at the moment but will try to find one for you.

About the *Sir Roger de Coverley Papers*, we happen to have in stock a volume of eighteenth century essays which includes a good selection of them as well as essays by Chesterfield and Goldsmith. It is edited by Austin Dobson and is quite a nice edition and as it is only $1.15 we have sent it off to you by Book Post. If you want a more complete collection of Addison & Steele let me know and I will try to find one.

There are six of us in the shop, not including Mr. Marks and Mr. Cohen.

Faithfully yours,

Frank Doel
For MARKS & CO.

MARKS & CO., Booksellers
84, Charing Cross Road
London, W.C. 2

9TH APRIL, 1951

Miss Helene Hanff
14 East 95th Street
New York 28, New York
U.S.A.

Dear Miss Hanff,

I expect you are getting a bit worried that we have not written to thank you for your parcels and are probably thinking that we are an ungrateful lot. The truth is that I have been chasing round the country in and out of various stately homes of England trying to buy a few books to fill up our sadly depleted stock. My wife was starting to call me the lodger who just went home for bed and breakfast, but of course when I arrived home with a nice piece of MEAT, to say nothing of dried eggs and ham, then she thought I was a fine fellow and all was forgiven. It is a long time since we saw so much meat all in one piece.

We should like to express our appreciation in some way or other, so we are sending by Book Post today a little book which I hope you will like. I remember you asked me for a volume of Elizabethan love poems some time ago – well, this is the nearest I can get to it.

Yours faithfully,

Frank Doel
For MARKS & CO.

14 East 95th St.
New York City

APRIL 16, 1951

To All at 84, Charing Cross Road:

Thank you for the beautiful book. I've never owned a book before with pages edged all round in gold. Would you believe it arrived on my birthday?

I wish you hadn't been so over-courteous about putting the inscription on a card instead of on the flyleaf. It's the bookseller coming out in you all, you were afraid you'd decrease its value. You would have increased it for the present owner. (And possibly for the future owner. I love inscriptions on flyleaves and notes in margins, I like the comradely sense of turning pages someone else turned, and reading passages some one long gone has called my attention to.)

And why didn't you sign your names? I expect Frank wouldn't let you, he probably doesn't want me writing love letters to anybody but him.

I send you greetings from America – faithless friend that she is, pouring millions into rebuilding Japan and Germany while letting England starve. Some day, God willing, I'll get over there and apologize personally for my country's sins (and by the time i come home my country will certainly have to apologize for mine).

Thank you again for the beautiful book, I shall try very hard not to get gin and ashes all over it, it's really much too fine for the likes of me.

Yours,

Helene Hanff

SEPTEMBER 10, 1951

Dearheart –

It is the loveliest old shop straight out of Dickens, you would go absolutely out of your mind over it.

There are stalls outside and I stopped and leafed through a few things just to establish myself as a browser before wandering in. It's dim inside, you smell the shop before you see it, it's a lovely smell, I can't articulate it easily, but it combines must and dust and age, and walls of wood and floors of wood. Toward the back of the shop at the left there's a desk with a work-lamp on it, a man was sitting there, he was about fifty with a Hogarth nose, he looked up and said 'Good afternoon?' in a North Country accent and I said I just wanted to browse and he said please do.

The shelves go on forever. They go up to the ceiling and they're very old and kind of grey, like old oak that has absorbed so much dust over the years they no longer are their true color. There's a print section, or rather a long print table, with Cruikshank and Rackham and Spy and all those old wonderful English caricaturists and illustrators that I'm not smart enough to know a lot about, and there are some lovely old, old illustrated magazines.

I stayed for about half an hour hoping your Frank or one of the girls would turn up, but it was one-ish when I went in, I gather they were all out to lunch and I couldn't stay any longer.

As you see, the notices were not sensational but we're told they're good enough to assure us a few months' run, so I went apartment-hunting yesterday and found a nice little 'bed-sitter' in Knightsbridge, I don't have the address here, I'll send it or you can call my mother.

We have no food problems, we eat in restaurants and hotels, the best places like Claridge's get all the roast beef and chops they want. The prices are astronomical but the exchange rate is so good we can afford it. Of course if I were the English I would loathe us, instead of which they are absolutely wonderful to us, we're invited to everybody's home and everybody's club.

The only thing we can't get is sugar or sweets in any form, for which I personally thank God, I intend to lose ten pounds over here.

Write me,

Love,

Maxine

WALTER BENJAMIN

UNPACKING MY LIBRARY

A TALK ABOUT BOOK COLLECTING

(1931)

Translated by Harry Zohn

I AM UNPACKING my library. Yes, I am. The books are not yet on the shelves, not yet touched by the mild boredom of order. I cannot march up and down their ranks to pass them in review before a friendly audience. You need not fear any of that. Instead, I must ask you to join me in the disorder of crates that have been wrenched open, the air saturated with the dust of wood, the floor covered with torn paper, to join me among piles of volumes that are seeing daylight again after two years of darkness, so that you may be ready to share with me a bit of the mood – it is certainly not an elegiac mood but, rather, one of anticipation – which these books arouse in a genuine collector. For such a man is speaking to you, and on closer scrutiny he proves to be speaking only about himself. Would it not be presumptuous of me if, in order to appear convincingly objective and down-to-earth, I enumerated for you the main sections or prize pieces of a library, if I presented you with their history or even their usefulness to a writer? I, for one, have in mind something less obscure, something more palpable than that; what I am really concerned with is giving you some insight into the relationship of a book collector to his possessions, into collecting rather than a collection. If I do this by elaborating on the various ways of acquiring books, this is something entirely arbitrary. This or any other procedure is merely a dam against the spring tide of memories which surges toward any collector as he contemplates his possessions. Every passion borders on the chaotic, but the collector's passion borders on the chaos of memories. More than that: the chance, the fate, that suffuse the past before my eyes are conspicuously present in the accustomed confusion of these books. For what else is this collection but a disorder to which habit has accommodated itself to such an extent that it can appear as order? You have all heard of people whom the loss of their books has turned into invalids, or of those who in order to acquire them became criminals. These are the very areas in which any order is a balancing act of extreme precariousness. 'The only exact knowledge there is,' said Anatole France, 'is the knowledge of the date of publication and the format of books.' And indeed, if there is a counterpart to the confusion of a library, it is the order of its catalogue.

Thus there is in the life of a collector a dialectical tension between the poles of disorder and order. Naturally, his existence is tied to many other things as well: to a very mysterious relationship to ownership, something about which we shall have more to say later; also, to relationship to objects which does not emphasize their functional, utilitarian value – that is, their usefulness – but studies and loves them as the scene, the stage, of their fate. The most profound enchantment for the collector is the locking of individual items within a magic circle in which they are fixed as the final thrill, the thrill of acquisition, passes over them. Everything remembered and thought, everything conscious, becomes the pedestal, the frame, the base, the lock of his property. The period, the region, the craftsmanship, the former ownership – for a true collector the whole background of an item adds up to a magic encyclopedia whose quintessence is the fate of his object. In this circumscribed area, then, it may be surmised how the great physiognomists – and collectors are the physiognomists of the world of objects – turn into interpreters of fate. One has only to watch a collector handle the objects in his glass case. As he holds them in his hands, he seems to be seeing through them into their distant past as though inspired. So much for the magical side of the collector – his old-age image, I might call it.

Habent sua fata libelli: these words have been intended as a general statement about books. So books like *The Divine Comedy*, Spinoza's *Ethics*, and *The Origin of Species* have their fates. A collector, however, interprets this Latin saying differently. For him, not only books but also copies of books have their fates. And in this sense, the most important fate of a copy is its encounter with him, with his own collection. I am not exaggerating when I say that to a true collector the acquisition of an old book is its rebirth. This is the childlike element which in a collector mingles with the element of old age. For children can accomplish the renewal in a hundred unfailing ways. Among children, collecting is only one process of renewal; other processes are the painting of objects, the cutting out of figures, the application of decals – the whole range of childlike modes of acquisition, from touching things to giving them names. To renew the old world – that is the collector's deepest desire when he is driven to acquire new things, and that is why a collector of older books is closer to the wellsprings of collecting than the acquirer of luxury editions. How do books cross the threshold of a collection and become the property of a collector? The history of their acquisition is the subject of the following remarks.

Of all the ways of acquiring books, writing them oneself is regarded as the most praiseworthy method. At this point many of you will remember with pleasure the large library which Jean Paul's poor little schoolmaster Wutz gradually acquired by writing, himself, all the works whose titles interested him in book-fair catalogues; after all, he could not afford to buy them. Writers are really people who write books not because they are poor, but because they are dissatisfied with the books which they could buy but do not like. You, ladies and gentlemen, may regard this as a whimsical definition of a writer. But everything said from the angle of a real collector is whimsical. Of the customary modes of acquisition, the one most appropriate to a collector would be the borrowing of a book with its attendant non-returning. The book borrower of real stature whom we envisage here proves himself to be an inveterate collector of books not so much by the fervor with which he guards his borrowed treasures and by the deaf ear which he turns to all reminders from the everyday world of legality as by his failure to read these books. If my experience may serve as evidence, a man is more likely to return a borrowed book upon occasion than to read it. And the non-reading of books, you will object, should be characteristic of collectors? This is news to me, you may say. It is not news at all. Experts will bear me out when I say that it is the oldest thing in the world. Suffice it to quote the answer which Anatole France gave to a philistine who admired his library and then finished with the standard question, 'And you have read all these books, Monsieur France?' 'Not one-tenth of them. I don't suppose you use your Sèvres china every day?'

Incidentally, I have put the right to such an attitude to the test. For years, for at least the first third of its existence, my library consisted of no more than two or three shelves which increased only by inches each year. This was its militant age, when no book was allowed to enter it without the certification that I had not read it. Thus I might never have acquired a library extensive enough to be worthy of the name if there had not been an inflation. Suddenly the emphasis shifted; books acquired real value, or, at any rate, were difficult to obtain. At least this is how it seemed in Switzerland. At the eleventh hour I sent my first major book orders from there and in this way was able to secure such irreplaceable items as *Der blaue Reiter* and Bachofen's *Sage von Tanaquil*, which could still be obtained from the publishers at that time.

Well – so you may say – after exploring all these byways we should finally reach the wide highway of book acquisition, namely, the purchasing of books. This is indeed a wide highway, but not a comfortable one. The purchasing done by a book collector has very little in common with that done in a bookshop by a student getting a textbook, a man of the world buying a present for his lady, or a businessman intending to while away his next train journey. I have made my most memorable purchases on trips, as a transient. Property and possession belong to the tactical sphere. Collectors are people with a tactical instinct; their experience teaches them that when they capture a strange city, the smallest antique shop can be a fortress, the most remote stationery store a key position. How many cities have revealed themselves to me in the marches I undertook in the pursuit of books!

By no means all of the most important purchases are made on the premises of a dealer. Catalogues play a far greater part. And even though the purchaser may be thoroughly acquainted with the book ordered from a catalogue, the individual copy always remains a surprise and the order always a bit of a gamble. There are grievous disappointments, but also happy finds. I remember, for instance, that I once ordered a book with colored illustrations for my old collection of childen's books only because it contained fairy tales by Albert Ludwig Grimm and was published at Grimma, Thuringia. Grimma was also the place of publication of a book of fables edited by the same Albert Ludwig Grimm. With its sixteen illustrations my copy of this book of fables was the only extant example of the early work of the great German book illustrator Lyser, who lived in Hamburg around the middle of the last century. Well, my reaction to the consonance of the names had been correct. In this case too I discovered the work of Lyser, namely *Linas Märchenbuch*, a work which has remained unknown to his bibliographers and which deserves a more detailed reference than this first one I am introducing here.

The acquisition of books is by no means a matter of money or expert knowledge alone. Not even both factors together suffice for the establishment of a real library, which is always somewhat impenetrable and at the same time uniquely itself. Anyone who buys from catalogues must have flair in addition to the qualities I have mentioned. Dates, place names, formats, previous owners, bindings, and the like: all these details must tell him something – not as dry, isolated facts, but as a harmonious whole; from the quality and intensity of this harmony he must be able to recognize whether a book is for him or not. An auction requires yet another set of qualities in a collector. To the reader of a catalogue the book itself must speak, or possibly its previous ownership if the provenance of the copy has been established. A man who wishes to participate at an auction must pay equal attention to the book and to his competitors, in addition to keeping a cool enough head to avoid being carried away in the competition. It is a frequent occurrence that someone gets stuck with a high purchase price because he kept raising his bid – more to assert himself than to acquire the book. On the other hand, one of the finest memories of a collector is the moment when he rescued a book to which he might never have given a thought, much less a wishful look, because he found it lonely and abandoned on the market place and bought it to give it its freedom – the way the prince bought a beautiful slave girl in *The Arabian Nights*. To a book collector, you see, the true freedom of all books is somewhere on his shelves.

To this day Balzac's *Peau de chagrin* stands out from long rows of French volumes in my library as a memento of my most exciting experience at an auction. This happened in 1915 at the Rümann auction put up by Emil Hirsch, one of the greatest of book experts and most distinguished of dealers. The edition in question appeared in 1838 in Paris, Place de la Bourse. As I pick up my copy, I see not only its number in the Rümann collection, but even the label of the shop in which the first owner bought the book over ninety years ago for one-eightieth of today's price. 'Papeterie I. Flanneau,' it says. A fine age in which it was still possible to buy such a de luxe edition at a stationery dealer's! The steel engravings of this book were designed by the foremost French graphic artist and executed by the foremost engravers. But I was going to tell you how I acquired this book. I had gone to Emil Hirsch's for an advance inspection and had handled forty or fifty volumes; that particular volume had inspired in me the ardent desire to hold on to it forever. The day of the auction came. As chance would have it, in the sequence of the auction this copy of *La Peau de chagrin* was preceded by a complete set of its illustrations printed separately on India paper. The bidders sat at a long table; diagonally across from me sat the man who was the focus of all eyes at the first bid, the famous Munich collector Baron von Simolin. He was greatly interested in this set, but he had rival bidders; in short, there was a spirited contest which resulted in the highest bid of the entire auction – far in excess of three thousand marks. No one seemed to have expected such a high figure, and all those present were quite excited. Emil Hirsch remained unconcerned, and whether he wanted to save time or was guided by some other consideration, he proceeded to the next item, with no one really paying attention. He called out the price, and with my heart pounding and with the full realization that I was unable to compete with any of those big collectors I bid a somewhat higher amount. Without arousing the bidders' attention, the auctioneer went through the usual routine – 'Do I hear more?' and three bangs of his gavel, with an eternity seeming to separate each from the next – and proceeded to add the auctioneer's charge. For a student like me the sum was still considerable. The following morning at the pawnshop is no longer part of this story, and I prefer to speak about another incident which I should like to call the negative of an auction. It happened last year at a Berlin auction. The collection of books that was offered was a miscellany in quality and subject matter, and only a number of rare works on occultism and natural philosophy were worthy of note. I bid for a number of them, but each time I noticed a gentleman in the front row who seemed only to have waited for my bid to counter with his own, evidently prepared to top any offer. After this had been repeated several times, I gave up all hope of acquiring the book which I was most interested in that day. It was the rare *Fragmente aus dem Nachlass eines jungen Physikers* [Posthumous Fragments of a Young Physicist] which Johann Wilhelm Ritter published in two volumes at Heidelberg in 1810. This work has never been reprinted, but I have always considered its preface, in which the author-editor tells the story of his life in the guise of an obituary for his supposedly deceased unnamed friend – with whom he is really identical – as the most important sample of personal prose of German Romanticism. Just as the item came up I had a brain wave. It was simple enough: since my bid was bound to give the item to the other man, I must not bid at all. I controlled myself and remained silent. What I had hoped for came about: no interest, no bid, and the book was put aside. I deemed it wise to let several days go by, and when I appeared on the premises after a week, I found the book in the secondhand department and benefited by the lack of interest when I acquired it.

Once you have approached the mountains of cases in order to mine the books from them and bring them to the light of day – or, rather, of night – what memories crowd in upon you! Nothing highlights the fascination of unpacking more clearly than the difficulty of stopping this activity. I had started at noon, and it was midnight before I had worked my way to the last cases. Now I put my hands on two volumes bound in faded boards which, strictly speaking, do not belong in a book case at all: two albums with stick-in pictures which my mother pasted in as a child and which I inherited. They are the seeds of a collection of children's books which is growing even today, though no longer in my garden. There is no living library that does not harbour a number of booklike creations from fringe areas. They need not be stick-in albums or family albums, autograph books or portfolios containing pamphlets or religious tracts; some people become attached to leaflets and prospectuses, others to handwriting facsimiles or typewritten copies of unobtainable books; and certainly periodicals can form the prismatic fringes of a library. But to get back to those albums: Actually, inheritance is the soundest way of acquiring a collection. For a collector's attitude toward his possessions stems from an owner's feeling of responsibility toward his property. Thus it is, in the highest sense, the attitude of an heir, and the most distinguished trait of a collection will always be its transmissibility. You should know that in saying this I fully realize that my discussion of the mental climate of collecting will confirm many of you in your conviction that this passion is behind the times, in your distrust of the collector type. Nothing is further from my mind than to shake either your conviction or your distrust. But one thing should be noted: the phenomenon of collecting loses its meaning as it loses its personal owner. Even though public collections may be less objectionable socially and more useful academically than private collections, the objects get their due only in the latter. I do know that time is running out for the type that I am discussing here and have been representing before you a bit *ex officio*. But, as Hegel put it, only when it is dark does the owl of Minerva begin its flight. Only in extinction is the collector comprehended.

Now I am on the last half-emptied case and it is way past midnight. Other thoughts fill me than the ones I am talking about – not thoughts but images, memories. Memories of the cities in which I found so many things: Riga, Naples, Munich, Danzig, Moscow, Florence, Basel, Paris; memories of Rosenthal's sumptuous rooms in Munich, of the Danzig Stockturm where the late Hans Rhaue was domiciled, of Süssengut's musty book cellar in North Berlin; memories of the rooms where these books had been housed, of my student's den in Munich, of my room in Bern, of the solitude of Iseltwald on the Lake of Brienz, and finally of my boyhood room, the former location of only four or five of the several thousand volumes that are piled up around me. O bliss of the collector, bliss of the man of leisure! Of no one has less been expected, and no one has had a greater sense of well-being than the man who has been able to carry on his disreputable existence in the mask of Spitzweg's 'Bookworm.' For inside him there are spirits, or at least little genii, which have seen to it that for a collector – and I mean a real collector, a collector as he ought to be – ownership is the most intimate relationship that one can have to objects. Not that they come alive in him; it is he who lives in them. So I have erected one of his dwellings, with books as the building stones, before you, and now he is going to disappear inside, as is only fitting.

ERNEST RHYS

From

EVERYMAN
REMEMBERS
(1931)

.

Everyman, I will go with thee and be thy guide,
In thy most need to go by thy side.

Old Play

IT WAS AT the rooms in Gray's Inn of Edward Garnett, already known as the author of *The Paradox Club*, that one evening I met a man he had described as 'an original East End bookbinder called Dent, with an ambition, a rosy face and a long black beard.'

When he brought his new acquaintance over to me, his own overtopping lanky boyish figure rather dwarfed the other by contrast, but I noticed the rosy cheeks, long beard, limping gait and eager manner of the new-comer.

Of Edward Garnett, who has crossed these pages before, one could easily write a long chapter, but as he is happily still living and of the *genus irritabile*, he might resent it. He, to be sure, is the Mystery Man of English Literature in our day, who has discovered as many stars in the firmament (including Joseph Conrad, W. H. Hudson, John Galsworthy and Cunninghame Graham) as there are in Orion's Belt.

He had told me that this unconventional bookbinder-publisher had printed two or three books experimentally in a cock-loft in Great Eastern Street; and before the evening was over we had arranged a visit there. It proved to be the most original publisher's office that could well be imagined. There was a bookbindery above, and below one heard all the racket of a book factory pouring out bales of goods.

The publisher himself sat in a little den upstairs boarded off from the rest of the warehouse. An hour spent in his cubicle talking over new books or old authors was true entertainment; for here was a man, with no working capital, who had every desire to become another John Murray. Our first talk led to a lunch at the Old Crosby Hall (now removed from Bishopsgate to Chelsea), and so to a series called the Lyric Poets, into whose printing and contriving he threw himself with zest, having the craft as well as the desire to produce books tempting to look upon.

Now when I look over the lyric volumes they appear almost too pretty-pretty in their pale blue and gold and too small of print for my notion of a viable poetry book. They did not prove market-makers, and about half-way J. M. D. grew impatient about his profits and startled me by suggesting the editor should take lower fees than those first agreed upon; for he seemed to have an ingenuous idea that an editor ought not to care about his emoluments, a touch of 'the artist's temperament' in him, along with a dash of Yorkshire shrewdness. But he was always at heart an optimist. His sheer driving power was extraordinary, and in the next five or six years he had worked out one bold scheme after another, including the Temple Shakespeare and the Temple Classics with a very able man, the late Sir Israel Gollancz, as editor.

Meanwhile, the old Camelot Series had run its term, and then there occurred to me a larger scheme, a collection of the great literatures beginning with the English, so co-ordinated that if its readers began with one creative book they would want another and another till the great public had the world literature within its grasp. It was a prodigious, hardly practicable idea. How was one to find a collaborator able and keen enough to work it out? Having made out some ambitious experimental lists at the old book factory, the Reading Room of the British Museum, I went off to Ventnor, in the Isle of

Wight, and wrote a piquant letter to J. M. Dent, enclosing my programme, and asking him if he did not want to become 'the Napoleon of Publishers'?

A week passed, and then I wrote again, asking to have the scheme returned if it was not a possible one. Then he replied, asking me to call and see him when next in London. I did so, and he told me he had been busy planning a similar series of books, which, in fact, had been discussed in some detail with his son Hugh. It was a strange coincidence and indeed a piece of singular good fortune to have put the idea before a publisher who had already conceived one of similar effect. In the end, when we had talked over the literary side, he asked me to become editor.

Once embarked on the scheme, he made endless plans and experiments, and drew out charts of the viable world on a magnificent scale. His enthusiasm for it was without bounds, and it soon became the ruling passion of his life. He decided to send out the army of books, not in single spies, but in battalions of fifty volumes. In the first year we brought out a hundred in all, and that with the most meagre editorial staff: he and I, his son Hugh Dent, and two or three British Museum foragers.

Good titles like good lyrics drop from heaven. The finding of one, arresting and explicit, was the grand crux. We must have made up a score of possible names for the new series, among them, the New Century Series, the Masterpiece Library and the Atlantic Library, but not one of them quite satisfied us. Then one day, walking along Garrick Street past the doors of the Garrick Club, not thinking of anything in particular, I recalled a line of the old Mystery Play – 'Everyman, I will go with thee and be thy guide,' . . . which gave the cue. It sent me marching into the office where the old chief sat. '*Eureka!*' I said, quoting the line: 'here's our title

– *Everyman's Library.*' He stared a moment incredulously, and then said: 'Why yes: you have it!'

We were soon in the thick of the struggle, spending arduous days when we began early in the forenoon, lunching on bread and cheese and apples in the midst of a fearful litter of books and papers, and not closing down till fifty or sixty volumes were put into the fighting line. For every author in turn was hotly discussed, and at times fought over. We had no great trouble in deciding on the first volume of all – Boswell's *Life of Johnson.* The trouble was that Dent grew so enthusiastic over a book like Boswell's that he was tempted to spend half an hour in quoting favourite passages. It must have been during one of those Boswell discussions, when he had been led into several curious reminiscences, that I suggested his own life ought to be written, Boswell fashion.

'But,' he rejoined, turning a little red in the face, 'I shall never find a Boswell.'

'Then you must be your own Boswell; but be sure you put in all your troubles and foibles.'

The thought of it may have made him uncomfortable, for he closed the subject and did not return to it till years later, when he said he was dictating his *Memoirs.* Since then they have appeared, congenially edited by his son Hugh Dent; but, as so often happens, its writer was not able to see himself always in the colours that best expressed his unique personality. It would have been too much to expect that any man but a Benvenuto Cellini or Goldoni, with so complex a self, could paint his own live and life-like portrait. For he had in him a strange mixture – book lover, artist, mystic, craftsman, small tradesman and rosy promiser. What made dealing with him, on the intimate terms that must exist between editor and publisher, so exciting, was that one was never quite sure which of these characters would come uppermost. Often in the course of an hour he would make a complete quick change from one role to another. In these mercurial moods he often became so wrought up that, in order to bring himself back to normal, he would clench with two hands the front of his desk as if he were afraid of suddenly being whirled away into limbo.

And if it chanced that an unlucky author interrupted him in one of these ecstasies, he fell into a state of wrath like a prophet interrupted at his devotions. On one occasion I went in and found him fuming just after he had been interviewed by a very famous personage indeed, who had written a book for him.

'Did you meet Lord—— as you entered the office, Mr. Rhys? He walked in without waiting to know if I could see him . . .!' He added what Disraeli once said of Gladstone: 'Poof! he is no gentleman.'

Another day when I asked for a cheque which was due, he seemed to be so confounded that I could not help feeling intense commiseration for him. He put his two elbows on the desk and his hands over his eyes and seemed to be praying for divine guidance in this crucial matter, and presently I saw the tears dropping through his fingers. The stoic in one has a feeling against men who weep, and so one sat on sternly and waited till Providence had supplied the necessary scrip.

One day afterward I met H. G. Wells and asked him if he had ever seen a publisher weep?

'Yes, I did once,' he replied, 'in the house of Dent.'

There was some reason for these perturbations and anxieties, because this simple bookbinder transformed into a book Napoleon was often cruelly hampered by the small capital he had at command, and had to borrow money from his bank or his friends when he was going through the first exacting stages of Everyman's Library. He had the power of exciting not only sympathy but affection, in a curious degree. In spite of a natural resentment at his strange neglect of the customary code of give-and-take, one's final feeling was of deep concern for a man who was fighting a terrific battle against odds.

As he explained in the story of the series he wrote afterward, the very success of the first hundred volumes meant a hundred-and-one difficulties. 'A large part of the hundred was sold before the end of the half-year, but it meant that in about two months reprints were called for, and reprinting meant stereotyping as well as the actual machining, providing the paper and so forth; and money must be found for increased weekly wages. How arrange for the heavy printers' and bookbinders' bills? There was money due to many people, and their accounts had to be put forward while they waited. It was a difficult and uncomfortable time for the first few months. One of the great paper houses, who had been very chivalrous in their dealings, said they could not afford to give further credit. Luckily another house was so good as to give credit for any sum required for the purpose. That was one of the kindest things a papermaker ever did for a publisher; and by that means we were able to pay our other papermakers' accounts when due without any delay.'

In all this trying campaign he never lost sight of his master purpose – to build up the most complete library for the common man the world had seen. His desire was based on his early memories of a time when it was precious hard to find the money to buy the book he wanted to read, and on his sympathy for the man who could not afford to go beyond the Democratic Shilling.

In truth publisher, and editor along with him, were aiming at something almost impracticable, almost quixotic, in this enterprise. Victor Hugo said a library was an act of faith, and an unknown writer spoke of one so beautiful, so perfect, so harmonious in all its parts, that he who made it or he who read in its volumes would be smitten with a passion. In that faith we had planned Everyman's Library, and our idea, so doing, was to make it conform, as far as buying public and book market would allow, to a perfect design. However, perfection is a thing to be aimed at and not easily achieved in this troublesome world; and as time went on we were often faced by difficulties that threatened to set up what the political journalists call 'strained relations.' A batch of fifty volumes, to be produced by a definite date without reprieve, meant that a small army of authors, writers of introductions, newspaper men and bosom friends, had to be kept in good humour while the last ounce of efficiency was being taken out of their lukewarm anatomy. The courage and resource of the old chief under these desperate conditions used to rouse me to feelings of wonder. Left to myself I should not have had the determination or the devotion to carry it through. There were so many other things going on in the world: one's own books, one's romances, critiques and ballads to be written, one's Celtic and medieval studies to be followed up, and one's weekly articles for the *Manchester Guardian*, dealing with Irish and Welsh topics, to be kept going. Many a morning when I hurried from the Reading Room of the British Museum, leaving there a pile of old authors or others not so old who might be converted into Everyman volumes, I would find the old chief fuming because there seemed no way out of some impasse. Perhaps it was a question of a history book by Carlyle or Macaulay, for which I was supposed to bring an introduction by some well-known writer or man of affairs. Then would come the disturbing admission that the inevitable introductor had not been found.

'I told you the book was to be published on the twenty-fifth. This is getting *crucical*!' (delicious word, 'crucical': one of those strange words that J. M. D. sometimes struck off in a heated moment). 'You must get Lord Rosebery to write.'

'At such short notice? That is like asking Cæsar to tea!'

'This is no laughing matter. We cannot carry on a series with bad jokes. I can quote too. I am in a tartar-limbo, worse than hell, and you laugh about it.'

'I smiled to reassure you. I'm *not* one who believes in lowering the temperature. Let us find our man.'

'You said your friend Lloyd George could get John Morley to write the introduction to Burke's *Speeches*.'

'I did ask L. G. if he could prompt it, but here's a post card from John Morley saying he regrets he can't do it.'

'That's bad, very bad! Why didn't you call on Morley and persuade him to do it? What about Woodrow Wilson? He is another Burke man, isn't he?'

The end of it was I looked up Woodrow Wilson's *Essays* and asked him to let me reprint one of his pages. So this harassing game of chess went on, with frequent crises when we felt like upsetting the chess-board. But the grand crisis, which we could not possibly have foreseen, was still to come. We had got about half-way either in planning or in publishing our successive book battalions, with the goal of a Thousand Volumes looming up auspiciously, when the tragic break came that was to shake the world fabric alike of books and men.

The War, indeed, was a calamity in more senses than one, for it involved a long pause in the series, and it had the effect too of preventing the old bibliolater from being able to realize his darling idea.

As for my share in the catastrophe, the trouble was not only a literary, or even a financial one. When, long before,

I had pointed out that considering the enormous sales of the series my reward was a very meagre one, he responded with enthusiasm and said in so many words: 'If you will be content to put all you know into the library you can trust to my honour to see that in the end you have your fair share.'

Unluckily, when the War came and like so many other writers I felt the pinch, and reminded him this would be the moment to make good his promises, J. M. D. only looked uncomfortable, opened and shut his mouth as if he were going to speak, and then said – *nothing*! (Let me add that after his death – whether it may have been in any degree of his prompting I cannot say – the house of Dent did remember those promises.) But at that critical moment he only turned aside to look at some letters, and I understood the episode was ended. Next day I had to consider ruefully which of my rare books and first editions I should sacrifice. There was a friendly bookseller, Everard Meynell, who kept what he called the 'Serendipity Shop.' He came and carried off some sixty pounds' worth. A cruel sacrifice and even there the constriction of the War made itself felt, for he explained if it had not been war-time he could have given me twice or thrice as much.

But out of that tragedy arose another event more mysterious. In a month or so there was a worse crisis to be met: one night things looked so threatening I remember walking out last thing under the stars, noticing how bright they were, and thinking how like a rat in a pit I was, with tax-collectors, tradesmen, and other exigent people asking to be paid next day at latest. There seemed no way out of the pit; but who dare say there is not a special Providence that looks after the improvident?

Next morning brought a single letter, an exceedingly curious one. It was from the Serendipity bookseller asking me if I could manage to see him that very forenoon? When I reached his shop he asked me, with an air of mystery, to step into his private room, and made a surprising gesture. A certain shipowner, who had world-wide dealings in merchant shipping and made a fortune out of them in the War, had decided to put aside a sum for the benefit of painters, poets, and other artistic folk who had suffered in the hard times. With that explanation, Meynell produced a cheque and made it out to me on one condition: I was not to know the name of the donor or make any acknowledgement whatsoever. There was a sort of Arabian Nights air about the whole transaction that greatly appealed to my sense of the unexpected, and I walked out into the street thinking that London, after all, was not such a cruel den to live in.

To take up again the story of Everyman's Library, it is amusing now to recall how often we were thrown into swithers by the failure of contributors to come up to time. You who know what authors are and what penmen like Hilaire Belloc, G. K. Chesterton, Edward Garnett, and Laurence Binyon feel about the exigencies of the pen, will appreciate the tertian ague of an editor who has to run a mixed team of fifty old authors and twenty new ones.

When we were in the very thick of the Battle of the Books, it was a nerve-racking experience to settle which out of a batch of possible authors were to be pushed into the front line. Supposing one arrived a few minutes late in Bedford Street with a notebook crammed with out-of-the-way information, one would find the old chief fuming with impatience because the bookbinders or papermakers had failed him. He suffered far more than any ordinary man from paroxysms of anxiety and disgust. A well-known Swedish doctor he once called in to diagnose his symptoms said to me after a visit:

446

'Your Mr. Dent! He suffer much from "termination of blood to the head." He ought to keep a pail of cold water in his office and whenever he feels his head burning he ought to plunge it in – slosh! It would not be surprising if some day a stroke of apoplexy should carry off the impatient patient.' But he was wrong, as other doctors have been in their diagnoses.

There were indeed no half-measures with this determined book-producer: it was all or nothing in his game with the gods. One of his colleagues said he was 'ruthless' in getting his way when along that way lay his one chance of getting the scheme through. Sometimes people, especially in America, have credited me with the main contriving and driving home of the project; but I should never have had the trust or courage to persevere against odds that this intrepid self-educated bookbinder had. There was a touch of the transcendental in him: it was as if he was the instrument of a force greater than he himself understood.

And, mind you, it was backed by a genuine belief in the book, beautiful and ideal, which should be the instrument of the living word, and by means of a collective Golden Commonwealth resolve itself into a League of Books and help to bring about the Peace of the World. It was an idea worth living for, and the best monument to him who served to make it good, will be the Thousand Books he projected, but, alas! was not destined to see completed.

It was a heartening sight, when some particular batch of volumes had been finished and published and sent out to the booksellers, to watch this intrepid entrepreneur take up and fondle one of the books that particularly appealed to him. For that might be the destined poet or proseman who should entangle the reader so artfully in the meshes of the Library that once he had begun he would be bound to go on until he was master of the whole labyrinth. The principle was that of Blake's induction:

> I give you the end of a golden string,
>   Only wind it into a ball
> It will lead you in at Heaven's gate,
>   Built in Jerusalem's wall.

BUILDING A
LIBRARY

Demetrius of Phalerum, the president of the king's
[Ptolemy I's] library, received vast sums of money, for
the purpose of collecting together, as far as he possibly
could, all the books in the world.

Letter of Aristeas (2nd century BCE)

JOHN EVELYN

From *Instructions Concerning Erecting of a Library* (1661)

THE SEVENTH POINT, and which seems absolutely necessary to be treated of after the precedent, is that of the Order
and Disposition which Books ought to observe in a Library;
for without this, doubtless, all inquiring is to no purpose, and
our labour fruitless; seeing Books are for no other reason laid
and reserved in this place, but that they may be serviceable
upon such occasions as present themselves; Which thing it is
notwithstanding impossible to effect, unless they be ranged,
and disposed according to the variety of their subjects, or
in such other sort, as that they may easily be found, as soon
as named. I affirm, moreover, that without this Order and
disposition, be the collection of Books whatever, were it of
fifty thousand Volumes, it would no more merit the name
of a Library, than an assembly of thirty thousand men the
name of an Army, unless they be martiall in their several
quarters, under the conduct of their Chiefs and Captains;
or a vast heap of stones and materials, that of a Palace or a
house, till they be placed and put together according to rule,
to make a perfect and accomplished structure. . . .

Making no more esteem of an order that can onely be
followed by an Author, which will not be understood, I
conceive that to be alwayes the best which is most facil,
the least intricate, most natural, practised, and which
follows the Faculties of Theologie, Physick, Iurisprudence,
Mathematicks, Humanity, and others, which should be
subdivided each of them into particulars, according to
their several members, which for this purpose ought to be
reasonably well understood by him who has the charge of

the Library; as for example, in Divinity, you should ever place the Bibles first, according to the order of the tongues, next these, the Councells, Synods, Decrees, Canons, and all that concerns the Ecclesiastical constitutions; forasmuch as they retain the second place of authority amongst us; After these, the Fathers, Greek and Latine; then the Commentators, Scholasticks, Mix'd Doctors, Historians, and finally, the Heretiques. In Philosophy, to begin with that of Trismegistus as the most antient, follow by that of Plato, of Aristotle, of Raymondus Lullius, Ramus, and finish with the Novators, Telesius, Patricius, Campanella, Verulamius, Gilbert, Iordanus Brunus, Gassendus, Bassonus, Gomesius, Carpenter, Gorleus, which are the principal amongst a thousand others: and so to observe the like in all Faculties, with these cautions, sedulously observed: the first, that the most universal and antient, do alwayes march in front; the second, that the Interpreters and Commentators be placed apart, and rang'd according to the order of the Books which they explicate; the third, that the particular Treatises follow the rank and disposition of their matter and subject, in the Arts and Sciences; the fourth and last, that all Books of like argument and subject be precisely reduced, & disciplin'd in their destin'd places; since in so doing, the memory is so refreshed, that it would be easie in a moment onely to find out whatever Book one would choose or desire, in a Library that were as vast as that of Ptolomy . . .

And however, I conceive, that this order being the most practised will ever be esteemed much better and easier than that of the Ambrosian Library, and some others, where all the Books are indifferently ranged pellmesle, according to the order of their Volumes and Ciffers, and onely distinguished in a Catalogue, wherein every piece is found under the name of its Author; forasmuch as that to avoid the

452

precedent inconveniencies, it draws along with it an Iliad of others, to many whereof one may yet prescribe a remedy, by a Catalogue faithfully compiled according to the Classes, and each Faculty subdivided to the most precise and particular of their parts.

There now remains only Manuscripts to be spoken of, which cannot be better placed then in some quarter of the Library, there being no occasion to separate and sequester them from it; since they compose the best part and the most curious, and esteemed; to this add, that divers easily perswade themselves, when they do not see them amongst the rest of the bookes, that all those Chambers where we use to say they are lock't up, are onely imaginary, and only destin'd to excuse such as indeed have none. . . .

[*Evelyn's book is a translation of* Advis pour dresser une bibliothèque *(1627) by Gabriel Naudé.*]

SENECA

From *De Tranquillitate Animi* (*c.* 49 CE)

OUTLAY UPON STUDIES, best of all outlays, is reasonable so long only as it is kept within certain limits. What is the use of books and libraries innumerable, if scarce in a lifetime the master reads the titles? A student is burdened by a crowd of authors, not instructed; and it is far better to devote yourself to a few, than to lose your way among a multitude.

Forty thousand books were burnt at Alexandria. I leave others to praise this splendid monument of royal opulence, as for example Livy, who regards it as 'a noble work of royal taste and royal thoughtfulness.' It was not taste, it was not thoughtfulness, it was learned extravagance – nay not even learned, for they had bought their books for the sake of show, not for the sake of learning – just as with many who are ignorant even of the lowest branches of learning books are not instruments of study, but ornaments of dining-rooms. Procure then as many books as will suffice for use; but not a single one for show. You will reply: 'Outlay on such objects is preferable to extravagance on plate or paintings.' Excess in all directions is bad. Why should you excuse a man who wishes to possess book-presses inlaid with *arbor-vitae* wood or ivory; who gathers together masses of authors either unknown or discredited; who yawns among his thousands of books; and who derives his chief delight from their edges and their tickets?

You will find then in the libraries of the most arrant idlers all that orators or historians have written – book-cases built up as high as the ceiling. Nowadays a library takes rank with a bathroom as a necessary ornament of a house. I could forgive such ideas, if they were due to extravagant desire for learning. As it is, these productions of men whose genius we revere, paid for at a high price, with their portraits ranged in line above them, are got together to adorn and beautify a wall.

Translated by John Willis Clark

J. W. VON GOETHE

From *Conversations with Goethe* (1848) by Johann Peter Eckermann

Monday, March 15, 1830

THIS EVENING, passed a short hour at Goethe's. He spoke a great deal of Jena, and of the arrangements and improvements he had made in the different branches of the University. For chemistry, botany, and mineralogy, formerly treated only so far as they belonged to pharmacy, he had introduced special chairs. Above all, he had done much good for the museum of natural history and the library. He again related to me, with much self-satisfaction and good humour, the history of his violent seizure of a room adjoining the library, of which the medical faculty had taken possession, and which they would not give up.

'The library,' said he, 'was in very bad condition. The situation was damp and close, and by no means fit to contain its treasures; particularly as, through the purchase of the Büttner library on the part of the Grand Duke, thirteen thousand additional volumes lay in large heaps upon the floor. An addition should have been made to the building, but for this the means were wanting; besides, this addition could easily be avoided, since adjoining the library there was a large room standing empty, and well calculated to supply all our necessities. However, this room was not in possession of the library; but was occupied by the medical faculty, who sometimes used it for conferences. I therefore applied to these gentlemen, civilly requesting that they would give up this room to me for the library. They would not agree. They said they were willing to give it up if I would have a new room built for their conferences, and that immediately. I replied that I should be very ready to have another place prepared for them but could not promise them a new building immediately. This answer did not appear to satisfy; for when I sent the next morning for the key, I was told that it could not be found!

'There now remained no other course but to enter as conqueror. I sent for a bricklayer, and took him into the library, to the wall of the said adjoining room. "This wall, my friend," said I, "must be very thick, for it separates two different parts of the dwelling: just try how strong it is." The bricklayer went to work, and scarcely had he given five or six hearty blows, when bricks and mortar fell in, and we could see, through the opening, some venerable perukes with which the room had been decorated. "Go on, my friend," said I; "I cannot see clearly enough yet. Act just as if you were in your own house." This friendly encouragement so animated the bricklayer that the opening was soon large enough to serve for a door; when my library attendants rushed into the room, each with an armful of books, which they threw upon the ground as a sign of possession.

'Benches, chairs, and desks vanished in a moment; and my assistants were so quick and active that in a few days all the books were arranged in the most beautiful order along the walls of their repository. The doctors, who soon afterwards entered their room, *in corpore*, through their usual door, were confounded by the great and unexpected change. They did not know what to say, and retired in silence; but they all harboured a secret grudge against me. Still, when I see them singly, and particularly when I have any one of them to dine with me, they are quite charming, and my very dear friends. When I related to the Grand Duke the course of this adventure, which was certainly achieved with his consent and perfect approbation, it amused him right royally, and we have very often laughed at it since.

'We had our share of trouble in doing good. Afterwards, when, on account of the great dampness in the library, I wished to take down and remove the whole of the old city-wall, which was quite useless, I found no better success. My entreaties, good reasons, and rational representations found no hearing, and I was at last obliged here also to go to work as a conqueror. When the city authorities saw my workmen at work upon their old wall, they sent a deputation to the Grand Duke, who was then at Dornburg, with the humble request that his highness would be pleased, by a word of command, to check my violent destruction of their venerable city-wall. But the Grand Duke, who had secretly authorized me to take this step, answered very wisely – "I do not meddle in Goethe's affairs. He knows what he has to do, and must act as he thinks right. Go to him, and speak to him yourself, if you have the courage!"

'However, nobody made his appearance at my house,' continued Goethe, laughing; 'I went on pulling down as much of the old wall as was in my way, and had the happiness of seeing my library dry at last.'

Translated by John Oxenford

AZAR NAFISI

THE *GATSBY* TRIAL

From

READING LOLITA IN TEHRAN
(2003)

IT WAS LATE; I had been at the library. I was spending a great deal of time there now as it was becoming more and more difficult to find 'imperialist' novels in bookstores. I was emerging from the library with a few books under my arm when I noticed him standing by the door. His two hands were joined in front of him in an expression of reverence for me, his teacher, but in his strained grimace I could feel his sense of power. I remember Mr. Nyazi always with a white shirt, buttoned up to the neck – he never tucked it in. He was stocky and had blue eyes, very closely cropped light brown hair and a thick, pinkish neck. It seemed as if his neck were made of soft clay; it literally sat on his shirt collar. He was always very polite.

'Ma'am, may I talk to you for a second?' Although we were in the middle of the semester, I had not as yet been assigned an office, so we stood in the hall and I listened. His complaint was about Gatsby. He said he was telling me this for my own good. For my own good? What an odd expression to use. He said surely I must know how much he respected me, otherwise he would not be there talking to me. He had a complaint. Against whom, and why me? It was against Gatsby. I asked him jokingly if he had filed any official complaints against Mr. Gatsby. And I reminded him that any such action would in any case be useless as the gentleman was already dead.

But he was serious. No, Professor, not against Mr. Gatsby

461

himself but against the novel. The novel was immoral. It taught the youth the wrong stuff; it poisoned their minds – surely I could see? I could not. I reminded him that Gatsby was a work of fiction and not a how-to manual. Surely I could see, he insisted, that these novels and their characters became our models in real life? Maybe Mr. Gatsby was all right for the Americans, but not for our revolutionary youth. For some reason the idea that this man could be tempted to become Gatsby-like was very appealing to me.

There was, for Mr. Nyazi, no difference between the fiction of Fitzgerald and the facts of his own life. *The Great Gatsby* was representative of things American, and America was poison for us; it certainly was. We should teach Iranian students to fight against American immorality, he said. He looked earnest; he had come to me in all goodwill.

Suddenly a mischievous notion got hold of me. I suggested, in these days of public prosecutions, that we put *Gatsby* on trial: Mr. Nyazi would be the prosecutor, and he should also write a paper offering his evidence. I told him that when Fitzgerald's books were published in the States, there were many who felt just as he did. They may have expressed themselves differently, but they were saying more or less the same thing. So he need not feel lonely in expressing his views.

The next day I presented this plan to the class. We could not have a proper trial, of course, but we could have a prosecutor, a lawyer for the defense and a defendant; the rest of the class would be the jury. Mr. Nyazi would be the prosecutor. We needed a judge, a defendant and a defense attorney.

After a great deal of argument, because no one volunteered for any of the posts, we finally persuaded one of the leftist students to be the judge. But then Mr. Nyazi and his friends objected: this student was biased against the prosecution.

After further deliberation, we agreed upon Mr. Farzan, a meek and studious fellow, rather pompous and, fortunately, shy. No one wanted to be the defense. It was emphasized that since I had chosen the book, I should defend it. I argued that in that case, I should be not the defense but the defendant and promised to cooperate closely with my lawyer and to talk in my own defense. Finally, Zarrin, who was holding her own conference in whispers with Vida, after a few persuasive nudges, volunteered. Zarrin wanted to know if I was Fitzgerald or the book itself. We decided that I would be the book: Fitzgerald may have had or lacked qualities that we could detect in the book. It was agreed that in this trial the rest of the class could at any point interrupt the defense or the prosecution with their own comments and questions.

I felt it was wrong for me to be the defendant, that this put the prosecutor in an awkward position. At any rate, it would have been more interesting if one of the students had chosen to participate. But no one wanted to speak for *Gatsby*. There was something so obstinately arrogant about Mr. Nyazi, so inflexible, that in the end I persuaded myself I should have no fear of intimidating him.

A few days later, Mr. Bahri came to see me. We had not met for what seemed like a long time. He was a little out-raged. I enjoyed the fact that for the first time, he seemed agitated and had forgotten to talk in his precise and leisurely manner. Was it necessary to put this book on trial? I was somewhat taken aback. Did he want me to throw the book aside without so much as a word in its defense? Anyway, this is a good time for trials, I said, is it not?

*

All through the week before the trial, whatever I did, whether talking to friends and family or preparing for classes, part of my mind was constantly occupied on shaping my arguments for the trial. This after all was not merely a defense of *Gatsby* but of a whole way of looking at and appraising literature – and reality, for that matter. Bijan, who seemed quite amused by all of this, told me one day that I was studying *Gatsby* with the same intensity as a lawyer scrutinizing a textbook on law. I turned to him and said, You don't take this seriously, do you? He said, Of course I take it seriously. You have put yourself in a vulnerable position in relation to your students. You have allowed them – no, not just that; you have forced them into questioning your judgment as a teacher. So you have to win this case. This is very important for a junior member of the faculty in her first semester of teaching. But if you are asking for sympathy, you won't get it from me. You're loving it, admit it – you love this sort of drama and anxiety. Next thing you know, you'll be trying to convince me that the whole revolution depends on this.

But it does – don't you see? I implored. He shrugged and said, Don't tell me. I suggest you put your ideas to Ayatollah Khomeini.

On the day of the trial, I left for school early and roamed the leafy avenues before heading to class. As I entered the Faculty of Persian and Foreign Languages and Literature, I saw Mahtab standing by the door with another girl. She wore a peculiar grin that day, like a lazy kid who has just gotten an A. She said, Professor, I wondered if you would mind if Nassrin sits in on the class today. I looked from her to her young companion; she couldn't have been more than thirteen or fourteen years old. She was very pretty, despite her own best efforts to hide it. Her looks clashed with her solemn expression, which was neutral and adamantly impenetrable. Only her body seemed to express something: she kept leaning on one leg and then the other as her right hand gripped and released the thick strap of her heavy shoulder bag.

Mahtab, with more animation than usual, told me that Nassrin's English was better than most college kids', and when she'd told her about *Gatsby*'s trial, she was so curious that she'd read the whole book. I turned to Nassrin and asked, What did you think of *Gatsby*? She paused and then said quietly, I can't tell. I said, Do you mean you don't know or you can't tell me? She said, I don't know, but maybe I just can't tell you.

That was the beginning of it all. After the trial, Nassrin asked permission to continue attending my classes whenever she could. Mahtab told me that Nassrin was her neighbor. She belonged to a Muslim organization but was a very interesting kid, and Mahtab was working on her – an expression the leftists used to describe someone they were trying to recruit.

I told Nassrin she could come to my class on one condition: at the end of term, she would have to write a fifteen-page paper on *Gatsby*. She paused as she always did, as if she didn't quite have sufficient words at her command. Her responses were always reluctant and forced; one felt almost guilty for making her talk. Nassrin demurred at first, and then she said: I'm not that good. You don't need to be good, I said. And I'm sure you are – after all, you're spending your free time here. I don't want a scholarly paper; I want you to write your own impressions. Tell me in your own words what *Gatsby* means to you. She was looking at the tip of her shoes, and she muttered that she would try.

From then on, every time I came to class I would look for Nassrin, who usually followed Mahtab and sat beside her. She would be busy taking notes all through the session, and she even came a few times when Mahtab did not show up. Then suddenly she stopped coming, until the last class, when I saw her sitting in a corner, busying herself with the notes she scribbled.

Once I had agreed to accept my young intruder, I left them both and continued. I needed to stop by the department office before class to pick up a book Dr. A had left for me. When I entered the classroom that afternoon, I felt a charged silence follow me in. The room was full; only one or two students were absent – and Mr. Bahri, whose activities, or disapproval, had kept him away. Zarrin was laughing and swapping notes with Vida, and Mr. Nyazi stood in a corner talking to two other Muslim students, who repaired to their seats when they caught sight of me. Mahtab was sitting beside her new recruit, whispering to her conspiratorially.

I spoke briefly about the next week's assignment and proceeded to set the trial in motion. First I called forth Mr. Farzan, the judge, and asked him to take his seat in my usual chair, behind the desk. He sauntered up to the front of the class with an ill-disguised air of self-satisfaction. A chair was placed near the judge for the witnesses. I sat beside Zarrin on the left side of the room, by the large window, and Mr. Nyazi sat with some of his friends on the other side, by the wall. The judge called the session to order. And so began the case of the Islamic Republic of Iran versus *The Great Gatsby*.

Mr. Nyazi was called to state his case against the defendant. Instead of standing, he moved his chair to the center of the room and started to read in a monotonous voice from his paper. The judge sat uncomfortably behind my desk and appeared to be mesmerized by Mr. Nyazi. Every once in a while he blinked rather violently.

A few months ago, I was finally cleaning up my old files and I came across Mr. Nyazi's paper, written in immaculate handwriting. It began with 'In the Name of God,' words that later became mandatory on all official letterheads and in all public talks. Mr. Nyazi picked up the pages of his paper one by one, gripping rather than holding them, as if afraid that they might try to escape his hold. 'Islam is the only religion in the world that has assigned a special sacred role to literature in guiding man to a godly life,' he intoned. 'This becomes clear when we consider that the Koran, God's own word, is the Prophet's miracle. Through the Word you can heal or you can destroy. You can guide or you can corrupt. That is why the Word can belong to Satan or to God.

'Imam Khomeini has relegated a great task to our poets and writers,' he droned on triumphantly, laying down one page and picking up another. 'He has given them a sacred mission, *much* more exalted than that of the materialistic writers in the West. If our Imam is the shepherd who guides the flock to its pasture, then the writers are the faithful watch-dogs who must lead according to the shepherd's dictates.'

A giggle could be heard from the back of the class. I glanced around behind me and caught Zarrin and Vida whispering. Nassrin was staring intently at Mr. Nyazi and absentmindedly chewing her pencil. Mr. Farzan seemed to be preoccupied with an invisible fly, and blinked exaggeratedly at intervals. When I turned my attention back to Mr. Nyazi, he was saying, 'Ask yourself which you would prefer: the guardianship of a sacred and holy task or the materialistic reward of money and position that has corrupted –' and here he paused, without taking his eyes off his paper, seeming to drag the sapless words to the surface – 'that has *corrupted*,' he repeated, 'the Western writers and deprived their work of spirituality and purpose. *That* is why our Imam says that the pen is mightier than the sword.'

The whispers and titters in the back rows had become more audible. Mr. Farzan was too inept a judge to pay attention, but one of Mr. Nyazi's friends cried out: 'Your Honor, could you please instruct the gentlemen and ladies in the back to respect the court and the prosecutor?'

'So be it,' said Mr. Farzan, irrelevantly.

'Our poets and writers in this battle against the Great Satan,' Nyazi continued, 'play the same role as our faithful soldiers, and they will be accorded the same reward in heaven. We students, as the future guardians of culture, have a heavy task ahead of us. Today we have planted Islam's flag of victory inside the nest of spies on our own soil. Our task, as our Imam has stated, is to purge the country of the decadent Western culture and . . .'

At this point Zarrin stood up. 'Objection, Your Honor!' she cried out.

Mr. Farzan looked at her in some surprise. 'What do you object to?'

'This is supposed to be about *The Great Gatsby*,' said Zarrin. 'The prosecutor has taken up fifteen precious minutes of our time without saying a single word about the defendant. Where is this all going?'

For a few seconds both Mr. Farzan and Mr. Nyazi looked at her in wonder. Then Mr. Nyazi said, without looking at Zarrin, 'This is an Islamic court, not *Perry Mason*. I can present my case the way I want to, and I am setting the context. I want to say that as a Muslim I cannot accept *Gatsby*.'

Mr. Farzan, attempting to rise up to his role, said, 'Well, please move on then.'

Zarrin's interruptions had upset Mr. Nyazi, who after a short pause lifted his head from his paper and said with some excitement, 'You are right, it is not worth it . . .'

We were left to wonder what was not worth it for a few seconds, until he continued. 'I don't have to read from a paper, and I don't need to talk about Islam. I have enough

468

evidence – every page, *every* single page,' he cried out, 'of this book is its own condemnation.' He turned to Zarrin and one look at her indifferent expression was enough to transform him. 'All through this revolution we have talked about the fact that the West is our enemy, it is the Great Satan, not because of its military might, not because of its economic power, but because of, because of' – another pause – 'because of its sinister assault on the very roots of our culture. What our Imam calls cultural aggression. This I would call a rape of our culture,' Mr. Nyazi stated, using a term that later became the hallmark of the Islamic Republic's critique of the West. 'And if you want to see cultural rape, you need go no further than this very book.' He picked his *Gatsby* up from beneath the pile of papers and started waving it in our direction.

Zarrin rose again to her feet. 'Your Honor,' she said with barely disguised contempt, 'these are all baseless allegations, falsehoods . . .'

Mr. Nyazi did not allow his honor to respond. He half rose from his seat and cried out: 'Will you let me finish? You will get your turn! I will tell you why, I will tell you why . . .' And then he turned to me and in a softer voice said, 'Ma'am, no offense meant to you.'

I, who had by now begun to enjoy the game, said, 'Go ahead, please, and remember I am here in the role of the book. I will have my say in the end.'

'Maybe during the reign of the corrupt Pahlavi regime,' Nyazi continued, 'adultery was the accepted norm.'

Zarrin was not one to let go. 'I object!' she cried out. 'There is no factual basis to this statement.'

'Okay,' he conceded, 'but the values were such that adultery went unpunished. This book preaches illicit relations between a man and woman. First we have Tom and his mistress, the scene in her apartment – even the narrator, Nick, is implicated. He doesn't like their lies, but he has no objection to their fornicating and sitting on each other's laps, and, and, those parties at Gatsby's . . . remember, ladies and gentlemen, this Gatsby is the hero of the book – and who is he? He is a charlatan, he is an adulterer, he is a liar . . . this is the man Nick celebrates and feels sorry for, this man, this destroyer of homes!' Mr. Nyazi was clearly agitated as he conjured the fornicators, liars and adulterers roaming freely in Fitzgerald's luminous world, immune from his wrath and from prosecution. 'The only sympathetic person here is the cuckolded husband, Mr. Wilson,' Mr. Nyazi boomed. 'When he kills Gatsby, it is the hand of God. He is the only victim. He is the genuine symbol of the oppressed, in the land of, of, of the Great Satan!'

The trouble with Mr. Nyazi was that even when he became excited and did not read from his paper, his delivery was monotonous. Now he mainly shouted and cried out from his semi-stationary position.

'The one good thing about this book,' he said, waving the culprit in one hand, 'is that it exposes the immorality and decadence of American society, but we have fought to rid ourselves of this trash and it is high time that such books be banned.' He kept calling Gatsby 'this Mr. Gatsby' and could not bring himself to name Daisy, whom he referred to as 'that woman.' According to Nyazi, there was not a single virtuous woman in the whole novel. 'What kind of model are we setting for our innocent and modest sisters,' he asked his captive audience, 'by giving them such a book to read?'

As he continued, he became increasingly animated, yet he refused throughout to budge from his chair. 'Gatsby is dishonest,' he cried out, his voice now shrill. 'He earns his money by illegal means and tries to buy the love of a married woman. This book is supposed to be about the American dream, but what sort of a dream is this? Does the author mean to suggest that we should all be adulterers and bandits? Americans are decadent and in decline because this is their dream. They are going down! This is the last hiccup of a dead culture!' he concluded triumphantly, proving that Zarrin was not the only one to have watched *Perry Mason*.

'Perhaps our honorable prosecutor should not be so harsh,' Vida said once it was clear that Nyazi had at last exhausted his argument. 'Gatsby dies, after all, so one could say that he gets his just deserts.'

But Mr. Nyazi was not convinced. 'Is it just Gatsby who deserves to die?' he said with evident scorn. '*No!* The whole of American society deserves the same fate. What kind of a dream is it to steal a man's wife, to preach sex, to cheat and swindle and to . . . and then that guy, the narrator, Nick, he claims to be moral!'

Mr. Nyazi proceeded in this vein at some length, until he came to a sudden halt, as if he had choked on his own words. Even then he did not budge. Somehow it did not occur to any of us to suggest that he return to his original seat as the trial proceeded.

*

Zarrin was summoned next to defend her case. She stood up to face the class, elegant and professional in her navy blue pleated skirt and woolen jacket with gold buttons, white cuffs peering out from under its sleeves. Her hair was tied back with a ribbon in a low ponytail and the only ornament she wore was a pair of gold earrings. She circled slowly around Mr. Nyazi, every once in a while making a small sudden turn to emphasize a point. She had few notes and rarely looked at them as she addressed the class.

As she spoke, she kept pacing the room, her ponytail, in

harmony with her movements, shifting from side to side, gently caressing the back of her neck, and each time she turned she was confronted with Mr. Nyazi, sitting hard as rock on that chair. She began with a passage I had read from one of Fitzgerald's short stories. 'Our dear prosecutor has committed the fallacy of getting too close to the amusement park,' she said. 'He can no longer distinguish fiction from reality.'

She smiled, turning sweetly towards 'our prosecutor,' trapped in his chair. 'He leaves no space, no breathing room, between the two worlds. He has demonstrated his own weakness: an inability to read a novel on its own terms. All he knows is judgment, crude and simplistic exaltation of right and wrong.' Mr. Nyazi raised his head at these words, turning a deep red, but he said nothing. 'But is a novel good,' continued Zarrin, addressing the class, 'because the heroine is virtuous? Is it bad if its character strays from the moral Mr. Nyazi insists on imposing not only on us but on all fiction?'

Mr. Farzan suddenly leapt up from his chair. 'Ma'am,' he said, addressing me. 'My being a judge, does it mean I cannot say anything?'

'Of course not,' I said, after which he proceeded to deliver a long and garbled tirade about the valley of the ashes and the decadence of Gatsby's parties. He concluded that Fitzgerald's main failure was his inability to surpass his own greed: he wrote cheap stories for money, and he ran after the rich. 'You know,' he said at last, by this point exhausted by his own efforts, 'Fitzgerald said that the rich are different.'

Mr. Nyazi nodded his head in fervent agreement. 'Yes,' he broke in, with smug self-importance, clearly pleased with the impact of his own performance. 'And our revolution is opposed to the materialism preached by Mr. Fitzgerald. We do not need Western materialisms, or American goods.' He paused to take a breath, but he wasn't finished. 'If anything, we *could* use their technical know-how, but we *must* reject their morals.'

Zarrin looked on, composed and indifferent. She waited a few seconds after Mr. Nyazi's outburst before saying calmly, 'I seem to be confronting two prosecutors. Now, if you please, may I resume?' She threw a dismissive glance towards Mr. Farzan's corner. 'I would like to remind the prosecutor and the jury of the quotation we were given at our first discussion of this book from Diderot's *Jacques le Fataliste*: "To me the freedom of [the author's] style is almost the guarantee of the purity of his morals." We also discussed that a novel is not moral in the usual sense of the word. It can be called moral when it shakes us out of our stupor and makes us confront the absolutes we believe in. If that is true, then *Gatsby* has succeeded brilliantly. This is the first time in class that a book has created such controversy.

'*Gatsby* is being put on trial because it disturbs us – at least some of us,' she added, triggering a few giggles. 'This is not the first time a novel – a non-political novel – has been put on trial by a state.' She turned, her ponytail turning with her. 'Remember the famous trials of *Madame Bovary*, *Ulysses*, *Lady Chatterley's Lover* and *Lolita*? In each case the novel won. But let me focus on a point that seems to trouble his honor the judge as well as the prosecutor: the lure of money and its role in the novel.

'It is true that Gatsby recognizes that money is one of Daisy's attractions. He is in fact the one who draws Nick's attention to the fact that in the charm of her voice is the jingle of money. But this novel is *not* about a poor young charlatan's love of money.' She paused here for emphasis. 'Whoever claims this has not done his homework.' She turned, almost imperceptibly, to the stationary prosecutor to her left, then walked to her desk and picked up her copy of *Gatsby*. Holding it up, she addressed Mr. Farzan, turning her back on Nyazi, and said, 'No, Your Honor, this novel is not about "the rich are different from you and me," although they are: so are the poor, and so are you, in fact, different from me. It is about wealth but not about the vulgar materialism that you and Mr. Nyazi keep focusing on.'

'You tell them!' a voice said from the back row. I turned around. There were giggles and murmurs. Zarrin paused, smiling. The judge, rather startled, cried out, 'Silence! Who said that?' Not even he expected an answer.

'Mr. Nyazi, our esteemed prosecutor,' Zarrin said mockingly, 'seems to be in need of no witnesses. He apparently is both witness and prosecution, but let us bring our witnesses from the book itself. Let us call some of the characters to the stand. I will now call to the stand our most important witness.

'Mr. Nyazi has offered himself to us as a judge of Fitzgerald's characters, but Fitzgerald had another plan. He gave us his own judge. So perhaps we should listen to him. Which character deserves to be our judge?' Zarrin said, turning towards the class. 'Nick, of course, and you remember how he describes himself: "Everyone suspects himself of at least one of the cardinal virtues, and this is mine: I am one of the few honest people that I have ever known." If there is a judge in this novel, it is Nick. In a sense he is the least colorful character, because he acts as a mirror.

'The other characters are ultimately judged in terms of their honesty. And the representatives of wealth turn out to be the most dishonest. Exhibit A: Jordan Baker, with whom Nick is romantically involved. There is a scandal about Jordan that Nick cannot at first remember. She had lied about a match, just as she would lie about a car she had borrowed and then left out in the rain with the top down. "She was incurably dishonest," Nick tells us. "She wasn't able to endure being at a disadvantage, and given this unwillingness I suppose she had begun dealing in subterfuges when she was very young in order to keep that cool insolent smile turned to the world and yet satisfy the demands of her hard jaunty body."

'Exhibit B is Tom Buchanan. His dishonesty is more obvious: he cheats on his wife, he covers up her crime and he feels no guilt. Daisy's case is more complicated because, like everything else about her, her insincerity creates a certain enchantment: she makes others feel they are complicit in her lies, because they are seduced by them. And then, of course, there is Meyer Wolfshiem, Gatsby's shady business partner. He fixes the World Cup. "It never occurred to me that one man could start to play with the faith of fifty million people – with the single-mindedness of a burglar blowing a safe." So the question of honesty and dishonesty, the way people are and the way they present themselves to the world, is a sub-theme that colors all the main events in the novel. And who are the most dishonest people in this novel?' she asked, again focusing on the jury. 'The rich, of course,' she said, making a sudden turn towards Mr. Nyazi. 'The very people our prosecutor claims Fitzgerald approves of.

'But that's not all. We are not done with the rich.' Zarrin picked up her book and opened it to a marked page. 'With Mr. Carraway's permission,' she said, 'I should like to quote him on the subject of the rich.' Then she began to read: ' "They were careless people, Tom and Daisy – they smashed up things and creatures and then retreated back into their money or their vast carelessness, or whatever it was that kept them together, and let other people clean up the mess they had made . . ."

'So you see,' said Zarrin, turning again to Mr. Farzan, 'this is the judgment the most reliable character in the novel makes about the rich. The rich in this book, represented primarily by Tom and Daisy and to a lesser extent Jordan Baker, are careless people. After all, it is Daisy who runs over Myrtle and lets Gatsby take the blame for it, without even sending a flower to his funeral.' Zarrin paused, making a detour around the chair, seemingly oblivious to the judge, the prosecutor and the jury.

'The word *careless* is the key here,' she said. 'Remember when Nick reproaches Jordan for her careless driving and she responds lightly that even if she is careless, she counts on other people being careful? *Careless* is the first adjective that comes to mind when describing the rich in this novel. The dream they embody is an alloyed dream that destroys whoever tries to get close to it. So you see, Mr. Nyazi, this book is no less a condemnation of your wealthy upper classes than any of the revolutionary books we have read.' She suddenly turned to me, and said with a smile, 'I am not sure how one should address a book. Would you agree that your aim is not a defense of the wealthy classes?'

I was startled by Zarrin's sudden question but appreciated this opportunity to focus on a point that had been central to my own discussions about fiction in general. 'If a critique of carelessness is a fault,' I said, somewhat self-consciously, 'then at least I'm in good company. This carelessness, a lack of empathy, appears in Jane Austen's negative characters: in Lady Catherine, in Mrs. Norris, in Mr. Collins or the Crawfords. The theme recurs in Henry James's stories and in Nabokov's monster heroes: Humbert, Kinbote, Van and Ada Veen. Imagination in these works is equated with empathy; we can't experience all that others have gone through, but we can understand even the most monstrous individuals in works of fiction. A good novel is one that shows the complexity of individuals, and creates enough space for all these characters to have a voice; in this way a novel is called democratic – not that it advocates democracy but that by nature it is so. Empathy lies at the heart of *Gatsby*, like so many other great novels – the biggest sin is to be blind to others' problems and pains. Not seeing them means denying their existence.' I said all this in one breath, rather astonished at my own fervor.

'Yes,' said Zarrin, interrupting me now. 'Could one not say in fact that this blindness or carelessness towards others is a reminder of another brand of careless people?' She threw a momentary glance at Nyazi as she added, 'Those who see the world in black and white, drunk on the righteousness of their own fictions.

'And if,' she continued with some warmth, 'Mr. Farzan, in real life Fitzgerald was obsessed with the rich and with wealth, in his fiction he brings out the corrupt and decaying power of wealth on basically decent people, like Gatsby, or creative and lively people, like Dick Diver in *Tender Is the Night*. In his failure to understand this, Mr. Nyazi misses the whole point of the novel.'

Nyazi, who for some time now had been insistently scrutinizing the floor, suddenly jumped up and said, 'I object!'

'To what, exactly, do you object?' said Zarrin with mock politeness.

'Carelessness is not enough!' he shot back. 'It doesn't make the novel more moral. I ask you about the sin of adultery, about lies and cheating, and you talk about carelessness?'

Zarrin paused and then turned to me again. 'I would now like to call the defendant to the stand.' She then turned to Mr. Nyazi and, with a mischievous gleam in her eyes, said, 'Would you like to examine the defendant?' Nyazi murmured a defiant no. 'Fine. Ma'am, could you please take the stand?' I got up, rather startled, and looked around me. There was no chair. Mr. Farzan, for once alert, jumped up and offered me his. 'You heard the prosecutor's remarks,' Zarrin said, addressing me. 'Do you have anything to say in your defense?'

I felt uncomfortable, even shy and reluctant to talk. Zarrin had been doing a great job, and it seemed to me there was no need for my pontifications. But the class was waiting, and there was no way I could back down now.

I sat awkwardly on the chair offered me by Mr. Farzan. During the course of my preparations for the trial, I had found that no matter how hard I tried, I could not articulate in words the thoughts and emotions that made me so excited about *Gatsby*. I kept going back to Fitzgerald's own explanation of the novel: 'That's the whole burden of this novel,' he had said, 'the loss of those illusions that give such color to the world so that you don't care whether things are true or false as long as they partake of the magical glory.' I wanted to tell them that this book is not about adultery but about the loss of dreams. For me it had become of vital importance that my students accept *Gatsby* on its own terms, celebrate and love it because of its amazing and anguished beauty, but what I had to say in this class had to be more concrete and practical.

'You don't read *Gatsby*,' I said, 'to learn whether adultery is good or bad but to learn about how complicated issues such as adultery and fidelity and marriage are. A great novel heightens your senses and sensitivity to the complexities of life and of individuals, and prevents you from the self-righteousness that sees morality in fixed formulas about good and evil . . .'

'But, ma'am,' Mr. Nyazin interrupted me. 'There is nothing complicated about having an affair with another man's

478

wife. Why doesn't Mr. Gatsby get his own wife?' he added sulkily.

'Why don't you write your own novel?' a muffled voice cracked from some indefinable place in the middle row. Mr. Nyazi looked even more startled. From this point on, I hardly managed to get a word in. It seemed as if all of a sudden everyone had discovered that they needed to get in on the discussion.

At my suggestion, Mr. Farzan called for a ten-minute recess. I left the room and went outside, along with a few students who felt the need for fresh air. In the hall I found Mahtab and Nassrin deep in conversation. I joined them and asked them what they thought of the trial.

Nassrin was furious that Nyazi seemed to think he had a monopoly on morality. She said she didn't say she'd approve of Gatsby, but at least he was prepared to die for his love. The three of us began walking down the hallway. Most of the students had gathered around Zarrin and Nyazi, who were in the midst of a heated argument. Zarrin was accusing Nyazi of calling her a prostitute. He was almost blue in the face with anger and indignation, and was accusing her in turn of being a liar and a fool.

'What am I to think of your slogans claiming that women who don't wear the veil are prostitutes and agents of Satan? You call this morality?' she shouted. 'What about Christian women who don't believe in wearing veils? Are they all – every single one of them – decadent floozies?'

'But this is an Islamic country,' Nyazi shouted vehemently. 'And this is the law, and whoever . . .'

'The law?' Vida interrupted him. 'You guys came in and changed the laws. Is it the law? So was wearing the yellow star in Nazi Germany. Should all the Jews have worn the star because it was the blasted law?'

'Oh,' Zarrin said mockingly, 'don't even try to talk to him about that. He would call them all Zionists who deserved what they got.' Mr. Nyazi seemed ready to jump up and slap her across the face.

'I think it's about time I used my authority,' I whispered to Nassrin, who was standing by, transfixed. I asked them all to calm down and return to their seats. When the shouts had died down and the accusations and counteraccusations had more or less subsided, I suggested that we open the floor to discussion. We wouldn't vote on the outcome of the trial, but we should hear from the jury. They could give us their verdict in the form of their opinions.

A few of the leftist activists defended the novel. I felt they did so partly because the Muslim activists were so dead set against it. In essence, their defense was not so different from Nyazi's condemnation. They said that we needed to read fiction like *The Great Gatsby* because we needed to know about the immorality of American culture. They felt we should read more revolutionary material, but that we should read books like this as well, to understand the enemy.

One of them mentioned a famous statement by Comrade Lenin about how listening to 'Moonlight Sonata' made him soft. He said it made him want to pat people on the back when we needed to club them, or some such. At any rate, my radical students' main objection to the novel was that it distracted them from their duties as revolutionaries.

Despite, or perhaps because of, the heated arguments, many of my students were silent, although many gathered around Zarrin and Vida, murmuring words of encouragement and praise. I discovered later that most students had supported Zarrin, but very few were prepared to risk voicing their views, mainly because they lacked enough self-confidence to articulate their points as 'eloquently,' I was told, as the defense and the prosecutor. Some claimed in private that they personally liked the book. Then why didn't they say so? Everyone else was so certain and emphatic in their position, and they couldn't really say why they liked it – they just did.

Just before the bell rang, Zarrin, who had been silent ever since the recess, suddenly got up. Although she spoke in a low voice, she appeared agitated. She said sometimes she wondered why people bothered to claim to be literature majors. Did it mean anything? she wondered. As for the book, she had nothing more to say in its defense. The novel was its own defense. Perhaps we had a few things to learn from it, from Mr. Fitzgerald. She had not learned from reading it that adultery was good or that we should all become shysters. Did people all go on strike or head west after reading Steinbeck? Did they go whaling after reading Melville? Are people not a little more complex than that? And are revolutionaries devoid of personal feelings and emotions? Do they never fall in love, or enjoy beauty? This is an amazing book, she said quietly. It teaches you to value your dreams but to be wary of them also, to look for integrity in unusual places. Anyway, she enjoyed reading it, and that counts too, can't you see?

In her 'can't you see?' there was a genuine note of concern that went beyond her disdain and hatred of Mr. Nyazi, a desire that even *he* should see, definitely see. She paused a moment and cast a look around the room at her classmates. The class was silent for a while after that. Not even Mr. Nyazi had anything to say.

I felt rather good after class that day. When the bell rang, many had not even noticed it. There had been no formal verdict cast, but the excitement most students now showed was the best verdict as far as I was concerned. They were

all arguing as I left them outside the class – and they were
arguing not over the hostages or the recent demonstrations
or Rajavi and Khomeini, but over Gatsby and his alloyed
dream.

RAY BRADBURY

THE LIBRARY
(1943)

THE PEOPLE POURED into the room. Health officials reeking of disinfectant, sprinklers in their hands. Police officials, fierce with blazing badges. Men with metal torches and roach exterminators, piling one on another, murmuring, shouting, bending, pointing. The books came down in avalanched thunders. The books were torn and rent and splintered like beams. Whole towns and towers of books collapsed and shattered. Axes beat at the windows, drapes fell in black sooty clouds of dust. Outside the door, the boy with the golden eyes looked in, stood silently, draped in his robin's egg sari, his rocket father and plastics mother behind him. The health official pronounced pronunciations. A doctor bent. 'He's dying,' was said, faintly, in the din. Antiseptic men lifted him on a stretcher, carried him through the collapsing room. Books were being piled into a portable incinerator; they were crackling and leaping and burning and twisting and vanishing into paper flame.

'No! No!' screamed A. 'Don't do it! The last ones in the world! The last ones!'

'Yes, yes,' soothed the health official mechanically.

'If you burn them, burn them, there are no other copies!'

'We know, we know. The law, the law,' said the health official.

'Fools, idiots, dolts! Stop!'

The books climbed and stoned down into baskets which

were carried out. There was the brisk suction of a vacuum cleaner.

'And when the books are burned, the last books' – A. was weakening – 'then there will be only myself, and the memories in my mind. And when I die, then it will all be gone. All of it gone forever. All of us gone. All us dark nights and Halloweens and white bone masks and closeted skeletons, all the Bierces and the Poes, Anubis and Set and the Niebelungen, the Machens and the Lovecrafts and the Frankensteins and the black vampire bats hovering, the Draculas and the Golems, gone, all gone.'

'We know, gone, gone,' whispered the official.

He shut his eyes. 'Gone. Gone. Tear my books, burn my books, cleanse, rip, clean away. Unearth the coffins, incinerate, do away with. Kill us, oh, kill us, for we are bleak castles on midnight mornings, we are blowing wind webs and scuttling spiders, and we are doors that swing unoiled and banging shutters banging, and we are darknesses so vast that ten million nights of darkness are held in one braincell. We are buried hearts in murdered bedrooms, hearts glowing under floorboards. We are clanking chains and gossamer veils, and vapors of enchanted and long dead and lovely ladies on grand castle stairs, float, afloat, windy and whispering and wailing. We are the Monkey's Paw, and the catacomb and the gurgling Amontillado bottle and the mortared brick, and the three wishes. We are the caped figure, the glass eye, the bloodied mouth, the sharp fang, the veined wing, the autumn leaf in the cold black sky, the wolf shining its white rimed morning pelt, we are the old days that come not again upon the earth, we are the red wild eye and the sudden instrument of knife or gun. We are all things violent and black. We are winds that keen and sad snows falling. We are October, burning down the lands into fused ruin, all flame, all blue and melancholy smoke. We are deep frozen winter. We are monumented mound yard, we are the chiseled marble name and the birth and death years. We are the tapping awake coffin and we are the scream in the night.'

'Yes, yes,' whispered the official.

'Carry me away, burn me up, let flames take me. Put me in a catacomb of books, brick me in with books, mortar me up with books and burn the whole of us together.'

'Rest easily,' whispered the official. 'I'm dying,' said Mr. A.

'No, no.'

'Yes, I am. You're carrying me.'

The stretcher was moving. His heart paled within him, fainter, fainter. 'Dying. In a moment now – dead.'

'Rest, please.'

'All of it gone, forever, and nobody to know it ever lived, the dark nights, Poe, Bierce, the rest of us. Gone, all gone.'

'Yes,' said the official in the moving dark.

There was a crackle of flame. They were burning out the room scientifically, with controlled fire. There was a vast blowing wind of flame that tore away the interior of darkness. He could see the books explode like so many kernels of dark corn.

'For the love of God, Montresor!'

The sedge withered, the vast ancient lawn of the room sizzled and flumed.

'Yes, for the love of God,' murmured the official.

'A very good joke indeed – an excellent jest! We will have many a rich laugh about it at the palazzo – over our wine! Let us be gone –'

In the dimness, the health official: 'Yes. Let us be gone.'

A. fell down in soft blackness. All black, all gone. He heard his own dry lips repeat, repeat the only thing thought of to repeat as he felt his old heart cease and grow cold within him:

'Requiescat in pace.'

He dreamed that he was walling himself in with bricks and more bricks of books.

For the love of god, Montresor!

Yes, for the love of God!

He went down into the soft blackness, and before it was all black and all gone he heard his own dry lips repeating and repeating the only thing he could think of to repeat as he felt his heart cease and desist within him.

'Requiescat in pace.'

ACKNOWLEDGMENTS

ISAAC BABEL: 'The Public Library' from *Complete Works of Isaac Babel* by Isaac Babel, edited by Nathalie Babel, translated by Peter Constantine. Copyright © 2002 by Peter Constantine. Used by permission of W. W. Norton & Company, Inc. 'The Public Library', translated by Peter Constantine, from *The Collected Stories of Isaac Babel*. Pan Macmillan UK. Reproduced with permission of the Licensor through PLSclear.

MAX BEERBOHM: 'Enoch Soames' from *Seven Men*. Reprinted with permissions from Berlin Associates.

WALTER BENJAMIN: 'Unpacking My Library' from *Illuminations*, Harcourt Brace Jovanovich, 1968. Reprinted with permission from HarperCollins Publishers. Penguin Random House UK.

ALAN BENNETT: From *The Uncommon Reader*. Published by Faber and Faber Limited. Reprinted with permission. Extract from *The Uncommon Reader* by Alan Bennett (© Forelake Ltd 2007) is printed by permission of United Agents (www.unitedagents.co.uk) on behalf of Forelake Ltd.

JORGE LUIS BORGES: 'The Library of Babel' from *Ficciones* by Jorge Luis Borges, English translation copyright © 1962 by Grove Press, Inc. Used by permission of Grove/Atlantic, Inc. Any third-party use of this material, outside of this publication, is prohibited. The Wylie Agency.

RAY BRADBURY: 'Exchange' © 1996 by Ray Bradbury; first published in *Quicker Than the Eye*. 'The Library' © 2007 by